Whe⟩

The Story o

By

Guy Thorne

BOOK I

"The mystery of iniquity doth already work."

[1]
WHEN IT WAS DARK

CHAPTER I

AN INCIDENT BY WAY OF PROLOGUE

Mr. Hinchcliffe, the sexton, looked up as Mr. Philemon, the clerk, unlocked the great gates of open ironwork which led into the street. Hinchcliffe was cutting the lettering on a tombstone, supported by heavy wooden trestles, under a little shed close to the vestry door of the church.

The clerk, a small, rotund man, clerical in aspect, and wearing a round felt hat, pulled out a large, old-fashioned watch. "Time for the bell, William," he said.

The parish church was a large building in sham perpendicular. It stood in a very central position on the Manchester main road, rising amid a bare triangle of flat gravestones, and separated from the street pavement only by high iron railings.

It was about half-past four on a dull autumn afternoon. The trams swung ringing down the black, muddy road, and the long procession of great two-wheeled carts, painted vermilion, carried coal from the collieries six miles away to the great mills and factories of Salford.

The two men went into the church, and soon the tolling of a deep-voiced bell, high up in the pall of smoke[2] which lay over the houses, beat out in regular and melancholy sound.

Inside the building the noise of the traffic sank into a long, unceasing note like the bourdon note of a distant organ.

Hinchcliffe tolled the bell in the dim, ugly vestibule with his foot in a loop in the rope, sitting on the chest which held the dozen loaves which were given away every Sunday to the old women in the free seats.

The clerk opened the green baize swing-doors and strode up the aisle towards the vestry, waking mournful echoes as the nails in his boots struck the tiled floor.

Saint Thomas's Church, the mother church of Walktown, was probably the ugliest church in Lancashire. The heavy galleries, the drab walls, the terrible gloom of the vast structure, all spoke eloquently of a chilly, dour Christianity, a grudging and suspicious Sunday religion which animated its congregation.

In the long rows of cushioned seats, each labelled with the name of the person who rented it, Sunday by Sunday the moderately prosperous and wholly vulgar Lancashire people sat for two hours. During the prayers they leaned forward in easy and comfortable concession to convention. Few ever knelt. During the hymn times they stood up in their places listening carefully to a fine choir of men and women—a choir which, despite its vocal excellence, was only allowed to perform the most stodgy and commonplace evangelical music.

When the incumbent preached he was heard with the jealous watchfulness which often assails an educated man. The renters of the pews desired a Low Church aspect of doctrine and were intelligent to detect any divergence from it.

The colour of the building was sombre. The brick-red and styx-like grey of the flooring, the lifeless chocolate[3] front of the galleries, the large and ugly windows filled with glass which was the colour of a ginger-beer bottle, had all a definite quality of cheerless vulgarity.

Philemon came out of the vestry door with a lighted taper. He lit two or three jets of the corona over the reading-desk. Then he sat down in a front pew close to the chancel steps and waited.

The bell outside stopped suddenly, and a tall young man in a black Inverness cape walked hurriedly up the side aisle under the gallery towards the vestry.

In less than a minute he came out again in surplice, stole, and hood,—the stole and hood were always worn at Walktown,—went to the reading-desk, and began to say Evensong in a level, resonant voice.

At the end of each psalm Mr. Philemon recited the doxology with thunderous assertion and capped each prayer with an echoing "Amen."

The curate, Basil Gortre, was a young fellow with a strong, impressive face. His eyes had the clearness of youth and looked out steadily on the world under his black hair. His face was of that type men call a "thoroughly honest" face, but, unlike the generality of such faces, it was neither stubborn nor stupid. The clean-shaven jaw was full of power, the mouth was refined and, artistic, without being either sensual or weak.

During the Creed he turned towards the east, and the clerk's uncompromising voice became louder and more acid as he noticed the action; and when the clergyman, almost imperceptibly, made the sign of the Cross at the words "The resurrection of the body," the old man gave a loud snort of disapprobation.

In deference to the congregation on Sundays, and at the wish of his vicar, Gortre omitted these simple signs of reverence. But alone, at Matins or Evensong, he followed his usual habit.

[4]

During the last low prayers, as dusk crept into the great church, and the clank and bells of the trams outside seemed to be more remote, a part, indeed, of that visible but not symbolic ugliness which the gloom was hiding, a note of fervour crept into the young man's praying which had only been latent there before.

He was reading the third collect when the few gas jets above his head began to whistle, burnt blue for a few seconds, and then faded out with three or four faint pops.

Some air had got into the pipes. Old Mr. Philemon rose noisily from his knees, and shuffled off to the vestry coughing and spluttering. Outside, with startling suddenness, a piano organ burst into a gay, strident melody. After a few bars the music stopped with a jerk. A police constable had spoken to the organ-grinder and moved him on.

Gortre's voice went on in a deep, fervent monotone, unmoved by the darkness or the dissonance—

"Lighten our darkness, we beseech Thee, O Lord; and by Thy great mercy defend us from all perils and dangers of this night; for the love of Thy only Son, our Saviour Jesus Christ."

The faithful, quiet voice, enduring through the dark, was a foreshadowing of the great cloud which was breaking over the world, big with disaster, imminent with gloom. It foreshadowed the divinely aided continuance of Truth through such a terror as men had never known before.

It meant many things, that firm and beautiful voice—hope in the darkest hour for thousands of dying souls, a noble woman's happiness in time of dire stress and evil temptations and a death worse than the death Judas[5] died—for Mr. Schuabe the millionaire and Robert Llwellyn the scholar, taking tea together in the Athenæum Club three hundred miles away in London.

"—by Thy great mercy defend us from all perils and dangers of this night."

Mr. Philemon returned with a taper, an old and wrinkled acolyte, in time with his loud and sonorous AMEN.

[6]
CHAPTER II

IN THE VICAR'S STUDY

The vicarage of Walktown was a new and commodious house with tall chimneys, pointed windows, and a roof of red tiles.

It was more than a mile from the church, in the residential quarter of the town. Here were no shops and little traffic. The solid houses of red brick stood in their own rather dingy grounds, where, though the grass was never really green, and spring came in a veil of smoky vapour when the wind blew from the town, there was yet a rural suggestion.

The trees rose from neatly kept lawns, the gravel sweeps of the drives were carefully tended, and there was distant colour in the elaborate conservatories and palm-houses which were to be seen everywhere.

Mr. Pryde, the great Manchester solicitor, had his beautiful modern house here. Sir John Neele, the wealthy manufacturer of disinfectants, lived close by, and a large proportion of the well-to-do Manchester merchants were settled round about.

Not all of them were parishioners of Mr. Byars, the vicar of Walktown. Many attended the more fashionable church of Pendleborough, a mile away in what answered to the "country"; others were leaders in the Dissenting and especially the Unitarian worlds.

Walktown was a stronghold of the Unitarians. The wealthy Jews of two generations back, men who made[7] vast fortunes in the black valley of the Irwell, had chosen Walktown to dwell in. Their grandsons had found it more politic to abjure their ancient faith. A few had become Christians,—at least in name, inasmuch as they rented pews at St. Thomas's,—but others had compromised by embracing a faith, or rather a dogma, which is simply Judaism without its ritual and ceremonial obligations. The Baumanns, the Hildersheimers, the Steinhardts, flourished in Walktown.

It was people of this class who supported the magnificent concerts in the Free Trade Hall at Manchester, who bought the pictures and read the books. They had brought an alien culture to the neighbourhood. The vicar had two strong elements to contend with,—for his parochial life was all contention,—on the one hand the Lancashire natives, on the other the wealthy Jewish families.

The first were hard, uncultured people, hating everything that had not its origin and end in commerce. They disliked Mr. Byars because he was a gentleman, because he was educated, and because—so they considered—the renting of the pews in his church gave them the right to imagine that he was in some sense a paid servant of theirs.

The second class of parishioners were less Philistine, certainly, but even more hopeless from the parish priest's point of view. In their luxurious houses they lived an easy, selfish, and sensual life, beyond his reach, surrounded by a wall of indifferentism, and contemptuous of all that was not tangible and material. At times the rector and the curate confessed to each other that these people seemed more utterly lost than any others with whom the work of the Church brought them in contact.

Mr. Byars was a widower with one son, now at Oxford,[8] and one daughter, Helena, who was engaged to Basil Gortre, the curate.

3

About six o'clock the vicar sat in his study with a pile of letters before him. The room was a comfortable, bookish place, panelled in pitch pine where the walls were not covered with shelves of theological and philosophical works.

The arm-chairs were not new, but they invited repose; the large engraving over the pipe-littered mantel was a fine autotype of Giacomo's St. Emilia. The room was brightly lit with electric light.

Mr. Byars was a man of medium height, bald, his fine, domed forehead adding to his apparent age, and wore a pointed grey beard and moustache. He was an epitome of the room around him.

The volumes on his shelves were no ancient and musty tomes, but represented the latest and newest additions to theological thought.

Lathom and Edersheim stood together with Renan's Vie de Jésus and Clermont-Ganneau's Recueil d'Arch. Orient, and Westcott guarded them all.

The ivory crucifix which stood on the writing-table completed the impression of the man.

Ambrose Byars at forty-five was thoroughly acquainted with modern thought and literature. His scholarship was tempered with the wisdom of an active and clear-headed man of the world. His life and habits were simple but unbigoted, and his broad-mindedness never obscured his unalterable convictions. He lived, as he conceived it his duty to live in his time and place, in thorough human and intellectual correspondence with his environment, but one thought, one absolute certainty informed his life.

As year by year his knowledge grew greater, and the scientific criticism of the Scriptures undermined the[9] faith of weaker and less richly endowed minds, he only found in each discovery a more vivid proof of the truth of the Incarnation and the Resurrection.

It was his habit in discussions to reconcile all apparently conflicting antichristian statements and weave them into the fabric of his convictions. He held that, even scientifically, historically, and materially, the evidence for the Resurrection was too strong to be ever overthrown. And beyond these intellectual evidences he knew that Christ must have risen from the dead, because he himself had found Christ and was found in Him.

His attitude was a careful one with all its conciseness. An anecdote illustrates this.

One day, when walking home from a meeting of the School Board, of which he was a member, he had met a parishioner named Baxter, the proprietor of a small engineering work in the district. The man, who never came to church, on what he called "principle," but spent his Sundays in bed with a sporting paper, was one of those half-educated people who condemn Christianity by ridiculing the Old Testament stories.

They walked together, Baxter quoting the Origin of Species, which he knew from a cheap epitomised handbook.

"Do you really think, Mr. Byars," he had said, "do you really believe, after Darwin's discovery, that we were made by a sort of conjuring trick by a Supreme Power? Seven days of cooking, so to speak, and then a world! Why, it's childish to expect thinking people to believe it. We are simply evolved by scientific evolution out of the primæval protoplasm."

"Very possibly," said the vicar; "and who made the protoplasm, Mr. Baxter?"

The man was silent for a minute. "Then, Mr. Byars,"[10] he said at length, "you do not believe the Old Testament—the Adam and Eve part, for instance. You do not believe the Book on which your creed is founded."

"There are such things as allegories," he had answered. "The untutored brain must be taught the truth in such a way as it can receive it."

4

The vicar lit his pipe and began to open his letters with a slight sigh. Of all men, he sometimes felt, he was the least possible one for Walktown. For twelve years he had worked there, and he seemed to make little headway. He longed for an educated congregation. Here methods too vulgar for his temperament seemed to be the only ones.

The letters were all from applicants for the curacy which Gortre's impending departure would shortly leave vacant.

"It will be a terrible wrench to lose Basil," he said to himself; "but it must be. He will have his chance and be far happier in London, in more congenial environment. He would never be a great success in Walktown. He has tried nobly, but the people won't understand him. They would never like him; he's too much of a gentleman. How they all hate breeding in Walktown! There is nothing for it, I can see. I must get an inferior man this time. An inferior man will go down with them better here. I only hope he will be a really good fellow. If he isn't, it will be Jerrold over again—vulgar cabals against me, and all the women in the place quarrelling and taking sides."

He read letter after letter, and saw, with a humorous shrug of disgust, that he would have little difficulty in engaging the "inferior" man of his thoughts.

The best men would not come to the North. Men of family with decent degrees, Oxford men, Cambridge men, accustomed to decent society and intellectual[11] friends, knew far too much to accept a title in the Manchester district.

The applications were numerous enough, but obviously from second-rate men, or at any rate from men who appeared to be so at first glance.

A Durham graduate, 40, with five children, begged earnestly for the £120 a year which was all Mr. Byars could offer. A few young men from theological colleges wanting titles, a Dublin B.A., announcing himself as "thoroughly Protestant in views"—they were a weary lot. A non-collegiate student from Oxford with a second class in Theology, a Manchester Grammar-School boy, whose father lived at Higher Broughton, seemed to promise the best. He would be able to get on with the people, probably. "I suppose I must have him, accent and all," the vicar said with a sigh, "though I suppose it's prejudice to dislike the lessons read with the Lancashire broad 'a' and short 'o.' St. Paul probably spoke with a terrible local twang! and yet, I don't know, he was too great to be vulgar; one doesn't like to think that——"

Mr. Byars was certainly a difficult person for his congregation to appreciate.

He picked up the letter and was re-reading it when the door opened and his daughter came in.

Helena Byars was a tall girl, largely made and yet slender. Her hair was luxuriant and of a traditional "heroine" gold. She was dressed with a certain richness, though soberly enough, a style which, with its slight hint of austerity, accentuated a quiet and delicate charm. So one felt on meeting her for the first time. Sweet-faced she was and with an underlying seriousness even in her times of laughter. Her mouth was rather large, her nose straight and beautifully chiselled. The eyes were placid, intelligent, but without keenness.[12] There was an almost matronly dignity about her quiet and yet decided manner.

The vicar looked up at her with a smile, thinking how like her mother the girl was—that grave and gracious lady who looked out of the picture by the door, St. Cecilia in form and face. "Eh, but Helena she favours her mother," Hinchcliffe, the sexton, had said with the frank familiarity of the Lancashire workman soon after Mrs. Byars's funeral four years ago.

"I've brought Punch, father," she said, "it's just come. Leave your work now and enjoy yourself for half an hour before dinner. Basil will be here by the time you're finished."

She stirred the fire into a bright glow, and, singing softly to herself, left the study and went into the dining-room to see that the table looked inviting for the coming meal.

About seven o'clock Gortre arrived, and soon afterwards the three sat down to dine. It was a simple meal, some fish, cold beef, and a pudding, with a bottle of beer for the curate and a glass of claret for the vicar. The housemaid did not wait upon them, for they found the meal more intimate and enjoyable without her.

"I've got some news," said Gortre. "The great question of domicile is settled. You know there is no room in the clergy-house at St. Mary's. Moreover, Father Ripon thought it well that I should live outside. He wanted one of the assistant clergy, at least, to be in constant touch with lay influences, he said when I saw him."

"What have you arranged, dear?" said Helena.

"Something very satisfactory, I think," he answered. "My first thought was to take ordinary rooms in Bloomsbury. It would be near St. Mary's and the schools. Then I thought of chambers in one of the Inns of Court. At any rate I wrote to Harold Spence to ask his[13] advice. He was at Merton with me, you know, lived on the same staircase in 'Stubbins,' and is just one of the best fellows in the world. We haven't corresponded much during the last three years, but I knew a letter to the New Oxford and Cambridge would always find him. So I wrote up. He's been University Extension lecturing for a time, you know, and writing too. Now he tells me that he is writing leaders for the Daily Wire and doing very well. I'll read you what he says."

He took a letter from his pocket, glanced down it for the paragraph he wanted, and began to read:

... "—and I am delighted to hear that you have at last made up your mind to leave the North country and have accepted this London curacy. I asked Marsh, our ecclesiastical editor, about St. Mary's last night. He tells me that it is a centre of very important Church work, and has some political and social influence. Of all the 'ritualistic' parishes—I use the word as a convenient label—it is thought to be the sanest. Here you will have a real chance. I know something of the North, and came in contact with all sorts and conditions of people when I was lecturing on the French Revolution round Liverpool and Manchester for the Extension. They are not the people for you to succeed with, either socially or from a clergyman's point of view—at least, that's my opinion, old man. You ask me about rooms. I have a proposal to make to you in this regard. I am now living in Lincoln's Inn with a man named Hands—Cyril Hands. You may know his name. He is a great archæologist, was a young Cambridge professor. For three years now he has been working for The Palestine Exploring Society. He is in charge of all the excavations now proceeding near Jerusalem, and constantly making new and valuable Biblical discoveries."

The vicar broke in upon the reading. "Hands!"[14] he said; "a most distinguished man! His work is daily adding to our knowledge in a marvellous way. He has just recently discovered some important inscriptions at El-Edhamîyeh—Jeremiah's grotto, you know, the place which is thought may be Golgotha, you know. But go on, I'm sorry to interrupt."

Gortre continued:

"Hands is only at home for three months in the year, when he comes to the annual meeting of the Society and recuperates at the seaside. His rooms, however, are always kept for him. The chambers we have are old-fashioned but very large. There are three big bedrooms, a huge sitting-room, two smaller rooms and a sort of kitchen, all inside the one oak. I have a bedroom and one small room where I write. Hands has only one bedroom and uses the big general room. Now if you care to come and take up your abode in the Inn with us, I can only say you will be heartily welcome. Your share of the expenses would be less than if you lived alone in rooms as you propose, and you would be far more comfortable. You could have your study to work in. Our laundress is nearly always about, and there is altogether a pleasant suggestion of Oxford and the old days in the life we lead. Of course I need hardly tell you that we are very quiet and quite untroubled by any of the rowdy people, all of whom live away from our court altogether. You would be only five minutes' walk from St. Mary's. What do you think of the idea? Let me know and I will give you all further details. I hope you will decide on joining us. I should find it most pleasant.—Ever yours,

"Harold Masterman Spence."

"An extremely genial letter," said the vicar. "I suppose you'll accept, Basil? It will be pleasant to be with friends like that."

[15]

"Isn't it just a little, well, bachelor?" said Helena rather nervously.

Gortre smiled at the question.

"No, dear," he said. "I don't think you need be afraid. I know the sort of visions you have. The sort of thing in Pendennis, isn't it? The boy sent out for beer to the nearest public-house, and breakfast at twelve in the morning, cooked in the sitting-room. You don't know Harold. He is quite bourgeois in his habits, despite his intellect, hates a muddle, always dresses extremely well, and goes to church like any married man. He was a great friend of the Pusey House people at Oxford."

"The days when you couldn't be a genius without being dirty are gone," said the vicar. "I am glad of it. I was staying at St. Ives last summer, where there is quite an artistic settlement. All the painters carried golf-clubs and looked like professional athletes. They drink Bohea in Bohemia now."

Gortre talked a little about his plans for the future. He had a sympathetic audience. During the four years of his curacy at Walktown he had become very dear to Mr. Byars. He had arrived in the North from Oxford, after a year at Litchfield Theological College, just about the time that Mrs. Byars had died. His help and sympathy at such a time had begun a friendship with his vicar that had been firmly cemented as the time went on, and had finally culminated in his engagement to Helena. He had been the vicar's sole intellectual companion all this time, and his loss would be irreparable. But both men felt that his departure was inevitable. The younger man's powers were stifled and confined in the atmosphere of the place. He had private means of his own, and belonged to an old West-country family, and, try as he would he failed to identify himself socially with the Walktown[16] people. His engagement to Helena Byars had increased his unpopularity. He would be far happier at St. Mary's in London, at the famous High Church, where he would find all those exterior accompaniments of religion to which he had been accustomed, and which, though he did not exalt the shadow into the substance, always made him happier when he was surrounded by them.

He was to wait a year and then he would be married. There were no money obstacles in the way and no reason for further delay. Only the vicar looked forward with a sort of horror to his future loneliness, and tried to put the thought from him whenever it came.

After dinner Helena left the two men to smoke alone in the study. There was a concert in the Town Hall to which she was going with Mrs. Pryde, the solicitor's wife, a neighbour. Her friend's carriage called for her about eight, and Gortre settled down for a long talk with the vicar on parochial affairs.

They sat on each side of the dancing fire, with coffee on a table between them, quietly enjoying the after-dinner pipe, the best and finest of the five cardinal pipes of the day. It was a comfortable scene. The room was lighted only by a single electric reading-lamp with a green shade, and the firelight flickered and played over the dull gold and crimson of the books on the shelves, and threw red lights on the shining ivory of the sculptured Christ.

"I daresay this North-country man will do all right," said the vicar. "He will be more popular than you, Basil."

The young man sighed. "God knows I have tried hard enough to win their confidence," he said sadly, "but it was not to be. I can't get in touch with them, vicar. They dislike my manners, my way of speaking—everything about me. Even the landlady of my rooms[17] distrusts me because I decline to take tea with my evening chop, and charges me three shillings a week extra because I have what she calls 'late dinner'!"

The vicar laughed. "At any rate," he said, "you have got hold of Leef, your landlord; he comes to church regularly now."

"Oh, Leef illustrates more than any one else how impossible it is, for me, at any rate, to do much good. Last week he said to me, 'It's a fine thing, religion, when you've got it at last, Mr. Gortre. When I look back at my unregenerate years I wonder at myself. Religion tells me to give up certain things. It only 'armonises with the experience of any sensible man of my age. I don't want to drink too much, for instance. My health is capital, and I'm not such a fool as to spoil it. To think that all those years I never knew that religion was as easy as winking, and with a certainty of everlasting glory afterwards. I'll always back you up, Mr. Gortre, in saying that religion's the finest thing out.'"

"Well, dear boy, you will be in another environment altogether soon. It's no use being discouraged. Tot homines, quot sententiæ! We can't alter these things. The Essenes used to speak disrespectfully enough of 'Ye men of Galilee,' no doubt. Sometimes I think I would rather have these stubborn people than those of the South, men as easy and commode as an old glove, and worth about as much. Have you seen the Guardian to-day?"

"No, I haven't. I've been at the schools all the morning, visiting in Timperley Street till Evensong, home for a wash, and then here."

"I see Schuabe is going to address a great meeting in the Free Trade Hall on the Education Bill."

"Then he is at Mount Prospect?"

"He arrived from London yesterday."

[18]

The two men looked at each other in silence. Mr. Byars seemed ill at ease. His foot tapped the brass rail of the fender. Then, a sure sign of disturbance with him, he put down his pipe, which was nearly smoked away, and took a cigarette from a box on the table and smoked in short, quick puffs.

Gortre's face became dark and gloomy. The light died out of it, the kindliness of expression, which was habitual, left his eyes.

"We have never really told each other what we think of Schuabe and how we think of him, vicar," he said. "Let us have it out here and now while we are thinking of him and while we have the opportunity."

"In a question of this sort," said Mr. Byars, "confidences are extremely dangerous as a rule, but between you and me it is different. It will clear our brains mutually. God forbid

8

that you and I, in our profession as Christ's priests and our socio-political position as clerks in Holy Orders, should bear rancour against any one. But we are but human. Possibly our mutual confidence may help us both."

There was a curious eagerness in his manner which was reflected by that of the other. Both were conscious of feelings ill in accord with their usual open and kindly attitude towards the world. Each was anxious to know if the other coincided with himself.

Men are weak, and there is comfort in community.

"From envy, hatred, malice, and all uncharitableness—" said Gortre.

"Good Lord deliver us," replied the vicar gravely.

There was a tense silence for a time, only broken by the dropping of the coals in the grate. The vicar was the first to break it.

"I'll sum up my personal impression of the man for and against," he said.

[19]

Gortre nodded.

"There can be no doubt whatever," said Mr. Byars, "that among all the great North-country millionaires—men of power and influence, I mean—Schuabe stands first and pre-eminent. His wealth is enormous to begin with. Then he is young—can hardly be forty yet, I should say. He belongs to the new generation. In Walktown he stands entirely alone. Then his brilliancy, his tremendous intellectual powers, are equalled by few men in England. His career at Oxford was marvellous, his political life, only just beginning as it is, seems to promise the very highest success. His private life, as far as we know—and everything about the man seems to point to an ascetic temperament and a refined habit—is without grossness or vice of any kind. In appearance he is one of the ten most striking-looking men in England. His manners are fascinating."

Gortre laughed shortly, a mirthless, bitter laugh.

"So far," he said, "you have drawn a picture which approaches the ideal of what a strong man should be. And I grant you every detail of it. But let me complete it. You will agree with me that mine also is true."

His voice trembled a little. Half unconsciously his eyes wandered to the crucifix on the writing-table. In the red glow of the fire, which had now ceased to crackle and flame, the drooping figure on the cross showed distinct and clear in all its tremendous appeal to the hearts of mankind. Tears came into the young man's eyes, his face became drawn and pained. When he spoke, his voice was full of purpose and earnestness.

"Yes," he said, with an unusual gesture of the hand, "Schuabe is all that you say. In a hard, godless, and material age he is an epitome of it. The curse of indifferentism is over the land. Men have forgotten that this world is but an inn, a sojourning place for a few hours. O[20] fools and blind! The terror of death is always with them. But this man is far more than this—far, far more. To him has been given the eye to see, the heart to understand. He, of all men living in England to-day, is the mailed, armed enemy of Our Lord. No loud-mouthed atheist, sincere and blatant in his ignorance, no honest searcher after truth. All his great wealth, all his attainments, are forged into one devilish weapon. He is already, and will be in the future, the great enemy of Christianity. Oh, I have read his book! 'Even now there are many antichrists.' I have read his speeches in Parliament. I know his enormous influence over those unhappy people who call themselves 'Secularists.' Like Diocletian, like Julian, he hates Christ. He is no longer a Jew. Judaism is nothing to him—one can reverence a Montefiore, admire an Adler. His attacks on the faith are something quite different to those of other men. As his skill is greater, so his intention is more evil. And yet how helpless are we who know! The mass of Christians—the lax, tolerant Christians—think he is a kind of John Morley. They praise his charities, his efforts for social amelioration. They quote, 'And God fulfils Himself in many ways.' I say again, O fools and blind! They do not know, they cannot see, this man as he is at heart, accursed and antichrist!" His voice dropped, tired with its passion and vehemence. He continued in a lower and more intimate vein:

"Do you think I am a fanatic, vicar? Am I touched with monomania when I tell you that of late I have thought much upon the prophetic indications of the coming of 'the Man of Sin,' the antichrist in Holy Writ? Can it be, I have asked myself, as I watch the comet-like brilliance of this man's career, can it be that in my own lifetime and the lifetime of those I love, the veritable enemy of our Saviour is to appear? Is this[21] man, this Jew, he of whom it is said in Jacob's words, 'Dan shall be a serpent by the way, an adder in the path'—the tribe of which not one was sealed?"

"You are overwrought, Basil," said the elder man kindly. "You have let yourself dwell too much on this man and his influences. But I do not condemn you. I also have had my doubts and wonderings. The outside world would laugh at us and people who might be moved as we are at these things. But do we not live always with, and by help of, the Unseen? God alone knows the outcome of the trend of these antichristian influences, of which, I fear, Schuabe is the head. The Fathers are clear enough on the subject, and the learned men of mediæval times also. Let me read to you."

He got up from his arm-chair, glad, it seemed, at opportunity of change and movement, and went to the book-shelves which lined the wall. His scholar's interest was aroused, his magnificent reading and knowledge of Christian history and beliefs engaged and active.

He dipped into book after book, reading extracts from them here and there.

"Listen. Marchantius says the ship of the Church will sink and be lost in the foam of infidelity, and be hidden in the blackness of that storm of desolation which shall arise at the coming of Antichrist. 'The sun shall be darkened and the stars shall fall from heaven.' He means, of course, the sun of faith, and that the stars, the great ecclesiastical dignitaries, shall fall into apostasy. But, he goes on to say, the Church will remain unwrecked, she will weather the storm and come forth 'beautiful as the moon, terrible as an army with banners.'"

His voice was eager and excited, his face was all alight with the scholar's eagerness, as he took down book after book with unerring instinct to illustrate his remarks.

[22]

"Opinions as to the nature and personality of Antichrist have been very varied," he continued. "Some of the very early Christian writers say he will be a devil in a phantom body, others that he will be an incarnate demon, true man and true devil, in fearful and diabolic parody of the Incarnation of our Lord. There is a third view also. That is that he will be merely a desperately wicked man, acting upon diabolic inspirations, just as the saints act upon Divine inspirations.

"Listen to St. John Damascene upon the subject. He is very express. 'Not as Christ assumed humanity, so will the Devil become human; but the Man will receive all the inspiration of Satan, and will suffer the Devil to take up his abode within him.'"

Gortre, who was listening with extreme attention, made a short, sharp exclamation at this last quotation.

He had risen from his seat and stood by the mantel-shelf, leaning his elbow upon it.

One of the ornaments of the mantel was a head of Christ, photographed on china, from Murillo, and held in a large silver frame like a photograph frame.

Just as the vicar had finished reading there came a sudden knock at the door. It startled Gortre, and he moved suddenly. His elbow slid along the marble of the shelf and

10

dislodged the picture, which fell upon the floor and was broken into a hundred pieces, crashing loudly upon the fender.

The housemaid, who had knocked, stood for a moment looking with dismay upon the breakage. Then she turned to the vicar.

"Mr. Schuabe from Mount Prospect to see you, sir," she said. "I've shown him into the drawing-room."

[23]
CHAPTER III

"I THINK HE IS A GOOD MAN"

The servant had turned on the lights in the drawing room, where a low fire still glowed red upon the hearth, and left Constantine Schuabe alone to await the vicar's arrival.

On either side of the fireplace were heavy hangings of emerald and copper woven stuff, a present to Helena from an uncle, who had bought them at Benares. Schuabe stood motionless before this background.

The man was tall, above the middle height, and the heavy coat of fur which he was wearing increased the impression of proportioned size, of massiveness, which was part of his personality. His hair was a very dark red, smooth and abundant, of that peculiar colour which is the last to show the greyness of advancing age. His features were Semitic, but without a trace of that fulness, and sometimes coarseness, which often marks the Jew who has come to the middle period of life. The eyes were large and black, but without animation, in ordinary use and wont. They did not light up as he spoke, but yet the expression was not veiled or obscured. They were coldly, terribly aware, with something of the sinister and untroubled regard one sees in a reptile's eyes.

The jaw, which dominated the face and completed its remarkable ensemble, was very massive, reminding people of steel covered with olive-coloured parchment. Handsome was hardly the word which fitted him. He[24] was a strikingly handsome man; but that, like "distinction," was only one of the qualities which made up his personality. Force, power—the relentless and conscious power suggested by some great marine engine—surrounded him in an almost indescribable way. They were like exhalations. Most people, with the casual view, called him merely indomitable, but there were others who thought they read deeper and saw something evil and monstrous about the man; powerless to give an exact and definite reason for the impression, and dubious of voicing it.

Nevertheless, now and again, two or three people would speak of him to each other without reserve, and on such occasions they generally agreed to this feeling of the sinister and malign, in much the same manner as the vicar and his curate had been agreeing but half an hour before his arrival at the house.

The door opened with a quick click of the handle, and the vicar entered with something of suddenness. One might almost have supposed that he had lingered, hesitant, in the hall, and suddenly nerved himself for this encounter.

Mr. Byars advanced to take the hand of his visitor. Beside the big man he seemed shrunken and a little ineffectual. He was slightly nervous in his manner also, for Basil's impassioned and terror-ridden words still rang in his ears and had their way with him.

The coincidence of the millionaire's arrival was altogether too sudden and bizarre.

11

When they had made greetings, cordial enough on the surface, and were seated on either side of the fire, Schuabe spoke at once upon the object of his visit.

"I have come, Mr. Byars," he said, in a singularly clear, vibrant voice, "to discuss certain educational proposals with you. As you probably know, just at present[25] I am taking a very prominent part in the House of Commons in connection with the whole problem of primary education. Within the last few weeks I have been in active correspondence with your School Board, and you will know all about the scholarships I have founded.

"But I am now coming to you to propose something of the same sort in connection with your own Church schools. My opinions on religious matters are, of course, not yours. But despite my position I have always recognised that, with whatever means, both the clergy and my own party are broadly working towards one end.

"Walktown provides me with very many thousands a year, and it is my duty in some way or another to help Walktown. My proposal is roughly this: I will found and endow two yearly scholarships for two boys in the national schools. The money will be sufficient, in the first instance, to send them to one of the great Northern Grammar Schools, and afterwards, always providing that the early promise is maintained, to either university.

"My only stipulation is this. The tests shall be purely and simply intellectual, and have nothing whatever to do with the religious teaching of the schools, with which I am not in sympathy. Nevertheless, it is only fair that a clever boy in a Church school should have the same opportunities as in a secular school. I should tell you that I have made the same offer to the Roman Catholic school authorities and it has been declined."

The vicar listened with great attention. The offer was extremely generous, and showed a most open-minded determination to put the donor's personal prejudices out of the question. There could be no doubt as to his answer—none whatever.

"My dear sir," he said, "your generosity is very great. I see your point about the examinations. Religion is to form no part of them exactly. But by the time one of[26] our boys submits himself for examination we should naturally hope that he would already be so firmly fixed in Christian principles that his after-career would have no influence upon his faith. Holding the opinions that you do, your offer shows a great freedom from any prejudice. I hope I am broad-minded enough to recognise that philanthropy is a fine, lovely thing, despite the banner under which the philanthropist may stand. I accept your generous offer in the spirit that it is made. Of course, the scheme must be submitted to the managers of the schools, of whom I am chief, but the matter practically lies with me, and my lead will be followed."

"I am only too glad," said the big man, with a sudden and transforming smile, "to help on the cause of knowledge. All the details of the scheme I will send you in a few days, and now I will detain you no longer."

He rose to go.

During their brief conversation the vicar had been conscious of many emotions. He blamed himself for his narrowness and the somewhat fantastic lengths to which his recent talk with Gortre had gone. The man was an infidel, no doubt. His intellectual attacks upon Christian faith were terribly damaging and subversive. Still, his love for his fellow-men was sincere, it seemed. He attacked the faith, but not the preachers of it. And—a half thought crossed his brain—he might have been sent to him for some good purpose. St. Paul had not always borne the name of Paul!

These thoughts, but half formulated in his brain, had their immediate effect in concrete action.

"Won't you take off your coat, Mr. Schuabe," he said, "and smoke a cigar with me in my study?"

The other hesitated a moment, looked doubtful, and then assented. He hung his coat up in the hall and went into the other room with the vicar.

[27]

During the conversation in the drawing-room Helena had come back from the concert, and Basil, hearing her, had left the study and gone to her own private sanctum for a last few minutes before saying good-night.

Helena sat in a low chair by the fire sipping a bowl of soup which the maid had brought up to her. She was a little tired by the concert, where a local pianist had been playing a nocturne of Chopin's as if he wanted to make it into soup, and the quiet of her own sitting-room, the intimate comfort of it all, and the sense of happiness that Basil's presence opposite gave her were in delightful contrast.

"It was very stupid, dear," she said. "Mrs. Pryde was rather trying, full of dull gossip about every one, and the music wasn't good. Mr. Cuthbert played as if he was playing the organ in church. His touch is utterly unfitted for anything except the War March from Athalie with the stops out. He knows nothing of the piano. I was in a front seat, and I could see his knee feeling for the swell all the time. He played the sonata as if he was throwing the moonlight at one in great solid chunks. I'm glad to be back. How nice it is to sit here with you, dearest!—and how good this Bovril is!" she concluded with a little laugh of content and happiness at this moment of acute physical and mental ease.

He looked lovingly at her as she lay back in rest and the firelight played over her white arms and pale gold hair.

"It's wonderful to think," he said, with a little catch in his voice, "it's wonderful to me, an ever-recurring wonder, to think that some day you and I will always be together for all our life, here and afterwards. What supreme, unutterable happiness God gives to His children! Do you know, dear, sometimes as I read prayers or stand by the altar, I am filled with a sort of rapture[28] of thankfulness which is voiceless in its intensity. Tennyson got nearer to expressing it than any one in that beautiful St. Agnes' Eve of his—a little gem which, with its simplicity and fervour, is worth far more than Keats's poem with all its literary art."

"It is good to feel like that sometimes," she answered; "but it is well, I think, not to get into the way of inducing such feelings. The human brain is such a sensitive thing that one can get into the way of drugging it with emotion, as it were. I think I am tinged a little with the North-country spirit. I always think of Newman's wonderful lines—

"'The thoughts control that o'er thee swell and throng;
They will condense within the soul and turn to purpose strong.
But he who lets his feelings run in soft luxurious flow,
Shrinks when hard service must be done, and faints at every blow.'

I only quote from memory. But you look tired, dear boy; you are rather white. Have you been overworking?"

He did not answer immediately.

"No," he said slowly, "but I've been having a long talk with the vicar. We were talking about Mr. Schuabe and his influence. Helena, that man is the most active of God's enemies in England. Almost when I was mentioning his name, by some coincidence, or perhaps for some deeper, more mysterious, psychical reason which men do not yet understand, the maid announced him. He had come to see your father on business, and—don't think I am unduly fanciful—the Murillo photograph, the head of Christ, on the mantel-shelf, fell down and was broken. He is here still, I think."

13

"Yes," said Helena; "Mr. Schuabe is in the study with father. But, Basil dear, it's quite evident to me[29] that you've been doing too much. Do you know that I look upon Mr. Schuabe as a really good man! I have often thought about him, and even prayed that he may learn the truth; but God has many instruments. Mr. Schuabe is sincere in his unbelief. His life and all his actions are for the good of others. It is terrible—it is deplorable—to know he attacks Christianity; but he is tolerant and large-minded also. Yes, I should call him a good man. He will come to God some day. God would not have given him such power over the minds and bodies of men otherwise."

Gortre smiled a little sadly,—a rather wan smile, which sat strangely upon his strong and hearty face—, but he said no more.

He knew that his attitude was illogical, perhaps it could be called bigoted and intolerant—a harsh indictment in these easy, latitudinarian days; but his conviction was an intuition. It came from within, from something outside or beyond his reason, and would not be stifled.

"Well, dear," he said, "perhaps it is as you say. Nerves which are overwrought, and a system which is run down, certainly have their say, and a large say, too, in one's attitude towards any one. Now you must go to bed. I will go down and say good-night to the rector and Mr. Schuabe—just to show there's no ill-feeling; though, goodness knows, I oughtn't to jest about the man. Good-night, sweet one; God bless you. Remember me also in your prayers to-night."

She kissed him in her firm, brave way—a kiss so strong and loving, so pure and sweet, that he went away from that little room of books and bric-à-brac as if he had been sojourning in some shrine.

As Basil came into the study he found Mr. Byars and Schuabe in eager, animated talk. A spirit decanter had[30] been brought in during his absence, and the vicar was taking the single glass of whisky-and-water he allowed himself before going to bed. Basil, who was in a singularly alert and observant mood, noticed that a glass of plain seltzer water stood before the millionaire.

Gortre's personal acquaintance with Schuabe was of the slightest. He had met him once or twice on the platform of big meetings, and that was all. A simple curate, unless socially,—and Schuabe did not enter into the social life of Walktown, being almost always in London,—he would not be very likely to come in the way of this mammoth.

But Schuabe greeted him with marked cordiality, and he sat down to listen to the two men.

In two minutes he was fascinated, in five he realised, with a quick and unpleasant sense of inferiority, how ignorant he was beside these two. In Schuabe the vicar found a man whose knowledge was as wide and scholarship as profound as his own.

From a purely intellectual standpoint, probably Gortre and Schuabe were more nearly on a level, but in pure knowledge he was nowhere. He wondered, as he listened, if the generation immediately preceding his own had been blessed with more time for culture, if the foundation had been surer and more comprehensive, when they were alumni of the "loving mother" in the South.

They were discussing archæological questions connected with the Holy Land.

Schuabe possessed a profound and masterly knowledge of the whole Jewish background to the Gospel picture, not merely of the archæology, which in itself is a life study, but of the essential characteristics of Jewish thought and feeling, which is far more.

Of course, every now and again the conversation[31] turned towards a direction that, pursued, would have led to controversy. But, with mutual tact, the debatable ground was avoided. That Christ was a historic fact Schuabe, of course, admitted and implied, and

14

when the question of His Divinity seemed likely to occur he was careful and adroit to avoid any discussion.

To the young man, burning with the zeal of youth, this seemed a pity. Unconsciously, he blamed the vicar for not pressing certain points home.

What an opportunity was here! The rarity of such a visit, the obvious interest the two men were beginning to take in each other—should not a great blow for Christ be struck on such an auspicious night? Even if the protest was unavailing, the argument overthrown, was it not a duty to speak of the awful and eternal realities which lay beneath this vivid and brilliant interchange of scholarship?

His brain was on fire with passionate longing to speak. But, nevertheless, he controlled it. None knew better than he the depth and worth of the vicar's character. And he felt himself a junior; he had no right to question the decision of his superior.

"You have missed much, Mr. Byars," said Schuabe, as he arose to go at last, "in never having visited Jerusalem. One can get the knowledge of it, but never the colour. And, even to-day, the city must appear, in many respects, exactly as it did under the rule of Pilate. The Fellah women sell their vegetables, the camels come in loaded with roots for fuel, the Bedouin, the Jews with their long gowns and slippers—I wish you could see it all. I have eaten the meals of the Gospels, drunk the red wine of Saron, the spiced wine mixed with honey and black pepper, the 'wine of myrrh' mentioned in the Gospel of Mark. I have dined with Jewish tradesmen and gone through the same formalities of[32] hand-washing as we read of two thousand years ago; I have seen the poor ostentatiously gathered in out of the streets and the best part of the meal given them for a self-righteous show. And yet, an hour afterwards, I have sat in a café by King David's Tower and played dice with Turkish soldiers armed with Martini rifles!"

The vicar seemed loath to let his guest go, though the hour was late, but he refused to stay longer. Mr. Byars, with a somewhat transparent eagerness, mentioned that Gortre's road home lay for part of the way in the same direction as the millionaire's. He seemed to wish the young man to accompany him, almost, so Basil thought, that the charm of his personality might rebuke him for his tirade in the early part of the evening.

Accordingly, in agreement with the vicar's evident wish, but with an inexplicable ice-cold feeling in his heart, he left the house with Schuabe and began to walk with him through the silent, lamp-lit streets.

[33]
CHAPTER IV

THE SMOKE CLOUD AT DAWN

The two men strode along without speaking for some way. Their feet echoed in the empty streets.

Suddenly Schuabe turned to Basil. "Well, Mr. Gortre," he said, "I have given you your opportunity. Are you not going to speak the word in season after all?"

The young man started violently. Who was this man who had been reading his inner thoughts? How could his companion have fathomed his sternly repressed desire as he sat in the vicarage study? And why did he speak now, when he knew that some chilling influence had him in its grip, that his tongue was tied, his power weakened?

"It is late, Mr. Schuabe," he said at length, and very gravely. "My brain is tired and my enthusiasm chilled. Nor are you anxious to hear what I have to say. But your taunt is ungenerous. It almost seems as if you are not always so tolerant as men think!"

15

The other laughed—a cold laugh, but not an unkindly one. "Forgive me," he said, "one should not jest with conviction. But I should like to talk with you also. There are lusts of the brain just as there are lusts of the flesh, and to-night I am in the mood and humour for conversation."

They were approaching a side road which led to[34] Gortre's rooms. Schuabe's great stone house was still a quarter of a mile away up the hill.

"Do not go home yet," said Schuabe, "come to my house, see my books, and let us talk. Make friends with the mammon of unrighteousness, Mr. Gortre! You are disturbed and unstrung to-night. You will not sleep. Come with me."

Gortre hesitated for a moment, and then continued with him. He was hardly conscious why he did so, but even as he accepted the invitation his nerves seemed recovered as by some powerful tonic. A strange confidence possessed him, and he strode on with the air and manner of a man who has some fixed purpose in his brain.

And as he talked casually with Schuabe, he felt towards him no longer the cold fear, the inexplicable shrinking. He regarded him rather as a vast and powerful enemy, an evil, sinister influence, indeed, but one against which he was armed with an armour not his own, with weapons forged by great and terrible hands.

So they entered the drive and walked up among the gaunt black trees towards the house.

Mount Prospect was a large, castellated modern building of stone. In a neighbourhood where architectural monstrosities abounded, perhaps it outdid them all in its almost brutal ugliness and vulgarity. It had been built by Constantine Schuabe's grandfather.

The present owner was little at Walktown. His Parliamentary and social duties bound him to London, and when he had time for recreation the newspapers announced that he had "gone abroad," and until he was actually seen again in the midst of his friends his disappearances were mysterious and complete.

In London he had a private set of rooms at one of the great hotels.
[35]
But despite his rare visits, the hideous stone palace in the smoky North held all the treasures which he himself had collected and which had been left to him by his father.

It was understood that at his death the pictures and library were to become the property of the citizens of Manchester, held in trust for them by the corporation.

Schuabe took a key from his pocket and opened the heavy door in the porch.

"I always keep the house full of servants," he said, "even when I am away, for a dismantled house and caretakers are horrible. But they will be all gone to bed now, and we must look after ourselves."

Opening an inner door, they passed through some heavy padded curtains, which fell behind them with a dull thud, and came out into the great hall.

Ugly as the shell of the great building was, the interior was very different.

Here, set like a jewel in the midst of the harsh, forbidding country, was a treasure-house of ordered beauty which had few equals in England.

Gortre drew a long, shuddering breath of pleasure as he looked round. Every æsthetic influence within him responded to what he saw. And how simple and severe it all was! Simply a great domed hall of white marble, brilliantly lit by electric light hidden high above their heads. On every side slender columns rose towards the dome, beyond them were tall archways leading to the rooms of the house; dull, formless curtains, striking no note of colour, hung from the archways.

16

In the centre of the vast space, exactly under the dome, was a large pool of still green water, a square basin with abrupt edges, having no fountain nor gaudy fish to break its smoothness.

And that was all, literally all. No rugs covered the[36] tesselated floor, not a single seat stood anywhere. There was not the slightest suggestion of furniture or habitation. White, silent, and beautiful! As Gortre stood there, he knew, as if some special message had been given him, that he had come for some great hidden purpose, that it had been foreordained. His whole soul seemed filled with a holy power, unseen powers and principalities thronged round him like sweet but awful friends.

He turned inquiringly towards his host. Schuabe's face was very pale; the calm, cruel eyes seemed agitated; he was staring at the priest. "Come," he said in a voice which seemed to be without its usual confidence; "come, this place is cold—I have sometimes thought it a little too bare and fantastic—come into the library; let us eat and talk."

He turned and passed through the pillars on the right. Gortre followed him through the dark, heavy curtains which led to the library.

They found themselves in an immense low-ceilinged room. The floor was covered with a thick carpet of dull blue, and their feet made no sound as they passed over it towards the blazing fire, which glowed in an old oak framework of panelling and ingle-nook brought from an ancient manor-house in Norfolk.

At one end of the room was a small organ, cased, modern as the mechanism was, in priceless Renaissance painted panels from Florence and set in a little octagonal alcove hung with white and yellow.

The enormous writing-table of dark wood stood in front of the fireplace and was covered with books and papers. By it was a smaller circular table laid with a white cloth and shining glass and silver for a meal.

"My valet is in bed," said Schuabe; "I hate any one about me at night, and I prefer to wait on myself then. 'From the cool cisterns of the midnight air my spirit[37] drinks repose.' If you will wait here a few moments I will go and get some food. I know where to find some. Pray amuse yourself by looking at my books."

He left the room noiselessly, and Basil turned towards the walls. From ceiling to floor the immense room was lined with shelves of enamelled white wood, here and there carved with tiny florid bunches of fruit and flowers—Jacobean work it seemed.

A few pictures here and there in spaces between the shelves—the hectic flummery of a Whistler nocturne; a woman avec cerises, by Manet; a green silk fan, painted with fêtes gallantes, by Conder—alone broke the many-coloured monotony of the books.

Gortre had, from his earliest Oxford days, been a lover of books and a collector in a moderate, discriminating way. As a rule he was roused to a mild enthusiasm by a fine library. But as his practised eye ran over the shelves, noting the beauty and variety of the contents, he was unmoved by any special interest. His brain, still, so it seemed, under some outside and compelling instinct or influence, was singularly detached from ordinary interests and rejected the books' appeal.

Close to where he stood the shelves were covered with theological works. Müller's Lectures on the Vedanta Philosophy, Romane's Reply to Dr. Lightfoot, De la Saussaye's Manual, stood together. His hand had been wandering unconsciously over the books when it was suddenly arrested, and stopped on a familiar black binding with plain gold letters. It was an ordinary reference edition of the Holy Bible, the "pearl" edition from the Oxford University Press.

There was something familiar and homely in the little dark volume, which showed signs of constant use. A few feet away was a long shelf of Bibles of all kinds, rare editions, expensive copies bound up with famous commentaries—all [38] the luxuries and éditions de luxe of Holy Writ. But the book beneath his fingers was the same size and shape as the one which stood near his own bedside in his rooms—the one which his father had given him when he went to Harrow, with "Flee youthful lusts" written on the fly-leaf in faded ink. It was homelike and familiar.

He drew it out with a half smile at himself for choosing the one book he knew by heart from this new wealth of literature.

Then a swift impulse came to him.

Gortre could not be called a superstitious man. The really religious temperament, which, while not rejecting the aids of surface and symbol, has seen far below them, rarely is "superstitious" as the word has come to be understood.

The familiar touch, the pleasant sensation of the limp, rough leather on his finger-balls gave him a feeling of security. But that very fact seemed to remind him that some danger, some subtle mental danger, was near. Was this Bible sent to him? he wondered. Were his eyes and hands directed to it by the vibrating, invisible presences which he felt were near him? Who could say?

But he took the book in his right hand, breathed a prayer for help and guidance—if it might so be that God, who watched him, would speak a message of help—and opened it at random.

He was about to make a trial of that old mediæval practice of "searching"—that harmless trial of faith which a modern hard-headed cleric has analysed so cleverly, so completely, and so entirely unsatisfactorily.

He opened the book, with his eyes fixed in front of him, and then let them drop towards it. For a moment the small type was all blurred and indistinct, and then one text seemed to leap out at him.

It was this—

[39] "TAKE YE HEED, WATCH AND PRAY: FOR YE KNOW NOT WHEN THE TIME IS."

This, then, was his message! He was to watch, to pray, for the time was at hand when—

The curtain slid aside, and Schuabe entered with a tray. He had changed his morning coat for a long dressing-gown of camel's-hair, and wore scarlet leather slippers.

Basil slipped the Bible back into its place and turned to face him.

"I live very simply," he said, "and can offer you nothing very elaborate. But here is some cold chicken, a watercress salad, and a bottle of claret."

They sat down on opposite sides of the round table and said little. Both men were tired and hungry. After he had eaten, the clergyman bent his head for a second or two in an inaudible grace, and made the sign of the Cross before he rose from his chair.

"Symbol!" said Schuabe, with a cold smile, as he saw him.

The truce was over.

"What is that Cross to which all Christians bow?" he continued. "It was the symbol of the water-god of the Gauls, a mere piece of their iconography. The Phœnician ruin of Gigantica is built in the shape of a cross; the Druids used it in their ceremonies; it was Thor's hammer long before it became Christ's gibbet; it is used by the pagan Icelanders to this day as a magic sign in connection with storms of wind. Why, the symbol of Buddha on the reverse of a coin found at Ugain is the same cross, the 'fylfot' of Thor. The cross was carved by Brahmins a thousand years before Christ in the caves of Elephanta. I have seen it in India with my own eyes in the hands of Siva Brahma and Vishnu! The[40] worshipper of Vishnu attributes as many virtues to it as the pious Roman Catholic here in

18

Salford to the Christian Cross. There is the very strongest evidence that the origin of the cross is phallic! The crux ansata was the sign of Venus: it appears beside Baal and Astarte!"

"Very possibly, Mr. Schuabe," said Gortre, quietly. "Your knowledge on such points is far wider than mine; but that does not affect Christianity in the slightest."

"Of course not! Who ever said it did? But this reverence for the cross, the instrument of execution on which an excellent teacher, and, as far as we know, a really good man, suffered, angers me because it reminds me of the absurd and unreasoning superstitions which cloud the minds of so many educated men like yourself."

"Ah," said Gortre, quietly, "now we are 'gripped.' We have come to the point."

"If you choose, Mr. Gortre," Schuabe answered; "you are an intellectual man, and one intellectual man has a certain right to challenge another. I was staying with Lord Haileybury the other day, and I spent two whole mornings walking over the country with the Bishop of London, talking on these subjects. He very ably endeavoured to bring physical and psychological science into a single whole. But all he seemed to me to prove was this, crystallised into an axiom or at least a postulate. Conscious volition is the ultimate source of all force. It is his belief that behind the sensuous and phenomenal world which gives it form, existence, and activity, lies the ultimate invisible, immeasurable power of Mind, conscious Will, of Intelligence, analogous to our own; and—mark this essential corollary—that man is in communication with it, and that was positively all he could do for me! I met him there easily enough, but when he tried to prove a revelation—Christianity—he utterly broke down. We parted very good friends, and I gave him a thousand[41] pounds for the East London poor fund. But still, say what you will to me. I am here to listen."

He looked calmly at the young man with his unsmiling eyes. He held a Russian cigarette in his fingers, and he waved it with a gentle gesture of invitation as if from an immeasurable superiority.

And as Gortre watched him he knew that here was a brain and intelligence far keener and finer than his own. But with all that certainty he felt entirely undismayed, strangely uplifted.

"I have a message for you, Mr. Schuabe," he began, and the other bowed slightly, without irony, at his words. "I have a message for you, one which I have been sent here—I firmly believe—to deliver, but it is not the message or the argument that you expect to hear."

He stopped for a short time, marshalling his mental forces, and noticing a slight but perceptible look of surprise in his host's eyes.

"I know you better than you imagine, sir," he said gravely, "and not as many other good and devout Christians see you. I tell you here to-night with absolute certainty that you are the active enemy of Christ—I say active enemy."

The face opposite became slightly less tranquil, but the voice was as calm as ever.

"You speak according to your lights, Mr. Gortre," he said. "I am no Christian, but there is much good in Christianity. My words and writings may have helped to lift the veil of superstition and hereditary influences from the eyes of many men, and in that sense I am an enemy of the Christian faith, I suppose. My sincerity is my only apology—if one were needed. You speak with more harshness and less tolerance than I should have thought it your pleasure or your duty to use."

Gortre rose. "Man," he cried, with sudden sternness,[42] "I know! You hate our Lord, and would work Him evil. You are as Judas was, for to-night it is given me to read far into your brain."

19

Schuabe rose quickly from his chair and stood facing him. His face was pallid, something looked out of his eyes which almost frightened the other.

"What do you know?" he cried as if in a swift stroke of pain. "Who—?" He stopped as if by a tremendous effort.

Some thought came to reassure him.

"Listen," he said. "I tell you, paid priest as you are, a blind man leading the blind, that a day is coming when all your boasted fabric of Christianity will disappear. It will go suddenly, and be swept utterly away. And you, you shall see it. You shall be left naked of your faith, stripped and bare, with all Christendom beside you. Your pale Nazarene shall die amid the bitter laughter of the world, die as surely as He died two thousand years ago, and no man or woman shall resurrect Him. You know nothing, but you will remember my words of to-night, until you also become as nothing and endure the inevitable fate of mankind."

He had spoken with extraordinary vehemence, hissing the words out with a venom and malice, general rather than particular, from which the Churchman shrunk, shuddering. There was such unutterable conviction in the thin, evil voice that for a moment the pain of it was like a spasm of physical agony.

Schuabe had thrown down the mask; it was even as Gortre said, the soul of Iscariot looked out from those eyes. The man saw the clergyman's sudden shrinking.

The smile of a devil flashed over his face. Gortre had turned to him once more and he saw it. And as he watched an awful certainty grew within him, a thought so appalling that beside it all that had gone before sank into utter insignificance.

[43]

He staggered for a moment and then rose to his full height, a fearful loathing in his eyes, a scorn like a whip of fire in his voice.

Schuabe blanched before him, for he saw the truth in the priest's soul.

"As the Lord of Hosts is my witness," cried Gortre loudly, "I know you now for what you are! You know that Christ is God!"

Schuabe shrank into his chair.

"Antichrist!" pealed out the accusing voice. "You know the truth full well, and, knowing, in an awful presumption you have dared to lift your hand against God."

Then there was a dead silence in the room. Schuabe sat motionless by the dying fire.

Very slowly the colour crept back into his cheeks. Slowly the strength and light entered his eyes. He moved slightly.

At last he spoke.

"Go," he said. "Go, and never let me see your face again. You have spoken. Yet I tell you still that such a blinding blow shall descend on Christendom that——"

He rose quickly from his chair. His manner changed utterly with a marvellous swiftness.

He went to the window and pulled aside the curtain. A chill and ghostly dawn came creeping into the library.

"Let us make an end of this," he said quietly and naturally. "Of what use for you and me, atoms that we are, to wrangle and thunder through the night over an infinity in which we have neither part nor lot? Come, get you homewards and rest, as I am about to do. The night has been an unpleasant dream. Treat it as such. We differ on great matters. Let that be so and we will forget it. You shall have a friend in me if you will."

Gortre, hardly conscious of any voluntary movements,[44] his brain in a stupor, the arteries all over his body beating like little drums, took the hat and coat the other handed to him, and stumbled out of the house.

20

It was about five o'clock in the morning, raw, damp, and cold.

With a white face, drawn and haggard with emotion, he strode down the hill. The keen air revived his physical powers, but his brain was whirling, whirling, till connected thought was impossible.

What was it? What was the truth about that nightmare, that long, horrid night in the warm, rich room? His powers were failing; he must see a doctor after breakfast.

When he reached the foot of the hill, and was about to turn down the road which led to his rooms, he stopped to rest for a moment.

From far behind the hill, over the dark, silhouetted houses of the wealthy people who lived upon it, a huge, formless pall of purple smoke was rising, and almost blotting out the dawn in a Titanic curtain of gloom. The feeble new-born sun flickered redly through it, the colour of blood. There was no wind that morning, and the fog and smoke from the newly lit factory chimneys in the Irwell valley could not be dispersed. It crept over the town like doom itself—menacing, vast, unconquerable.

He pulled out his latch-key with trembling hand, and turned to enter his own door. The cloud was spreading.

"Lighten our darkness," he whispered to himself, half consciously, and then fell fainting on the door-step, where they found him soon, and carried him in to the sick-bed, where he lay sick of a brain-fever a month or more.

Lighten our darkness!

[45]
CHAPTER V

A LOST SOUL

In his great room at the British Museum, great, that is, for the private room of an official, Robert Llwellyn sat at his writing-desk finishing the last few lines of his article on the Hebrew inscription in mosaic, which had been discovered at Kefr Kenna.

It was about four in the afternoon, growing dark with the peculiarly sordid and hopeless twilight of a winter's afternoon in central London. A reading lamp upon the desk threw a bright circle of light on the sheet of white unlined paper covered with minute writing, which lay before the keeper of Biblical antiquities in the British Museum.

The view from the tall windows was hideous and almost sinister in its ugliness. Nothing met the eye but the gloomy backs of some of the great dingy lodging-houses which surround the Museum, bedroom windows, back bedrooms with dingy curtains, vulgarly unlovely.

The room itself was official looking, but far from uncomfortable. There were many book-shelves lining the walls. Over them hung large-framed photographs and drawings of inscriptions. On a stand by itself, covered with a glass shade, was a duplicate of Dr. Schick's model of the Haram Area during the Christian occupation of Jerusalem.

A dull fire glowed in the large open fireplace.

[46]
Llwellyn wrote a final line with a sigh of relief and then leaned far back in his swivel chair. His face was gloomy, and his eyes were dull with some inward communing, apparently of a disturbing and unpleasant kind.

The door opened noiselessly (all the dwellers in the mysterious private parts of the Museum walk without noise, and seem to have caught in their voices something of that almost religious reverence emanating from surroundings out of the immemorial past), and Lambert, the assistant keeper and secretary, entered.

He drew up a chair to the writing-desk.

"The firman has been granted!" he said.

A quick interest shone on Professor Llwellyn's face.

"Ah!" he said, "it has come at last, then, after all these months of waiting. I began to despair of the Turkish Government. I never thought it would be granted. Then the Society will really begin to excavate at last in the prohibited spots! Really that is splendid news, Lambert. We shall have some startling results. Results, mind you, which will be historical, historical! I doubt but that the whole theory of the Gospel narrative will have to be reconstructed during the next few years!"

"It is quite possible," said Lambert. "But, on the other hand, it may happen that nothing whatever is found."

Llwellyn nodded. Then a sudden thought seemed to strike him. "But how do you know of this, Lambert?" he said, "and how has it happened?"

Lambert was a pleasant, open-faced fellow, young, and with a certain air of distinction. He laughed gaily, and returned his chief's look of interest with an affectionate expression in his eyes.

"Ah!" he said, "I have heard a great deal, sir, and I have some thing to tell you which I am very happy about. It is gratifying to bring you the first news. Last night I[47] was dining with my uncle, Sir Michael Manichoe, you know. The Home Secretary was there, a great friend of my uncle's. You know the great interest he takes in the work of the Exploration Society, and his general interest in the Holy Land?"

"Oh, of course," said Llwellyn. "He's the leader of the uncompromising Protestant party in the House; owes his position to it, in fact. He breakfasts with the Septuagint, lunches off the Gospels, and sups with Revelations. Well?"

"It is owing to his personal interest in the work," continued Lambert, "that the Sultan has granted the firman. After dinner he took me aside, and we had a longish talk. He was very gracious, and most eager to hear of all our recent work here, and additions to the collections in our department. I was extremely pleased, as you may imagine. He spoke of you, sir, as the greatest living authority—wouldn't hear of Conrad Schick or Clermont-Ganneau in the same breath with you. He went on to say in confidence, and he hinted to me that I had his permission to tell you, though he didn't say as much in so many words, that they are going to offer you knighthood in a few days!"

A sudden flush suffused the face of the elder man. Then he laughed a little.

"Your news is certainly unexpected, my dear boy," he said, "and, for my part, knighthood is no very welcome thing personally. But it would be idle to deny that I'm pleased. It means recognition of my work, you see. In that way only, it is good news that you have brought."

"That's just it, Professor," the young man answered enthusiastically. "That's exactly it. Sir Robert Llwellyn, or Mr. Llwellyn, of course, cannot matter to you personally. But it is a fitting and graceful recognition of the work. It is a proper thing that the greatest living[48] authority on the antiquities and history of Asia Minor should be officially recognised. It encourages all of us, you see, Professor."

The young man's generous excitement pleased Llwellyn. He placed his hand upon his shoulder with a kindly, affectionate gesture.

At that moment a messenger knocked and entered with a bundle of letters, which had just arrived by the half-past-four post, and, with a congratulatory shake of the hand, Lambert left his chief to his correspondence.

22

The great specialist, when he had left the room, rose from his chair, went towards the door with swift, cat-like steps, and locked it. Then he returned to the desk, opened a deep drawer with a key which he drew from his watch-pocket, and took a silver-mounted flask of brandy from the receptacle. He poured a small dose of brandy into the metal cup and drank it hurriedly.

Then he leaned back once more in his chair.

Professor Llwellyn's face was familiar to all readers of the illustrated press. He was one of the few famous savants whose name was a household word not only to his colleagues and the learned generally, but also to the great mass of the general public.

In every department of effort and work there are one or two men whose personality seems to catch the popular eye.

His large, clean-shaven face might have belonged to a popular comedian; his portly figure had still nothing of old age about it. He was sprightly and youthful in manner despite his fat. The small, merry, green eyes—eyes which had yet something furtive and "alarmed" in them at times—stood for a concrete personification of good humour. His somewhat sensual lips were always smiling and jolly on public occasions. His enormous erudition and acknowledged place among the learned of[49] Europe went so strangely with his appearance that the world was pleased and tickled by the paradox.

It was a fine thing to think that the spectacled Dry-as-dust was gone. That era of animated mummy was over, and when The World read of Professor Llwellyn at a first night of the Lyceum, or the guest of honour at the Savage Club, it forgot to jeer at his abstruse erudition.

Scholars admitted his scholarship, and ordinary men and women welcomed him as homme du monde.

The Professor replaced the flask in the drawer and locked it. His hand trembled as he did so. The light which shone on the white face showed it eloquent with dread and despair. Here, in the privacy of the huge, comfortable room, was a soul in an anguish that no mortal eyes could see.

The Professor had locked the door.

The letters which the messenger had brought were many in number and various in shape and style.

Five or six of them, which bore foreign stamps and indications that they came from the Continental antiquarian societies, he put on one side to be opened and replied to on the morrow.

Then he took up an envelope addressed to him in firm black writing and turned it over. On the flap was the white, embossed oval and crown, which showed that it came from the House of Commons. His florid face became paler than before, the flesh of it turned grey, an unpleasant sight in so large and ample a countenance, as he tore it open. The letter ran as follows:

"House of Commons.

"Dear Llwellyn,—I am writing to you now to say that I am quite determined that the present situation shall not continue. You must understand, finally, that my patience is exhausted, and that, unless the large sum[50] you owe me is repaid within the next week, my solicitors have my instructions, which are quite unalterable, to proceed in bankruptcy against you without further delay.

"The principal and interest now total to the sum of fourteen thousand pounds. Your promises to repay, and your innumerable requests for more time in which to do so, now extend over a period of three years. I have preserved all your letters on the subject at issue between us, and I find that, so far from decreasing your indebtedness when your promises

23

became due, you have almost invariably asked me for further sums, which, in foolish confidence, as I feel now, I have advanced to you.

"It would be superfluous to point out to you what bankruptcy would mean to you in your position. Ruin would be the only word. And it would be no ordinary bankruptcy. I have a by no means uncertain idea where these large sums have gone, and my knowledge can hardly fail to be shared by others in London society.

"I have still a chance to offer you, however, and, perhaps, you will find me by no means the tyrant you think.

"There are certain services which you can do me, and which, if you fall in with my views, will not only wipe off the few thousands of your indebtedness, but provide you with a capital sum which will place you above the necessity for any such financial manœuvres in the future as your—shall I say infatuation?—has led you to resort to in the past.

"If you care to lunch with me at my rooms in the Hotel Cecil, at two o'clock, the day after to-morrow—Friday—we may discuss your affairs quietly. If not, then I must refer you to my solicitors entirely.

"Yours sincerely,

"Constantine Schuabe."

The big man gave a horrid groan—half snarl, half[51] groan—the sound which comes from a strong animal desperate and at bay.

He crossed over to the fireplace and pushed the letter down into a glowing cavern among the coals, holding it there with the poker until it was utterly consumed and fluttered up the chimney from his sight in a sheet of ash—the very colour of his relaxed and pendulous cheeks.

He opened another letter, a small, fragile thing written on mauve paper, in a large, irregular hand—a woman's hand:—

"15 Bloomsbury Court Mansions.

"Dear Bob—I shall expect you at the flat to-night at eleven, without fail. You'd better come, or things which you won't like will happen.

"You've just got to come.

Gertrude."

He put this letter into his pocket and began to walk the room in long, silent strides.

A little after five he put on a heavy fur coat and left the now silent and gloomy halls of the Museum.

The lamps of Holborn were lit and a blaze of light came from Oxford Circus, where the winking electric advertisements had just begun their work on the tops of the houses.

A policeman saluted the Professor as he passed, and was rewarded by a genial smile and jolly word of greeting, which sent a glow of pleasure through his six feet.

Llwellyn walked steadily on towards the Marble Arch and Edgeware Road. The continual roar of the traffic helped his brain. It became active and able to think, to plan once more. The steady exercise warmed his blood and exhilarated him.

There began to be almost a horrid pleasure in the stress of his position. The danger was so immediate and fell; the blow would be so utterly irreparable, that he was near[52] to enjoying his walk while he could still consider the thing from a detached point of view.

Throughout life that had always been his power. A strange resilience had animated him in all chances and changes of fortune.

He was that almost inhuman phenomenon, a sensualist with a soul.

24

For many years, while his name became great in Europe and the solid brilliancy of his work grew in lustre as he in age, he had lived two lives, finding an engrossing joy in each.

The lofty scientific world of which he was an ornament had no points of contact with that other and unspeakable half-life. Rumours had been bruited, things said in secret by envious and less distinguished men, but they had never harmed him. His colleagues hardly understood them and cared nothing. His work was all-sufficient; what did it matter if smaller people with forked tongues hissed horrors of his private life?

The other circles—the lost slaves of pleasure—knew him well and were content. He came into the night-world a welcome guest. They knew nothing of his work or fame beyond dim hintings of things too uninteresting for them to bother about.

He turned down the Edgeware Road and then into quiet Upper Berkeley Street, a big, florid, prosperous-looking man, looking as though the world used him well and he was content with all it had to offer.

His house was but a few doors down the street and he went up-stairs to dress at once. He intended to dine at home that night.

His dressing-room, out of which a small bedroom opened, was large and luxurious. A clear fire glowed upon the hearth; the carpet was soft and thick. The great dressing-table with its three-sided mirror was[53] covered with brushes and ivory jars, gleaming brightly in the rays of the little electric lights which framed the mirror. A huge wardrobe, full of clothes neatly folded and put away, suggested a man about town, a dandy with many sartorial interests. An arm-chair of soft green leather, stamped with red-gold pomegranates, stood by a small black table stencilled with orange-coloured bees. On the table stood a cigarette-box of finely plaited cream-coloured straw, woven over silver and cedar-wood, and with Llwellyn's initials in turquoise on one lid.

He threw off his coat and sank into the chair with a sigh of pleasure at the embracing comfort of it. Then his fingers plunged into the tea which filled the box on the table and drew out a tiny yellow cigarette.

He smoked in luxurious silence.

He had already half forgotten the menacing letter from Constantine Schuabe, the imperative summons to the flat in Bloomsbury Court Mansions. This was a moment of intense physical ease. The flavour of his saffron Salonika cigarette, a tiny glass of garnet-coloured cassis which he had poured out, were alike excellent. All day long he had been at work on a brilliant monograph dealing with the new Hebrew mosaics. Only two other living men could have written it. But his work also had fallen out of his brain. At that moment he was no more than a great animal, soulless, with the lusts of the flesh pouring round him, whispering evil and stinging his blood.

A timid knock fell upon the door outside. It opened and Mrs. Llwellyn came slowly in.

The Professor's wife was a tall, thin woman. Her untidy clothes hung round her body in unlovely folds. Her complexion was muddy and unwholesome; but the unsmiling, withered lips revealed a row of fair, white, even teeth. It was in her eyes that one read the[54] secret of this lady. They were large and blue, once beautiful, so one might have fancied. Now the light had faded from them and they were blurred and full of pain.

She came slowly up to her husband's chair, placing one hand timidly upon it.

"Oh, is that you?" he said, not brutally, but with a complete and utter indifference. "I shall want some dinner at home to-night. I shall be going out about ten to a supper engagement. See about it now, something light. And tell one of the maids to bring up some hot water."

25

"Yes, Robert," she said, and went out with no further word, but sighing a little as she closed the door quietly.

They had been married fifteen years. For fourteen of them he had hardly ever spoken to her except in anger at some household accident. On her own private income of six hundred a year she had to do what she could to keep the house going. Llwellyn never gave her anything of the thousand a year which was his salary at the Museum, and the greater sums he earned by his work outside it. She knew no one, the Professor went into none but official society, and indeed but few of his colleagues knew that he was a married man. He treated the house as a hotel, sleeping there occasionally, breakfasting, and dressing. His private rooms were the only habitable parts of the house. All the rest was old, faded, and without comfort. Mrs. Llwellyn spent most of her life with the two servants in the kitchen.

She always swept and tidied her husband's rooms herself. That afternoon she had built and coaxed the fire with her own hands.

She slept in a small room at the top of the house, next to the maids, for company. This was her life.

[55]

Over the head of the little iron bedstead of her room hung a great crucifix.

That was her hope.

When Llwellyn was rioting in nameless places she prayed for him during the night. She prayed for him, for herself, and for the two servant girls, very simply—that Heaven might receive them all some day.

The maid brought up some dinner for the Professor—a little soup, a sole, and some camembert.

He ate slowly, and smoked a short light-brown cigar with his coffee. Then he bathed, put on evening clothes, dressing himself with care and circumspection, and left the house.

In the Edgeware Road he got into a hansom and told the man to drive him to Bloomsbury Court Mansions.

[56]
CHAPTER VI

THE WHISPER

Robert Llwellyn paid the cabman outside the main gateway which led into the courtyard, and dismissed him.

The Court Mansions were but a few hundred yards from the British Museum itself, though he never visited them in the day time. A huge building, like a great hotel, rose skyward in a square. In the quadrangle in the centre, which was paved with asphalt, was an ornamental fountain surrounded by evergreen plants in tubs.

The Professor strode under the archway, his feet echoing in the stillness, and passed over the open space, which was brilliantly lit with the hectic radiance of arc lamps. He entered one of the doorways, and turning to the right of the ground-floor, away from the lift which was in waiting to convey passengers to the higher storeys, he stopped at No. 15.

He took a latch-key from his pocket, opened the door, and entered. It was very warm and close inside, and very silent also. The narrow hall was lit by a crimson-globed electric lamp. It was heavily carpeted, and thick curtains of plum-coloured plush, edged with round, fluffy balls of the same colour, hung over the doors leading into it.

26

He hung his hat up on a peg, and stood perfectly silent for a moment in the warm, scented air. He could hear no sound but the ticking of a French clock. The[57] flat was obviously empty; and pulling aside one of the curtains, he went into the dining-room.

The place was full of light. Gertrude Hunt, or her maid, had, with characteristic carelessness, forgotten to turn off the switches. Llwellyn sat down and looked around him. How familiar the place was! The casual visitor would have recognised at a glance that the occupant of the room belonged to the dramatic profession.

Photographs abounded everywhere. The satinwood overmantel was crowded with them in heavy frames of chased silver. Bold enlargements hung on the crimson walls; they were upright, and stacked in disorderly heaps upon the grand piano.

All were of one woman—a dark Jewish girl with eyes full of a fixed fascination, a trained regard of allurement.

The eyes pursued him everywhere; bold and inviting, he was conscious of their multitude, and moved uneasily.

The dining-table was in a curious litter. Half-empty cups of egg-shell china stood upon a tray of Japanese lacquer inlaid with ivory and silver; a cake basket held pink and honey-coloured bon-bons, among which some cigarette ends had fallen. Two empty bottles, which had held champagne, stood side by side, cheek by jowl, with a gilt tray, on which was a miniature methyl lamp and some steel curling tongs.

The arm-chairs were upholstered in pink satin. On one of them was a long fawn-coloured tailor-made coat, hanging collar downwards over the back. A handful of silver and a tiny gun-metal cigarette case had dropped out of a pocket on to the seat of the chair.

The whole place reeked with a well-known perfume—an evil, sickly smell of ripe lilies and the acrid smoke of Egyptian tobacco. A frilled dressing jacket covered with yellowish lace lay in a tumbled heap upon the hearth-rug.

[58]

The room would have struck an ordinary visitor with a sense of nausea almost like a physical blow. There was something sordidly shameless about it. The vulgarest and most material of Circes held sway among all this gaudy and lavish disorder. The most sober-living and innocent-minded man, brought suddenly into such a place, would have known it instantly for what it was, and turned to fly as from a pestilence.

A week or two before, a picture of this den had appeared in one of the illustrated papers. Underneath the photograph had been printed—

"THE BOUDOIR OF ONE OF LONDON'S POPULAR FAVOURITES.

MISS GERTRUDE HUNT AT HOME."

Below had been another picture—"Miss Hunt in her new motor-car." Robert Llwellyn had paid four hundred pounds for the machine.

The big man seemed to fit into these surroundings as a hand into a glove. In his room at the Museum, on a platform at the Royal Society, his intellect always animated his face. In such places his personality was eminent, as his work also.

Here he was changed. Silenus was twin to him; he sniffed the perfume with pleasure; he stretched himself to the heat and warmth like a great cat. He was an integral part of the mise-en-scène—lost, and arrogant of his degradation.

A key clicked in the lock, there was a rustling of silk, and Gertrude Hunt swept into the room.

"So you're come to time, then," she said in a deep, musical voice, but spoilt by an unpleasing Cockney twang. "I'm dead tired. The theatre was crammed; I had to[59] sing

27

the Coon of Coons twice. Get me a brandy-and-soda, Bob. There's a good boy—the decanter's in the sideboard."

She threw off her long cloak and sank into a chair. The sticky grease-paint of the theatre had hardly been removed. She looked, as she said, worn out.

They chatted for a few moments on indifferent subjects, and she lit a cigarette. When she took it from her lips, Llwellyn noticed that the end was crimsoned by the paint upon them.

"Well," she said at length, "somehow or other you must pay those bills I sent on to you. They must be paid. I can't do it. I'm only getting twenty-five pounds from the theatre now, and that's just about enough to pay my drink bill!"

Llwellyn's face clouded. "I'm just about at my last gasp myself," he said. "I'm threatened with bankruptcy as it is."

"Oh, cheer up!" she cried. "Here, have a B. and S. I do hate to hear any one talk like that. It gives me the hump at once. Now look here, Bob. You know that I like you better than any one else. We've been pals for seven or eight years now, and I'd rather have you a thousand times than the others. You understand that, don't you?"

He nodded back at her. His face was pleased at her expression of affection, at the kindness of this dancing-girl to the great scholar!

"But," she continued, "you know me, and you know that I can't go on unless I have what I want all the time. And I want a lot, too. If you can't give it me, Bob, it must be some one else—that's all. Captain Parker's ready to do anything, any time. He's almost a millionaire, you know. Can't you raise any 'oof anyhow? If I'd a thousand at once, and another in a week[60] or two, I could manage for a bit. But I must have a river-house at Shepperton. That cat, Lulu Wallace, has one, and an electric launch and all. What about your German friend—the M.P.? He's got tons of stuff. Touch him for a bit more."

"Had a letter from him this afternoon," said Llwellyn, "with a demand for about fourteen thousand that I owe him now. Threatens to sell me up. But there was something which looked brighter at the end of the letter, though I couldn't quite make out what he was driving at."

"What was that?"

"The tone of the letter changed; it had been nasty before. He said that I could do him a service for which he would not only wipe out the old debt, but for which I could get a lot more money."

"You'll go to him at once, Bob, won't you?"

"I suppose I must. There's no way out of it. I can't think, though, how I can do him any service. He's a dabbler, an amateur in my own work, but he's not going to pay a good many thousands for any help in that."

"Let it alone till you find out," she said, with the instinctive dislike of her class to the prolonged discussion of anything unpleasant. She got up and rang the bell for her maid and supper.

For some reason Llwellyn could eat nothing. A weight oppressed him—a presage of danger and disaster. The unspeakable mental torments that the vicious man who is highly educated undergoes—torments which assail him in the very act and article of his pleasures—have never been adequately described. "What a frail structure his honours and positions were," he thought as the woman chatted of the coulisses and the blackguard news of the demi-monde. His indulgent life had acted[61] on the Professor with a dire physical effect. His nerves were unstrung and he became childishly superstitious. The slightest hint of misfortune set his brain throbbing with a horrid fear. The spectre of overwhelming disaster was always waiting, and he could not exorcise it.

The two accidental and trivial facts that the knives at his place were crossed, and that he spilt the salt as he was passing it to his mistress, set him crossing himself with nervous rapidity.

The girl laughed at him, but she was interested nevertheless. For the moment they were on an intellectual level. He explained that the sign of the Cross was said to avert misfortune, and she imitated him clumsily.

Llwellyn thought nothing of it at the time, but the meaningless travesty came back afterwards when he thought over that eventful night.

Surely the holy sign of God's pain was never so degraded as now.

Their conversation grew fitful and strained. The woman was physically tired by her work at the theatre, and the dark cloud of menace crept more rapidly into the man's brain. The hour grew late. At last Llwellyn rose to go.

"You'll get the cash somehow, dear, won't you?" she said with tired eagerness.

"Yes, yes, Gertie," he replied. "I suppose I can get it somehow. I'll get home now. If it's a clear night I shall walk home. I'm depressed—it's liver, I suppose—and I need exercise."

"Have a drink before you go?"

"No, I've had two, and I can't take spirits at this time."

He went out with a perfunctory and uninterested kiss. She came to the archway with him.

London was now quite silent in its most mysterious[62] and curious hour. The streets were deserted, but brilliantly lit by the long row of lamps.

They stood talking for a moment or two in the quadrangle.

"Queer!" she said; "queer, isn't it, just now? I walked back from the Covent Garden ball once at this time. Makes you feel lonesome. Well, so long, Bob. I shall have a hot bath and go to bed."

The Professor's feet echoed loudly on the flags as he approached the open space. Never had he seemed to hear the noises of his own progress so clearly before. It was disconcerting, and emphasised the fact of his sole movement in this lighted city of the dead.

On the island in the centre of the cross-roads he suddenly caught sight of a tall policeman standing motionless under a lamp. The fellow seemed a figure of metal hypnotised by the silence.

Llwellyn walked onwards, when, just as he was passing the Oxford Music Hall, he became conscious of quick footsteps behind him. He turned quickly, and a man came up. He was of middle size, with polite, watchful eyes and clean shaven.

The stranger put his hand into the pocket of his neat, unobtrusive black overcoat and drew out a letter.

"For you, sir," he said in calm, ordinary tones.

The Professor stared at him in uncontrollable surprise and took the envelope, opening it under a lamp. This was the note. He recognised the handwriting at once.

"Hotel Cecil.

"Dear Llwellyn,—Kindly excuse the suddenness of my request and come down to the Cecil with my valet. I have sent him to meet you. I want to settle our business to-night, and I am certain that we shall be able to[63] make some satisfactory arrangement. I know you do not go to bed early.—Most sincerely yours,

"Constantine Schuabe."

29

"This is a very sudden request," he said to the servant rather doubtfully, but somewhat reassured by the friendly signature of the note. "Why, it's two o'clock in the morning!"

"Extremely sorry to trouble you, sir," replied the valet civilly, "but my master's strict orders were that I should find you and deliver the note. He told me that you would probably be visiting at Bloomsbury Court Mansions, so I waited about, hoping to meet you. I brought the coupé, sir, in case we should not be able to get you a cab."

Following the direction of his glance, Llwellyn saw that a small rubber-tired brougham to seat two people was coming slowly down the road. The coachman touched his hat as the Professor got in, and, turning down Charing Cross Road, in a few minutes they drove rapidly into the courtyard of the hotel.

Schuabe had not been established at the Cecil for any length of time. Though he owned a house in Curzon Street, this was let for a long period to Miss Mosenthal, his aunt, and he had hitherto lived in chambers at the Albany.

But he found the life at the hotel more convenient and suited to his temperament. His suite of rooms was one of the most costly even in that great river palace of to-day, but such considerations need never enter into his life.

The utter unquestioned freedom of such a life, its entire liberation from any restraint or convention, suited him exactly.

Llwellyn had never visited Schuabe in his private apartments before at any time. As he was driven easily[64] to the meeting he nerved himself for it, summoning up all his resolution. He swept aside the enervating influences of the last few hours.

Schuabe was waiting in the large sitting-room with balconies upon which he could look down upon the embankment and the river. It was his favourite among all the rooms of the suite.

He looked gravely and also a little curiously at the Professor as he entered the room. There was a question in his eyes; the guest had a sensation of being measured and weighed with some definite purpose.

The greeting was cordial enough. "I am very sorry, Llwellyn, to catch you suddenly like this," Schuabe said, "but I should like to settle the business between us without delay. I have certain proposals to make you, and if we agree upon them there will be much to consider, as the thing is a big one. But before we talk of this let me offer you something to eat."

The Professor had recovered his hunger. The chill of the night air, the sudden excitement of the summons, and, though he did not realise it, the absence of patchouli odours in his nostrils, had recalled an appetite.

The space and air of the huge room, with its high roof, was soothing after Bloomsbury Court Mansions.

Supper was spread for two on a little round table by the windows. Schuabe ate little, but watched the other with keen, detective eyes, talking meanwhile of ordinary, trivial things. Nothing escaped him, the little gleam of pleasure in Llwellyn's eyes at the freshness of the caviare, the Spanish olives he took with his partridge—rejecting the smaller French variety—the impassive watchful eyes saw it all.

It was too late for coffee, Llwellyn said, when the man brought it, in a long-handled brass pan from Constantinople, but he took a kümmel instead.

[65]

The two men faced each other on each side of the table. Both were smoking. For a moment there was silence; the critical time was at hand. Then Schuabe spoke. His voice was cold and steady and very businesslike. As he talked the voice seemed to wrap round

30

Llwellyn like steel bands. There was something relentless and inevitable about it; bars seemed rising as he spoke.

"I am going to be quite frank with you, Llwellyn," he said, "and you will find it better to be quite frank with me."

He took a paper from the pocket of his smoking jacket and referred to it occasionally.

"You owe me now about fourteen thousand pounds?"

"Yes, it is roughly that."

"Please correct me if I am wrong in any point. Your salary at the British Museum is a thousand pounds a year, and you make about fifteen hundred more."

"Yes, about that, but how do you——"

"I have made it my business to know everything, Professor. For example, they are about to offer you knighthood."

Llwellyn stirred uneasily, and the hand which stretched out for another cigarette shook a little.

"I need hardly point out to you," the cold words went on, and a certain sternness began to enforce them, "I need hardly point out that if I were to take certain steps, your position would be utterly ruined."

"Bankruptcy need not entirely ruin a man."

"It would ruin you. You see I know where the money has gone. Your private tastes are nothing to me, and it is not my business if you choose to spend a fortune on a cocotte. But in your position, as the very mainspring and arm of the Higher Criticism of the Bible, the revelations which would most certainly be made would[66] ruin you irreparably. Your official posts would all go at once, your name would become a public scandal everywhere. In England one may do just what one likes if only one does not in any way, by reason of position or attainments, belong to the nation. You do belong to the nation. You can never defy public opinion. With the ethical point of view I have nothing personally to do. But to speak plainly, in the eyes of the great mass of English people you would be stamped as an irredeemably vicious man, if everything came out. That is what they would call you. At one blow everything—knighthood, honour, place—all would flash away. Moreover, you would have to give up the other side of your life. There would be no more suppers with Phryne or rides to Richmond in the new motor-car."

He laughed, a low, contemptuous laugh which stung. Llwellyn's face had grown pale. His large, white fingers picked uneasily at the table-cloth.

His position was very clearly shown to him, with greater horror and vividness than ever it had come to him before, even in his moments of acutest depression.

The overthrow would be indeed utter and complete. With the greedy imagination of the sensualist he saw himself living in some cheap foreign town, Bruges perhaps, or Brussels, upon his wife's small income, bereft alike of work and pleasure.

"All you say is true," he murmured as the other made an end. "I am in your power. It is best to be plain about these things. What is your alternative?"

"My alternative, if you accept it, will mean certain changes to you. First of all, it will be necessary for you to obtain a year's leave from the British Museum. I had thought of asking you to resign your position, but that will not be necessary, I think, now. This can be arranged with a specialist easily enough. Even if[67] your health does not really warrant it, a word from me to Sir James Fyfe will manage that. You will have to travel. In return for your services and your absolute secrecy—though when you hear my proposals you will realise that perhaps in the whole history of the world never was secrecy so important to any man's safety—I will do as follows. I will wipe off your debt at once. I will pay you

31

ten thousand pounds in cash this week, and during the year, as may be agreed upon between us, I will make over forty thousand pounds more to you. In all fifty thousand pounds, exclusive of your debt."

His voice had not been raised, nor did it show any excitement during this tremendous proposal. The effect on Llwellyn was very different. He rose from his chair, trembling with excitement, staring with bloodshot eyes at the beautiful chiselled face below.

"You—you mean it?" he said huskily.

The millionaire made a single confirmatory gesture.

Then the whole magnitude and splendour of the offer became gradually plain to him in all its significance.

"I suppose," he said, "that, as the payment is great, the risk is commensurate."

"There will be none if you do what I shall ask properly. Only two other men living would do it, and, first and foremost, you will have to guard against their vigilance."

"Then, in God's name, what do you ask?" Llwellyn almost shouted. The tension was almost unbearable.

Schuabe rose from his seat. For the first time the Professor saw that he was terribly agitated. His eyes glowed, the apple in his throat worked convulsively.

"You are to change the history of the world!"

He drew Llwellyn into the very centre of the room, and held him firmly by the elbows. Tall as the Professor was, Schuabe was taller, and he bent and whispered into the other's ear for a full five minutes.

[68]

There was no sound in the room but the low hissing of his sibilants.

Llwellyn's face became white, and then ashen grey. His whole body seemed to shrink from his clothes; he trembled terribly.

Then he broke away from his host and ran to the fireplace with an odd, jerky movement, and sank cowering into an arm-chair, filled with an unutterable dread.

As morning stole into the room the Professor took a bundle of bills and acknowledgements from Schuabe and thrust them into the fire with a great sob of relief.

Then he turned into a bedroom and sank into the deep slumber of absolute exhaustion.

He did not go to the Museum that day.

[69]
CHAPTER VII

LAST WORDS AT WALKTOWN

The great building of the Walktown national schools blazed with light. Every window was a patch of vivid orange in the darkness of the walls. The whole place was pervaded by a loud, whirring hum of talk and laughter and an incredible rattle of plates and saucers.

In one of the classrooms down-stairs Helena Byars, with a dozen other ladies of the parish, presided over a scene of intense activity. Huge urns of tea ready mixed with the milk and sugar, were being carried up the stone stairs to the big schoolroom by willing hands. Piles of thick sandwiches of ham, breakfast-cups of mustard, hundreds of slices of moist wedge-shaped cake covered the tables, lessening rapidly as they were carried away to the crowded rooms above.

A Lancashire church tea-party was in full swing, for this was the occasion when Basil Gortre was to say an official farewell to the people among whom he had worked in the North.

In the tea-room itself several hundred people were making an enormous meal at long tables, under flaring, naked gas-lights, which sent shimmering vapours of heat up to the pitch-pine beams of the room above.

On the walls of the schoolroom hung long, map-like pictures, heavily glazed. Some of them were representations of foreign animals, or trees and plants, with the names printed below each in thick black type. Others[70] represented scenes from the life of Christ, and though somewhat stiff and wooden, showed clearly the immense strides that educational art has taken during the past few years.

At one end of the room was a platform running along its length. Some palms and tree-ferns in pots, chairs, a grand piano, and some music stands, promised a concert when tea should be over.

All the ladies of the parish were acting as attendants, or presiding at the urns on each table. There could be no doubt that the people were in a state of high good humour and enjoyment. Every now and again a great roar of laughter would break through the prevailing hum from one table or another. Despite the almost stifling heat and a mixed odour of humanity and ham, which a sensitive person might have shrunk from, the rough, merry Lancashire folk were happy as may be.

Basil Gortre, in his long, black coat, his skin somewhat pale from his long illness, walked from table to table, spending a few minutes at each. His face was wreathed in perpetual smiles, and roars of laughter followed each sally of his wit, a homely cut-and-thrust style of humour adapted to his audience. The fat mothers of families, wives of prosperous colliers and artisans, with their thick gold earrings and magenta frocks, beamed motherhood and kindliness at him. The Sunday-school teachers giggled and blushed with pleasure when he spoke.

The vicar, smiling paternally as was his wont, walked up and down the gangways also, toying with the pince-nez at his breast, and very successfully concealing the fact from every one that he was by no means in the seventh heaven of happiness. Tea-parties, so numerous and popular in the North, were always somewhat of a trial to him.

[71]

Basil and Mr. Byars met in the middle of the room when the tea was nearly over. Tears were gleaming in the eyes of the younger man.

"It is hard to leave them all," he said. "How good and kind they are, how hearty! And these are the people I thought disliked me and misunderstood me. I resented what I thought was a vulgar familiarity and a coarse dislike. But how different they are beneath the surface!"

"They have warm, loyal hearts, Basil," said the vicar. "It is a pity that such uncouth manners and exteriors should go with them. Surface graces may not mean much, but there is no doubt they have a tremendous influence over the human mind. During your illness the whole parish thought of little else, I really believe. And to-night you will have very practical evidence of their friendship. You know, of course, that there is going to be a presentation?"

"Yes. I couldn't help knowing that much, though I wish they wouldn't."

"It is very good of them. Now I shall call for grace."

The vicar made his way on to the platform and loudly clapped his hands. The tumult died suddenly away into silence, punctuated here and there by a belated rattle of a teacup and the spasmodic choking of some one endeavouring to bolt a large piece of cake in a hurry.

"We will now sing grace," Mr. Byars said in a clear and audible voice,—"the Old Hundred, following our usual custom."

As he spoke a little, bearded man in a frock-coat clambered up beside him. This was Mr. Cuthbert, the organist of the parish church. The little man pulled a tuning-fork from his pocket and struck it on the back of a chair.

[72]

Then he held it to his ear for a moment. The people had all risen, and the room was now quite silent.

"La!" sang the little organist, giving the note in a long, melodious call.

He raised his hand, gave a couple of beats in the air, and the famous old hymn burst out royally. The great volume of sound seemed too fierce and urgent even for that spacious room. It pressed against the ear-drums almost with pain, though sung with the perfect time and tune which are the heritage of the sweet-voiced North-country folk:—

"All people that on earth do dwell,
Sing to the Lord with cheerful voice!"

How hearty it was! How strong and confident!

As Basil Gortre listened his heart expanded in love and fellowship towards these brother Christians. The dark phantoms which had rioted in his sick brain during the long weeks of his illness lay dead and harmless now. The monstrous visions of a conventional and formal Christianity, covering a world of secret and gibing atheism, seemed incredibly far removed from the glorious truth, as these strong, homely people sang a full-voiced ave to the great brooding Trinity of Power and Love unseen, but all around them.

Who was he to be refined and too dainty for his uses? There seemed nothing incongruous in the picture before his eyes. The litter of broken ham, the sloppy cups, the black-coated men with brilliant sky-blue satin ties, the women with thick gnarled hands and clothes the colour of a copper kettle, what were they now but his very own brethren, united in this burst of praise?

And he joined in the doxology with all his heart and voice, his clear tenor soaring joyously above the rest:

[73]

"To FATHER, SON, and HOLY GHOST,
The GOD Whom Heaven and earth adore,
From men and from the Angel-host
Be praise and glory evermore. Amen."

It ceased with suddenness. There was the satisfied silence of a second, and then the attendant helpers, assisted by the feasters, fell swiftly upon the tables. Cloths and crockery vanished like snow melting in sunlight, and as each table was laid bare it was turned up by a patent arrangement, and became a long bench with a back, which was added to the rows of seats facing the platform. As each iron-supported seat was pushed noisily into its place it was filled up at once with a laughing crowd, replete but active, smacking anticipatory chops over the entertainment and speech-making to come.

Mr. Cuthbert, a painstaking pianist, whose repertoire was noisily commonplace, opened the concert with a solo.

Songs and recitations followed. All were well received by an audience which was determined to enjoy itself, but it was obvious that the real event of the gathering was eagerly awaited.

34

At last the eventful moment arrived. A table covered with green baize and bearing some objects concealed by a cloth was carried on the platform, and a row of chairs placed on either side of it.

The vicar, Basil, a strange clergyman, and a little group of black-coated churchwardens and sidesmen filed upon the platform amid tumultuous cheering and clapping of hands.

Mr. Pryde, the solicitor, rose first, and pronounced a somewhat pompous but sincere eulogy upon Basil's work and life at Walktown, which was heard in an absolute and appreciative silence, only broken by the scratching pencil of the reporter from a local paper.

[74]

Then he called upon the vicar to make the presentation.

Basil advanced to the table.

"My dear friends and fellow-workers," said Mr. Byars, "I am not going to add much to what Mr. Pryde has said. As most of you know, Mr. Gortre stands and is about to stand to me in even a nearer and more intimate relation than that of assistant priest to his parish priest. But before giving Mr. Gortre the beautiful presents which your unbounded generosity has provided, and in order that you may have as little speech-making from me as possible, I want to take this opportunity of introducing the Reverend Henry Nuttall to you to-night."

He bowed towards the stranger clergyman, a pleasant, burly, clean-shaven man.

"I am going from among you for a couple of months, as I believe you have been told, and Mr. Nuttall is to take my place as your temporary pastor for that time. My doctor has ordered me rest for a time. So my daughter and myself, together with Mr. Gortre, who sadly needs change after his illness, and who is not to take up his duties in London for several weeks, going away together for a holiday. And now I will simply ask Mr. Gortre to accept this tea-service and watch in the name of the congregation of St. Thomas as a token of their esteem and good-will."

He pulled the cloth away and displayed some glittering silver vessels. Then he handed the agitated young man a gold watch in a leather case.

Basil faced the shouting, enthusiastic crowd, staring through dimmed eyes at the long rows of animated faces.

When there was a little silence he began to speak in a voice of great emotion.

[75]

Very simply and earnestly he thanked them for their good-will and kindness.

"This may be," he said, "the last time I shall ever have the privilege and pleasure of speaking to you. I want to give you one last message. I want to urge one and all here to-night to do one thing. Keep your faith unspotted, unstained by doubts, uninfluenced by fears. Do that and all will be well with you here and hereafter." His voice sank a full tone and he spoke with marked emphasis. "I have sometimes thought and felt of late that possibly the time may be at hand, we who are here to-night may witness a time, when the Powers and Principalities of evil will make a great and determined onslaught upon the Christian Faith. I may not read the signs of the times aright, my premonitions—for they have sometimes amounted even to that—may be unfounded or imaginary. But if such a time shall come, if the 'horror of great darkness,' a spiritual horror, that we read of in Genesis, descend upon the world and envelop it in its gloom and terror, oh! let us have faith. Keep the light burning steadily. 'Let nothing disturb thee; let nothing affright thee. All passeth: God only remaineth.' And now, dear brothers and sisters in the Holy Faith, thank you, God bless you, and farewell."

35

There was a tense silence as his voice dropped to a close.

Here and there a woman sobbed.

There was something peculiar about his warning. He spoke almost in prophecy, as if he knew of some terror coming, and saw its advance from afar. His face, pale and thin from fever, his bright, earnest eyes, not the glittering eyes of a fanatic, but the saner, wiser ones of the earnest single-minded man, had an immense influence with them there.

[76]

And that night, as they trudged home to mean dwellings, or suburban villas, or rolled away in carriages, each person heard the intense, quiet voice warning them of the future, exhorting them to be steadfast in the Faith.

Seed which bore most fragrant blossom in the time which, though they knew it not, was close at hand was sown that night.

[77]
CHAPTER VIII

A DINNER AT THE PANNIER D'OR

Helena stood with her hand raised to her eyes, close by the port paddle-box, staring straight in front of her at a faint grey line upon the horizon.

A stiff breeze was blowing in the Channel, though the sun was shining brightly on the tossing waters, all yellow-green with pearl lights, like a picture by Henry Moore.

By the tall, graceful figure of the girl, swaying with the motion of the steamer and bending gracefully to the sudden onslaughts of the wind, stood a thick-set man of middle height, dressed in a tweed suit. His face was a strong one. Heavy reddish eyebrows hung over a pair of clear grey eyes, intellectual and kindly. The nose was beak-like and the large, rugged, red moustache hid the mouth.

This was Harold Spence, the journalist with whom Gortre was to live after the holiday was over and he began his work in Bloomsbury. Spence was snatching a few days from his work in Fleet Street, in order to accompany Gortre and Mr. and Miss Byars to Dieppe. It had been his first introduction to the vicar and his daughter.

"So that is really France, Mr. Spence!" said Helena; "the very first view of a foreign country I've ever had. I don't suppose you've an idea of what I'm feeling now? It seems so wonderful, something I've been waiting for all my life."

[78]

Spence smiled kindly, irradiating his face with good humour as he did so.

"Well, my sensations or emotions at present, Miss Byars, are entirely confined to wondering whether I am going to be seasick or not."

"Don't speak of it!" said a thin voice, a voice from which all the blood seemed to be drained, and, turning, they saw the vicar at their elbow.

His face was livid, his beard hung in lank dejection, a sincere misery poured from his pathetic eyes.

"Basil," he said, "Basil is down in the saloon eating greasy cold chicken and ham and drinking pale ale! I told him it was an outrage—" His feelings overcame him and he staggered away towards the stern.

"Poor father," said the girl. "He never could stand the sea, you know. But he very soon gets all right when he is on dry land again. Oh, look! that must be a church tower! I can see it quite distinctly, and the sun on the roofs of the houses!"

"That is St. Jacques," said Spence, "and that dome some way to the right, is St. Remy. Farthest of all to the right, on the cliffs, you can just see the château where the garrison is."

Helena gazed eagerly and became silent in her excitement. Basil, who came up from the saloon and joined them, the healthy colour beginning to glow out on his cheeks once more, watched her tenderly. There was something childishly sweet in her delight as the broad, tub-like boat kicked its way rapidly towards the quaint old foreign town.

In smoky Walktown he had not often seen her thus. Life was a more sober thing there, and her nature was graver than that of many girls, attuned to her environment. But, at the beginning of this holiday time, under a brilliant spring sun, which she was already beginning[79] to imagine had a foreign charm about it, she too was happy and in a holiday mood.

Basil pulled out his new and glorious gold watch, which had replaced the battered old gun-metal one he usually wore. Though not a poor man, he was simple in all his tastes, and the new toy gave him a recurring and childish pleasure whenever he looked at it.

"We ought to be in in about twenty minutes," he said. "Have you noticed that the tossing of the ship has almost stopped? The land protects us. How clear the town is growing! I wonder if you will remember any of your French, Helena? I almost wish I was like you, seeing a foreign country for the first time. Spence is the real voyageur though. He's been all over the world for his paper."

The vicar came up to them again, just as there was a general movement of the passengers towards the deck. A hooting cry from the steam whistle wailed over the water and the boat began to move slowly.

In a few more minutes they had passed the breakwater and were gliding slowly past the wharves towards the landing-stage.

Suddenly Helena clutched hold of Basil's arm.

"O Basil," she whispered, "how beautiful—look! Guarding the harbour!"

He turned and followed the direction of her glance.

An enormous crucifix, more than life size, planted in the ground, rose from the low cliffs on the right for all entering the harbour to see.

They watched the symbol in silence as the passengers chattered on every side and gathered up their rugs and hand-bags.

Gortre slipped his arm through Helena's.

The reminder was so vivid and sudden it affected them powerfully. They were both people of the world, living[80] in it and enjoying the pleasures of life that came in their way. Gortre was not one of those narrow, and even ill-bred, young priests with a text for ever on his lips, a sort of inopportune concordance, with an unpleasant flavour of omniscience. His religion and Helena's was too deep and fibrous a thing for commonplaces about it. It did not continually effervesce within and break forth in minute and constant bubbles, losing all its sincerity and beauty by the vulgar wear and tear of a verbal trick.

But it was always and for ever with him a transmuting force which changed his life each hour in a way of which the nominal believer has no conception.

A letter he had once written to Helena during a holiday compressed all his belief, and his joy in his belief, into a few short lines. Thus had run the sincere and simple statement, unadorned by any effort of literary grace to give it point and force:—

"Day by day as your letters come I go on saying my prayers for you, and with you, in fresh faith and confidence. You know that I absolutely trust the Lord Jesus Christ, who is,

37

I believe, the God who made the worlds, and that I pray to Him continually, relying on His promises.

"I keep on reading all sides of the question, as your father does also, and while admitting all that honest criticism and sincere intellectual doubt can teach me, and freely conceding that there is no infallible record in the New Testament, I grow more and more convinced that the Gospels and Paul's letters relate facts and not imaginations or hallucinations. And the more strongly my intellect is convinced, so much more does my heart delight in the love of God, who has given Himself for me. How magnificent is that finale of St. John's Gospel! 'Thomas saith unto Him, My Lord and my God.' And, then, how exquisite is the supplement about the manifestation [81] at the lake side! Imagine the skill of the literary man who invented that! Fancy such a man existing in a.d. 150 or thereabouts! I see Mrs. Humphry Ward says 'it was a dream which the old man at Ephesus related, and his disciples thought it was fact.' And she is a literary person!"

So, as the lovers glided slowly past the high symbol of God's pain, the worship in their hearts found but little utterance on their lips, though they were deeply touched.

It seemed a good omen to welcome them to France!

Spence remained to look after the luggage and to see it through the Customs, and the three others resolved to walk to the rooms which they had taken in the Faubourg de la Barre on the steep hill behind the château.

They passed over the railway line in the middle of the road, and past the cafés which cluster round the landing-stage, into the quaint market-place, with the great Gothic Cathedral Church of St. Jacques upon one side, and the colossal statue of Duquesne surrounded by baskets of spring flowers in the centre.

To Helena Byars that simple progress was one of unalloyed excitement and delight. The small and wiry soldiers in their unfamiliar uniforms; an officer sipping vermouth in a café, with spurs, sword, and helmet shining in the sun; two black priests, with huge furry hats—all the moving colour of the scene gave her new and delightful sensations.

"It's all so different!" she said breathlessly. "So bright and gay. What is that red thing over the tobacco shop, and that little brass dish over the hair-dresser's? Think of Walktown or Salford, now!"

The house in the Faubourg de la Barre was kept by a Madame Varnier, who spoke English well, and was in[82] the habit of letting her rooms to English people. A late déjeuner was ready for them.

The omelette was a revelation to Helena, and the rognons sautés filled her with respect for such cooking, but she was impatient, nevertheless, to be out and sight-seeing.

The vicar was tired, and proposed to stay indoors with the Spectator, and Spence had some letters to write, so Basil and Helena went out alone.

"The vicar and I will meet you at six," Spence said, "at the Café des Tribuneaux, that big place with the gabled roof in the centre of the town. At six the l'heure verre begins, the time when everyone goes out for an apéritif, the appetiser before dinner; afterwards I'll take you to dine at the Pannier d'Or, a jolly little restaurant I know of, and in the evening we'll go to the Casino."

Madame Varnier, the patronne, was in her kitchen sitting-room at the bottom of the stairs, and they looked in through the hatchway as they passed to tell her that they were not dining indoors.

On the floor a little girl, with pale yellow hair, an engaging button of three, was playing with a live rabbit, plump and mouse-coloured.

"How sweet!" said Helena, who was in a mood which made her ready to appreciate everything. "Look at the little darling with its pet. Has baby had the rabbit long, Madame Varnier?"

The Frenchwoman smiled lavishly. "Est-elle gentille l'enfant! hein! I bring the lapin chez moi from the magazin yesterday. There was very good lapins yesterday. I buy when I can. Je trouverai ça plus prudent. He is for the déjeuner of mademoiselle to-morrow. I take him so,"—she caught up the animal and suited the action to the word,—"I press his throat till his mouth[83] open, and I pour a little cognac into him. Il se meurt, and the flesh have a delicious flavour from the cognac!"

"How perfectly horrible!" said Helena as they came out into the street and walked down the hill. "Fancy seeing one's lunch alive and playing about like that, and then killing it with brandy, too! What pigs these French people are!"

Soon after the cool gloom of St. Remy enveloped them. Under the big dome they lingered for a time, walking from chapel to chapel, where nuns were praying. But it dulled them rather, and they had more pleasure in the grey and Gothic twilight of St. Jacques. Here the eye was uplifted by more noble lines, there was a more mediæval and romantic feeling about the place.

"We will come here to Mass on Sunday," said Basil. "I shall not go to the English Church at all. I never do abroad, and the vicar agrees with me. You see one belongs to the Catholic Church in England. In France one belongs to it, too. The 'Protestant' Church, as they call it, with an English clergyman, is, of course, a Dissenting church here."

"I see your point," said Helena, "though I don't know that I quite agree with it. But I have never been to a Roman Catholic church in England, and I want to see some of the services. 'Bowing down in the House of Rimmon,' Mr. Philemon would call it at Walktown."

They turned down a narrow street of quiet houses, and came out on to the Plage. There were a good many people walking up and down the great promenade from the Casino to the harbour mouth. An air of fulness and prosperity floated round the magnificent hotels which faced the sea.

It was a spring season, owing to the unusual mildness of the weather, and Dieppe was full of people. The Casino was opened temporarily after the long sleep of the[84] winter, and a company was performing there, having come on from the theatre at Rouen.

"What a curious change from the churches and market-place," said Helena. "This is tremendously smart and fashionable. How well-dressed every one is. Look at that red-haired woman with the furs. This is being quite in the world again."

They began a steady walk towards the pier and lighthouse. The wind was fresh, though not troublesome, and at five o'clock the sun, low in the sky, was still bright, and could give his animation to the picture.

The two young people amused themselves by speculations about the varied types of people who passed and repassed them. Gortre wore a suit of very dark grey, with a short coat and an ordinary tweed cap—his holiday suit, he called it—and, except for his clerical collar, there was little to show his calling. He was pleased, with a humorous sense of proprietorship, a kind of vicarious vanity, to notice the attention and admiration excited by the beautiful English girl at his side.

Helena Byars held her own among the cosmopolitan crowd of women who walked on the Plage. Her beauty was Saxon, very English, and not of a type that is always appreciated to its full value on the Continent, but it shone the more from Latin contrasts, and could not escape remark.

Every now and again they turned, at distances of a quarter of a mile or so, and during the recurrence of their beat they began to notice a person whom they met several times, coming and going.

He was an enormously big man, broad and tall, dressed expensively and with care. His size alone was sufficient to mark him out of the usual, but his personality seemed to them no less arresting and strange.

His large, smooth face was fat, the eyes small and brilliant,[85] with heavy pouches under them. His whole manner was a trifle florid and Georgian. Basil said that he seemed to belong to the Prince Regent's period in some subtle way. "I can imagine him on the lawns at Brighton or dining in the Pavilion," he said. "What a sensual, evil face the man has! Of course it may mean nothing, though. The Bishop of ——, one of the saints of the time, whose work on the Gospels is the most wonderful thing ever done in the way of Christian apologetics, has a face like one of the grotesque devils carved on the roof of Notre Dame or Lincoln Cathedral. But this man seems by his face to have no soul. One can't feel it is there, as one does, thank God! with most people."

"But what an intellect such a man must have! Look at him now. Look at the shape of his head. And besides, you can see it in his face, despite its sensuality and materialism. He must be some distinguished person. I seem to remember pictures of him, just lately, too, in the illustrated papers, only I can't get a name to them. I'm certain he's English, and some one of importance."

The big man passed them again with a quiet and swift glance of appreciation for Helena. He seemed lonely. Basil and Helena realised that he would have welcomed a chance word of greeting, some overture of friendship, which is not so impossible between English people abroad—even in adjacent Dieppe—as in our own country.

But neither of them responded to the unspoken wish they felt in the stranger. They were quite happy with each other, and presently they saw him light a cigar and turn into one of the great hotels.

They discussed the man for a few minutes—he had made an odd impression on them by his personality—and then found that it was time for the rendezvous at the Café des Tribuneaux.

[86]

By this time dusk was falling, and the sea moaned with a certain melancholy. But the town began to be brilliant with electric lights, and the florid Moorish building of the Casino was jewelled everywhere.

They turned away to the left, leaving the sea behind them, and, passing through a narrow street by the Government tobacco factory, came into the town again, and, after a short walk, to the café.

The place was bright and animated—lights, mirrors, and gilding, the stir and movement of the pavement, combined to make a novel and attractive picture for the English girl. The night was not cold, and they sat under the awning at a little round table watching the merry groups with interest. In a few minutes after their arrival they saw Spence and the vicar, now quite restored and well, coming towards them. They had forborne to order anything before the arrival of their companions.

The journalist took them under his wing at once. It amused him to be a cicerone to help them to a feeling of being at home. Gortre and Mr. Byars had been in Switzerland, and the latter at Rome on one occasion, but under the wing of a bishop's son who made his livelihood out of personally conducting parties to Continental towns of interest for a fixed fee. There was little freedom in these cut-and-dried tours, with their lectures en route and the very dinners in the hotel ordered for the tourists, and everything so arranged that they need not speak a word of any foreign language.

For the vicar, Spence prescribed a vermouth sec; Gortre, a courtesy invalid, was given a minute glass of an amber-coloured liquid with quinine in it—"Dubonnet" Spence called it; and Helena had a sirop of menthe.

They were all very happy together in the simple-minded, almost childish, way of quiet, intellectual people. Their enjoyment of the novel liqueurs, in a small café at[87] tourist-haunted Dieppe, was as great as that of any sybarite at the Hotel Ritz in Paris, or at a rare dinner at Ciro's in Monte Carlo.

Spence ordered an absinthe for himself.

The vicar seemed slightly perturbed. "Isn't that stuff rather dangerous, Spence?" he said, shrinking a little from the glass when the waiter brought it. "I've heard terrible things of it."

"Oh, I know," said the journalist, laughing, "people call it the French national vice and write tirades against it. Of course if it becomes a regular habit it is dangerous, and excess in absinthe is worse than most things. But one glass taken now and again is a wonderful stomachic and positively beneficial. I take one, perhaps, five times in a year and like it. But, like all good things, it is terribly abused both by the people who use it and those who don't."

Suddenly Helena turned to Gortre.

"Oh, look, Basil!" she said. "There is our friend of the Plage—Quinbus Flestrin, the mountain of flesh, you remember your Swift?"

The big stranger, now in evening dress and a heavy fur coat, had just come into the café and was sitting there with a cigarette and a Paris paper. He seemed lost in some sort of anxious speculation—at least so it seemed by the drooping of the journal in his massive fingers and the set expression of abstraction which lingered in his eyes and spread a veil over his countenance.

They had all turned at Helena's exclamation and looked towards the other side of the café, where the man was sitting.

"Why, that's Sir Robert Llwellyn," said Spence.

The vicar looked up eagerly. "The great authority on the antiquities of the Holy Land?" he said.

"Yes, that's the man. They knighted him the other[88] day. He's supposed to be the greatest living authority, you know."

"Do you know him, then?" asked the vicar.

"Oh, yes," said Spence, carelessly. "One knows every one in my trade. I have to. I've often gone to him for information when anything very special has been discovered. And I've met him in clubs and at lectures or at first nights at the theatre. He is a great play-goer."

"A decent sort of man?" said Gortre in a tone which certainly implied a doubt.

Spence hesitated a moment. "Oh, well, I suppose so," he said carelessly. "There are tales about his private life, but probably quite untrue. He's a man of the world as well as a great scholar, and I suppose the rather unusual combination makes people talk. But he is right up at the top of the tree,—goes everywhere; and he's just been knighted for his work. I'll go over and speak to him."

"If he'll come over," said the vicar, his eyes alight with anticipation and the hope of a talk with this famous expert on the subjects nearest his own heart, "bring him, please. There is nothing I should like better than a chat with him. I know his Modern Discoveries and Holy Writ almost by heart."

41

They watched Spence go across to Sir Robert's table. The big man started as he was spoken to, looked up in surprise, then smiled with pleasure, and extended a welcoming hand. Spence sat down beside him and they were soon in the middle of a brisk conversation.

"The poor man looked very bored until Mr. Spence spoke to him," said Helena. "Father, I'm sure you'll have your wish. He seems glad to have some one to talk to."

She was right. After a minute or two the journalist[89] returned with Llwellyn, and the five of them were soon in a full flood of talk.

"I was going to dine alone at my hotel," said the Professor, at length; "but Spence says that he knows of a decent restaurant here. I wonder if you would let me be one of your party? I'm quite alone in Dieppe for a couple of days. I'm waiting for a friend with whom I am going to travel."

"Oh, do come, Sir Robert," said the vicar, with manifest pleasure. "Are you going to be away from England for long?"

"I have leave from the British Museum for a year," said the Professor. "My doctor says that I require absolute rest. I am en route for Marseilles and from there to Alexandria."

The Pannier d'Or proved a pleasant little place, and the dinner was excellent. The Professor surprised and then amused the others by his criticism of the viands. He made the dinner his especial business, sent for the cook and had a serious conversation with him, chose the wines with extreme care.

His knowledge of the culinary art was enormous, and he treated it with a kind of reverence, addressing himself more particularly to Helena.

"Yes, Miss Byars, you must be most careful in the preparation of really good crayfish soup. This is excellent. The great secret is to flavour with a little lobster spawn and to mix the crumb of a French roll with the stock—white stock of course—before you add the powdered shells and anchovies."

Many times, despite his impatience to get to deeper and more congenial subjects, the vicar smiled at the purring of this gourmet, who seemed to prefer a sauce to an inscription and rissoles to research.

But with the special coffee—covered with fine yellow[90] foam and sweetened with crystals of amber sugar—the vicar's hour came. Sir Robert realised that it was inevitable and with a half sigh gave the required opening.

Once started, his manner changed utterly. The mask of materialism peeled away from his face, which became younger, brighter, as thought animated it, and new, finer lines cames out upon it as knowledge poured from him.

The conversation threatened to be a long one. Spence saw that and proposed to go on to the Casino with Helena, leaving the two clergymen with Llwellyn. It was when they had gone that the trio settled down completely.

It resolved itself at first into a duologue between the two elder men. Gortre's knowledge was too general and superficial on these purely antiquarian matters to allow him to take much part in it. He sat sipping his coffee and listening with keen attention and great enjoyment to this talk of experts. He had not liked Llwellyn from the first and could not do so even now, but he was forced to recognise the enormous intellectual activity and power of the big, purring creature before him.

Step by step the two archæologists went over the new discoveries being made in the ground between the City Wall of Jerusalem and the Hill of "Jeremiah's Grotto." They talked of the blue and purple mosaics found on the Mount of Olives, of all that had been done by the English and German excavators during the past years.

Gradually the discussion became more intimate and began to touch on great issues.

Mr. Byars was in a state of extraordinary interest. His knowledge was wide, and Llwellyn early realised[91] this, speaking to him as an equal, but beside the Professor's all-embracing achievements it was as nothing. The clergyman learnt something fresh, some sudden illuminating point of view, some irradiating fact, at every moment.

"I suppose," Mr. Byars said at length, "that the true situation of the Holy Sepulchre is still a matter of considerable doubt, Professor. Your view would interest me extremely."

"My view," said Llwellyn, with remarkable earnestness and with an emphasis which left no doubt about his convictions, "is that the Sepulchre has not yet been located."

"And your view is authoritative of course," said Mr. Byars.

The Professor bowed.

"That is as it may be," he said, "but I have no doubt upon the subject. The Church of the Holy Sepulchre is quite out of the question. There is really no historical evidence for it beyond a foolish dream of the Empress Helena, in a.d. 326. The people who know dismiss the traditional site at once. Of course it is generally believed, but one cannot expect the world at large to be cognisant of the doings of the authorities. Canon MacColl has said that the traditional site is the real one, and as his name has never been out of the public eye since what were called 'The Bulgarian Atrocities,' they are content to follow his lead. Then there is the question of the second site, in which a great many people believe they have found the true Golgotha and Sepulchre. 'The Gordon Tomb,' as it has been called, excited a great deal of attention at the time of its discovery. You may remember that I went to Jerusalem on behalf of the Times to investigate the matter. You may recollect that I proved beyond dispute that the[92] tomb was not Jewish at all, but indubitably Christian and long subsequent to the time of Christ. As a matter of fact, when the tomb was excavated in 1873 it was full of human bones and the mould of decomposed bodies, and there were two red-painted crosses on the walls. The tomb was close to a large Crusading hospice, and I have no doubt that it was used for the burial of pilgrims. Besides, my excavations proved that the second "city wall" must have included the new site, so that the Gospel narrative at once demolishes the new theory. I embodied twenty-seven other minor proofs in my letters to the Times also. No, Mr. Byars, my conviction is that we are not yet able to locate in any way the position of Golgotha and the Holy Tomb."

"You think that is to come?" asked Gortre.

"I feel certain," answered the Professor, with great deliberation and meaning—"I feel certain that we are on the eve of stupendous discoveries in this direction."

His tones were so impressive and so charged with import that the two clergymen looked quickly at each other. It seemed obvious that Llwellyn was aware of some impending discoveries. He must, they knew, be in constant touch with all that was being done in Palestine. Curiously enough, his words gave each of them a certain sense of chill, of uneasiness. There seemed to be something behind them, something of sinister suggestion, which they could not divine or formulate, but merely felt as an action upon the nerves.

It was a rare experience to sit with the greatest living authority upon a subject, and hear his views—views which it would be folly not to accept. His knowledge was so sure and so profound, a sense of power flowed from him.

But though both men felt a dim premonition of what[93] his words might possibly convey, neither could bring himself to a deliberate question. Nor did Llwellyn appear to invite it. During the whole of their talk he had sedulously avoided any religious questions. He had dealt solely with historical aspects.

His position in the religious world was singular. His knowledge of Biblical history was one of its assets, but he was not known definitely as a believer.

His attitude had always been absolutely non-committal. He did the work he had to do without taking sides.

It had become generally understood that no definite statement of his own personal convictions was to be asked or expected from him.

The general consensus of opinion was that Sir Robert Llwellyn was not a believer in the divinity of Christ; but it was merely an opinion, and had never been confirmed by him.

There was rather a tense silence for a short time.

The Professor broke it.

"Let me show you," he said, taking a gold pencil-case from his pocket, "a little map which I published at the time of the agitation about Gordon's Tomb. I can trace the course of the city walls for you."

He felt in his pocket for some paper on which to make the drawing, and took out a letter.

Gortre and the vicar drew their chairs closer.

Suddenly a curious pain shot through Basil's head and all his pulses throbbed violently. He experienced a terribly familiar sensation—the sick fear and repulsion of the night before his illness in the great library. The aroma of some utterly evil and abominable personality seemed to come into his brain.

For, as he had looked down at the paper on which the great white fingers were now tracing thin lines, he had[94] seen, before Llwellyn turned it over, a firm, plain signature, thus:

Constantine Schuabe

With some excuse about the heat of the room, he left it and went out into the night.

His brain was busy with terrible intuitive forebodings, he seemed to be caught up in the fringe of some great net, the phantoms of his illness came round him once more, the dark air was thick with their wings—vague, and because of that more hideous.

He passed the lighted kiosk at the Casino entrance with a white, set face.

He was going home to pray.

[95]
CHAPTER IX

INAUGURATION

It was at Victoria Station that Basil said good-bye to Helena. Spence had been back again in London for a fortnight. Mr. Byars and his daughter were to go straight back to Manchester the same day, and Gortre was to take possession of his new quarters in Lincoln's Inn and enter on his duties at St. Mary's without delay.

It had been a pleasant holiday, they all agreed, as the train brought them up from Newhaven; how pleasant they had hardly realised till it was all over. They had been all brought more intimately together than ever before. Gortre had come to know Mr. Byars with far more completeness than had been possible during their busy parochial life at Walktown. The elder man's calm and steadfast belief, his wide knowledge and culture, the Christian sanity of his life, were never more manifest than in the uninterrupted communion of this time of rest and pleasure.

44

He saw in his future father-in-law such a man as he himself humbly hoped that he might become. The impulsiveness of an eager youth had toned down into the mature judgment of middle age. The enthusiasms of life's springtime had solidified into quiet strength and force, and faith and intellect had combined into a deep and immovable conviction. And Mr. Byars's was no simple, childlike nature to whom goodness and belief were easy, a natural attribute of the man. He was subtle[96] rather, complex, and the victory over himself had cost him more than it costs most men. So much Gortre realised, and his love and admiration for the vicar were tempered with that joyous awe that one fine nature is privileged to feel at the contact with another.

To Helena also this time of holiday had been very precious. To mark the fervour of her chosen one, the energy he threw into Life, Love, and Religion, to find him a man and yet a priest, to follow him in thought to the ivory gates of his Ideals—these were her uplifting occupations; and to all these as they walked and talked, listened to the music at the Casino, explored the ancient forest and castle at Arques, or knelt with bowed heads as the sacring bell rang and the priests moved about the altar—these had been the united bond of the great knowledge and hope they shared together.

After the farewells had been said in the noisy station, and Basil's cab drove him rapidly towards his new home, he felt wonderfully ready and prepared for his new work.

The moving panorama of Victoria Street, the sudden stately vision of Palace Yard, the grandeur of the Embankment—all spoke to the young man of a vivid, many-coloured, and pulsating life which was waiting for him and his activities. Here, indeed, was a fine battlefield and theatre for the Holy War.

The cab moved slowly up Chancery Lane and then turned into the sudden quiet of Lincoln's Inn. It was almost like going back to Oxford, he thought, with a quick glow of pleasure to see himself surrounded by mellow, ancient buildings once more.

All his heavy personal effects had been sent up from Walktown some days before, and when he had carried up his two portmanteaus he knocked at the "oak" or outside door of the chambers, which was shut, and waited for a response. He saw that his name was[97] freshly painted on the lintel of the door under the two others:

Mr. Harold M. Spence.
Mr. Cyril Hands.
Rev. Basil Gortre.

In a minute he heard footsteps. The inner door was opened and he saw a tall, thin man, bearded and brown, peering at him through spectacles.

"Ah! Gortre, I suppose," said the other. "We were expecting you. I'm Hands, you know, home for another month yet. Give me these bags. Come in, come in."

He followed the big, stooping fellow with a sense of well-being at the cheery bohemianism of his greeting.

He found himself in a very large room indeed, panelled from floor to ceiling, the woodwork painted a sage green. Three great windows, each with a cushioned seat in its recess, looked down into the quadrangle below. Curtained doors faced him on all sides of the room, which was oddly shaped and full of nooks and angles. Books and newspapers covered two or three writing-tables and were piled on shelves between the doors. A bright fire burned in a large grate and the mantel above was covered with Oxford photographs, pipes, and tobacco jars. There was a note of comfort everywhere, of luxurious comfort though not of luxury. The furniture was not new and it bore the signs of long use no less than careful choice. Bohemia it was, but not a squalid Bohemia. If a room can have a personality, this was a gentlemanly room. One saw that gentlemen lived here, men who, without daintiness or a tinge[98] of the sybarite, yet liked a certain order and fitness around them. At once Basil felt in key with the place. There was no jarring note anywhere.

"I've got you a sort of meal, Gortre," said Hands, pleasantly, "though we were rather in doubt as to what a man could want at four o'clock in the afternoon! Spence suggested afternoon tea, as you'll be wanting to dine later on. But Mrs. Buscall, our laundress, suggested cold beef and Bass's beer—after a sea voyage which she regards as a sort of Columbus adventure. So fall to—here you are. Harold is just getting up."

Indeed, as he spoke there came a noise of vigorous splashing from behind one of the closed doors and Spence's voice bellowed out a greeting.

Basil looked puzzled for a moment and Hands laughed as he saw it.

"You must remember that Spence doesn't get back from the office till three in the morning," he said. "He's writing four leaders a week now, and on his late nights, when he comes back, his brain is too alert and excited to sleep, so he has some Bovril and just works away at other stuff till morning. He won't interfere with us, though. I never hear him come in, nor will you. These chambers are a regular rabbit warren for size and ramification."

Basil went into the bedroom he was to have, a spacious, clean, and simply furnished place, and when he came out again for his meal found Spence, in a loose suit of flannels, smoking a cigarette. The journalist joined him at the table.

In a very short time Gortre felt thoroughly at home. He knew by a kind of instinct that he should be happy in Lincoln's Inn. Hands had still a month to spend in London before he went back to Palestine to continue his work for the Exploring Society, and he looked for[99]ward to many interesting talks with him, the actual agent and superintendent of the work at Jerusalem, the trained eye and arm of the great and influential English Society.

And as for Spence, he had known him intimately ever since his first Oxford days, many years ago now. Harold Spence was like a brother to him—had always been that.

The first hour's conversation, desultory as it was, in a sense, showed him how full and varied his new life promised to be. After the noisy seclusion of Walktown he felt that he was now in the centre of things. Both Spence and Hands were thoroughly cultured men, and both were distinguished above the crowd in their respective spheres.

Basil heard keen, critical, "inside" talk for almost the first time. His two companions knew everybody, were at the hub of things. Two nights ago Spence had been talking to the Prime Minister for ten minutes.—The Daily Wire was the unofficial Government organ. Hands had been at Lambeth with the Archbishop, the president and patron of the Palestine Society. They were absolute types of the keen, vigorous, and young mental aristocracy which is always on the active service of English life. They belonged to the executive branch.

"I'm sorry, Basil," Spence said suddenly, "I've got a note for you from Father Ripon. I forgot to give it to you. He sent it down by a special messenger this morning. Here it is."

Father Ripon was the vicar of St. Mary's, Gortre's new chief.

He took the note and opened it, reading as follows:

"The Clergy House,

"St Mary's, Bloomsbury.

"Dear Mr. Gortre,—Friend Spence says that you will[100] arrive in London this afternoon. I don't believe in wasting time and I want a good long talk with you before you begin your work with us. To-night I am due at Bethnal Green to give a lecture. I shall be driving home about ten and I'll call at Lincoln's Inn on my way. If this will not be too late for you, we can then talk matters over.—Sincerely yours in Christ,

46

Arthur Ripon."

Basil passed the note to Spence.

"That'll be all right," he said. "I shall be at work, and Hands will be in his own room. What a man Ripon is! He's just the incarnation of breezy energy. Brusque, unconventional as Dr. Parker himself, but one of the sincerest Christians and best men I ever met or ever shall meet. He signs his note like that because he means it. He hates cant, and what in some men would appear cant, or at least a rather unnecessary form of ending, is to him just an ordinary every-day fact. You will get on with Father Ripon, Basil, I'm sure. You'll get to love the man as we all do. I never knew any one so absolutely joyous as he is. He's about the happiest man in town, I should say. His private income is nearly two thousand a year, and his living's worth something too, and yet I don't suppose his own expenses are fifty pounds. He lives more or less on porridge—when he remembers to eat at all—and his only extravagance is hansom cabs, so that he can cram more work into the day."

They all laughed, and Spence began to tell anecdotes of the famous "ritualistic" parson who daily filled more stomachs, saved more souls, and shocked more narrow-minded people than any two men in Crockford.

At seven o'clock they all went out together—Spence to his adjacent office in Fleet Street, the other two to dine quietly at the University Club.

"London depresses me," said Hands, when they were[101] seated on the top of an omnibus and rolling westward through the Strand. "I am afraid that I shall never be in love with London any more. I always dislike my vacations, or rather my business visits to town. It's necessary that I attend the annual meeting of the Society and see people in authority, and I have to give a few lectures too. But I hate it all the same. I love the simple life of the East, the sun, the deep blue shadows, my silent Arabs. I know of no more beautiful sight than the Holy City—why do they call Rome the 'Holy City'? Jerusalem is the Holy City—when the hills are covered with the January snows. It is a wonderful, immemorial land, Gortre, a silent, beautiful country. Just before I came over here I spent a fortnight working at some inscriptions in a very ancient Latin monastery. I never knew such peace. The monks are all sad-faced, courteous Syrians, and they move along the rock balconies like benignant ghosts. And then one comes back and is plunged into this!"

He threw out his hand over the side of the omnibus with a note of disgust in his rather dreamy voice. The Strand was all brilliantly lit and waiting crowds stood by all the theatre doors. Men and women passed in and out of the bright orange light of bars and restaurants, and small filthy boys stabbed the deep roar of the traffic with their shrill voices as they called out the evening papers.

They dined quietly and simply at the big warm club in Piccadilly. Hands did most of the talking and Gortre was content to listen to the pleasant monotony of the low, level voice and to fall under the man's peculiar spell or charm—a charm that he always exercised upon another artistic temperament.

Hands was a poet by nature and sentiment. His strange, lonely life among the evidences of the past[102] under the Eastern sky had toned, mellowed, and orientalised his vision.

As he listened Gortre also began to feel something of the mystery and magic influence of that country of God's birth.

It was half-past nine when they got back to the chambers again. Hands went at once to his own room to work and Basil sat down in front of a red, glowing fire, gazing into the hot caverns, lost in reverie. It was as though he had taken some opiate and there was nothing better in life than to sit thus and dream in the warm silence of the firelit room.

47

A few minutes after ten he was suddenly called out of the clouds by a furious knocking at the door of the chambers.

The sound cut into his dreams like a knife.

He went to open the door, and Father Ripon, his new vicar, came in like a whirlwind. His voluminous black cloak brought cold air in its folds; his breezy, genial personality was so actual a fact, struck such a strident, material note, that dreams and reverie fled before it.

Gortre turned up the gas-jets and flooded the room with light.

Father Ripon was a tall, well-made man, too active to be portly, but with hints of a tendency towards plumpness, which was never allowed to ripen. His iron-grey hair was cropped close to his large, well-shaped head. The shrewd, merry eyes, of a rare red-hazel colour, were shaded by heavy grey brows, which gave them a singular directness and penetration. The nose was aquiline, the lips thin, though the mouth was large, and the chin massive and somewhat protruding. The mobile face, lined and seamed by the strenuous life of its owner, was very seldom in repose. It glowed and flashed continually with changing expression. On those occasions when the[103] play of feature sank to rest for a moment, at the giving of a benediction or the saying of a solemn prayer in church, a nobility and asceticism transformed the face into something saintly. But in the ordinary business of life the large humanity of the man gave him a readier title to the hearts of his people than their knowledge of the underlying saintliness of his character.

"Whisky?" he said, as Gortre asked him to take some. "No, thanks. Teetotaler for sake of example, always have been—and don't like the stuff either, never did. But I'll have some coffee and some bread and butter, if you've got it, and some of those oranges I see there. Forgot to lunch and had no time to dine!"

He began ravenously upon the oranges and with little further preamble plunged at once into the business of the parish. To emphasise a point, he flung a piece of orange peel savagely into the fire now and again.

"Our congregation," he said, "is peculiar to the church. You'll realise that when you get among them. I don't suppose in the whole of London there is a more difficult class of people to reach than our own. In the first place, it's a young congregation, speaking generally. 'Good,' you'll say; 'ductible material, plenty of enthusiasm to work on.' Not a bit of it. Most of the men are engaged in the City as clerks upon a small wage. They are mentally rather "small" men. Their lives are hard and monotonous, their outlook upon life petty and vulgar. The lowest and the highest classes are far easier to get at because they are temperamentally more alike. The anarchists have some right on their side when they condemn the bourgeoisie! It's difficult to show a small brain a big thing. Our difficulty is to explain the stupendous truths of Christianity to flabby and inert, machine-like fellows. When we do get hold of them, the very monotony of their lives makes religion a[104] more valuable thing to them. But the temptations of this class are terribly strong, living alone in lodgings as they do. The cheap music-hall and bar attract them; dissipation forms their society. Their views of women are taken from their association with the girls of the streets and the theatres. As they have no settled place in society, they are horribly afraid of ridicule. They are a far more difficult lot than their colleagues who live in the suburbs and have chances for healthier recreations.

"Then much of our work lies among women who seem irretrievably lost, and, I fear, very often are so. The Bloomsbury district is honeycombed with well-conducted dens of impurity. The women of a certain class have fixed upon the parish as their home. I don't mean the starving prostitute that one meets in the East End, I mean the fairly prosperous, utterly vicious, lazy women. You will meet with horrors of vice, a marvellous and stony

48

indifference, in the course of your work. To reach some of these well-dressed, well-fed, well-housed girls, to show them the spiritual and even the economic and material end of their lives, requires almost superhuman powers. If an angel came some of them would not believe. And in the great and luxurious buildings of flats which have sprung up in all the squares, the well-known London demi-mondaines—people who dance upon the stage and whose pictures glare upon one from every hoarding—have made their homes and constantly parade before the eyes of others the wealth which is the reward of lust.

"This is a wicked part of London, Gortre. And yet, day by day, in our beautiful church, where the Eucharist is celebrated and prayers go up unceasingly, we have evidences that our work is acceptable and that the Power is with us. Magdalen still comes with her jewels and her tears of repentance. I ask and beg of you to re[105]member certain things—keep them always before your eyes—during your ministry among us. Whenever a man or woman comes to you, either at confession or otherwise, and tells of incredible sins, welcome the very slightest movement towards the light. Cultivate an all-embracing sympathy. I firmly believe that more souls have been lost by a repellent manner on the part of a priest, or an apparent lack of understanding, than any one has any idea of. Remember that when a thoroughly evil and warped nature has made a great effort and laid its spiritual case before a priest, it expects in its inner consciousness a pat on the back for its new efforts. It wants commendation. One must fight warily, with a thorough psychological knowledge, with a broad humanity. To take even the slightest signs of repentance as a matter of course, to throw any doubt upon its reality or permanence, is to accept an awful responsibility. Err rather on the side of sentiment. Who are we to judge?"

Gortre had listened with deep attention to Father Ripon's earnest words. He began to realise more clearly the difficulties of his new life. And yet the obstacles did not daunt him. They seemed rather a trumpet note for battle. Ripon's enthusiasm was contagious; he felt the exhilaration of the tried soldier at a coming contest.

"One more thing," said the vicar. "In all your teaching and preaching hammer away at the great central fact of the Incarnation. No system of morals will reach these people—however plausible, however pure—unless you constantly bring the supernatural side of religion before them. Preach the Incarnation day in, day out. Don't, like so many men, regard it as an accepted fact merely, using it as a postulate on which to found a scheme of conduct. Once get the central truth of all into the hearts of a congregation, and then all else will follow. Now, good-night. I've kept you late, but I wished to[106] have a talk with you. A good deal will devolve upon you. I have especially arranged that you should not live in the Clergy House with Stokes, Carr, and myself. I would rather that your environment should be more secular. Stokes and Carr are perhaps a little too priestly, too "professional" in manner, if you understand what I am driving at. Keep yourself from that. If you go among the young men, see them at home, smoke with them, and take what they offer you in the way of refreshment. Well, good-bye. You are to preach at Sunday Evensongs you know. Sir Michael Manichoe, our patron, will be there, and there will be a large congregation."

He turned, said good-night with sudden abruptness, as if he had been lingering too long and was displeased with himself, and hurried away. It was his usual manner of farewell.

A few minutes afterwards Gortre went to bed. He found it difficult to believe that he had walked down the Faubourg de la Barre that morning. It had been a crowded day.

[107]
CHAPTER X

49

THE RESURRECTION SERMON

Sir Michael Manichoe was the great help and standby of St. Mary's. His father had been a wealthy banker in Rome, and a Jew. The son, who had enormously increased his inherited wealth, was an early convert to Christianity during his Oxford days in England. He was the Conservative member for a division in Lincolnshire, where his great country house was situated, and had become a pillar of the Church and State in England. In the House of Commons he presented the somewhat curious spectacle of a Jew by birth leading the moderate "Catholic" party. He was the great antagonist of Constantine Schuabe, and with equal wealth and position, though Schuabe was by far the more brilliant of the two men, he devoted all his energies to the opposition of the secular and agnostic influences of his political rival.

Every Sunday during the session, when he was in London, Sir Michael drove to St. Mary's for both morning and evening service. He was church warden, and intimately concerned in all the parochial business, while his purse was always open at Father Ripon's request.

Gortre had been introduced to Sir Michael during the week, and he knew the great man purposed attending to hear his first sermon at St. Mary's on the Sunday evening.

He prepared his discourse with extreme care. A natural wish to make a good first impression animated[108] him; but, as he sat late on the Saturday night, finally arranging his notes, he began to be conscious of new and surprising thoughts about the coming event. Earlier in the evening he had been talking to Hands, but the archæologist had gone to bed and left him alone.

The day had been a gloomy one. A black pall of fog fell over London at dawn, and had remained all day, almost choking him as he said evensong in the almost empty church.

All day long he had felt strangely overweighted and depressed. A chance paragraph in an evening paper, stating that Mr. Schuabe, M.P., had returned from a short Continental trip, started an uneasy and gloomy train of thought. The memory of the terrible night at Walktown recurred to him with a horrible sense of unreality, the picture blurred somewhat, as if the fingers of the disease which had struck him down had already been pressing on his brain when he had been alone with the millionaire. Much of what he remembered of that dread interview must have been delusion. And yet in all other matters he was sane and unprejudiced enough. Many times he had met and argued with unbelievers. They had saddened him, but no more. Why was it that this man, notorious atheist as he was, filled him with a shuddering fear, a horror for which he had no name?

Then also, what had been the significance of the incident at Dieppe—its true significance? Sir Robert Llwellyn had also inspired him with a feeling of utter loathing and abhorrence, though perhaps in a less degree. There was the sudden glimpse of Schuabe's signature on the letter. What was the connection between the two men? How could the Antichristian be in friendly communion with the greatest Higher Critic of the time?

He recalled an even more sinister occurrence, or so it had seemed to him. Two days after his first introduction[109] to Llwellyn and the dinner at the Pannier d'Or he had seen him enter the Paris train with Schuabe himself, who had just arrived from England. He had said nothing of the incident to Mr. Byars or Helena. They would have regarded it as ordinary enough. They knew nothing of what had passed between him and Schuabe. The deliberate words of Sir Robert at the restaurant recurred to him again and again, taking possession of his brain and ousting all other thoughts. What new discoveries was the Professor hinting at?

What did the whole obsession of his brain mean?

Curiously enough, he felt certain that these thoughts were in no way heralds of a new attack of brain fever. He knew this for a certainty. It seemed as if the persistent whisperings within him were rather the results of some spiritual message, as if the unseen agency which prompted them had some definite end and purpose in view.

The more he prayed the stronger his premonitions became; added force was given to them, as if they were the direct causes of his supplications.

It almost seemed that God was speaking to him.

He had questioned Hands cautiously, trying to learn if any new and important facts bearing upon Biblical history were indeed likely to be discovered in the near future.

But the answer did not amount to very much. The new and extensive excavations, under the permission of the lately granted firman from the Turkish Government, were only just beginning. The real work was to commence when Hands had finished his work in London and had returned to take charge of the operations.

Of course, Hands had said there were possibilities of discovery of first-class importance, but he doubted it. The locality of Golgotha and the Holy Sepulchre was[110] already established, in Hands's opinion. He had but little doubt of the authenticity of the established sites. Llwellyn's theories he scouted altogether, while agreeing with him in his negation of the Gordon Tomb.

So there had been very little from Hands that was in any way satisfactory to Basil.

But as he sat in the great silence of the night and read over the heads of the sermon a great sense of comfort came to him. He felt a mysterious sense of power, not merely because he knew the work was good, but something beyond that. He was conscious that for some reason or other that particular sermon which he was about to preach was one on which much depended. He could not say how or why he knew the thing was fraught with destiny to himself or others. He only knew it.

Many years afterwards he remembered that quiet night, and the help which seemed to come to him suddenly, a renewed hope and confidence after the mental misery of the day.

When he looked back on the terrible and stupendous events in which he had played so prominent a part, he was able to see clearly the chain of events, and to place his experience about what he always afterwards called his "Resurrection sermon" in their proper sequence.

Looking back through the years, he saw that a more than mortal power was guiding him towards the fulfilment of a Divine purpose.

But that night as he said his prayers before going to sleep he only felt a sweet security as he glanced at the MS. on the chair by his bedside.

The future was not yet revealed to him. God spared him the torture of foreknowledge.

The pulpit was high above the heads of the people,[111] much higher than is usual, a box of stone set in the great arch of the chancel.

As Gortre stood for a moment, after the prayer, he kissed the stole and placed it, as a yoke, upon his shoulders. He looked down the great building and saw the hundreds of watchful, expectant faces, with an uplifting sense of power. He felt as if he were a mouthpiece of strange, unseen forces. The air seemed full of wings.

51

For a moment the preacher paused and sent a keen glance over the congregation below. He saw Sir Michael Manichoe, dark, aquiline, Semitic, sitting in his front pew. A few seats behind him, with a sudden throb of surprise but nothing else, the calm and evil beauty of Constantine Schuabe's face looked up at him.

The strangeness of the appearance and the shock of it had at that moment no menace or intimidation for him. Standing there to deliver God's message, in God's house, his enemy seemed to have no power to throw his brain into its old fear and tumult.

Another face, unknown to him, arrested his attention.

The sexes were not separated for worship in St. Mary's. In the same seat where Schuabe sat was a woman, dark, handsome, expensively dressed.

She also was Jewish in appearance, though it was obvious that there was no connection between her and the millionaire. Her face, as the young clergyman's eyes rested on it for a second, seemed to be curiously familiar, as if he saw it every day of his life, but it nevertheless struck no personal note.

Gortre began to speak, taking for his text part of a verse from the Epistle of St. Paul to the Romans—"Declared to be the Son of God with power, according to the spirit of holiness, by the resurrection of the dead."

"In this world of to-day," he began calmly, and with a[112] certain deliberation and precision in his utterance, "what men in general are hungering after is a positive assurance of actual spiritual agency in the world. They crave for something to hold by which is outside themselves, and which cannot have grown out of the inner persuasions of men. They cannot understand people who tell them that, whether the events of the Gospels actually passed upon earth or not, they may fashion their own dispositions all the same, on the supposition that these events occurred. If I can to-night show that any appearance of the Risen Lord is attested in the same way as are certain facts commonly accepted as history, I shall have accomplished as much as I can hope."

Then, very carefully, Gortre went through the scientific and historical evidences for the truth of the Resurrection. Gradually, as he marshalled his proofs and brought forth one after the other, he began, by a sort of unconscious hypnotism of the eye, to make the seat where Schuabe and the strange woman sat his objective.

Many speakers have this automatic habit of addressing one or two persons as if they were the ear of the whole congregation. It is said that by such means, even if unconsciously employed, the brain becomes more concentrated and clearer for the work in hand.

Slowly the preacher's voice became more resonant and triumphant. To many of the congregation the overwhelming and stupendous evidences for the truth of the Gospel narratives which the study of late years has collected was entirely new. The Higher Criticism, the fact that it is not only in science that "discoveries" can be made, the excavations in the East and the newly discovered MSS., with their variations of reading, the possibility that the lost Aramaic original of St. Matthew's Gospel may yet be discovered, were all things which[113] came to them for the first time in their lives. Gortre's words began to open up to them an entirely new train of thought. Their interest was profoundly quickened.

Very few clergymen of middle age are cognisant of the latest theological thought. Time, money, and lack of education alike prevent them. The slight mental endowment and very ordinary education which are all that is absolutely necessary for an ordination candidate, are not realised by the ordinary member of a church congregation. The mass of the English clergy to-day are content to leave such questions alone, to do their duty simply, to impose upon their flock the necessity of "faith," and to deny the right of individual judgment and speculation.

They do not realise that the world of their middle age is more educated, and so more intelligent, than the world of their youth, and that, if the public intellect is nurtured by the public, those whose duty it is to keep it within the fold of Christianity must provide it with a food suited to its development.

Gortre, in his sermon, had crystallised and boiled down into pregnant paragraphs, without circumlocution or obscurity, all the brilliant work of Latham, Westcott, Professor Ramsay, and Homersham Cox. He quoted Renan's passage from Les Apôtres, dealing with the finding of the empty tomb, and showed the flaws and fallacies in that brilliant piece of antichristian suggestion.

As he began to bring his arguments to a close he was conscious that the people were with him. He could feel the brains around him thinking in unison; it was almost as if he heard the thoughts of the congregation. The dark, handsome woman stared straight up at him. Trouble was in her eyes, an awakened consciousness, and Gortre knew that the truth was dropping steadily into her mind, and that conviction was unwelcome and alarming.

[114]

And he felt also the bitter antagonism which was alive and working behind the impassive face and half-closed eyes of the millionaire below. It was a silent duel between them. He knew that his words were full of meaning, even of conviction, to the man, and yet he was subjectively conscious of some reserve of force, some hidden sense of fearful power, a desperate resolve which he could not overcome.

His soul wrestled in this dark, mysterious conflict as with a devil, but could not prevail.

He finished all his argument, the last of his proofs. There was a hushed silence in the church.

Then swiftly, with a voice which trembled with the power that was given him, he called them to repentance and a new life. If, he said, his words had carried conviction of the truth of Christ's resurrection, of His divinity, then, believing that, there was but one course open to them all. For to know the truth, and to believe it, and to continue in indifference, was to kill the soul.

It was over. Father Ripon had pronounced the blessing, the great organ was thundering out the requiem of another Sunday, and Sir Michael was shaking hands warmly with Basil in the vestry.

Gortre was tired and shaken by the long, nervous strain, but the evident pleasure of Father Ripon and Sir Michael, the knowledge that he had acquitted himself well, was comforting and sustaining.

He walked home, down quiet Holborn, curiously dead without the traffic of a week day and the lights of the shop fronts, and not reanimated by the strolling pedestrians, young people of the lower classes from the East End, who thronged it.

Lincoln's Inn was wonderfully soothing and quiet as his footsteps echoed in the old quadrangle. After a lonely, tranquil supper—Hands was at a dinner-party[115] somewhere in Mayfair and Spence was at the office of The Daily Wire preparing for Monday's paper—he wheeled a small writing-desk up to the fireside and began a long letter of news and thankfulness to Helena.

He pictured the pleasant dining-room at Walktown, the Sunday night's supper,—an institution at the Vicarage after the labours of the busiest day in the week,—with a guest or two perhaps.

He knew they would be thinking of him, as he of them, and pictured the love-light in his lady's sweet, calm eyes.

[116]
CHAPTER XI

"NEITHER DO I CONDEMN THEE"

Autumn came to London, a warm, lingering season. There was a hint of the South in the atmosphere of town. All business moved with languor; there was more enjoyment in life as people went and came through the streets under so ripe and genial a sun.

Gortre had settled down to steady, regular work. At no time before had a routine been so pleasant to him. His days were full of work, which, hard as it was, came to him with far more appeal than his duties at Walktown. Nothing ever stagnated here, at the very hub and centre of things.

The splendid energy and force of Father Ripon, the magnificent unconvention of his methods, animated his staff to constant and unflagging exertions.

Gortre felt that he was suddenly "grown up," that his life before had been spent in futile playtime compared to the present.

One central fact in St. Mary's parish held all the great organisation together. This was the daily services in the great church. Priests, deacons, sisters of mercy, school teachers, and lay helpers all drew their strength and inspiration from this source. The daily Eucharist, matins, evensong, were both a stimulus and stimulant of enormous power.

Church brought the mysteries in which they lived, moved, and had their being into intimate relation with every circumstance of daily life.

[117]
The extraordinary thing, which many of Father Ripon's staff were almost unable to understand, was that more people did not avail themselves of what they regarded— viewing the thing from a standpoint of personal experience—such helpful opportunities.

"They are always coming to me," Father Ripon had said on one occasion, "and complaining that they find such a tremendous difficulty in leading a holy life—say that the worldly surroundings and so forth kill their good impulses—and yet they won't come to church. People are such fools! My young men imagine that they can become good Christians by a sort of sudden magic—a low beast on Saturday night, the twentieth of August, and, after a nerve storm in church and a few tears in the vestry, a saint for evermore! And then when they get drunk or do something beastly the next week, they rail against the Christian Faith because it isn't a sort of spiritual hand cuffs! And yet if you told them you could manage a bank after merely experience in a shipping office, they would see the absurdity of that at once. Donkeys!"

This with a genial smile of tenderness and compassion, for this Whirlwind in a Cassock loved his flock.

So from the very first Basil had found his life congenial. Privately he blessed his good fortune in living in Lincoln's Inn with Spence. On the nights when the journalist was free from the office, and not otherwise engaged, the two men sat late with pipes and coffee, enjoying that vigorous communion of two keen, young, and virile brains which is one of the truly stimulating pleasures of life.

Gortre admired Spence greatly for some of his qualities. His intellect was, of course, first class—his high position on the great daily paper guaranteed that. His reading and sympathies were wide. Moreover, the[118] clergyman found a great refreshment in the fact that, in an age of indifference, at a time when the best intellects of younger London life were professedly agnostic, Harold Spence was an avowed Christian and Churchman. As Gortre got to know him better, when the silence and detachment of midnight in the old Inn broke down reticence, he realised with a sense of thankfulness, and sometimes of fear also, how a thorough belief in religion kept the writer straight and captain of his own soul.

For the man was a creature of strong passions and wayward desires. He had not always been the clean gentleman of the present. As is so often the case with a refined and cultured temperament, he had a dark and ugly side to his nature. The coarse vices of the blood called to him long and often with their hollow siren voices. Evil came to him with swift invitation and cunning allurement. He had hinted to Basil of days of sin and secret shame. And now, very soberly and without any emotion, he clung to Christ for help.

And he had conquered.

This was ever a glorious fact to Basil, another miracle in those thousands of daily miracles which were happening all around him. But his fear for Harold came from his realisation of his friend's exact spiritual grip. Spence's Christianity was rather too utilitarian for safety. Perhaps the deep inward conviction was weak. It seemed sometimes as if it were a barren, thorny thing—too much fetish, too much a return for benefits received, a sort of half-conscious bargain. He often prayed long that nothing should ever occur to shake Spence's belief; for he felt, if that should happen, the disaster would prove irreparable. A dammed river is a dangerous thing.

But he kept all these thoughts locked in his heart, and never spoke of them to Harold.

[119]

Since the evening of his first sermon he had never seen Schuabe again. Now and then the thought of him passed through his brain, and his mental sight seemed obscured for a moment, as though great wings hid the sun from him. But since the silent duel in the church, the curious and malign influence of the millionaire had waned. It was prominent no longer, and when it troubled him it did so without power and force. Fine health, the tonic of constant work, the armour of continual prayer, had their way and were able to banish much of what he now looked back on as morbidity, sinister though it had been.

Nevertheless, one thing often reminded him of that night. The dark, Jewish-looking lady he had seen sitting in the same pew with Schuabe often came to church on Sunday nights when he was preaching. The bold and insolently beautiful face looked up at him with steady interest. The fierce regard had something passionate and yet wistful in it.

Sometimes Basil found himself preaching almost directly to the face and soul of the unknown woman. There was an understanding between them. He knew it; he felt it most certainly.

Sometimes she would remain in her seat after the mass of the congregation had shuffled away into the night. She did not pray, but sat still, with her musing eyes fixed on the huge ten-foot crucifix that swung down from the chancel arch.

Once, as he passed the pew on the way to baptise the child of a poor woman of the streets—brought in furtively after the Sunday evensong—she made a movement as if to speak to him. He had waited in expectation for a moment, but she remained still, and he passed on to the font, with its sad cluster of outcasts, its dim gas-jets, and the tiny child of shame with its thin cry of distress.

He was asking the tremendous question—

[120] "Dost thou, in the name of this child, renounce the devil and all his works, the vain pomp and glory of the world, with all covetous desires of the same, and the carnal desires of the flesh, so that thou wilt not follow nor be led by them?"

when he saw that the unknown woman was standing by within the shadow of a pillar. A gleam of yellow light fell through the dark on her rich dress, her eye glittered behind her white veil. He thought there was a tear in it. But when he was saying the exhortation he saw that the tall, silent figure had departed.

He often wondered who the woman was,—if he should ever know her.

Something told him that she wanted help. Something assured him that he should some day give it to her.

And beyond this there was an unexplained conviction within him that the stranger was in some way concerned and bound up in the part he was to play in life.

Long ago he had realised that it was idle to deny the interference of supernatural personalities in human life. Accepting the Incarnation, he accepted the Communion of Saints. And he was always conscious of hidden powers moulding, directing him.

The episode of the cigarettes happened in this way.

Stokes, one of Gortre's fellow-curates, came to supper one night in Lincoln's Inn.

Spence was there also, as it was one of his free nights.

About ten o'clock supper was over and they proposed to have a little music. Stokes was a fine pianist, and he had brought some of the nocturnes and ballads of Chopin with him, to try on the little black-cased piano which stood at an obtuse angle with the end of the large sitting-room.

"Will you smoke, Stokes?" Spence said.

"Thank you, I'll have a cigarette," the young man[121] replied. "I can't stand cigars, and I've left my pipe at the Clergy House."

They looked for cigarettes in the silver box lined with cedar which stood on the mantel-shelf, but some one had smoked them all and the box was empty.

"Never mind," Spence said; "I've been meaning to run out and get a late Westminster and I'll buy some cigarettes, too. There's a shop at the Holborn end of the Lane, next to the shop where the oysters come from, and it won't be shut yet."

In a few minutes he came back with several packets of cigarettes in his hand. "I've brought Virginian," he said; "I know you can't stand Egyptian, none of us can, and if these are cheap, they're good, too."

Till eleven o'clock Stokes played to them—Chopin's wild music of melancholy and fire—and as the hour struck he went home.

Gortre and Spence sat and talked casually after he had gone, about the music they had heard, the cartoon in the evening paper, anything that came.

Basil had not been smoking during the evening. He had been too intent upon the nocturnes, and now he felt a want of tobacco. One of the packets of cigarettes lay by him on the table. He pulled up the flaps and took one. Without thinking what he was doing he drew a little photograph, highly finished and very clear, from the tiny cardboard case.

He glanced at it casually.

The thing was one of those pictures of burlesque actresses which are given away with this kind of tobacco. A tall girl with short skirts and a large picture hat was shown in a coquettish attitude that was meant to be full of invitation.

Basil looked at it steadily with a curious expression on his face. Then he took a large reading-glass from the[122] table and examined it again, magnifying it to many times its original size.

He scrutinised it with great care. It was the portrait of the strange girl who came to St. Mary's.

Basil had told Spence of this woman, and now he passed the photograph on to him.

"Harold, that is the girl who comes to church and looks so unhappy. She is an actress, of course. The name is underneath—Miss Gertrude Hunt. Who is Miss Gertrude Hunt?"

Spence took the thing. "How very queer!" he said, "to find your unknown like this. Gertrude Hunt? Why, she is a well-known musical comedy girl, sings and dances at the Regent, you know. There are all the usual stories about the lady, but possibly they are all lies. I'm sure I don't know. I've chucked that sort of society long ago. Are you sure it's the same person?"

"Oh, quite sure! Of course, this shows the girl in a different dress and so on, but it's she without a doubt. I am glad she comes to church. It is not what one expects from what one hears of that class of woman, and it's not what one generally finds in the parish."

He sighed, thinking of the many chilling experiences of the last few months in the vice-haunted streets and squares of Bloomsbury.

"Well," said Spence, "experiments with that type are generally failures, and sometimes dangerous to the experimenter. You remember Anatole France's Thaïs? But this damsel is no Thaïs certainly, and you aren't a bit like Paphuntius. I hope you will be able to do some good. Personally, anything of the sort would be quite impossible to me. Good-night, old man. I'm going to turn in. I've a hard day's work to-morrow. Sleep well."

He went out of the room with a yawn.

[123]

When he was left alone, with his little mystery solved in so commonplace a fashion, Basil was conscious of a curious disappointment. It was an anti-climax.

He had no narrow objection to the theatre. Now and then he had been to see famous actors in great plays. His occasional visits to the theatres of Irving or Wyndham had given him pleasure, nevertheless he had always felt a slight instinctive dislike to the trade of a mime. All voluntary sacrifices of personal dignity affect the average English temperament in this way more or less. However much the apologists of the stage may cry "art" or "beneficial influence," your British thinker is not convinced that there is anything very worthy in painting the face and making the body a public show for a wage. And there is sometimes a kind of wonder in the heart of a sincere Christian who attends a theatre as he remembers that the body is the Temple of the Holy Spirit.

Still Basil was tolerant enough. But this case which had thrust itself before him was quite different. He knew that the burlesque, the modern music play, made, first and foremost, a frank appeal to the senses. Its hopeless vulgarity and coarseness of sentiment, its entire lack of appeal to anything that was not debased and materialistic, were ordinary indisputable facts of every-day life. And so his lady of evensong was a high-priestess of nothing better than this cult of froth and gaudy sensuality. More than all others, his experiences of late had taught him that women of this class seemed to be very nearly soulless. Their souls had dissolved in champagne, their consciences were burnt up by the feverish excitement and pleasure of their lives. They sold themselves for luxury and the adulation of coarse men.

His very chagrin made him bitter and contemptuous more than his wont.

Then his eye lit upon a photogravure hung upon the[124] opposite wall. It was the reproduction of a quaint, decorative, stilted picture by an artist of the early Umbrian school, and represented St. Mary Magdalene.

The coincidence checked his contemptuous thoughts.

He began to reconstruct the scene in his brain, a favourite and profitable exercise of his, using his knowledge and study of the old dim times to animate the picture and make it vivid.

They were all resting, or rather lying, around the table, the body resting on the couch, the feet turned away from the table in the direction of the wall, while the left elbow rested on the table.

And then, from the open courtyard, up the verandah step, perhaps through an antechamber, and by the open door, passed the figure of a woman into the festive reception-room and dining-hall. How had she gained access? How incongruous her figure must have been there! In those days the Jewish prejudice against any conversation with women—even those of the most lofty character—was extreme.

The shadow of her form must have fallen on all who sat at meat. But no one spoke, nor did she heed any but One only.

The woman had brought with her an alabastron of perfume. It was a flask of precious foliatum, probably, which women wore round the neck, and which hung over the breast. The woman stood behind Him at His feet, and as she bowed reverently a shower of tears, like sudden summer rain, "bedewed" His feet.

Basil went through the whole scene until the final, "Go into peace" not go in peace, as the logical dogmatics would have had it.

And so she, the first who had come to Him for spiritual healing, went out into the better light, and into the eternal peace of the Kingdom of Heaven.

[125]

Basil tore up the vulgar little photograph and forgot that aspect of the dancer. He remembered rather the dim figure by the font.

There was a sudden furious knocking on the outer door of the chambers, and he went to open it.

[126]
CHAPTER XII

POWERS OF GOOD AND EVIL

Gortre felt certain that his vicar stood without. His knocking was full of militant Christianity. The tumultuous energy of the man without communicated its own stir and disturbance to Basil's brain by the most subtle of all forms of telepathy—that "telepathy" which, in a few more years, will have its definite recipes and formulæ.

Father Ripon refused to live by any standard of measured time. He refused—so he said—to believe that a wretched little clock really knew what the great golden sun was doing. He had found it impossible to call on Gortre before this late hour, and he came regardless of it now. He wished to see Basil, and he came now with a supreme and simple carelessness of conventional time.

As usual, the worthy man was hungry, and the débris of supper on the table reminded him of that. He sat down at once and began to eat rapidly, telling his story between mouthfuls.

"I bring you news of a famous opportunity," he said. "If you go to work in the right way you may win a soul. It's a poor demi-mondaine creature, a dancer at the theatres. She came to me in her brougham, her furs, and finery, and had a chat in my study. I gave her tea and a cigarette—you know I always keep some cigarettes for the choir-men or teachers when they call. All these women smoke. It's a great thing to treat these

58

people[127] with understanding and knowledge, Gortre. Don't 'come the priest' over them, as a coster said to me last week. When they realise that one is a man, then they are fifty times more willing to allow the other and more important thing.

"Well, this poor girl told me all about it, the same very sordid story one is always hearing. She is a favourite burlesque actress, and she lives very expensively in those gorgeous new flats—Bloomsbury Court. Some wealthy scoundrel pays for it all. A man 'in a very high position,' as she said with a pathetic little touch of pride which made me want to weep. Oh, my dear fellow, if the world only knew what I know! Great and honoured names in the senate, the forum, the Court, unsullied before the eyes of men. And then these hideous establishments and secret ties! This is a wicked city. The deadly lusts which war against the soul are great, powerful, and militant all around us.

"This poor woman has been coming regularly to church on Sundays. The first time was when you preached your capital sermon on the Resurrection. Now, she is dying from a slow complaint. She will live a year or two, the doctors think, and that is all. It does not prevent her from living her ordinary life, but it will strike her down suddenly some day.

"She has expressed a wish to see you to talk things over with you. She thinks you can help her. Go to her and save her. We must."

He handed Gortre a visiting-card, on which he saw the name of Gertrude Hunt with a curious lack of surprise.

"Well, I must be off," said Father Ripon, rising from the table with a large hunk of bread and cheese in one hand.

"Go and see this poor woman to-morrow evening.[128] She tells me she isn't acting for a week or two,—rehearsing some new play. Isn't it wonderful to think of the things that are going on every day? Just think of the Holy Spirit pouring into this sinning creature's heart, catching her in the middle of her champagne and frivolity, and just turning her, almost compelling her towards Christ! And men like John Morley or Constantine Schuabe say there is no truth in Christianity!—I'll take one of these apples— poor fools! Now I must go and write my sermon."

He was gone in a clattering rush.

For a long time Basil sat thinking. The mysterious links of some great chain were being revealed inch by inch. Wonderful as these circumstances already seemed to him, he felt sure there was far more behind them than he knew as yet. There was some unseen tie, some influence that drew his thoughts ever more and more towards the library in the palace at Manchester.

The next evening a maid showed Gortre into the hall of the flat of Bloomsbury Court Mansions, eyeing him curiously as she did so.

He passed down the richly carpeted passage with a quickening of all his pulses, noticing the Moorish lamps of copper studded with turquoise which threw a dim crimson light over everything, marking the ostentatious luxury of the place with wonder.

Gertrude Hunt lay back in a low arm-chair. She was dressed in a long, dull red teagown of cashmere, with a broad white band round the neck opening of white Indian needlework, embroidered with dark green leaves.

Her face was pale and tired.

Despite the general warmth of the time, a fire burnt steadily on the hearth.

Gortre sat down at her invitation, and they fell into a[129] desultory conversation. He waited for her to open on the real subjects that had brought him there.

He watched the tired, handsome face. Coarse it certainly was, in expression rather than feature, but that very coarseness gave it power. This woman, who lived the life of a doll, had character. One saw that. Perhaps, he thought, as he looked at her, that the very eagerness and greed for pleasure marked in her face, the passionate determination to tear the heart and core out of life, might still be directed to purer and nobler ends.

Then she began to talk to him quite frankly, and with no disguise or slurring over the facts of her life.

"I'm sick and tired of it all, Mr. Gortre," she said bitterly. "You can't know what it means a bit—lucky for you. Imagine spending all your life in a room painted bright yellow, eating nothing but chocolate creams, with a band playing comic songs for ever and ever. And even then you won't get it."

Basil shuddered. There was something so poignant and forceful in her words that they hurt, stung like a whip-lash. He was being brought into terrible contact not only with sin and the satiety of sin, but with its results. The hideous staleness and torture of it all appalled him as he looked at this human personification of it in the crimson gown.

"That's how it was at first," she continued. "I knew there was something more than this in life, though. I could read it in people's faces. So I came to the service at your church one Sunday evening. I'd never made fun of religion and all that at any time. I simply couldn't believe it, that was all. Then I heard you preach on the Resurrection. I heard all the proofs for the first time. Of course, I could see there wasn't any doubt about the matter at all. Then, curiously, directly I began to believe in it I began to hate the way I was[130] going on, so I went to Father Ripon, who was very nice, and he said you'd call."

"I quite understand you, Miss Hunt," said Gortre. "That's the beauty of faith. When once you believe, then you've got to change. It's a great pity, a very great pity, that clergymen don't attempt to explain things more than they do. If one isn't built in a certain way, I can quite understand and sympathise with any one who isn't able to take a parson's mere statement on trust, so to speak. But that's beside the way. You believe at any rate. And now what are you going to do? I'm here to help you in every possible way. I want to hear your views, just as you have thought them out."

"I like that," she said. "That's practical and sensible. I've never cared very much for sentimental ways of looking at things. You know I can't live very long. I've got enough to live quietly on for some years, put away in a bank, money I've made acting. I haven't spent a penny of my salary for years—I've made the men pay for everything. I shall go quietly away to the country and be alone with my thoughts, close to a little quiet church. You'll find a place for me, won't you? That's what I want to do. But there's something in the way, and a big something, too."

"I'm here to help that," said Basil.

"It's Bob," she answered. "The man that keeps me. I'm afraid of him. He's been away for months, out of England, but he's coming back at once. To-morrow as likely as not, he couldn't say to a day. I had a letter from Brindisi last week. He's been to Palestine, via Alexandria."

A quick premonition took hold of the young man.

"Who is he?" he asked.

She took a photograph from the mantel-shelf and gave it to him. It was one of the Stereoscopic Company's[131] series of "celebrities." Under the portrait was printed—"Sir Robert Llwellyn."

Gortre started violently.

"I know him," he said thickly. "I felt when I met him—What does it all mean?"

He dropped his head into his hands, filled with the old, nameless, unreasoning fear.

She looked steadily at him, wondering at his manner.

There was a tense silence for a time.

60

In the silence suddenly they heard a sound, clear and distinct. A key was being inserted into the door of the flat.

They waited breathlessly. Gertrude Hunt grew very white. Without any words from her, Basil knew whose fingers were even now upon the handle of the door.

Llwellyn entered. His huge form was dressed in a light grey suit and he carried a straw hat in his hand. His face was burned a deep brown.

He stopped suddenly as he saw Gortre and an ugly look flashed out on the sensual, intellectual face. Some swift intuition seemed to give him the key of the situation or something near it.

"The curate of Dieppe!" he said in a cold, mirthless voice. "And what, Mr. Gortre, may I ask, are you doing here?"

"Miss Hunt has asked me to come and see her," answered Basil.

"Consoling yourself with the Church, Gertie, while your proprietor is away?" Llwellyn said with a sneer.

Then his manner changed suddenly.

He turned to Gortre. "Now then, my man," he snarled, "get out of this place at once. You may not know that I pay the rent and other expenses of this establishment. It is mine. I know all about you. Your reputation has reached me from sources you have little[132] idea of. And I saw you at Dieppe. I don't propose to resume our acquaintance in London; kindly go at once."

Basil looked at the woman. He saw pleading, a terrible entreaty in her eyes. If he left her now, the power of this man, his strength of will, might drag her back for ever into hell. He could see the girl regarded him with terror. There was a great surprise in her face also. The man seemed so strong and purposeful. Even Gortre remembered that he had worn no such indefinable air of confidence and triumph six months ago in France.

"Miss Hunt wants me to stay, sir," he answered quietly, "and so I'm going to stay. But perhaps you had better be given an explanation at once. Miss Hunt is going to leave you to-morrow. She will never see you again."

"And may I ask," the big man answered, "why you have interfered in my private affairs and why you think—for she is going to do nothing of the sort—Miss Hunt is going from here?"

"Simply because the Holy Spirit wills it so," said the clergyman.

Llwellyn looked steadily at him and then at the woman.

Something he saw in their faces told him the truth.

He laughed shortly. "Let me tell you," he said in a voice which quivered with ugly passion, "that in a short time all meddling priests will lose their power over the minds of others for ever. Your Christ, your God, the pale dreamer of the East, shall be revealed to you and all men at last!"

His manner had changed once more. Fierce as it was, there was an intense meaning and power in it. He spoke as one having authority, with also a concentrated hate in his words, so real and bitter that it gave them a certain fineness.

[133]

"Yes!" he continued, lifting his arm with a sudden gesture:

"'Far hence He lies
In the lorn Syrian town,
And on His grave, with shining eyes,
The Syrian stars look down.'"

Gortre answered him:

"You lie and you know you lie! and by the powers given to me I'll tell you so from God Himself. Christ is risen! And as the day follows the night so the Spirit of God remains upon the earth God once visited, and works upon the hearts of men."

"Are you going?" said Llwellyn, stepping towards Gortre.

"No," the young man answered in sharp, angry tones. "It's you that are going, Sir Robert. You know as well as I do that I can do exactly as I like with you if it comes to force. And really I am not at all disinclined to do so, despite my parson's coat. Then you will have your remedy, you know. The newly made knight fighting a clergyman under such very curious circumstances! If this thing is to become open talk, then let us have it so. You can do me no harm. I came here at my vicar's request and Miss Hunt's. You know best if you can stand a scandal of this kind in your position. Now I'm going to use my last argument. Are you going at once or shall I knock you down and kick you out?"

He could not help a note of exultation in his voice, try as he would. He was still a young man, full of power and virility. His life had brought no trace of effeminacy with it. And as he saw this splendid lying intellect, the slave of evil, and rejoicing in it, as he heard the arrogant denial of Christ's Godhead coming sonorously from those polluted lips, a wild longing flared up[134] in him. Like a sudden flame, the impulse to strike a clean, hard blow fired all his blood. The old Oxford days of athletic triumphs on field, flood, and river came back to him.

He measured the man scientifically with his eyes, judging his distance, alert to strike.

But Llwellyn made no further movement of aggression and uttered no word of menace. He did not seem in the least afraid of Gortre or in any way intimidated by him. Indeed, he laughed, a laugh which was very hollow, mirthless, and cold.

"Ah, my boy," he said, "I have a worse harm to work you than you can dream of yet. You will remember me some day. You can't frighten me now. I will go. I want no scandal. Good-bye, Gertrude. You also will remember and regret some day. Good-bye."

He went noiselessly out of the room, still with the strange flickering smile of prescience and fate upon his evil face.

When he had gone, Gertrude fell into a passion of weeping. The strain had been too great. Basil comforted her as well as he could, and before he went promised to see Father Ripon that night and make arrangements that she should quietly disappear the next day to some distant undiscoverable haven.

Then he also went out into the night, through the silent squares of sleeping houses towards the Clergy House of St. Mary's. Once more his nerves were unstrung and the old fears and the sense of waiting—Damocles-like for some blow to fall—poured over him.

Sir Robert walked swiftly to Oxford Street, where he found a cab. He ordered the man to drive him to the Sheridan Club. On the way he stopped at Charing Cross Station and ordered his luggage to be sent home[135] at once to his house in Upper Berkeley Street. He had only been in London two or three hours, having crossed from Calais that afternoon.

He washed when he had arrived at the famous club, and then went up-stairs to the grill-room for some supper. It was the hour when the Sheridan is full of the upper Bohemian world. Great actors and musicians, a judge on his way through town from one watering-place to another,—for it was now the long vacation,—a good many well-known journalists, all sorts and conditions of men. All were eminent in their work, for that was a condition of membership.

Llwellyn was welcomed on all sides, though men noticed that he seemed preoccupied. His healthy appearance was commented on, his face browned, as was supposed, by the sun of the Riviera, his general fitness of manner and carriage.

He took supper by himself at a small table, choosing the menu with his usual extreme care, and more than once summoning the head waiter to conference. Although he kept glancing at his watch, as if expecting an arrival, he made a good meal, mixing his own salad of crisp white lettuce with deliberation.

He had sent a page early on his arrival to find out if Mr. Constantine Schuabe was in the club.

He was standing at the desk in the middle of the room, paying his bill, when the swing-doors were pushed open and Schuabe entered. He was in evening dress and carried a light overcoat on his arm.

Llwellyn gathered up his change and went to meet him. Had there been an attentive observer to mark the meeting of the two men he would have perhaps been a little surprised at the fashion of it.

Although Llwellyn was a six-months' stranger to London, and the meeting between the two men was[136] obviously prearranged, neither of the two men smiled as they shook hands. Both were expectant of each other, pale, almost with some apprehension, it might have been fancied; and though the meeting seemed a relief to each, there was little human kindliness in it.

"Come down to the Hotel," said Schuabe; "we can't possibly say anything here, every room is full."

They walked out of the club together, two figures of noticeable distinction, very obviously belonging to the ruling classes of England. The millionaire's pale and beautiful face was worn and lined.

"Schuabe seems a bit done up," one man in the hall said to another as the two friends passed through.

"Heat, I suppose," answered his companion. "Handsome chap, though; doesn't seem to care for anything worth having, only books and politics and that. Wish I'd his money."

"So do I. But give me Bob Llwellyn of these two. Thoroughly decent sort he is. Invented two new omelettes and a white soup. Forgets all about his thing-um-bobs—old Egyptian or something—they knighted him for directly he leaves the Museum."

"That's the sort," answered a third man who had joined them. "I don't object to a Johnny having a brain, and knowing a devil of a lot, if he'll only jolly well keep it to himself. Bob does that. I'm going up-stairs to have a turn at poker. You fellows coming?"

Schuabe and Llwellyn walked to the Cecil, no great distance, saying little by the way, and presently they were in the millionaire's great room, with its spacious view over the river.

The place was beautifully cool and full of flowers. A great block of ice rose from a copper bowl placed on a pedestal. The carpet had been covered with light matting of rice straw, brought from Rawal-pindi. All the[137] windows leading to the balcony were wide open, and the balcony was covered with striped awning, underneath which the electric lights glowed on the leaves of Japanese palms, seeming as if they had been cunningly lacquered a metallic green colour, and on low chairs of white bleached rushes.

The two men sat down in the centre of the room on light chairs, with a small Turkish table and cool drinks between them.

"You've had all my letters, my last from Jaffa?" asked Sir Robert.

"Yes, all of them," said Schuabe; "each one was carefully destroyed after I had read it and memorialised the contents. Let me say now that you have done your work with extraordinary brilliance. It has been an intellectual pleasure of a high order to follow your proceedings and know your plans. There is not another man in the world who could do what you have done. Everything seems guarded against, all is secure."

"You are right, Schuabe," said Llwellyn, in a matter-of-fact voice. "You bade me make a certain thing possible. You paid me proportionately to the terrible risks and for my unrivalled knowledge. Well, you and I are going to shake the whole world as no two other men have ever done, and what will be the end?"

"The end!" cried Schuabe, in a high, strained, unnatural voice. "Who shall say? What man can know? For ever more the gigantic fable of the Cross and the Man God will be overthrown. The temples of the world will fall into the abomination of desolation, and you and I, latter-day bringers of light—Lucifers!—will kill the pale Nazarene more surely than the Sanhedrists and soldiers of the past."

There was a thin madness in his voice. The great figure of the savant shifted uneasily in its chair.

[138]

"That fellow Gortre, that abominable young priest, has been getting in my way to-night," he said with a savage curse. "I found him with Gertrude Hunt, the woman I've spent thousands on! The priests have got her; she's going to 'lead a new life.' She has 'found Christ'!"

Schuabe smiled horribly, a cunning smile of unutterable malice.

"He has crossed my path also," he said; "in some way, by a series of coincidences, he has become slightly involved in our lives. Leave the matter to me. So small a thing as the fanaticism of one obscure youth is nothing to trouble us. I will see to his future. But he shall live to know what is coming to the world. Then—it is easy enough. He thwarted me one night also."

They were silent for a minute or two. Sir Robert lifted a long glass to his lips. His hand shook with passion, and the ice in the liquid clinked and tinkled.

"Everything is now ready," he said at last, glancing at Schuabe. "Every detail. Ionides knows what he has to do when he receives the signal. He is a mere tool, and knows and cares nothing of what will happen. He is to direct the excavators in certain directions, that is all. It will be three months, so I calculate, after we have set the machinery in motion, before the blow will fall. It rests with you now to begin."

"The sign shall go at once," said Schuabe. His eyes glittered, his mouth worked with emotion.

"It is a letter with a single sign on it."

"What is the sign?"

"A drawing of a broken cross."

"Before the day dawns we will send the broken cross to Jerusalem."

END OF BOOK I

[139]

BOOK II

"A horror of great darkness."
[141]

64

CHAPTER I

WHILE LONDON WAS SLEEPING

In the winter, two or three weeks before Christmas, Gortre asked Father Ripon for a ten days' holiday, and went to Walktown to spend the time with Mr. Byars and Helena. Christmas itself could be no time of vacation for him,—the duties of St. Mary's were very heavy,—so he snatched a respite from work before the actual time of festival.

Harold Spence was left alone in the chambers at Lincoln's Inn. The journalist found himself discontented, lonely, and bored. He had not realised before how much Basil's society had contributed to his happiness during the past few months. It had grown to be a necessity to him gradually, and, as is the case with all gradual processes, the lack of it surprised him with its sense of incompleteness and loss.

He had spent a hard summer and autumn over very uncongenial work. For months there had been a curious lull and calm in the news-world. Yet day by day the Daily Wire had to be filled. Not that there was any lack of material,—even in the dullest season the expert journalist will tell one that his difficulty is what to leave out of his paper, not what to put in,—but that the material was uninteresting and dull.

He felt himself that his leaders were growing rather stale, lacking in spontaneity. His style did not glitter and ring quite as usual. And Basil had helped him through this time wonderfully.

[142] One Wednesday—he remembered the day afterwards—Spence awoke about mid-day. He had been late at the office the night before and afterwards had gone to a club, not going to bed till after four.

He heard the laundress moving about the chambers preparing his breakfast. He shouted to her, and in a minute or two she came in with his letters and a cup of tea. She went to the window and pulled up the blind, letting a dreary grey-yellow December light into the room.

"Nasty day, Mrs. Buscall," he said, sipping his tea.

"It is so, sir," the woman said, a lean, kindly-faced London drudge from a court in Drury Lane. "Gives me a frog in my throat all the time, this fog does. You'd better let me pour a drop of hot water in your bath, sir. I've got the kettle on the gas stove."

The laundress had an objection to baths, deep-rooted and a matter of principle. The daily cold tub she regarded as suicidal, and when Gortre had arrived, her pained surprise at finding him also—a clergyman too!—addicted to such adventurous and injudicious habits had been as extreme as her disappointment.

Spence agreed to humour her, and she began to prepare the bath.

"Letter from Mr. Cyril, I see, sir," she remarked. Mrs. Buscall loved the archæologist with more strenuousness than her other two charges. The unusual and mysterious has a real fascination for a certain type of uneducated Cockney brain. Hands's rare sojourns at the chambers, the Eastern dresses and pictures in his room, his strange and perilous life—as she considered it—in the veritable Bible land, where Satan actually roamed the desert in the form of a lion seeking whom he might devour, all these stimulated her crude imagination and brought colour into the dreary purlieus of Drury Lane.

[143] Most of the women around Mrs. Buscall drank gin. The doings of Cyril Hands were sufficient tonic for her.

Spence glanced at the bulky packet with its Turkish stamps and peculiar aroma—which the London fog had not yet killed—of ships and alien suns. Hands was a good correspondent. Sometimes he sent general articles on the work he was doing, not too technical, and Ommaney, the editor of Spence's paper, used and paid well for them.

But on this morning Spence did not feel inclined to open the packet. It could wait. He was not in the humour for it now. It would be too tantalising to read of those deep skies like a hard, hollow turquoise, of the flaming white sun, the white mosques and minarets throwing purple shadows round the cypress and olive.

"Neque enim ignari sumus," he muttered to himself, recalling the swing and freedom of his own travels, the vivid, picturesque life where, at great moments, he had been one of the eyes of England, flashing electric words to tell his countrymen of what lay before him.

And now, after the chill of his bath and the rasping torture of shaving in winter, he must light all the gas-jets as he sat down to breakfast in his sitting-room!

He opened the Wire and glanced at his own work of the night before. How lifeless it seemed to him!

"Many years ago Bagehot wrote that 'Parliament expresses the nation's opinions in words well, when it happens that words, not laws, are wanted. On foreign matters, where we cannot legislate, whatever the English nation thinks, or thinks it thinks, as to the critical events of the world, whether in Denmark, in Italy or America, and no matter whether it thinks wisely or unwisely, that same something, wise or unwise, will be thoroughly well said in Parliament.'

[144]

"We have never read a finer defence of such Parliamentary discussion as the recent events in certain Continental bureaucracies have given rise to, etc., etc."

Words! words! words! that seemed to him to mean little and matter nothing. Yet as he chipped his egg he remembered that the writing of this leader had meant considerable mental strain. Oh, for a big happening abroad, when he would be sent and another would take up this routine work! He knew he was a far better correspondent than leader writer. His heart was in that work.

There were one or two invitations among his letters, two books were sent by a young publisher, a friend of his, asking if he could get them "noticed" in the Wire, and a syllabus of some winter lectures to be given at Oxford House. His name was there. He was to lecture in January on "The Sodality of the Knights of St. John".

After breakfast, the lunch time of most of the world, he found it impossible to settle down to anything. He was not due at the office that night, and the long hours, without the excitement of his work, stretched rather hopelessly before him. He thought of paying calls in the various parts of the West End, where he had friends whom he had rather neglected of late. But he dismissed that idea when it came, for he did not feel as if he could make himself very agreeable to any one.

He wanted a complete change of some sort. He half thought of running down to Brighton, fighting the cold, bracing sea winds on the lawns at Hove, and returning the next day.

He was certainly out of sorts, liverish no doubt, and the solution to his difficulties presented itself to him in the project of a Turkish bath.

He put his correspondence into the pocket of his overcoat,[145] to be read at leisure, and drove to a hammam in Jermyn Street.

The physical warmth, the silence, the dim lights, and Oriental decorations induced a supreme sense of comfort and bien-être. It brought Constantinople back to him in vague reverie.

Perhaps, he thought, the Turkish bath in London is the only easy way to obtain a sudden and absolute change of environment. Nothing else brings detachment so readily, is so instinct with change and the unusual.

In delightful langour he passed from one dim chamber to another, lying prone in the great heat which surrounded him like a cloak. Then the vigorous kneading and massage, the gradual toning and renovating of each joint and muscle, till he stood drenched in aromatic foam, a new, fresh physical personality. The swift dive under the india-rubber curtain left behind the domed, dim places of heat and silence. He plunged through the bottle-green water of the marble pool into the hall, where lounges stood about by small inlaid octagonal tables, and a thin whip of a fountain tinkled among green palms. Wrapped from head to foot in soft white towels, he lay in a dream of contentment, watching the delicate spirals from his Cairene cigarette, and sipping the brown froth of a tiny cup of thick coffee.

At four a slippered attendant brought him a sole and a bottle of yellow wine, and after the light meal he fell once more into a placid, restorative sleep.

And all the while the letter from Jerusalem was in his overcoat pocket, forgotten, hung in the entrance-hall. The thing which was to alter the lives of thousands and ten thousands, that was to bring a cloud over England more dark and menacing than it had ever known, lay there with its stupendous message, its relentless influence,[146] while outside the church bells all over London were tolling for Evensong.

At length, as night was falling, Spence went out into the lighted streets with their sudden roar of welcome. He was immensely refreshed in brain and body. His thoughts moved quickly and well, depression had left him, the activity of his brain was unceasing.

As a rule, especially for the last year or two, Spence was by no means a man given to casual amusements. His work was too absorbing for him to have time or inclination to follow pleasure. But to-night he felt in the humour for relaxation.

He turned into St. James Street, where his club was, intending to find some one who would go to a music-hall with him. There was no one he knew intimately in the smoking-room, but soon after he arrived Lambert, one of the deputy curators from the British Museum, came in. Spence and Lambert had been at Marlborough together.

Spence asked Lambert, who was in evening dress, to be his companion.

"Sorry I can't, old man," he answered; "I've got to dine with my uncle, Sir Michael. It's a bore, of course, but it's policy. The place will be full of High Church bishops, minor Cabinet Ministers, and people of that sort. I only hope old Ripon will be there—he's my uncle's tame vicar, you know; uncle runs an expensive church, like some men run a theatre—for he's always bright and amusing. You're not working to-night, then?"

"No, not to-night. I've been and had a Turkish bath, and I thought I'd wind up a day of mild dissipation by going to the Alhambra."

"Sorry I can't go too—awful bore. I've had a tiring day, too, and a ballet would be refreshing. The[147] governor's been in a state of filthy irritation and nerves for the last fortnight."

"Sir Robert Llwellyn, isn't it?"

"Yes, he's my chief, and a very good fellow too, as a rule. He went away for several months, you know—travelled abroad for his health. When he first came back, three months ago, he looked as fit as a fiddle, and seemed awfully pleased with himself all round. But lately he's been decidedly off colour. He seems worried about something, does hardly any work, and always seems waiting and looking out for a coming event. He bothers me out of my life, always coming into my room and talking about nothing, or

67

speculating upon the possibility of all sorts of new discoveries which will upset every one's theories."

"I met him in Dieppe in the spring. He seemed all right then, just at the beginning of his leave."

"Well, he's certainly not that now, worse luck, and confound him. He interferes with my work no end. Good-bye; sorry I must go."

He passed softly over the heavy carpet of the smoking-room, and Spence was left alone once more.

It was after seven o'clock.

Spence wasn't hungry yet. The light meal in the hammam had satisfied him. He resolved to go to the Empire alone, not because the idea of going seemed very attractive, but because he had planned it and could substitute no other way of spending the evening for the first determination.

So, about nine o'clock, he strolled into the huge, garish music-hall.

He went into the Empire, and already his contentment was beginning to die away again. The day seemed a day of trivialities, a sordid, uneventful day of London gloom, which he had vainly tried to disperse with little futile rockets of amusement.

[148]

He sat down in a stall and watched a clever juggler doing wonderful things with billiard balls. After the juggler a coarsely handsome Spanish girl came upon the stage—he remembered her at La Scala, in Paris. She was said to be one of the beauties of Europe, and a king's favourite.

After the Spanish woman there were two men, "brothers" some one. One was disguised as a donkey—a veritable peau de chagrin!—the other as a tramp, and together they did laughable things.

With a sigh he went up-stairs and moved slowly through the thronged promenade. The hard faces of the men and women repelled him. One elderly Jewish-looking person reminded him of a great grey slug. He turned into the American bar at one extremity of the horse-shoe. It was early yet, and the big room, pleasantly cool, was quite empty. A man brought him a long, parti-coloured drink.

He felt the pressure of a packet in his pocket. It was Cyril Hands's letter, he found as he took it out. He thought of young Lambert at the club, a friend of Hands and fellow-worker in the same field, and languidly opened the letter.

Two women came in and sat at a table not far from him as he began to read. He was the only man in the place, and they regarded him with a tense, conscious interest.

They saw him open a bulky envelope with a careless manner. He would look up soon, they expected.

But as they watched they saw a sudden, swift contraction of the brows, a momentous convulsion of every feature. His head bent lower towards the manuscript. They saw that he became very pale.

In a minute or two what had at first seemed a singular paleness became a frightful ashen colour.

[149]

"That Johnny's going to be ill," one of the women said to the other.

As she spoke they saw the face change. A lurid excitement burst upon it like a flame. The eyes glowed, the mouth settled into swift purpose.

Spence took up his hat and left the room with quick, decided steps. He threaded his way through the crowd round the circle—like a bed of orchids, surrounded by heavy, poisonous scents—and almost ran into the street.

68

A cab was waiting. He got into it, and, inspired by his words and appearance, the man drove furiously down dark Garrick Street, and the blazing Strand towards the offices of the Daily Wire.

The great building of dressed stone which stood in the middle of Fleet Street was dark. The advertisement halls and business offices were closed.

Spence paid his man and dived down a long, narrow passage, paved, and with high walls on either side. At the end of the passage he pushed open some battered swing-doors. A commissionaire in a little hutch touched his cap as Spence ran up a broad flight of stone stairs.

The journalist turned down a long corridor with doors on either side. The glass fanlights over the doors showed that all the rooms were brilliantly lit within. The place was very quiet, save for the distant clicking of a typewriter and the thud of a "column-printer" tape machine as the wheel carrier shot back for a new line.

He opened a door with his own name painted on it and went inside. At a very large writing-table, on which stood two shaded electric lights, an elderly man, heavily built and bearded, was writing on small slips of paper. There was another table in the room, a great many books on shelves upon the walls, and a thick carpet. The big man looked up as Spence came in, lifted a cup of tea which was standing by him, and drank a little. He[150] nodded without speaking, and went on with his leading article.

Spence took off his hat and coat, drew the sheets of Hands's letter from his pocket, and went out into the passage. At the extreme end he opened a door, and passing round a red baize screen found himself in Ommaney's room, the centre of the great web of brains and machinery which daily gave the Wire to the world.

Ommaney's room was very large, warm, and bright. It was also extremely tidy. The writing-table had little on it save a great blotting-pad and an inkstand. The books on chairs and shelves were neatly arranged.

The editor sat at a table in the centre of the room, facing several doors which led into various departments of the staff. The chief sub-editor, a short, alert person, spectacled and Jewish in aspect, stood by Ommaney's side as Spence came in. He had proof of page three in his hand—that portion of the paper which consisted of news which had accumulated through the day. He was submitting it to the editor, so that the whole sheet might be finally "passed for press" and "go to the foundry," where the type would be pressed into papier-mâché moulds, from which the final curved plates for the roller machines would be cast.

"Not at all a bad make-up, Levita," Ommaney said, as he initialled the margin in blue pencil. The sub-editor hurried from the room.

Ommaney was slim and pale, carefully dressed, and of medium height. He did not look very old. His moustache was golden and carefully tended, his pale, honey-coloured hair waved over a high, white forehead.

"I shall want an hour," Spence said. "I've just got what may be the most stupendous news any newspaper has ever published."

The editor looked up quickly. A flash of interest[151] passed over his pale, immobile face and was gone. He knew that if Spence spoke like this the occasion was momentous.

He looked at his watch. "Is it news for to-night's paper?" he said.

"No," answered Spence. "I'm the only man in England, I think, who has it yet. We shall gain nothing by printing to-night. But we must settle on a course of action at once. That won't wait. You'll understand when I explain."

Ommaney nodded. On the writing-table was a mahogany stand about a foot square. A circle was described on it, and all round the circle, like the figures on the face of a clock, were little ivory tablets an inch long, with a name printed on each. In the centre of the circle a vulcanite handle moved a steel bar working on a pivot. Ommaney turned the handle till the end of the bar rested over the tablet marked

COMPOSING ROOM

He picked up the receiver and transmitter of a portable telephone and asked one or two questions.

When he had communicated with several other rooms in this way Ommaney turned to Spence.

"All right," he said, "I can give you an hour now. Things are fairly easy to-night."

He got up from the writing-table and sat down by the fire. Spence took a chair opposite.

He seemed dazed. He was trembling with excitement, his face was pale with it, yet, above and beyond this agitation, there was almost fear in his eyes.

"It's a discovery in Palestine—at Jerusalem," he said in a low, vibrating voice, spreading out the thin,[152] crackling sheets of foreign note-paper on his knee and arranging them in order.

"You know Cyril Hands, the agent of the Palestine Exploring Fund?"

"Yes, quite well by reputation," said Ommaney, "and I've met him once or twice. Very sound man."

"These papers are from him. They seem to be of tremendous importance, of a significance that I can hardly grasp yet."

"What is the nature of them?" asked the editor, rising from his chair, powerfully affected in his turn by Spence's manner.

Harold put his hand up to his throat, pulling at his collar; the apple moved up and down convulsively.

"The Tomb!" Spence gasped. "The Holy Tomb!"

"What do you mean?" asked Ommaney. "Another supposed burial-place of Christ—like the Times business, when they found the Gordon Tomb, and Canon MacColl wrote such a lot?"

His face fell a little. This, though interesting enough, and fine "news copy," was less than he hoped.

"No, no," cried Spence, getting his voice back at last and speaking like a man in acute physical pain. "A new tomb has been found. There is an inscription in Greek, written by Joseph of Arimathæa, and there are other traces."

His voice failed him.

"Go on, man, go on!" said the editor.

"The inscription—tells that Joseph—took the body of Jesus—from his own garden tomb—he hid it in this place—the disciples never knew—it is a confession——"

Ommaney was as white as Spence now.

"There are other contributory proofs," Spence continued. "Hands says it is certain. All the details are here, read——"

[153]

Ommaney stared fixedly at his lieutenant.

"Then, if this is true," he whispered, "it means?——"

"That christ never rose from the dead, that christianity is all a lie."

Spence slipped back in his chair a little and fainted.

With the assistance of two men from one of the other rooms they brought him back to consciousness before very long. Then while Ommaney read the papers Spence sat

70

nervously in his chair, sipping some brandy-and-water they had brought him and trying to smoke a cigarette with a palsied hand.

The editor finished at last. "Pull yourself together, Spence," he said sharply. "This is no time for sentiment. I know your beliefs, though I do not share them, and I can sympathise with you. But keep yourself off all private thoughts now. We must be extremely careful what we are doing. Now listen carefully to me."

The keen voice roused Spence. He made a tremendous effort at self-control.

"It seems," Ommaney went on, "that we alone know of this discovery. The secretary of the Palestine Exploring Society will not receive the news for another week, Hands says. He seems stunned, and no wonder. In about a fortnight his detailed papers will probably be published. I see he has already telegraphed privately for Dr. Schmöulder, the German expert. Of course you and I are hardly competent to judge of the value of this communication. To me—speaking as a layman—it seems extremely clear. But we must of course see a specialist before publishing anything. If this news is true—and I would give all I am worth if it were not, though I am no Christian—of course you realise that the future history of the world is changed? I hold in my hand something that will come to millions and millions of people as an utter extinction of hope and light. It's[154] impossible to say what will happen. Moral law will be abrogated for a time. The whole moral fabric of Society will fall into ruin at once until it can adjust itself to the new state of things. There will be war all over the world; crime will cover England like a cloud——"

His voice faltered as the terrible picture grew in his brain.

Both of them felt that mere words were utterly unable to express the horrors which they saw dawning.

"We don't know the truth yet," said Spence, at length.

"No," answered Ommaney. "I am not going to speculate on it either. I am beginning to realise what we are dealing with. One man's brain cannot hold all this. So let me ask you to regard this matter for the present simply from the standpoint of the paper, and through it, of course, from the standpoint of public policy——"

He broke off suddenly, for there was a knock at the door. A commissionaire entered with a telegram. It was for Spence. He opened the envelope, read the contents with a groan, and passed it to the editor.

The telegram was from Hands:

"Schmöulder entirely confirms discovery, is communicating first instance with Kaiser privately, fuller details in mail, confer Ommaney, make statement to Secretary Society, use Wire medium publicity, leave all to you, see Prime Minister, send out Llwellyn behalf Government immediately, meanwhile suggest attitude suspended decision, personally fear little doubt.—Hands."

"We must act at once," said Ommaney. "We have a fearful responsibility now. It's not too much to say[155] that everything depends on us. Have you got any of that brandy left? My head throbs like an engine."

A sub-editor who came in and was briefly dismissed told his colleagues that something was going on in the editor's room of an extraordinary nature. "The chief was actually drinking a peg, and his hand shook like a leaf."

Ommaney drank the spirits—he was an absolute teetotaler as a rule, though not pledged in any way to abstinence—and it revived him.

"Now let us try and think," he said, lighting a cigarette and walking up and down the room.

71

Spence lit a cigarette also. As he did so he gave a sudden, sharp, unnatural chuckle. He was smoking when the Light of the World—the whole great world!—was flickering into darkness.

Ommaney saw him and interpreted the thought. He pulled him up at once with a few sharp words, for he knew that Spence was close upon hysteria.

"From a news point of view," he continued, "we hold all the cards. No one else knows what we know. I am certain that the German papers will publish nothing for a day or two. The Emperor will tell them nothing, and they can have no other source of information; so I gather from this telegram. Dr. Schmöulder will not say anything until he has instructions from Potsdam. That means I need not publish anything in to-morrow's paper. It will relieve me of a great responsibility. We shall be first in the field, but I shall still have a few hours to consult with others."

He pressed a bell on the table. "Tell Mr. Jones I wish to see him," he told the boy who answered the summons.

A young man came in, the editor of the "personal" column.

[156]

"Is the Prime Minister in town, Mr. Jones?" he asked.

"Yes, sir; he's here for three more days."

"I shall send a message now," said Ommaney, "asking for an interview in an hour's time. I know he will see me. He knows that I would not come at this hour unless the matter were of national importance. As you know, we are very much in the confidence of the Cabinet just now. I dare not wait till to-morrow." He rapidly wrote a note and sent for Mr. Folliott Farmer.

The big-bearded man from Spence's room entered, smoking a briar pipe.

"Mr. Farmer," said Ommaney, "I suppose you've done your leader?"

"Sent it up-stairs ten minutes ago," said the big man.

"Then I want you to do me a favour. The matter is so important that I do not like to trust any one else. I want you to drive to Downing Street at once as hard as you can go. Take this letter for Lord ——. It is making an appointment for me in an hour's time. He must see it himself at once—take my card. One of the secretaries will try and put you off, of course. This is irregular, but it is of international importance. When I tell you this you will realise that Lord —— must see the note. Bring me back the answer as rapidly as you can."

The elderly man—his name was a household word as a political writer all over England and the Continent—nodded without speaking, took the letter, and left the room. He knew Ommaney, and realised that if he made a messenger boy of him, Folliott Farmer, the matter was of supreme importance.

"That is the only thing to do," said Ommaney. "No one else would be possible. The Archbishop would laugh. We must go to the real head. I only want to put myself on the safe side before publishing. If they[157] meet me properly, then for the next few days we can control public opinion. If not, then it is my duty to publish, and if I'm not officially backed up there may be war in a week. Macedonia would be flaming, Turkish fanatics would embroil Europe. But that will be seen at once in Downing Street, unless I'm very much mistaken."

"It's an awful, horrible risk we are running," said Spence. He was forgetting all personal impressions in the excitement of the work; the journalist was alive in him. "Hands's letter and diagrams seem so flawless; he has exhausted every means of disproving what he says; but still supposing that it is all untrue!"

72

"I look at it this way," said Ommaney. "It's perfectly obvious, at any rate, that the discovery is of the first importance, regarded as news. Hands has the reputation of being a thoroughly safe man, and now he is supported by Schmöulder. Schmöulder is, of course, a man of world-wide reputation. As these two are certain, even if later opinion or discovery proves the thing to be untrue, the paper can't suffer. Our attitude will, of course, be non-committal, until certainty one way or the other comes. At any rate, it seems to me that you have brought in the greatest newspaper 'scoop' that has ever been known or thought of. For my part, I have little doubt of the truth of this. Can't go into it now, but it seems so very, very probable. It explains, and even corroborates, and that's the wonderful thing, so much of the Gospel narrative. We shall see what Llwellyn says. I've more to go into, but, meanwhile, I must make arrangements for setting up Hands's papers. Then there are the inscriptions, too. Of course they must be reproduced in facsimile. As we can't print in half-tone, I must have the photograph turned into an absolutely correct line drawing, and have line blocks made. I shall[158] have pulls of the whole thing prepared and sent by post to-morrow at midnight to the editors of all the dailies in London and Paris, and to the heads of the Churches. I shall also prepare a statement, showing exactly how the documents have come into our possession and what steps we are taking. I shall write the thing to-night, after I have seen the Prime Minister."

He went to his writing-table once more, moved the telephone indicator, and summoned the foreman printer.

In a few moments a lean Scotchman in his shirt sleeves—one of the most autocratic and important people connected with the paper—came into the room.

"I want an absolutely reliable linotype operator, Burness," said Ommaney. "He will have to set up some special copy for me after the paper's gone to press. It'll take him till breakfast-time. I want a man who will not talk. The thing is private and important. And it must be a man who can set up from the Greek font by hand also. There are some quotations in Greek included in the text."

"Well, sirr," said the man, with a strong Scotch accent, "I can find ye a guid operrator to stay till morning, but aboot his silence—if it's of great moment—I wouldn't say, and aboot his aptitude for setting up Greek type I hae nae doot whatever. There's no a lino operrator in the building wha can do it. Some of the men at the case might, but that'll be keeping two men. Is it verra important, Mr. Ommaney?"

"More important than anything I have ever dealt with."

"Then ye'll please jist give the copy into my own hands, sirr. I'll do the lino and the case warrk mysel' and pull a galley proof for ye too. No one shall see the copy but me."

"Thank you, Burness," said the editor. "I'm very[159] much obliged. I shall be here till morning. I shall go out in an hour and be back by the time the machines are running down-stairs. Then the composing-room will be empty and you can get to work."

"I'll start directly the plates have gone down to the foundry and the men are off, just keeping one hand to see to the gas-engine."

"And, Burness, lock up the galley safely when you come down with the proof."

"I'll do it, sir," and the great man—indispensable, and earning his six hundred a year—went away with the precious papers.

"That is perfectly safe with Burness," said Spence, as the foreman compositor retired. "He will make no mistakes either. He is a capital Greek scholar, corrects the proof-readers themselves often."

"Yes," answered Ommaney, "I know. I shall leave everything in his hands. Then late to-morrow night, just before the forms go to the foundry, I shall shove the whole thing in before any one knows anything about it, and nothing can get round to any other office.

73

Burness will know about it beforehand, and he'll be ready to break up a whole page for this stuff. Of course, as far as leaders go and comment, I shall be guided very much by the result of my interview to-night and others to-morrow morning. I shall send off several cables before dawn to Palestine and elsewhere."

Once more the editor began to pace up and down the room, thinking rapidly, decisively, deeply. The slim, fragile body was informed with power by the splendid brain which animated it.

The rather languid, silent man was utterly changed. Here one could see the strength and force of the personality which directed and controlled the second, perhaps the first, most powerful engine of public opinion in the[160] world. The millionaires who paid this frail-looking, youthful man an enormous sum to direct their paper for them knew what they were about. They had bought one of the finest living executive brains and made it a potentate among its fellows. This man who, when he was not at the office, or holding some hurried colloquy with one of the rulers of the world, was asleep in a solitary flat at Kensington, knew that he had an accepted right to send a message to Downing Street, such as he had lately done. No one knew his face—no one of the great outside public; his was hardly even a name to be recognised in passing, yet he, and Spence, and Folliott Farmer could shake a continent with their words. And though all knew it, or would at least have realised it had they ever given it a thought, the absolute self-effacement of journalism made it a matter of no moment to any of them.

While Englishmen read their dicta, and unconsciously incorporated them into their own pronouncements, mouthing them in street, market, and forum, these men slept till the busy day was over, and once more with the setting of the sun stole out to their almost furtive and yet tremendous task.

Every now and then Ommaney strode to the writing-table and made a rapid note on a sheet of paper.

At last he turned to Spence.

"I am beginning to have our line of action well marked out in my brain," he said. "The thing is grouping itself very well. I am beginning to see my way. Now about you, Spence. Of course this thing is yours. At any rate you brought it here. Later on, of course, we shall show our gratitude in some substantial way. That will depend upon the upshot of the whole thing. Meanwhile, you will be quite wasted in London. I and Farmer and Wilson can deal with anything and everything here. Of[161] course I would rather have you on the spot, but I can use you far better elsewhere."

"Then?" said Spence.

"You must go to Jerusalem at once. Start for Paris to-morrow morning at nine; you'd better go round to your chambers and pack up now and then come back here till it's time to start. You can sleep en route. I shall be here till breakfast-time, and I can give you final instructions."

He used the telephone once more and his secretary came in.

"Mr. Spence starts for Palestine to-morrow morning, Marriott," he said. "He is going straight through to Jerusalem as fast as may be. Oblige me by getting out a route for him at once, marking all the times for steamers and trains, etc., in a clear scheme for Mr. Spence to take with him. Be very careful with the Continental timetables indeed. If you can see any delay anywhere which will be likely to occur, go down to Cook's early in the morning and make full inquiries. If it is necessary, arrange for any special trains that may be necessary. Mr. Spence must not be delayed a day. Also map out various points on the journey, with the proper times, where we can telegraph instructions to Mr. Spence. Go down to Mr. Woolford and ask him for a hundred pounds in notes and give them to Mr.

Spence. You will arrange about the usual letter of credit during the day and wire Mr. Spence at Paris after lunch."

The young man went out to do his part in the great organisation which Ommaney controlled.

"Then you'll be back between three and four?" Ommaney said.

"Yes, I'll go and pack at once," Spence answered. "My passport from the Foreign Office is all right now."

He rose to go, vigorous, and with an inexpressible[162] sense of relief at the active prospect before him. There would be no time for haunting thought, for personal fears yet. He was going, himself, to the very heart of things, to see and to gain personal knowledge of these events which were shadowing the world.

The door opened as he rose and Folliott Farmer strode in. With him was a tall, distinguished man of about five-and-thirty; he was in evening dress and rather bald.

It was Lord Trelyon, the Prime Minister's private secretary.

"I thought I would come myself with Mr. Farmer, Mr. Ommaney," he said, shaking hands cordially. "Lord —— will see you. He tells me to say that if it is absolutely imperative he will see you. I suppose there is no doubt of that?"

"None whatever, I'm sorry to say, Lord Trelyon," the editor answered. "Farmer, will you take charge till I return?"

He slipped on his overcoat and a felt hat and left the room with the secretary without looking back. Spence followed the two down the stairs—the tall, athletic young fellow and the slim, nervous journalist. These were just driving furiously towards the Law Courts as Spence turned into Fleet Street on his way to Lincoln's Inn.

Fleet Street was brilliantly lit and almost silent. A few cabs hovered about and that was all. Presently all the air would be filled with the dull roar and hum of the great printing machines in their underground halls, but the press hour was hardly yet.

The porter let him into the Inn, and in a few moments he was striking matches and lighting the gas. Mrs. Buscall had cleared away the breakfast things, but the fire had long since gone out. The big rooms looked very bare and solitary, unfamiliar almost, as the gas-jets hissed in the silence.

[163]

One or two letters were in the box. One envelope bore the Manchester post-mark. It was from Basil Gortre. A curious pang, half wonder and anticipation, half fear, passed through his mind as he saw the familiar handwriting of his friend. But it was a pang for Gortre, not for himself. He himself was wholly detached now that the time for action had arrived. Personal consideration would come later. At present he was starting out on the old trail—"The old trail, the long trail, the trail that is always new."

He felt a man again, with a fierce joy and exultation throbbing in all his veins after the torpor of the last few weeks.

He sat down at the table, first getting some bread and cheese from a cupboard, for he was hungry, and opening a bottle of beer. The beer tasted wonderfully good. He laughed exultingly in the flow of his high spirits.

He wrote a note to Mrs. Buscall, long since inured to these sudden midnight departures, and another to Gortre. To him he said that some great and momentous discoveries were made at Jerusalem by Hands, and that he himself was starting at once for the Holy City as special correspondent for the Wire. He would write en route, he explained, there was no time for any details now.

"Poor chap," he said to himself, "he'll know soon enough now. I hope he won't take it very badly."

Then he went into his bedroom and hauled down the great pig-skin kit-bag, covered with foreign labels, which had accompanied him half over the world.

He packed quickly and completely, the result of long practice. The pads of paper, the stylographic pens, with the special ink for hot countries which would not dry up or corrode, his revolvers, riding-breeches, boots and spurs, the kodak, with spare films and light-tight zinc cases, the old sun helmet—he forgot nothing.

[164]

When he had finished, and the big bag, with a small Gladstone also, was strapped and locked, he changed joyously from the black coat of cities into his travelling tweeds of tough cloth. At length everything seemed prepared. He sat on the bed and looked round him, willing to be gone.

His eye fell on the opposite wall. A crucifix hung there, carved in ebony and ivory. During his short holiday at Dieppe, nearly nine months ago now, he had gone into the famous little shop there where carved work of all kinds is sold. Basil and Helena were with him and they had all bought mementoes. Helena had given him that.

And as he looked at it now he wondered what his journey would bring forth. Was he, indeed, chosen out of men to go to this far country to tear Christ from that awful and holy eminence of the Cross? Was it to be his mission to extinguish the Lux Mundi?

As he gazed at the sacred emblem he felt that this could not be.

No, no! a thousand times no. Jesus had risen to save him and all other sinners. It was so, must be so, should be so.

The Holy Name was in itself enough. He whispered it to himself. No, that was eternally, gloriously true.

Humbly, faithfully, gladly he knelt among the litter of the room and said the Lord's Prayer, said it in Latin as he had said it at school—

Pater noster!

[165]
CHAPTER II

AVOIDING THE FLOWER PATTERN ON THE CARPET

Sir Michael Manichoe, the stay and pillar of "Anglicanism" in the English Church, was a man of great natural gifts. The owner of one of those colossal Jewish fortunes which, few as they are, have such far-reaching influence upon English life, he employed it in a way which, for a man in his position, was unique.

He presented the curious spectacle, to sociologists and the world at large, of a Jew by origin who had become a Christian by conviction and one of the sincerest sons of the English Church as he understood it. In political life Sir Michael was a steady, rather than a brilliant, force. He had been Home Secretary under a former Conservative administration, but had retired from office. At the present moment he was a private member for the division in which his country house, Fencastle, stood, and he enjoyed the confidence of the chiefs of his party.

His great talent was for organisation, and all his powers in that direction were devoted towards the preservation and unification of the Church to which he was a convert.

Sir Michael's convictions were perfectly clear and straightforward. He believed, with all his heart, in the Catholicity of the Anglican persuasion. Roman priests he spoke of as "members of the Italian mission"; Nonconformists as "adherents to the lawless bands of

Dissent." He allowed the validity of Roman orders and spoke of the Pope as the "Bishop of Rome," an Italian[166] ecclesiastic with whom the English communion had little or nothing to do.

In his intimate and private life Sir Michael lived according to rubric. His splendid private chapel at Fencastle enjoyed the services of a chaplain, reinforced by priests from a community of Anglican monks which Sir Michael had established in an adjacent village. In London, St. Mary's was, in some sense, his particular property. He spent fabulous sums on the big Bloomsbury Parish and the needs of its great, cathedral-like church. There was no vicar in London who enjoyed the command of money that Father Ripon enjoyed. Certainly there was no other priest in the ranks of the High Churchmen who was the confidential friend and spiritual director of so powerful a political and social personality.

Yet in his public life Sir Michael was diplomatic enough. He worked steadily for one thing, it is true, but he was far too able to allow people to call him narrow-minded. The Oriental strain of cunning in his blood had sweetened to a wise diplomacy. While he always remembered he was a Churchman, he did not forget that to be an effective and helpful one he must keep his political and social eminence. And so, whatever might take place behind the scenes in the library with Father Ripon, or in the Bloomsbury clergy house, the baronet showed the world the face of a man of the world, and neither obtruded his private views nor allowed them to disturb his colleagues.

The day after the news arrived in Fleet Street from Palestine—while nothing was yet known and Harold Spence was rushing through Amiens en route for Paris and the East—a house party began to collect at Fencastle, the great place in Lincolnshire.

For a day or two a few rather important people were to meet under Sir Michael's roof. Now and then the[167] palace in the fen lands was the scene of notable gatherings, much talked of in certain circles and commented on by people who would truthfully have described themselves as being "in the know."

These parties were, indeed, congresses of the eminent, the "big" people who quietly control an England which the ignorant and the vulgar love to imagine is in the hands of a corrupt society of well-born, "smart," and pleasure-seeking people.

The folk who gathered at Fencastle were as remote from the gambling, lecherous, rabbit-brained set which glitters so brightly before the eyes of the uninformed as any staid, middle-class reader of the popular journals.

In this stronghold of English Catholicism—"hot-bed of ritualists" as the brawling "Protestant" journals called it, one met a diversity of people, widely divided in views and only alike in one thing—the dominant quality of their brains and position.

Sir Michael thought it well that even his professed opponents should meet at his table, for it gave both him and his lieutenants new data and fresh impressions for use in the campaign. Sir Michael's convictions were perfectly unalterable, but to find out how others—and those hostile—really regarded them only added to the weapons in his armoury.

And, as one London priest once remarked to another, the combination of a Jewish brain and a Christian heart was one which had already revolutionised Society nearly two thousand years ago in the persons of eleven distinguished instances.

As Father Ripon drove to Liverpool Street Station after lunch, to catch the afternoon train to the eastern counties, he was reading a letter as his cab turned into Cheapside and crawled slowly through the heavy afternoon traffic of the city.

[168]

" ... It will be as well for you to see the man à huisclos and form your own opinions. There can be no doubt that he is a force to be reckoned with, and he is, moreover, as I think you will agree after inspection, far more brilliant and able than any other professed antichristian of the front rank. Then there will also be Mrs. Hubert Armstrong. She is a pseudo-intellectual force, but her writings have a certain heaviness and authoritative note which I believe to have real influence with the large class of semi-educated people who mistake an atmosphere of knowledge for knowledge itself. A very charming woman, by the way, and I think sincere. Matthew Arnold and water!

"The Duke of Suffolk will stop a night on his way home. He writes that he wishes to see you. As you know, he is just back from Rome, and now that they have definitely pronounced against the validity of Anglican orders he is most anxious to have a further chat with you in order to form a working opinion as to our position. From his letter to me, and the extremely interesting account he gives of his interview at the Vatican, I gather that the Roman Church still utterly misunderstands our attitude, and that hopes there are high of the ultimate "conversion" of England. I hope that as a representative of English Churchmen you will be able to define what we think in an unmistakable way. This will have value. Among my other guests you will meet Canon Walke. He is preaching in Lincoln Cathedral on the Sunday, fresh from Windsor. "Render unto Cæsar" will, I allow myself to imagine, not be an unlikely text for his homily.—I am, Father, yours most sincerely,

"M. M."

Still thinking carefully over Sir Michael's letter, Father Ripon bought his ticket and made his way to the platform.

[169]

He got into a first-class carriage. While in London the priest lived a life of asceticism and simplicity which was not so much a considered thing as the outcome of an absolute and unconscious carelessness about personal and material comfort; when he went thus to a great country house, he complied with convention because it was politic.

He was the grandson of a peer, and, though he laughed at these small points, he wished to meet his friend's opinions in any reasonable way, rather than to flout them.

The carriage was empty, though a pile of newspapers and a travelling rug in one corner showed Father Ripon that he was to have one companion at any rate upon the journey.

He had bought the Church Times at the bookstall and was soon deeply immersed in the report of a Bampton Lecture delivered during the week at the University Church in Oxford.

Some one entered the carriage, the door was shut, and the train began to move out of the station, but he was too interested to look up to see who his companion might be.

A voice broke in upon his thoughts as they were tearing through the wide-spread slums of Bethnal Green.

"Do you mind if I smoke, sir? This isn't a smoking carriage, but we are alone——"

It was an ordinary query enough. "Oh, dear, no!" said the priest. "Please do, to your heart's content. It doesn't inconvenience me."

Father Ripon's quick, breezy manner seemed to interest the stranger. He looked up and saw a personality. Obviously this clergyman was some one of note. The heavy brows, the hawk-like nose, the large, firm, and yet kindly mouth, all these seemed familiar in some vague way.

[170]

For his part, Father Ripon experienced much the same sensation as he glanced at the tall stranger. His hair, which could be seen beneath his ordinary hard felt hat, was dark red and somewhat abundant. His features were Semitic, but without a trace of that fulness, and often coarseness, which sometimes marks the Jew who has come to the period of middle life. The large black eyes were neither dull nor lifeless, but simply cold, irresponsive, and alert. A massive jaw completed an impression which was remarkable in its fineness and almost sinister beauty.

The priest found it remarkable but with no sense of strangeness. He had seen the man before.

Recognition came to Schuabe first.

"Excuse me," he said, "but surely you are Father Ripon? I am Constantine Schuabe."

Ripon gave a merry chuckle. "I knew I knew you!" he said, "but I couldn't think quite who you were for a moment. Sir Michael tells me you're going to Fencastle; so am I."

Schuabe leaned back in his seat and regarded Father Ripon with a steady and calm scrutiny, somewhat with the manner of a naturalist examining a curious specimen, with a suggestion of aloofness in his eyes.

Suddenly Father Ripon smiled rather sternly, and the deep furrows which sprang into his cheeks showed the latent strength and power of the face.

"Well, Mr. Schuabe," he said abruptly, "the train doesn't stop anywhere for an hour, so willy-nilly you're locked up with a priest!"

"A welcome opportunity, Father Ripon, to convince one that perhaps the devil isn't as black as he's painted."

"I've read your books," said Ripon, "and I believe you are sincere, Mr. Schuabe. It's not a personal question at all. At the same time, if I had the power,[171] you know I should cheerfully execute you or imprison you for life, not out of revenge for what you have done, but as a precautionary measure. You should have no further opportunity of doing harm." He smiled grimly as he spoke.

"Rather severe, Father," said Schuabe laughing. "Because I find that in a rational view of history there is no place for a Resurrection and Ascension you would give me your blessing and an auto da fé!"

"I rather believe in stern measures, sometimes," answered the clergyman, with an underlying seriousness, though he spoke half in jest. "Not for all heretics, you know— only the dangerous ones."

"You are afraid of intellect when it is brought to bear on these questions."

"I thought that would be your rejoinder. Superficially it is a very telling one, because there is nothing so insidious as a half-truth. In a sense what you say is true. There are a great many Christians whose faith is weak and whose natural inclinations, assisted by supernatural temptations, are towards a life of sin. Christianity keeps them from it. Now, your books come in the way of such people as these far more readily and easily than works of Christian apologetics written with equal power. An attack upon our position has all the elements of popularity and novelty. It is more seen. For example, ten thousand people have heard of your Christ Reconceived for every ten who know Lathom's Risen Master. You have said the last word for agnosticism and made it widely public, the Master of Trinity Hall has said the last word for Christianity and only scholars know of it. It isn't the strength of your case which makes you dangerous, it's the ignorance of the public and a condition of affairs which makes it possible for you to shout loudest."

[172]

"Well, there is at least a half-truth in what you say also, Mr. Ripon," said Schuabe. "But you don't seem to have brought anything to eat. Will you share my luncheon basket? There is quite enough for two people."

Father Ripon had been called away after the early Eucharist, and had quite forgotten to have any breakfast.

"Thank you very much," he said; "I will. I suddenly seem to be hungry, and after all there is scriptural precedent for spoiling the Egyptians!"

Both laughed again, sheathed their weapons, and began to eat.

Each of them was a man of the world, cultured, with a charming personality. Each knew the other was impervious to attack.

Only once, as the short afternoon was darkening and they were approaching their destination, did Schuabe refer to controversial subjects. The carriage was shadowed and dusky as they rushed through the desolate fenlands. The millionaire lit a match for a cigarette, and the sudden flare showed the priest's face, set and stern. He seemed to be thinking deeply.

"What would you say or do, Father Ripon," Schuabe asked, in a tone of interested curiosity,—"What would you do if some stupendous thing were to happen, something to occur which proved without doubt that Christ was not divine? Supposing that it suddenly became an absolute fact, a historical fact which every one must accept?"

"Some new discovery, you mean?"

"Well, if you like; never mind the actual means. Assume for a moment that it became certain as an historical fact that the Resurrection did not take place. I say that the ignorant love of Christ's followers wreathed His life in legend, that the true story was from the be[173]ginning obscured by error, hysteria, and mistake. Supposing something proved what I say in such a way as to leave no loophole for denial. What would you do? As a representative Churchman, what would you do? This interests me."

"Well, you are assuming an impossibility, and I can't argue on such a postulate. But, if for a moment what you say could happen, I might not be able to deny these proofs, but I should never believe them."

"But surely——"

"Christ is within; I have found Him myself without possibility of mistake; day and night I am in communion with Him."

"Ah!" said Schuabe, dryly, "there is no convincing a person who takes that attitude. But it is rare."

"Faith is weak in the world," said the priest, with a sigh, as the train drew up in the little wayside station.

A footman took their luggage to a carriage which was waiting, and they drove off rapidly through the twilight, over the bare brown fen with a chill leaden sky meeting it on the horizon, towards Fencastle.

Sir Michael's house was an immemorial feature of those parts. Josiah Manichoe, his father, had bought it from old Lord Lostorich. To this day Sir Michael paid two pounds each year, as "Knight's fee," to the lord of the manor at Denton, a fee first paid in 1236. As it stood now, the house was Tudor in exterior, covering a vast area with its stately, explicit, and yet homelike, rather than "homely," beauty.

The interior of the house was treated with great judgment and artistic ability. A successful effort had been made to combine the greatest measure of modern comfort without unduly disturbing the essential character of the place. Thus Father Ripon found himself in an ancient bedroom with a painted ceiling and panelled[174] walls. The furniture was in keeping with the design, but electric lamps had been fitted to the massive pewter sconces on the wall, and the towel-rail by the washing-stand was made of copper tubing through which hot water passed constantly.

The dinner-gong boomed at eight and Ripon went down into the great hall, where a group of people were standing round an open fire of peat and coal.

Mrs. Bardilly, a widowed sister of Sir Michael's, acted as hostess, a quiet, matronly woman, very Jewish in aspect, shrewd and placid in temper, an admirable châtelaine.

Talking to her was Mrs. Hubert Armstrong, the famous woman novelist. Mrs. Armstrong was tall and grandly built. Her grey hair was drawn over a massive, manlike brow in smooth folds, her face was finely chiselled. The mouth was large, rather sweet in expression, but with a slight hinting of "superiority" in repose and condescension in movement. When she spoke, always in full, well-chosen periods, it was with an air of somewhat final pronouncement. She was ever ex cathedra.

The lady's position was a great one. Every two or three years she published a weighty novel, admirably written, full of real culture, and without a trace of humour. In those productions, treatises rather than novels, the theme was generally that of a high-bred philosophical negation of the Incarnation. Mrs. Armstrong pitied Christians with passionate certainty. Gently and lovingly she essayed to open blinded eyes to the truth. With great condescension she still believed in God and preached Christ as a mighty teacher.

One of her utterances suffices to show the colossal arrogance—almost laughable were it not so bizarre—of her intellect:

"The world has expanded since Jesus preached in the [175] dim ancient cities of the East. Men and women of to-day cannot learn the complete lesson of God from him now—indeed they could not in those old times. But all that is most necessary in forming character, all that makes for pureness and clarity of soul—this Jesus has still for us as he had for the people of his own time."

After the enormous success of her book, John Mulgrave, Mrs. Armstrong more than half believed she had struck a final blow at the errors of Christianity.

Shrewd critics remarked that John Mulgrave described the perversion of the hero with great skill and literary power, while quite forgetting to recapitulate the arguments which had brought it about.

The woman was really educated, but her success was with half-educated readers. Her works excited to a sort of frenzy clergymen who realised their insidious hollowness. Her success was real; her influence appeared to be real also. It was a deplorable fact that she swayed fools.

By laying on the paint very thick and using bright colours, Mrs. Armstrong caught the class immediately below that which read the works of Constantine Schuabe. They were captain and lieutenant, formidable in coalition.

A short, carelessly dressed man—his evening tie was badly arranged and his trousers were ill cut—was the Duke of Suffolk. His face was covered with dust-coloured hair, his eyes bright and restless. The Duke was the greatest Roman Catholic nobleman in England. His vast wealth and eager, though not first-class, brain were devoted entirely to the conversion of the country. He was beloved by men of all creeds.

Canon Walke, the great popular preacher, was a handsome[176] man, portly, large, and gracious in manner. He was destined for high preferment, a persona grata at Court, suave and redolent of the lofty circles in which he moved.

Canon Walke was talking to Schuabe with great animation and a sort of purring geniality.

81

Dinner was a very pleasant meal. Every one talked well. Great events in Society and politics were discussed by the people who were themselves responsible for them.

Here was the inner circle itself, serene, bland, and guarded from the crowd outside. And perhaps, with the single exception of Father Ripon, who never thought about it at all, every one was pleasantly conscious of pulling the strings. They sat, Jove-like, kindly tolerant of lesser mortals, discussing, over a dessert, what they should do for the world.

At eleven nearly every one had retired for the night. Father Ripon and his host sat talking in the library for another hour discussing church matters. At twelve these two also retired.

And now the great house was silent save for the bitter winter wind which sobbed and moaned round the towers.

It was the eve of the twelfth of December. The world was as usual and the night came to England with no hintings of the morrow.

Far away in Lancashire, Basil Gortre was sleeping calmly after a long, quiet evening with Helena and her father.

Father Ripon had said his prayers and lay half dreaming in bed, watching the firelight glows and shadows on the panelling and listening to the fierce outside wind as if it were a lullaby.

Mrs. Hubert Armstrong was touching up an article[177] for the Nineteenth Century in her bedroom. An open volume of Renan stood by her side; here and there the lady deftly paraphrased a few lines. Occasionally she sipped a cup of black-currant tea—an amiable weakness of this paragon when engaged upon her stirring labours.

In the next room Schuabe, with haggard face and twitching lips, paced rapidly up and down. From the door to the dressing-table—seven steps. From there to the fireplace—ten steps—avoiding the flower pattern of the carpet, stepping only on the blue squares. Seven! ten! and then back again.

Ten, seven, turn. A cold, soft dew came out upon his face, dried, hardened, and burst forth again.

Seven, ten, stop for a glass of water, and then on again, rapidly, hurriedly; the dawn is coming very near.

Ten! seven! turn!

[178]
CHAPTER III

"I, JOSEPH"

At about nine o'clock the next morning there was a knock at Father Ripon's door and Lindner, Sir Michael's confidential man, entered.

He seemed slightly agitated.

"I beg your pardon, Father," he said, "but Sir Michael instructed me to come to you at once. Sir Michael begs that you will read the columns marked in this paper and then join him at once in his own room."

The man bowed slightly and went noiselessly away.

Impressed with Lindner's manner, Father Ripon sat up in bed and opened the paper. It was a copy of the Daily Wire which had just arrived by special messenger from the station.

The priest's eyes fell first upon the news summary. A paragraph was heavily scored round with ink.

"Page 7.—A communication of the utmost gravity and importance reaches us from Palestine, dealing with certain discoveries at Jerusalem, made by Mr. Cyril Hands, the agent of the Palestine Exploring Fund, and Herr Schmöulder, the famous German historian."

Ripon turned hastily to the seventh page of the paper, where all the foreign telegrams were. This is what he read:

"NOTE[179]
"In reference to the following statements, the Editor wishes it to be distinctly understood that he prints them without comment or bias. Nothing can yet be definitely known as to the truth of what is stated here until the strictest investigations have been made. Our special Commissioner left London for the East twenty-four hours ago. The Editor of this paper is in communication with the Prime Minister and His Grace the Archbishop of Canterbury. A special edition of the 'Daily Wire' will be published at two o'clock this afternoon.

"MOMENTOUS NEWS FROM JERUSALEM
"For the last three months, under a new firman granted by the Turkish Government, the authorities of the Palestine Exploring Society have been engaged in extensive operations in the waste ground beyond the Damascus Gate at Jerusalem.
"It is in this quarter, as archæologists and students will be aware, that some years ago the reputed site of Calvary and the Holy Sepulchre was placed. Considerable discussion was raised at the time and the evidence for and against the new and the traditional sites was hotly debated.
"Ten days ago, Mr. Cyril Hands, M.A., the learned and trusted English explorer, made a further discovery which may prove to be far-reaching in its influence on Christian peoples.
"During the excavations a system of tombs were discovered, dating from forty or fifty years before Christ, according to Mr. Hands's estimate. The tombs are indisputably Jewish and not Christian, a fact which is proved by the presence of kôkîm, characteristic of Jewish tombs in preference to the usual Christian arcosolia. They are Herodian in character.
"These tombs consist of an irregularly cut group of two chambers. The door is coarsely moulded. Both chambers are crooked, and in their floors are four-sided[180] depressions, 1 foot 2 inches deep in the outer, 2 feet in the inner chamber. The roof of the outer chamber is 6 feet above its floor, that of the inner 5 feet 2 inches.
"The doorway leading to the inner tomb was built up into stone blocks. Fragments of that coating of broken brick and pounded pottery, which is still used in Palestine under the name hamra, which lay at the foot of the sealed entrance, showed that it had at one time been plastered over, and was in the nature of a secret room.
"In the depression in the floor of the outer room was found a minute fragment of a glass receptacle containing a small quantity of blackish powder. This has been analysed by M. Constant Allard, the French chemist. The glass vessel he found to be an ordinary silicate which had become devitrified and coloured by oxide of iron. The contents were finely divided lead and traces of antimony, showing it to be one of the cosmetics prepared for purposes of sepulture.
"When the interior of the second tomb had been reached, a single loculus or stone slab for the reception of a body was found.

83

"Over the loculus the following Greek inscription in uncial characters was found in a state of good preservation, with the exception of two letters:

"[See drawing of inscription on this page, made from photographs in our possession. We print the inscription below in cursive Greek text, afterwards dividing it into its component words and giving its translation.—Editor, Daily Wire.]

FACSIMILE IN MODERN GREEK SCRIPT

Εγωιωσηφοαποαριμαθειαςλαβω
ντοσωματουιησουτουαπονα**
ρεταποτουμνημειουοπουτοπρωτ
ονεκειτοεντωτοπωτουτωενεκρυψα
** = lacunæ of two letters.

[181]
FINAL READING OF THE INSCRIPTION

Εγω Ιωσηφ ὁ ἀπο Αριμαθειας λαβων το σωμα του Ιησου του ἀπο Να[ζα]ρετ ἀπο του μνημειου ὁπου το πρωτον ἐκειτο ἐν τω τοπω τουτω ἐνεκρυψα
[ ] = letters supplied.

"TRANSLATION INTO ENGLISH OF THE INSCRIPTION

"I, JOSEPH OF ARIMATHÆA, TOOK THE BODY OF JESUS, THE NAZARENE, FROM THE TOMB WHERE IT WAS FIRST LAID AND HID IT IN THIS PLACE.

"The slight mould on the stone slab, which may or may not be that of a decomposed body, has been reverently gathered into a sealed vessel by Mr. Hands, who is waiting instructions.

"Dr. Schmöulder, the famous savant from Berlin, has arrived at Jerusalem, and is in communication with the German Emperor regarding the discovery.

"At present it would be presumptuous and idle to comment upon these stupendous facts. It seems our duty, however, to quote a final passage from Mr. Hands's communication, and to state that we have a cablegram in our possession from Dr. Schmöulder, which states that he is in entire agreement with Mr. Hands's conclusions.

"To sum up. There now seems no shadow of doubt that the disappearance of The Body of Christ from the first tomb is accounted for, and that the Resurrection as told in the Gospels did not take place. Joseph of Arimathæa here confesses that he stole away the body, probably in order to spare the Disciples and friends of the dead Teacher, with whom he was in sympathy, the shame and misery of the final end to their hopes.

"The use of the first aorist 'ἐνεκρυψα,' 'I hid,' seems[182] to indicate that Joseph was making a confession to satisfy his own mind, with a very vague idea of it ever being read. Were his confession written for future ages, we may surmise that the perfect 'κεκρυφα,' 'I have hidden,' would have been used."

So the simple, bald narrative ended, without a single attempt at sensationalism on the part of the newspaper.

Just as Father Ripon laid down the newspaper, with shaking hands and a pallid face, Sir Michael Manichoe strode into the room.

84

Tears of anger and shame were in his eyes, he moved jerkily, automatically, without volition. His right arm was sawing the air in meaningless gesticulation.

He glanced furtively at Father Ripon and then sank into a chair by the bedside.

The clergyman rose and dressed hastily. "We will speak of this in the library," he said, controlling himself by a tremendous effort. "Meanwhile——"

He took some sal volatile from his dressing-case, gave some to his host, and drank some also.

As they went down-stairs a brilliant sun streamed into the great hall. The world outside was bright and frost-bound.

The bell of the private chapel was tolling for matins.

The sound struck on both their brains very strangely. Sir Michael shuddered and grew ashen grey. Ripon recovered himself first.

He placed his arm in his host's and turned towards the passage which led to the chapel.

"Come, my friend," he said in low, sweet tones, "come to the altar. Let us pray together for Christendom. Peace waits us. Say the creed with me, for God will not desert us."

They passed into the vaulted chapel with the seven[183] dim lamps burning before the altar, and knelt down in the chancel stalls. Some of the servants came in and then the chaplain began the confession.

The stately monotone went on, echoing through the damp breath of the morning.

Father Ripon and Sir Michael turned to the east. The sun was pouring through the great window of stained glass, where Christ was painted ascending to heaven.

The two elderly men said the creed after the priest in firm, almost triumphant voices:

"I believe in God the Father ... and in Jesus Christ His only Son our Lord.... The third day he arose again from the dead. He ascended into heaven...."

And those two, as they came gravely out of church and walked to the library, knew that a great and awful lie was resounding through the world, for the Risen Christ had spoken with them, bidding them be of good courage for what was to come.

The voice of Peter called down the ages:

"This Jesus hath God raised up, whereof we are all witnesses."

[184]
CHAPTER IV

THE DOMESTIC CHAPLAIN'S TESTIMONY

When Mrs. Armstrong came down to breakfast her hostess told her, with many apologies, that Sir Michael had left for London with Father Ripon. They had gone by an early train. Matters of great moment were afoot.

As this was being explained Mr. Wilson, the private chaplain, Schuabe, and Canon Walke entered the room. The Duke of Suffolk did not appear.

A long, low room panelled in white, over which a huge fire of logs cast occasional cheery reflections, was used as a breakfast-room. Here and there the quiet simplicity of the place was violently disturbed by great gouts of colour, startling notes which, so cunningly had they been arranged in alternate opulence and denial, were harmonised with their background.

A curtain of Tyrian purple, a sea picture full of gloom and glory, red light and wind; a bronze head, with brilliant, lifelike enamel eyes, the features swollen and brutal, from Sabacio—these were the means used by the young artist employed by Sir Michael to decorate the room.

The long windows, hewn out of a six-foot wall, presented a sombre vista of great leafless trees standing in the trackless snow, touched here and there with the ruddiness of the winter sun.

The glowing fire, the luxurious domesticity of the[185] round table, with its shining silver and gleaming china, the great quiet of the park outside, gave a singular peace and remoteness to the breakfast-room. Here one seemed far away from strife and disturbance.

This was the usual aspect and atmosphere of all Fencastle, but as the members of the house-party came together for the meal the air became suddenly electrified. Invisible waves of excitement, of surmise, doubt, and fear radiated from these humans. All had seen the paper, and though at first not one of them referred to it, the currents of tumult and alarm were knocking loudly at heart and brain, varied and widely diverse as were the emotions of each one.

Mrs. Hubert Armstrong at length broke the silence. Her speech was deliberate, her words were chosen with extreme care, her tone was hushed and almost reverential.

"To-day," she said, "what I perceive we have all heard, may mean the sudden dawning of a New Light in the world. If this stupendous statement is true—and it bears every hall-mark of the truth even at this early stage—a new image of Jesus of Nazareth will be for ever indelibly graven on the hearts of mankind. That image which thought, study, and research have already made so vivid to some of us will be common to the world. The old, weary superstitions will vanish for all time. The real significance of the anthropomorphic view will be clear at last. The world will be able to realise the Real Figure as It went in and out among Its brother men."

She spoke with extreme earnestness. No doubt she saw in this marvellous historical confirmation of her attitude a triumph for the school of which she had become the vocal chieftainess, that would ring and glitter through the world of thought. The mental arrogance which had already led this woman so far was already busy, opening[186] a vista that had suddenly become extremely dazzling, imminently near.

At her words there was a sudden movement of relief among the others. The ice had been broken; formless and terrifying things assumed a shape that could be handled, discussed. Her words acted as a precipitate, which made analysis possible.

The lady's calm, intellectual face, with its clear eyes and smooth bands of hair, waited with interest, but without impatience, for other views.

Canon Walke took up her challenge. His words were assured enough, but Schuabe, listening with keen and sinister attention, detected a faint tremble, an alarmed lack of conviction. The courtier-Churchman, with his commanding presence, his grand manner, spoke without pedantry, but also without real force. His language was beautifully chosen, but it had not the ring of utter conviction, of passionate rejection of all that warred with Faith.

A chaplain of the Court, the husband of an earl's daughter, a friend of royal folk, a future bishop, there were those who called him time-serving, exclusively ambitious. Schuabe realised that not here, indeed, was the great champion of Christianity. For a brief moment the Jew's mind flashed to a memory of the young curate at Manchester, then, with a little shudder of dislike, he bent his attention to Canon Walke's words.

"No, Mrs. Armstrong," he was saying, "an article such as this in a newspaper will be dangerous; it will unsettle weak brains for a time until it is proved, as it will be proved, either a blasphemous fabrication or an ignorant mistake. It cannot be. Whatever the upshot of such rumours, they can only have a temporary effect. It may be that those at the head of the Church will have to sit close, to lay firm hold of principles, or anything[187] that will steady the vessel as the storm sweeps up. This may be an even greater tempest than that which broke upon the Church in the days of the first George, when Christianity was believed to be fictitious. What did Bishop Butler say to his chaplain? He asked: 'What security is there against the insanity of individuals? The doctors know of none. Why, therefore, may not whole communities be seized with fits of insanity as well as individuals?' It is just that which will account for so much history tells us of wild revolt against Truth. It may be—God grant that it will not—that we are once more upon the eve of one of these storms. But, despite your anticipations, Mrs. Armstrong, you will see that the Church, as she has ever done, will weather the storm. I myself shall leave for town at mid-day, and follow the example of our host. My place is there. The Archbishop will, doubtless, hold a conference, if this story from Palestine seems to receive further confirmation. Such dangerous heresies must not be allowed to spread."

Then Schuabe took up the discussion. "I fear for you, Canon Walke," he said, "and for the Church you represent. This news, it seems to me, is merely the evidence for the confirmation of what all thoughtful men believe to-day, though the majority of them do not speak out. There is a natural dislike to active propaganda, a timidity in combination to upset a system which is accepted, and which provides society as an ethical programme, though founded on initial error. But now—and I agree with Mrs. Armstrong in the extreme probability of this news being absolute fact, for Hands and Schmöulder are names of weight—everything must be reconstructed and changed. The churches will go. Surely the times are ripe, the signs unmistakable? We are face to face with what is called an anti-clerical wave—a dislike to the clergy as the representatives of the Church, a[188] dislike to the Church as the embodiment of religion, a dislike to religion as an unwelcome restraint upon liberty of thought. The storm which will burst now has been muttering and gathering here in England no less than on the Continent. You have heard its murmur in the debates on the Education Act, in the proposed State legislation for your Church. Your most venerable and essential forms are like trees creaking and groaning in the blast; public opinion is rioting to destroy. But perhaps until this morning it has never had a weapon strong enough to attack such a stronghold as the Church with any hope of victory. There has been much noise, but that is all. It has been a matter of feeling; conviction has been weak, because it could only be supported by probabilities, not by certainties. The antichristian movement has been guided by emotions, hardly by principles. At last the great discovery which will rouse the world to sanity appears to have been made. Even as I speak in this quiet room the whole world is thrilling with this news. It is awakening from a long slumber."

Walke heard his ringing words with manifest uneasiness. The man was unequal to the situation. He represented the earthly pomp and show of Christianity, wore the ceremonial vestments. He feared the concrete power, the vehement opposition of the mouthpiece of secularism. He saw the crisis, but from one side only. The deep spiritual love was not there.

"You are exultant, Mr. Schuabe," he said coldly, "but you will hardly be so long."

"You do not appreciate the situation, sir," Schuabe answered. "I can see further than you. A great intellectual peace will descend over the civilised world. Should one not exult at that, even though men must give up their dearest fetishes, their secret shrines; even though sentiment must be sacrificed to Truth? The religion[189] of Nature, which is based upon the determination not to believe anything which is unsupported by indubitable evidence, will become the faith of the future, the fulfilment of progress. It is as Huxley said, 'Religion ought to mean simply reverence and love for the Ethical Ideal, and the desire to realise that Ideal in life.' Miracles do not happen. There has been no supernatural revelation, and nothing can be known of what Herbert Spencer calls the Infinite and Eternal Energy save by the study of the phenomena about us. And I repeat that the discovery we hear of to-day makes a thorough intellectual sanity possible for each living man. Doubt will disappear."

"Yes, Mr. Schuabe," said Mrs. Armstrong, "you are right, incalculably right. It is to human intellect and that alone—the great Intellect of The Nazarene among others—that we must look from henceforth. Already by his unaided efforts man's achievements are everywhere breaking down superstition. The arts, the laws of gravitation, force, light, heat, sound, chemistry, electricity, and all that these imply—botany, medicine, bacteria, the circulation of the blood, the functions of the brain and nervous system (last-named abolishing all witchcraft and diabolic possession, such as we read of in the 'inspired' writings)—all these are but incidents in a progress never aided by the supernatural, but always impeded by the professors of it. Christians tortured the man who discovered the rotation of the earth, and in every church to-day absolutely false accounts of the origin of the world are publicly read. And as long as the world was content to believe that Jesus rose from the dead so long error has hindered development."

"Yes," replied Schuabe, "all this will, I believe, inevitably follow the discovery of the professors in Palestine. And what does Christianity, as it is at present[190] accepted, bring to the Christians? Localise it, and look at the English Church—Canon Walke's Church. At one time every one is a rigid Puritan and decries the bare accessories of worship, at another a Ritualist who twists and turns everything into fantastic shapes, as if he were furnishing an æsthetic bazaar. At another time these people are swayed with the doctrines of 'Christian Science,' and believe that pain is a pure trick of the diseased fancy, and matter the morbid creation of an unhealthy mind. Then we hear priests who tell us that the Old Testament (which in the same breath they announce to be witnessed to by Christ and His Apostles and the unbroken continuity of the Catholic Church) is an enlarged and plagiarised version of the days of a fantastic god discovered on a burnt brick at Babylon. And others sit anxiously waiting to know the precise value which this or that Gospel may possess, as its worth fluctuates like shares in the money market, with the last quotation from Germany! All this will cease."

The while these august ones had been speaking, Father Wilson, the domestic chaplain at Fencastle, had remained silent but attentive.

He was a lean, dark man, monk-like in appearance, somewhat saturnine on the surface. It was Sir Michael's wish, not the chaplain's, that he should sit with the guests as one of them, and make experience of the great ones of the world. For he had but little interest in worldly things or people.

Schuabe's voice died away. Every one was a little exhausted, great matters had been dealt with. There came a little clink and clatter as they sought food.

Suddenly Wilson looked up and began to speak. His voice was somewhat harsh and unsympathetic, his manner was uncompromising and without charm. As he spoke every one realised, with a sense of unpleasant[191] shock, that he cared little or nothing for the society he was in.

"It's very interesting, sir," he said, turning to Schuabe, "to hear all you have been saying. I have seen the paper and read of this so-called discovery too. Of course such a thing harmonises exactly with the opinions of those who want to believe it. But go and tell a devoted son of the Church that he has been fed with sacraments which are no sacraments, and all that he has done has been at best the honest mistake of a deceived man, and he will laugh in your face, as I do! There are memories, far back in his life, of confirmation, when his whole being was quickened and braced, which refuse to be explained as the hallucinations of a well-meaning but deceived man. There are memories when Christ drew near to his soul and helped him. Struggles with temptation are remembered when God's grace saved him. He also says, 'Whether He be a sorcerer or not I know not; one thing I know, that whereas I was blind, now I see.' It is easy to part with one in whom we have never really believed. We can easily surrender what we have never held. But you haven't a notion of the real Christian's convictions, Mr. Schuabe. Your estimate of the future is based upon utter ignorance of the Christian's heart. You are incapable of understanding the heart to which experience has made it clear that Jesus was indeed the very Christ. There are many people who are called Christians with whom your sayings and writings, and those of this lady here, have great power. It is because they have never found Christ. Unreal words, shallow emotions, unbalanced sentiment, leave such as these without armour in a time of tumult and conflicting cries. But if we know Him, if we can look back over a life richer and fuller because we have known Him, if we know, every man, the plague of his own heart, then your[192] explorers may discover anything and we shall not believe. It is easy to prophesy as you have been doing all this meal-time—it is popular once more to shout the malignant 'Crucify'—but events will show you how utterly wrong you are in your estimate of the Christian character."

They all stared at the chaplain. His sudden vigorous outburst, the harsh, unlovely voice, the contempt in it, was almost stupefying at first.

Indeed, though they had certainly no cue from Sir Michael, they had regarded the silent, rather forbidding priest, in his cassock and robe, a dress which typified his reserve and detachment from all their interests, in the light of an upper servant, almost. Nor was it so much his interference they resented as his manner of interfering. The supreme confidence of the man galled them; it was patronising in its strength.

Mrs. Armstrong heard the outburst with a slight frown of displeasure, which, as the priest continued, changed into a smile of kindly tolerance, the attitude of a housemaid who spares a spider. She remembered that, after all, her duty lay in being kind to those of less power than herself.

The speech touched Schuabe more nearly. He seemed to hear a familiar echo of a voice he hated and feared. There was something chilling in these men who drew a confidence and certainty, sublime in its immobility, from the Unseen. He felt, as he had felt before, the hated barrier which he could in no wise pass, this calm fanaticism which would not even listen to him, which was beyond his influence. The bitter hate which welled up in his heart, the terrible scorn which he had to repress at these insults to his evil and devilish egoism, gave him almost a sense of physical nausea. His pale face became pallid, but he showed no other sign of the[193] insane tempest within. He smiled slightly. That was all.

As for Canon Walke, his feelings were varied. His face flickered with them in rapid alternation. He was quite conscious of the lack of life, fire, and conviction in what he himself had said. His own windy commonplaces shrank to nothingness and failure before the witnessing of the undistinguished priest. Before the two hostile intellects, the man and the woman, he had left the burden of the fight to this nobody. He was quick and jealous to mark the strength of Wilson's words, and his own failure had put him in an entirely false position. And yet a shrewd blow had been struck at Schuabe and Mrs. Armstrong; there was consolation in the fact.

Father Wilson, when he had finished what he had to say, rose from his seat without more ado. "I will say a grace," he said. He made the sign of the Cross, muttered a short Latin thanksgiving, and strode from the room.

"A fanatic," said Mrs. Armstrong.

Neither Walke nor Schuabe replied.

It was getting late in the morning. The sun had risen higher and flooded the level wastes of snow without. The little party finished their meal in silence.

In the chapel Wilson knelt on the chancel step, praying that help and light might come to men and the imminent darkness pass away.

[194]
CHAPTER V

DEUS, DEUS MEUS, QUARE DERELIQUISTI!

The Prime Minister was a man deeply interested in all philosophic thought, and especially in the Christian system of philosophy. He had written two most important books, weighty, brilliant contributions to the mass of thought by which his school laboured to make theism increasingly credible to the modern mind.

He had proved that science, ethics, and theology are all open to the same kind of metaphysical difficulties, and that, therefore, to reject theology in the name of science was impossible. It was fortunate that, at this juncture, such a one should be at the head of affairs.

The vast network of cables and telegraph wires, those tentacles which may be called the nerves of the world's brain, throbbed unceasingly after the tremendous announcement for which Ommaney had undertaken the responsibility.

A battalion of special correspondents from every European and American paper of importance followed hot upon Harold Spence's trail.

Nevertheless, for the first two or three days the world at large hardly realised the importance of what was happening. Nothing was certain. The whole statement depended upon two men. To the mass of people these two names—Hands, Schmöulder—conveyed no meaning whatever. Nine tenths of the population of England[195] knew nothing of the work of archæologists in Palestine, had never even heard of the Exploring Society.

Had Consols fallen a point or two the effect would have been far greater, the fact would have made more stir.

The great dailies of equal standing with the Wire were making every private preparation for a supply of news and a consensus of opinion. But all this activity went on behind the scenes, and nothing of it was yet allowed to transpire generally. The article in the Wire was quoted from, but opinions upon it were printed with the greatest caution and reserve. Indeed, the general apathy of England at large was a source of extreme wonder to the unthinking, fearing minority.

The mass of the clergy, at any rate in public, affected to ignore, or did really honestly dismiss as impossible, the whole question. A few words of earnest exhortation and indignant denial were all they permitted themselves.

But beneath the surface, and among the real influencers of public opinion, great anxiety was felt.

The Patriarch of the Greek Church called a council of Bishops, and Dr. Procopides, an ephor of antiquities from Athens, was sent immediately to Palestine.

The following paragraph, in substance, appeared in the leader page of all the English papers. It was disseminated by the Press Association:

"We are in a position to state, that in order to allay the feeling of uneasiness produced among the churches by a recent article in the Daily Wire making extraordinary statements as to a discovery in Jerusalem, a conference was held yesterday at Lambeth. Their Graces the Archbishops of Canterbury and York, the Bishops of Manchester, Gloucester, Durham, Lincoln, and London were present. Other well-known Churchmen consisted[196] of Sir Michael Manichoe, Lord Robert Verulam, Canons Baragwaneth and Walke, the Dean of Christchurch and the Master of Trinity Hall. The Prime Minister was not present, but was represented by Mr. Alured King. Mr. Ommaney, the editor of the Daily Wire, was included in the conference. Although, from the names mentioned, it will be seen that the conference is considered to be of great importance, nothing has been allowed to transpire as to the result of its deliberations."

This paragraph appeared on the morning of the third day after the initial article. It began to attract great attention throughout the United Kingdom during the early part of the day.

The Westminster Gazette in its third edition then published a further statement. The public learned:

"Professor Clermont-Ganneau, the Professor of Biblical Antiquities at the French University of La Sorbonne, arrived in London yesterday night. He drove straight to the house of Sir Robert Llwellyn, the famous archæologist. Early this morning both gentlemen drove to Downing Street, where they remained closeted with the Prime Minister for an hour. While there, they were joined by Dr. Grier, the learned Bishop of Leeds, and Dr. Carr, the Warden of Wyckham College, Oxford. The four gentlemen were later driven to Charing Cross Station in a brougham. On the platform from which the Paris train starts they were met by Major-General Adams, the Vice-President of the Palestine Exploring Society, and Sir Michael Manichoe. The distinguished party entered a reserved saloon and left, en route for Paris, at mid-day. We are able to state on undeniable authority that the party, which represents all that is most authoritative in historical research and archæological[197] knowledge, are a committee from a recent conference at Lambeth, and are proceeding to Jerusalem to investigate the alleged discovery in the Holy City."

This was the prominent announcement, made on the afternoon of the third day, which began to quicken interest and excite the minds of people in England.

All that evening countless families discussed the information with curious unrest and foreboding. In all the towns the churches were exceptionally full at evensong. One fact was more discussed than any other, more particularly in London.

Although the six men who had left England so suddenly, almost furtively, were obviously on a mission of the highest importance, no reputable paper published more than the bare fact of their departure. Comment upon it, more detailed explanation of it, was sought in the columns of all the journals in vain.

The next morning was big with shadow and gloom. A shudder passed over the country. Certain telegrams appeared in all the papers which struck a chill of fear to the very heart of all who read them, Christian and indifferent alike.

It was as though a great and ominous bell had begun to toll over the world.

The faces of people in the streets were universally pale.

It was remarked that the noises of London, the traffic, the movement of crowds engaged upon their daily business, lost half their noise.

The shops were full of Christmas gifts, but no one seemed to enter them.

In addition to the telegrams a single leading article appeared in the Daily Wire, which burnt itself, as the extremest cold burns, into the brains of Englishmen.

[198]

"(1) TERRIBLE RIOTS IN JERUSALEM

"The French Consul-General and Staff, who were paying a ceremonial visit to the Latin Patriarch, have been attacked by fanatical Moslems, and only escaped from the fury of the crowd with great difficulty, aided by the Turkish Guards. A vast concourse of Armenian Christians, Russian pilgrims, and Aleppine Greeks afterwards gathered round the Church of the Holy Sepulchre. The strange discovery said to have been made by the English excavator, Mr. Hands, and the German Doctor Schmöulder, has aroused the mob to furious protest against it. For nearly an hour fervent cries of 'Hadda Kuber Saidna,' 'This is the tomb of our Lord,' filled all the air. The Mohammedans and lower-class Jews made a wild attack upon the protesting Christians in the courtyard of the church. Many hundreds are dead and dying.

"Reuter."

"Later.—Strong drafts of Turkish troops have marched into Jerusalem. By special order from the Sultan to the Governor of the city, the 'New Tomb,' discovered by Mr. Hands and Doctor Schmöulder, is guarded by a triple cordon of troops. The two gentlemen are guests of the Governor. The concentration of troops round the 'New Tomb' has left various portions of the city unguarded. Naked Mohammedan fanatics, armed with swords, are calling for a general massacre of Christians. The city is in a state of utter anarchy. By the Jaffa gate and round the Mosque of Omar the dervishes are preaching massacre."

"(2) SIR ROBERT LLWELLYN'S PARTY TO BE CONVEYED IN A WAR-SHIP

"Malta.—Orders have been received here from the Admiralty that the gunboat Velox is to proceed at once[199] to Alexandria, there to await the coming of Sir Robert Llwellyn and the other members of the English Commission by the Indian mail steamer from Brindisi. The Velox will then leave at once for Jaffa with the six gentlemen. At Jaffa an escort of mounted Turkish troops will accompany the party on the day's ride to Jerusalem."

"(3) Berlin.—The German Emperor has convened the principal clergy of the empire to meet him in conference at Potsdam. The conference will sit with closed doors."

"(4) Rome.—A decree, or short letter, has just been issued from the Vatican to all the 'Patriarchs, Primates, Archbishops, Bishops and other local ordinaries having peace and communion with the Holy See.' The decree deals with the alleged discoveries in Jerusalem. In it Catholics are forbidden to read newspaper accounts of the proceedings in Palestine, nor may they discuss them with their friends. The decree has had the effect of drawing great attention to the affairs in the East, and has excited much adverse comment among the secularist party, and in the Voce della Populo."

Quite suddenly, as if a curtain were withdrawn, the world began to realise the fact that something almost beyond imagination was taking place in the far-off Syrian town.

These detached and sinister messages which flashed along the cables, with their stories of princes and potentates alarmed and active, made the general silence, the lack of detail, more oppressive. The unknown, or dimly guessed at, rather, laid hold on men's minds like some mighty convulsion of nature, imminent, and presaged by fearful signs. Thus the Daily Wire:

[200]

92

"The story of the recent gathering of great Churchmen at Lambeth has not yet been made public, but there can be little doubt in the minds of those who watch events that it must eventually take a place among the great historical occurrences of the world's history. While the men and women of England were going to and fro about their business, the ecclesiastical princes of this realm were met together in doubt, astonishment, and fear, confronted with a problem so tremendous that we find comment upon it presents almost insuperable difficulties.

"We do not therefore propose to take the widest view of probable contingencies and events, for that would be impossible within the limits of a single article. It must be enough that with a sense of the profoundest responsibility, and with the deep emotions which must arise in the heart of every man who is confronted by a vast and sudden overthrow of one of the binding forces of life, we briefly recapitulate the events of the last few days, and attempt a forecast of what we fear must lie before us here in England.

"Four days ago we published in these columns the first account of a discovery made by Mr. Cyril Hands, M.A., and confirmed by Dr. Herman Schmöulder, in the red earth débris by the 'Tombs of the Kings,' beyond the Damascus gate of Jerusalem. The news arrived at this office through a private channel, in the form of a long and detailed account written by Mr. Hands, the archæologist and agent of the Palestine Exploring Society. Before publishing the statement the editor was enabled to discuss the advisability of doing so with the Prime Minister. A long series of telegrams passed between the office of this paper, the Foreign Office, and the gentlemen at Jerusalem during the day preceding our publication of the document. Hour by hour new details and a mass of contributory evidence came to hand.[201] All these papers, together with photographs, drawings, and measurements, were placed by us in the hands of the Archbishop of Canterbury. A conference of the greatest living English scholars was summoned. The result of that meeting has been that a committee representing the finest intellect and the most unsullied integrity is now on its way to Jerusalem. Upon the verdict of Sir Robert Llwellyn and his fellow-members, together with the distinguished foreign savants M. Clermont-Ganneau and Dr. Procopides, the Ephor-General of Antiquities in the Athens Museum, the Christian world must wait with terrible anxiety, but with a certainty that the highest human intelligence is concentrated on its deliberation.

"What that verdict will be, seems, it must be boldly said and faced, almost a foregone conclusion. We feel that we should be lacking in our duty to our readers were we to withhold from them certain facts. Not unnaturally His Grace the Archbishop and many of his advisers have wished the press to preserve a complete silence as to the result of the conference, a silence which should continue until the report of the International Committee of Investigation is published. We have endeavoured to preserve a reticence for two days, but at this juncture it becomes our duty to inform the people of England what we know. And we do not take this step without careful consideration.

"We have informed the Prime Minister of our intention, and may state that, despite the opposition of the Church Party, Lord —— is in sympathy with it.

"Briefly, then, Sir Robert Llwellyn, the acknowledged leader of archæological research, has given it as his opinion that Mr. Hands's discovery must be genuine. Sir Robert alone has had the courage to speak out bravely, though he did so with manifest emotion and reluctance. The other members of the conference have[202] refused to express an opinion, though of at least three from among their number there can be little doubt that they concur with Sir Robert's view.

"Private telegrams, which we have hitherto refrained from publishing, show that the cultured people of Germany, from the Emperor downwards, are persuaded that the story of Jesus of Nazareth has at last been told. Many of the most eminent public men of France agree with this view. These are statements borne out by the evidence of our correspondents in foreign capitals who have secured a series of interviews with those who represent public opinion of the expert kind.

"The Roman Church, on the other hand, with that supreme isolation and historic indifference to all that helps the cause of Progress and Truth, has not only loftily declined to recognise the fact that any discovery has been made at all, has not only absolutely declined to be represented at Jerusalem, but has issued a proclamation forbidding Roman Catholics to think of or discuss the events which are shaking the fabric of Christendom.

"In saying as much as we have already said, in placing our melancholy conviction on record in this way, we lay ourselves open to the charge of prejudging the most important decision affecting the welfare of mankind that any body of men have ever been called upon to make. Not even the startling and overwhelming mass of support we have received would have led us to do this were it not our conviction that it is the wisest course to pursue in regard to what we feel almost certain will happen in the future. It seems far better to prepare the minds of Christian English men and women for the terrible shock that they will have to endure by a more gradual system of disclosure than would be possible were we to adopt the suggestion of the bishops and keep silent.

"And now, in the concluding portion of this article,[203] we must briefly consider what the news that it has been our responsible and painful duty to give first to the world will mean to England.

"We fear that the mental anguish of countless thousands must for a time cloud the life of our country as it has never been clouded and darkened before. The proof that the Divinity of the Greatest and Wisest Teacher the world has ever known, or ever will know, is but a symbolic fable, will for a time overwhelm the world. A great upheaval of English society is beginning. Old and venerated institutions will be swept away, minds fed upon the Christian theory from youth, instinct with all its hereditary tradition, will be for a while as men groping in the dark. But the light will come after this great tempest, and it will be a broader, finer, more steadfast light than before, because founded on, and springing from, Eternal Truth. The mission of beneficent illusion is over. Error will yet linger for a generation or two. That much is certain. There will be more who will base their objections to the New Revelation upon 'the unassailable and ultimate reality of personal spiritual experience,' forgetting the psychological influences of hereditary training, which have alone produced those experiences. But, alas! the knell of the old and beautiful superstitions is ringing. The Doom is begun. The Judge is set, who shall stay it? Let us rather turn from the saddening spectacle of a fallen creed and rejoice that the 'Infinite and eternal energy' men have called God—Jah-weh, θεος—that mysterious law of Progress and evolution, is about to reveal man to himself more than ever completely in its destruction of an imagined revelation."

During the afternoon preceding the publication of the above article, the three principal proprietors had met at[204] the offices of the paper and had held a long conference with Mr. Ommaney, the editor.

It had been decided, as a matter of policy and in order to maintain the leading position already given to the paper by the first publication of Hands's dispatch, that a strong and definite line should be taken at once.

The other great journals were already showing signs of a cautious "trimming" policy, which would allow them to take up any necessary attitude events might dictate. They feared to be explicit, to speak out. So they would lose the greater glory.

Once more commercial and political influences were at work, as they had been two thousand years before. The little group of Jewish millionaires who sat in Ommaney's room had their prototypes in the times of Christ's Passion. Men of the modern world were once more enacting the awful drama of the Crucifixion.

Constantine Schuabe was among the group; his words had more weight than any others. The largest holding in the paper was his. The tentacles of this man were far-reaching and strong.

"For my part, gentlemen," Ommaney said, "I am entirely with Mr. Schuabe. I agree with him that we should at once take the boldest possible attitude. Sir Robert's opinion before he left was conclusive. We shall therefore publish a leader to-morrow taking up our standpoint. We will have it quite plain and simple. Strong and simple, but with no subtleties to puzzle and obscure the ordinary reader. It's no use to touch on history or metaphysics, or anything but pure simplicity."

"Then, Mr. Ommaney," Schuabe had said, "since we are exactly agreed on the best thing to do, and since these other gentlemen are prepared to leave the thing in our hands, if you will allow me I will write the leading article myself."

[205]
CHAPTER VI

HARNESS THE HORSES; AND GET UP, YE HORSEMEN, AND STAND FORTH WITH YOUR HELMETS; FURBISH THE SPEARS, AND PUT ON THE BRIGANDINES.—JER. XLVI: 4

Father Ripon sat alone in his study at the Clergy House of St. Mary's. The room was quite silent, save for the occasional dropping of a coal upon the hearth, where a bright, clear fire glowed.

Three walls of the room were lined with books. There was no carpet on the floor; the bare boards showed, except for a strip of worn matting in front of the little cheap brass fender. Over the mantel a great crucifix hung on the bare wall, painted, or rather washed with dark red colour.

The few chairs which stood about were all old-fashioned and rather uncomfortable. A great writing-table was covered with papers and books. Two candles stood upon it and gave light to the room. The only other piece of furniture was a deal praying-stool, with a Bible and prayer-book upon the ledge.

A rugged, ascetic place, four walls to work and pray in, with just the necessary tools and no more. Yet there was no affectation of asceticism, the effect was not a considered one in any way. For example, there was an oar, with college arms painted on one blade, leaning against the wall, a memory of old days when Father Ripon had rowed four and his boat at Oxford had got to the head[206] of the river one Eight's week. The oar looked as if it were waiting to be properly hung on the wall as a decorative trophy, which indeed it was. But it had been waiting for seven years. The priest never had time to nail it up. He did not despise comfort or decoration, pretend to a pose of rigidness; he simply hadn't the time for it himself. That was all. He was always promising himself to put up—for example—a pair of crimson curtains a sister had sent him months back. But whenever he really determined to get them out and hang them, some sudden call came and he had to rush out and save a soul.

Father Ripon looked ill and worn. A pamphlet, a long, thin book bound in blue paper, with the Royal Arms on the top of the folio, lay upon the table. It was the report of the Committee of Investigation, and the whole world was ringing with it.

95

The report had now appeared for two days.

The priest took up The Tower, a weekly paper, the official organ, not of the pious Evangelical party within the Church, but of the ultra-Protestant.

His hand shook with anger and disgust as he read, for the third time, the leading article printed in large type, with wider spaces than usual between the lines:

"We have hitherto refrained from any comment on the marvellous discovery in Jerusalem, being content simply to record the progress of the investigations, which have at last satisfied us that a genuine discovery has been made.

"In the daily special issues of the organs of the sacerdotal party we find much more freedom of expression. They have run the whole gamut—Disbelief, Doubt, Desolation, Detraction, Demoralisation, and Dismay. Rome and Ritualism have received a shock which demolishes[207] and destroys the very foundation of their sinful system.

"Carnal in its conception it cannot survive.

"'The worship of the corporeal presence of Christ's natural flesh and blood' (vide the so-called Black rubric at the end of the order of the administration of the Lord's Supper) was always prohibited in the Protestant Reformed Communion, but this idolatrous practice has been the glory and boast of Babylon, and the aim and object of the Traitors, within the Established Church of England, whom we have habitually denounced.'

"'The times of this ignorance God winked at, but now commandeth all men everywhere to repent.'

"Hidden by the Divine Providence till the fulness of time, a simple inscription has taught us the full meaning of Paul's mysterious words, 'Yea, though we have known Christ after the flesh, yet now henceforth know we Him no more.'—2 Cor. v. 16.

"Paul and Protestantism are vindicated at last. 'There is a natural body and there is a spiritual body.' The spiritual body that manifested the resurrection of Jesus to His disciples has too long been identified with the natural body that was piously laid to rest by Joseph and Nicodemus. Much that has been obscure in the Gospel narratives is now explained.

"Men have always wondered that the Apostles, in preaching their risen Lord, attempted no explanation of His manifestations of Himself.

"We can understand now why it was that they were divinely protected from imagining that the spiritual Body is a dead body revived.

"How often have perplexed believers been troubled by the questions of our modern scientists as to the physical possibilities of a future resurrection of the body! The material substance of humanity is resolved into its[208] elements, and again and again through the centuries is employed in other organisms.

96

"'How then,' men have asked, 'can you believe that the body you have deposited beneath the earth shall collect from the universe its dissipated particles and rise again?'

"Hitherto we have been content to put the question aside with a simple faith that 'with God all things are possible.' But to-day we are enabled to have a further comprehension of the Lord's words, 'It is the spirit that quickeneth, the flesh profiteth nothing.'

"Doubtless those who, even among our own company of Evangelical Protestants, have attached too much importance to the teaching of the so-called 'Fathers of the Church' (who so early corrupted the sweet simplicity of the Gospel) will find themselves compelled to a more spiritual explanation of some passages of Holy Scripture; but Faith will find little difficulty in rightly dividing and interpreting the word of Truth.

"The Protestant cause has little to fear from facts. We have been by God's Providence gradually prepared for a great elucidation of the truth about the Resurrection.

"Those who studied with attention the treatise of the late Frederick W. H. Myers (the man who, of all moderns, has best appreciated the personality of Paul the apostle) had come to a conviction on the survival of Human Personality after death on scientific grounds.

"The Resurrection of the Lord Jesus was no longer to them 'a thing incredible,' its unique character was recognised as consisting in its spiritual power.

"'Some doubted,' as on the mountain in Galilee. Protestantism on the Continent, especially in Germany, the home of what is misnamed the 'Higher Criticism,' has been hampered in this way by the study of the[209] 'letter,' and so in some degree has lost the assistance of 'the spirit which giveth life.'

"But the great heart of Protestant England is still sound, and whilst Rome and Ritualism are aghast as the foundation of their fabric of lies crumbles into dust, we stand sure and steadfast, rejoicing in hope.

"Some readjustment of formularies may be conceded to weak brethren.

"Our great Reformers drew up that marvellous manifesto of the Protestant faith— 'Articles agreed upon by the archbishops and bishops of Both Provinces, and the whole clergy in the Convocation holden at London in the year 1562 for the avoiding of diversities of opinions, and for the establishing of consent touching True Religion.'

"England was at that time—alas, how often has it been so!—inclined to compromise.

"There were timid men amongst the great divines who brought us out of Babylon, and the 4th article of the Thirty-nine was notoriously drawn up in antagonism to the teaching of the holy Silesian nobleman, Caspar Schwenckfeld, to satisfy the scruples of the sacerdotal party, which clung to the benefices of the Establishment then as now.

97

"The omission of twelve words would remove all doubt as to its interpretation. We may be content to affirm that 'Christ did truly rise again from death' without stating further 'and took again his body with flesh, bones, and all things appertaining.'

"It has always been the curse of Christendom that man desired to express in words the ineffable.

"'Intruding into those things which he hath not seen, vainly puffed up by his fleshly mind.'

"But it need not now be difficult with the aid of a Protestant Parliament, which has so recently and so[210] gloriously determined on the expulsion of sacerdotalists, to modify, in deference to pious scruples, too rigid definitions. Time will suffice for these necessary modifications of sixteenth-century theology.

"In the present, the gain is ours. We shall hear less of the cultus of the 'Sacred Heart' in future. The blasphemous mimicry of the Mass will perish from amongst us.

"No man, in England at least, will dare to affirm that the flesh in which the Saviour bore our sins upon the Cross is exposed for adoration on the so-called 'altar.'

"As Matthew Arnold put it, on the true grave of Jesus 'the Syrian stars look down,' but the risen Christ, glorious in His Spiritual Body, reigns over the hearts of his true followers, and we look forward in faith to our departure from the earthly tabernacle, which is dissolved day by day, knowing that we also have a spiritual house not made with hands eternal in the heavens."

As he read the clever trimming article and marked the bitterness of its tone, the priest's face grew red with anger and contempt.

This facile acceptance of the Great Horror, this insolent conversion of it to party ends, this flimsy pretence of reconciling statements, which, if true, made Christianity a thing of nought, to a novel and trumped-up system of adherence to it, filled him with bitter antagonism.

But, useful as the article was as showing the turn many men's minds were taking, there was no time to trouble about it now.

To-morrow the great meeting of those who still believed Christ died and rose again from the dead was to be held.

The terrible "Report" had been issued. During the forty hours of its existence everything was already beginning[211] to crumble away. To-morrow the Church Militant must speak to the world.

It was said, moreover, that the great wave of infidelity and mockery which was sweeping hourly over the country would culminate in a great riot to-morrow....

Everything seemed dark, black, hopeless....

He picked up the Report once more to study it, as he had done fifty times that day.

But before he opened it he knelt in prayer.

As he prayed, so sweet and certain an assurance came to him, he seemed so very near to the Lord, that doubt and gloom fled before that Presence.

What were logic, proofs of stone-work, the reports of archæologists, to This?

Here in this lonely chamber Christ was, and spoke with His servant, bidding him be of good comfort.

With bright eyes, full of the glow of one who walks with God, the priest opened the pamphlet once more.

[212]
CHAPTER VII

THE HOUR OF CHAOS

Although, during the first days of the Darkness, hundreds of thousands of Christian men and women were chilled almost to spiritual death, and although the lamp of Faith was flickering very low, it was not in London that the far-reaching effects of the discovery at Jerusalem were most immediately apparent.

In that great City there is an outward indifference, bred of a million different interests, which has something akin to the supreme indifference of Nature. The many voices never blend into one, so that the ear may hear them in a single mighty shout.

But in the grimmer North public opinion is heard more readily, and is more quickly visible. In the great centres of executive toil the vital truths of religion seem to enter more insistently into the lives of men and women whose environment presents them with fewer distractions than elsewhere. Often, indeed, this interest is a political interest rather than a deeply Christian one, a matter of controversy rather than feeling. Certain it is that all questions affecting religious beliefs loom large and have a real importance in the cities of the North.

It was Wednesday evening at Walktown.

Mr. Byars was reading the service. The huge, ugly church was lit with rows of gas-jets, arranged in coronæ painted a drab green. But the priest's voice, strained and worn, echoed sadly and with a melancholy cadence[213] through the great barn-like place. Two or three girls, a couple of men, and half a dozen boys made up the choir, which had dwindled to less than a fifth of its usual size. The organ was silent.

Right down the church, those in the chancel saw row upon row of cushioned empty seats. Here and there a small group of people broke the chilling monotony of line, but the worshippers were very few. In the galleries an occasional couple, almost secure from observation, whispered to each other. The church was warm, the seats not uncomfortable; it was better to flirt here than in the cold, frost-bound streets.

Never had Evensong been so cheerless and gloomy, even in that vast, unlovely building. There was no sermon. The vicar was suffering under such obvious strain, he looked so worn and ill, that even this lifeless congregation seemed to feel it a relief when the Blessing was said and it was free to shuffle out into the promenade of the streets.

The harsh trumpeting of Mr. Philemon, the vestry clerk's final "Amen," was almost jubilant.

As Mr. Byars walked home he saw that the three great Unitarian chapels which he had to pass en route were blazing with light. Policemen were standing at the doors to prevent the entrance of any more people into the overcrowded buildings. A tremendous life and energy pulsated within these buildings. Glancing back, with a bitter sigh, the vicar saw that the lights in St. Thomas were already extinguished, and the tower, in which the illuminated clock glowed sullenly, rose stark and cold into the dark winter sky.

The last chapel of all, the Pembroke Road Chapel, had a row of finely appointed carriages waiting outside the doors. The horses were covered with cloths, the grooms and coachmen wore furs, and the breaths of men[214] and beasts alike poured out in streams of blue vapour. These men stamped up and down the gravel sweep in front of the chapel and swung their arms in order to keep warm.

On each side of the great polished mahogany doors were large placards, printed in black and red, vividly illuminated by electric arc lights. These announced that on that night Mr. Constantine Schuabe, M.P., would lecture on the recent discovery in Jerusalem. The title of the lecture, in staring black type, seemed to Mr. Byars as if it possessed an almost physical power. It struck him like a blow.

THE DOWNFALL OF CHRISTIANITY
And then in smaller type,
Anthropomorphism an Exploded Superstition
He walked on more hurriedly through the dark.

All over the district the Church seemed tottering. The strong forces of Unitarianism and Judaism, always active enemies of the Church, were enjoying a moment of unexampled triumph. Led by nearly all the wealthy families in Walktown, all the Dissenters and many lukewarm Church people were crowding to these same synagogues. At the very height of these perversions, when Christianity was forsworn and derided on all sides, Schuabe had returned to Mount Prospect from London.

His long-sustained position as head of the antichristian party in Parliament, in England indeed, his political connection with the place, his wealth, the ties of family and relationship, all combined to make him the greatest power of the moment in the North.
[215]

His speeches, of enormous power and force, were delivered daily and reported verbatim in all the newspapers. He became the Marlborough of a campaign.

On every side the churches were almost deserted. Day by day ominous political murmurs were heard in street and factory. The time had come, men were saying, when an established priesthood and Church must be forced to relinquish its emoluments and position. The Bishop of Manchester, as he rolled through the streets in his carriage, leaning back upon the cushions, lost in thought, with his pipe between his lips, according to the wont and custom which had almost created a scandal in the neighbourhood, was hissed and hooted as he went on his way.

With a sickness of heart, an utter weariness that was almost physical nausea, the vicar let himself into his house with a latch-key.

There was a hushed, subdued air over the warm, comfortable house, felt quite certainly, though not easy to define. It was as though one lay dead in an upper chamber.

Mr. Byars turned into his study. Helena rose to meet him. The beautiful, calm face was very pale and worn as if by long vigils. Minute lines of care had crept round the eyes, though the eyes themselves were as calm and steadfast as of old.

"Basil feels much stronger to-night, Father," she said. "He is dressing now, and will come down to supper. He wishes to have a long talk with you, he says."

For two weeks Gortre had lain prostrate in the house of his future father-in-law.

It was as though he had watched the waters gradually rising round him until at last he was submerged in a merciful unconsciousness. The doctor said that he was enduring a very slight attack of brain-fever, but one[216] which need cause no one any alarm, and which was, in fact, nothing at all in comparison to his former illness.

His fine physical strength asserted itself and helped him to an easy bodily recovery.

To Basil himself, with returning health and a clearer brain came a renewal of mental power. A great strain was removed, the strain of waiting and watching, the tension of a sick anticipation.

"It was almost as if I was conscious of this terrible thing that has happened," he said to Helena. "I am sure that I felt it coming instinctively in some curious psychic way. But now that we know the worst, I am my own man again. Soon, dear, I shall be up and about again, ready to fight against this blackness, to take my place in the ranks once more."

To her loving solicitude he seemed to have some definite plan or purpose, but when she questioned him his reserve was impenetrable, even to her.

During the days of darkness Helena's lot was hard, her heart heavy. While Mr. Byars was at least active, militant, she must eat her heart out in sorrow at home. The doctor had forbidden any talk on those subjects which were agitating the world, between her and Basil. She was denied that consolation. So while her father was attending the conferences at the Bishop's palace, speaking at meetings, visiting the sick with passionate, and, alas, how often useless! assurance that the Truth would prevail and the Light of the World once more shine out undimmed, she must live and pray alone.

Helena's faith had never weakened. All through the trying days and nights it had burned steadily, clear, and pure. But all around her she saw the enemies of Christ prevailing. Nor was it with the slow movement of ordinary secularism, but with a great shout of triumph and exultation which resounded through the world. Men[217] were deserting their posts, the Church she loved seemed tottering, a horrid confusion and anarchy was everywhere.

And all that she could do was to pray. But as the girl moved about her simple household duties, as she tended the sick man with an almost wifely care, her prayers went on unceasingly and every action was interwoven with supplication.

Pale, subdued, but with a quiet clearness and resolution in his eye, Basil came down to the meal. There was but little conversation during it. Afterwards, Helena went to her own room, knowing that her father and Gortre wished to be left alone.

In the study the two men sat on either side of the fireplace. Basil wore a long dressing-gown of camel's-hair. He would not smoke, the doctor had forbidden it, but Mr. Byars lit his pipe with a sigh of satisfaction.

"To think, Basil," the older man said in a broken voice, "to think that Christmas is upon us now! It's the vigil of Christmas, and never since our Lord's Passion has the world been in such a state. And worse than all is our utter impotence!" His voice grew almost angry. "We know, know as surely as we know anything, that this terrible business is some stupendous mistake or fraud. But there isn't the slightest possibility of any one listening to us. On one side the weightiest expert proof, on the other nothing but a conviction to oppose to what appear to be the hardest facts. I cannot blame any non-Christian for acquiescing in this discovery. Viewing the thing clearly and without prejudice, I can't blame any one. It is only the smallest minority, even of professing Christians, whose faith is strong enough to keep them from an utter denial of our Lord's Divinity. It is simply a matter of long personal experience that gives you and me and Helena our confidence in this utter[218] darkness. But in comparison to the rest of the world, how many have that confidence?"

He put down his pipe on the table and rested his head in his outstretched hands, a grey and venerable head. "It's awful, Basil," he said in a broken voice, and with his eyes full of tears. "In my old age I have seen this. I wish that I had gone with my dear wife. 'Help, Lord; for the godly man ceaseth; for the faithful fail from among the children of men.' But what is so bitter to me, my dear boy, is the sight of the utter overthrow of

Faith. It all shows how terribly weak the majority of Christians are. Surface and symbol! symbol and surface!"

"It will not last long," said Gortre, gravely. "For my part, Father, I think that this terrible trial is allowed and permitted by God to bring about a great and future triumph for His Son, which will marshal, organise, and consolidate Faith as nothing has ever done before. I am convinced of it."

"Yes, it must be that," answered the vicar; "undoubtedly that is God's purpose. But I would that the light might come in my time. And I fear I shall not live to see it. I'm an old man now, Basil; this has aged me very much, and I shall not live much longer. It is God's will, but it is hard to know that one will die seeing Christ dethroned in the hearts of men, the Cross broken."

"While I have been quietly up-stairs," said Gortre, "many strange thoughts have come to me, of which I want to speak to you to-night. I have things to tell you which I have mentioned to no one as yet. But before I go into these matters—very dark and terrible ones, I fear—I want you to give me a résumé of the position of things as they are now. The present state is not clear in my mind. I have not read many of the papers, and I want a sort of bird's-eye view of what is going on."

[219]

"The position at present," said Mr. Byars, "from our point of view, is a kind of anarchy. Within every denomination those who absolutely refuse to credit the truth of the discovery are in the minority. Abroad, in France especially, wild free-thought of the rabid Tom Paine order has broken out everywhere in a kind of hysterical rage against Christianity. The immediate social result has been an appalling increase in crimes of lust and cruelty. Great alarm is felt by the authorities. All the papers are taking a horribly cynical view. They say that the delusion of Christianity has clouded men's brains for so long that they are now incapable of bearing the truth, and that the best way to govern the State is to go on making believe. On the other hand, the vast majority of Roman Catholics, both abroad and in England, have remained utterly uninfluenced. It is one of the most marvellous triumphs of discipline and order that history has ever witnessed. The Pope forbade the slightest notice of the discovery to be taken by priests or people in the first instance. Then, when the Report of the Committee was issued, with only one dissentient voice—Sir Michael Manichoe's—a Papal Bull was issued. Here it is, translated in The Tablet, magnificent in its brevity and serenity."

He took a paper from the table beside him and began to read:

"VENERABLE BRETHREN,—HEALTH AND APOSTOLIC BENEDICTION

"It has seemed good to Us to address you on certain points dealing with the decay of faith in divine things, which is the effect of pride and moral corruption. And this is the natural result of pride; for when this vice has taken possession of the heart it is inevitable that the[220] Christian Faith, which demands a most willing docility, should languish, and that a murky darkness in regard to divine truths should close upon the mind, so that in the case of many these words should be made good, 'whatever things they know not they blaspheme' (St. Jude). We, however, so far from being hereby turned aside from the design which We have taken in hand, are, on the contrary, determined all the more zealously and diligently to guide the well-disposed, so that they may be saved from the perils of secular unbelief.

"And, with the help of the united prayers of the faithful, We earnestly implore forgiveness for those who speak evil of holy things.

"And inasmuch as certain persons not being members of the Holy Catholic Church have in an extremity of criminal madness laid claim to discoveries which are pretended and put forth as affecting the eternal Truths of the Faith, We command you, Venerable Brethren, that it shall be stated in all the churches such pretences are void of truth and utterly abominable. The enemies of Christ cry out, 'We will not have this man to reign over us' (Luke xix. 14), and make themselves loudly heard with the utterance of that wicked purpose, 'Let us make away with Him.'

"We therefore charge all Christians having peace and communion with the Holy Church that they shall give no ear or countenance to these onslaughts upon the Faith. It is forbidden for them to speak of these things among themselves, or to listen to others concerning them.

"With these injunctions, Venerable Brethren, We, as a presage of the divine liberality, and as a pledge of our own charity, most lovingly bestow on each of you, and on the clergy and flock committed to the care of each, our Apostolic Benediction."

[221]

"That is the gist of it," said Mr. Byars, "though I have missed out a few paragraphs. The result has been that, with a few exceptions, the whole army of Romanists, so to speak, have closed ranks and utterly refused to listen to what is going on."

"It's very fine, very fine indeed, as a spectacle," Gortre answered. "I wish we had something like that unity and discipline. But is that submission, possibly without the fire of an inward conviction, worth very much? I doubt it."

"It is not for us to judge," answered the vicar. "But the result has been that the Catholic Church, both here and on the Continent, is undergoing a storm of persecution and popular hatred. There have been fearful fights in Liverpool, and riots between the Irish dock-labourers and a mob of people who called themselves Protestants last year and 'Rationalists' to-day.

"The attitude of the Low Church party is varied. Many of them are openly deserting to Unitarianism. Others have accepted the discovery as being a true one, and evolved an entirely new theory from it, while using it as a party weapon also. This attitude is reflected in The Tower in an article which says that, though the actual body of Christ is now proved never to have risen from the dead, the spiritual body was what the Disciples saw. It is a clever piece of work, which has attracted an immense number of people, and is directed entirely against the Holy Eucharist.[1] The Moderate and High Church parties are in some ways in a worse position than any other. They find themselves unable to compromise. "At the great meeting in the Albert Hall the other day, which ended up in something like a free fight, all the conclusion the majority of the clergy could come to was that it was utterly impossible to accept the discovery [222] and remain Christian. The result everywhere is chaos; men are resigning their livings, there have been several suicides—isn't it horrible to think of?—congregations are dwindling everywhere, and disestablishment seems a certainty in a very short time. The papers are full of nothing else, of course. We are fighting tooth and nail upon the standpoint of personal spiritual experience, which nothing can alter, but in a material way how little that helps! The Methodists and Wesleyans are more successful than any one. They are holding revival meetings all over the country. Very few of these two bodies have joined the infidel ranks. Dissent has always implied an act of choice, which, at any rate, means a man is not indifferent to the whole thing. I suppose that is why the Wesleyans seem to be making a firmer and more spiritual stand than any of us. To my shame I say it, but the Churchmen of England are not bearing witness as these others are."

"And the Bishops?"

"Most of them don't know what to do. Of course, the great leaders of spiritual thought, W——, for instance, and G——, have written that which has brought comfort and conviction to hundreds. But see the horror of the position. The only way in which this awful thing can be combated is by just the methods which only scholars and cultivated people can understand. How are people who read the hard, material, logical speeches of people like Schuabe, or that abominable woman, Mrs. Hubert Armstrong, going to be convinced by the subtleties of the intellect or by the reiteration of a personal conviction which they cannot share? Then the Court party, the Archbishop, Walke, and all those, are leaning more and more towards the 'spiritual' body theory, though they hesitate to commit themselves as yet. It is all to be shelved until Convocation meets. They want [223] to see how things will go in Parliament. The Erastian spirit is rampant. They are nearly all afraid of any ecclesiastical action. They are following the lead of Germany under the Kaiser."

"It is all very terrible to see how much less Christianity means to mankind than earnest Christians believed," said Gortre, sadly. "To see the edifice tumbling round one like a house of paper when one thought it so secure and strong. What a terrible lesson this will be in the future to every one; what frightful shame and humiliation will come to those who have denied their Lord when this is over!"

"When will that be, Basil?" said the vicar, wearily. "It seems as if the real hour of test were at hand, and that now, finally and for ever, God means to separate the true believers from the rest. I have thought that all this may be but a prelude to the Last Day of all, and that Christ's Second Coming is very near. But what I cannot understand, what is utterly beyond the power of any of us to appreciate, is what this all means. How can this new tomb have been discovered after all these years? Can all these great experts have been deceived? There have been historical forgeries before, but surely this cannot be one. And yet, I know, you know, that our Lord rose from the dead."

"I believe that to me, of all men in England, The Hand of God has given the key to the mystery," said Gortre.

Mr. Byars started and looked uneasily at him.

"Basil," he said, "I have been thoughtless. We've talked too long. You are not quite clear as to what you are saying. Let us read compline together and go to bed."

He watched Basil as he spoke, but before he had finished his sentence he saw something in the young man's [224] face which sent the blood leaping and tearing through his veins.

In a sudden, utterly unreasoning way, he saw a truth, a certain knowledge, in Gortre's eyes which flooded his whole heart and soul with exaltation and joy.

His good and almost saintly face looked as John's might have looked when, after the octave of the Resurrection Day, the eight heavy-hearted men were once more returning to the daily round and common task, and saw the Lord upon the shore.

[225]
CHAPTER VIII

THE FIRST LINKS

"Ihave been piecing things together gradually, as I lay silent up-stairs," said Gortre, drawing his chair a little closer to the fire.

"Slowly, little by little, I have added link and link to a chain of circumstantial evidence which has led me to an almost incredible conclusion. When you have heard what I have to say you will realise two things. One is that there are depths of human wickedness so abysmal and awful that the mind can hardly conceive of them. The other is that, for what reason it is not for us to try and divine, I have been led, by a most extraordinary series of events and coincidences, to something very near the truth about the discovery in Jerusalem. My story begins some months ago, on the night before I was struck down with brain-fever. You will remember that Constantine Schuabe"—he spoke the name with a shudder of horror that instinctively communicated itself to Mr. Byars— "that Schuabe called here on that night about the school scholarships. When I went away, I left the house with him. He invited me to go on to Mount Prospect and I did so. Earlier in the evening we had been talking of the antichrist and I had said to you that I saw in Schuabe a modern type of the old mediæval idea. My mind was peculiarly sensitive on these points that night, awake, alert, and inquiring. When Schuabe invited me to his house, something impelled me to go, [226] something outside of myself. I went, feeling that I was on the threshold of some discovery."

He paused for a moment, white and tired with the intensity of his narrative.

"When we got to Schuabe's house we began upon the controversial points which we had carefully avoided here. At first our talk was quite quiet, mere argument between two people having different points of view on religion. He went out to get some supper—the servants were all in bed. While he was gone, again I felt the strange assurance of something by me directing my actions. I felt a sense of direct spiritual protection. I went to the bookshelf and took down a Bible. I opened it, half ashamed of myself for the tinge of superstition, and my eyes fell upon the text:

"'WATCH AND PRAY.'

"I could not help taking it as a direct message. Schuabe came back. Gradually, as I saw his bitter hatred and contempt for our Lord and the Christian Church becoming revealed, I was uplifted to rebuke him. He had dropped the veil of an intellectual disagreement. Some power was given to me to see far into the man's soul. He knew that also, and all pretence between us was utterly swept away. Then I told him that his hate was real and active, that I saw him as he was. And these were the words in which he answered me, standing like Lucifer before me. For months they have haunted me. They are burnt in upon my brain for all time. 'I tell you, paid priest as you are, a blind man leading the blind, that a day is coming when all your boasted fabric of Christianity will disappear. It will go suddenly and be swept utterly away. And you, you shall see it. You shall be left naked of your [227] Faith, stripped and bare, with all Christendom beside you. Your pale Nazarene shall die among the bitter laughter of the world, die as surely as he died two thousand years ago, and no man nor woman shall resurrect him. You know nothing, but you will remember my words of to-night, until you also become as nothing and endure the inevitable fate of mankind!'"

Mr. Byars started. As yet he realised nothing of where Basil's story was to lead. "A prophecy!" he cried. "It is as if he were gifted to know the future. Something of what he said has already come to pass."

"My story is a long one, Father," said Gortre, "and as yet it is only begun. You will see plainer soon. Well, as he said these words I knew with certainty that this man was afraid of God. I saw his awful secret in his eyes, this man, antichrist indeed, believes in our Lord, and in terrible presumption dares to lift his hand against Him. Little more of importance happened upon that night. The next day, as you know, I fell ill and was so for some weeks. When I recovered and remembered perfectly all that had happened—do you remember how the picture of Christ fell and broke when Schuabe came?—I saw that I must keep all these things locked within my own brain. What could I do or say more than that I, a fanatical curate—that is what people would have said—had had a row with the famous agnostic millionaire and politician? I could not hope to explain to any one the reality of that evening, the certain knowledge I had of its being only a prelude to some horror that I could not foresee or name. So I kept my own counsel. Perhaps you may remember that on the night of the tea-party when I said good-bye to the people I urged them to keep fast hold on faith, made a special point of it?"

Again Mr. Byars showed his intense interest by a [228] sudden movement of the muscles of his face. But he did not speak, and Gortre continued:

"Now we come to Dieppe when we were all there together. You will, of course, remember how Spence introduced us to Sir Robert Llwellyn, and how we talked over dinner at the Pannier d'Or. Since then, we must remember, Sir Robert's evidence in favour of the absolute authenticity of Hands's discovery has had more weight with the world than that of any one else. He is, of course, known to be the greatest living expert. And that fact also has a very important bearing on my story. After dinner, the conversation turned upon discoveries in exactly the direction that the recent discovery has been made. Llwellyn expressed himself as believing that—I think I remember something like his actual words—'We are on the eve of stupendous discoveries in this direction.' None of us liked to pursue the discussion further. There was a little pause."

"Yes!" said the vicar, "I remember it perfectly now; it all comes back to me quite vividly. But do you know that, beyond of course remembering that we were introduced to Sir Robert at Dieppe, the subject of our conversation had almost escaped my memory. Certainly I never thought of it in detail. But go on, Basil."

"Well, then, Sir Robert drew a plan of the walls of Jerusalem on the back of a letter which he took from his pocket. As he turned the letter over I could not help seeing whom it was from. I read the signature quite distinctly, 'Constantine Schuabe.' This brings us up to a curious fact. Two eminent men, one antichristian, the other a famous archæologist, both express an opinion in my hearing. The first says openly that something is about to occur that will destroy faith in Christ, the other hints only at some wonderful impending discovery in the Holy Land. The connection between the two statements, [229] startling enough in any case, becomes still more so when it is discovered that these two eminent people are in correspondence one with the other. And there is more than this even. Two days after that dinner I was taking a stroll down by the quays when I saw Sir Robert and Mr. Schuabe, who had just landed from the Newhaven boat, get into the Paris train together."

A sudden short exclamation came from the chair on the opposite side of the fire. Very dimly and vaguely the vicar was beginning to see where Basil's story was tending. The fire had grown low, and Mr. Byars replenished it. The noise of the falling coals accentuated the tension which filled the quiet room like a gas.

Then Gortre's tired, but even and deliberate, voice continued:

"I will here ask you to consider one or two other points. Professor Llwellyn told us that he had a year's leave from the British Museum owing to ill health. So long a rest presupposes a real illness, does it not? Now, of course, one can never be sure of anything of this sort, but it is, at least, curious and worthy of remark that Sir Robert seemed outwardly in perfect health and with a hearty appetite. He also said that he was en route for Alexandria. Well, Alexandria is the nearest port to Jaffa, which is but one day's ride from Jerusalem. Now comes a still more curious part of my story. As I have told you, our parish in Bloomsbury is one in which a great class of undesirable people have made their home. It cannot be denied that it is a centre of some peculiarly shameless vice. Much of the work of the clergy lies among women of a certain class, and great tact and resolution is needed to deal with such problems as these people present. Some months ago a woman, whose face seemed in some vague way familiar to me, began to come to church.

106

Once or twice she seemed to show an inclination [230] to speak to me or my colleagues after the service, but she never actually did so. Eventually she called on Ripon, and confessed her way of life. Her repentance seemed sincere, and she was anxious to turn over a new leaf. It appeared that the girl was a rather well-known dancer at one of the burlesque theatres, and I must have seen her portrait on the hoardings and advertisements of these places. She had been touched by something in one of my sermons, it seems, and Ripon requested me to go and see her. I did so, in the flat where she lived, and we had a chat. The poor thing was suffering from an internal disease, and had only a year or two to live. She seemed a kindly, sensible creature enough, vulgar and pleasure-loving, but without any very great wickedness about her, despite her wretched life. She wanted to get right away, to bury herself in the country, and live a pure and quiet life until she died. The great difficulty in the way was the man whose mistress she was, and of whom she seemed in considerable fear. I explained to her that, with the help of Father Ripon and myself, no harm should come to her from him, and that her quiet disappearance from the scenes of her past life could be very easily managed. Then it came out that the man in whose power she was was none other than Sir Robert Llwellyn. She told me that he had been for some time in Palestine. She was expecting him back every day. While we were talking Sir Robert actually entered the room, fresh from his journey. We had a fearful row, of course, and he would not go until I threatened to use force, and then only because he was afraid of the scandal. But before he went he seemed filled with a sort of coarse triumph even in a moment of what must have been great discomfiture for him. I had to explain what had happened to him. I told him frankly that Miss Hunt—that was the woman's [231] name—was, by the grace of the Holy Spirit, about to lead a new and different life. Then this sort of triumph burst forth. He said that in a short time meddling priests would lose all their power over the minds of others. He said that Christ, 'the pale dreamer of the East,' should be revealed to all men at last. He quoted the verse about the grave from Matthew Arnold. And it was all done with a great confidence and certainty."

He stopped, worn out, and glanced inquiringly at Mr. Byars.

The vicar was evidently much moved and excited by the narrative. "The most curious point of all," he said, "in what you tell me is the fact of Sir Robert's private and secret visit to Palestine some months before the discovery was made. Such a recent visit is entirely unknown to the public, who have been so busy with his name of late. The newspapers have said nothing of it. Otherwise, I see no reason why, in some way or other, Mr. Schuabe and Sir Robert may not have known of this tomb in some way before it was discovered by Hands, and their hintings of a catastrophe to faith may have simply been because of this knowledge which they were unwilling to publish."

Gortre shook his head. "No, it is not that," he said. "It is not that. They would never have kept the knowledge secret. You have not been through the scenes with these men that I have. There are a hundred objections to that theory. I am absolutely persuaded that this 'discovery' is a forgery, executed with the highest skill, by the one man living capable of doing it at the instigation of the one man evil enough to suggest it. The hand of God is leading me towards the truth."

"But the proof!" said the vicar, "the proof! Think of the tremendous forces arrayed against us. What can we do? No one would listen to what you have told me."

[232] "God will show a way," said Gortre. "I know it. I had a letter from Harold Spence this morning. His work is done, and he has returned. At the end of the week the doctor says I shall be able to get back to Lincoln's Inn. I shall take counsel with Harold; he is brilliant, and a man of the world. Together we will work to overthrow these devils."

"And meanwhile," answered Mr. Byars, with a despairing gesture, "meanwhile hope and faith are dying out of millions of hearts, men are turning to sinful pleasures unafraid, hopeless, desolate."

The strain had been too great, he was growing older; he bent his head on his hands, while the darkness crept into his soul.

[233]
CHAPTER IX

PARTICULAR INSTANCES, CONTRASTING THE OLD LADY AND THE SPECIAL CORRESPONDENT

The long Manchester station was full of the sullen and almost unbearable roar of escaping steam. Every now and again the noise ceased with a suddenness that was pain, and the groups of people waiting to see the London train start on its four hours' rush could hear each other's voices strange and thin after the mighty vibration.

The feast of Christmas was over. Throughout the world the festival had fallen chill and cold on the hearts of mankind. The Adeste Fideles had summoned few to worship, and the praise had sounded thin and hollow. Even the faithful must keep their deep conviction as a hidden fire within them amid the din and crash of faith and the rising tides of negation and despair.

Gortre, Helena, and Mr. Byars stood together by the train side. They spoke but little; the same thought was in their brains. The jarring materialism of the scene, its steady, heedless industry, seemed an outrage almost in its cold disregard of the sadness which they felt themselves. The great engines glided in and out of the station, the porters and travellers moved with busy cheerfulness as if the world were not in the grip of a great darkness and horror, taking no account of it. They stood by the door of the carriage Basil had chosen, a forlorn group not quite able to realise the stir of life around them.

[234] Gortre was pale and worn, but visibly better and stronger. His face was fixed and resolute. The vicar seemed much older, shrunken somewhat, and his manner was more tremulous than before. His arm was in Helena's.

"Basil," said the vicar, "you are going from us into what must be the unknown— God grant a happy issue out of the perils and difficulties before you. For my part, I seem to be in an unhappy and doubting state. It may be that you have the key to this black mystery and can dispel the clouds. I shall pray daily that it may be so. It is in the hands of God."

He sighed heavily as he gripped Basil's hand in farewell. In truth, he had but little hope and had hardly been able to realise the young man's story. It was almost inconceivable to him, the abnormal wickedness it suggested, the possibility that this great cloud could come upon the world at the action of two men, both of whom he had known, found pleasant, cultured people, and rather liked. The thought was too big to grasp, it confused and stunned him. It is a curious fact that this good man, who could believe, despite all contrary evidence, in the eternal truths of the Gospel, could not believe in the malignancy which Basil's story had seemed to indicate.

Helena had not been told of Basil's suspicions, only of his hopes. She knew that there was that in his mind which might lead once more to light and disperse the clouds. No details were given to her, nor did she ask for them. She was too serene and fine for commonplace curiosity. The mutual trust between the lovers was absolute. Nothing could strain it, nothing could disturb it; and in her love and admiration for Basil, Helena saw nothing incongruous or incredible in the fact that the young man hoped himself to bring peace back to the world.

[235] To any one viewing the project with unbiassed eyes it might have seemed beyond possibility, would have provoked a smile, this spectacle of an obscure curate going up to London in a third-class carriage with hopes of saving his country's faith, in the expectation of overthrowing the gigantic edifice of learned opinion, of combating a Sanhedrin of the great. Such people would have said with facile pedantry that this girl possessed no sense of humour, imagining that they were reproaching her. For by some strange mental perversion most people would rather be told that they lack a sense of morals or duty than a sense of humour, and it is quite certain that this was said of John the Baptist as he preached in his unconventional raiment upon Jordan's banks.

Helena and Basil walked slowly up and down the platform, saying farewell.

Her words of love and hope, her serene and unquestioning confidence, uplifted him as nothing else could do. At this moment, big with his own passionate hopes and desires, yet dismayed at the immensity of the task before him, the trust and encouragement of one he loved were especially helpful and uplifting. It was the tonic he needed. And as the train slowly moved out of the station the bright and noble face of his lady was the last thing he saw.

He thought long of her as the train began to gather speed and rush through the smoky Northern towns. As many other people, Gortre found a stimulus to clear, ordered thought in the sensation of rapid motion. The brain worked with more power, owing to the exhilaration produced in it by speed.

As the ponderous machine which was carrying him back to the great theatre of strife and effort gathered momentum and power, so his mind became filled with high hopes, began to glow with eagerness to strike a great blow against the enemies of Christ.

[236] He looked at the carriage, noticing for the first time, at least consciously, the people who sat there. He had two fellow-passengers, a man and a woman. The man seemed to belong to the skilled artisan class, decently dressed, of sober and quiet manner. His well-marked features, the prominent nose, keen grey eyes, and thick reddish moustache, spoke eloquently of "character" and somewhat of thought. The woman was old, past sixty, a little withered creature, insignificant of face, her mouth a button, her hair grey, scanty, and ill-nourished.

The man was sitting opposite to Gortre and they fell into talk after a time on trivial subjects. The stranger was civil, but somewhat assertive. He did not use the ordinary "sir."

Suddenly, with a slight smile of anticipation, he seemed to gather himself up for discussion.

"Well," he said, "I don't wish individuals no particular harm, you'll understand, but speaking general, I suppose you realise that your job's over. The Church will be swept away for good 'n' all in a few months now, and to my way of thinking it'll be the best thing as 'as ever come to the country. The Church has always failed to reach the labourin' man."

"Because the labouring man has generally failed to reach the Church," said Gortre, smiling. "But you mean Disestablishment is near, I suppose?"

"That's it, mister," said the man. "It must come now, and about time, too, after all these centuries of humbug. I used to go to church years back and sing 'The Church's one foundation.' Its foundation's been proved a pack o' lies now, and down it comes. Disestablishment will prove the salvation of England. When religion's swept away by act o' Parliament, then men will have an opportunity of talking sense and seeing things clearly."

[237] He spoke without rudeness but with a certain arrogance and an obvious satisfaction at the situation. Here was a parson cornered, literally, forced to listen to him, with no way of escape. Gortre imagined that he was congratulating himself that this was not a corridor train.

"I think Disestablishment is very likely to come indeed," said Gortre, "and it will come the sooner for recent events. Of course I think that it will be most barefaced robbery to take endowments from the Church which are absolutely her own property, and use them for secular purposes, but I'm not at all sure that it wouldn't be an excellent thing for the Church after all. But you seem to think that Disestablishment will destroy religion. That is an entire mistake, as you will find."

"It's destroyed already," said the man, "let alone what's going to happen. Since what they've found out in Jerusalem the whole thing's gone puff! like blowin' out a match. You can't get fifty people together in any town what believe in religion any more. The religion of common sense has come now, and it's come to stay."

A voice with a curious singing inflection came from the corner of the carriage, a voice utterly unlike the harsh North-country accent of the workman. The old woman was beginning to speak.

Gortre recognised the curious Cornish tones at once, and looked up with sudden interest.

"You'm wrong, my son," said the old woman, "bitter wrong you be, and 'tis carnal vanity that spakes within you. To Lostwithul, where I bide, I could show 'ee different to what you do say."

The workman, a good-humoured fellow enough, smiled superior at the odd old thing. The wrinkled face had become animated, two deep lines ran from the nostrils to the corner of the lips, hard and uncompromising. The eyes were bright.

[238] "Well, Mother," he said, "let's hear what you've got ter say. Fair do's in argument is only just and proper."

"Ah!" she replied, "it's easy to go scat when you've not got love of the Lard in your heart. I be gone sixty years of age, and many as I can mind back-along as have trodden the path of sorrow. There be a brae lot o' fools about."

The workman winked at Gortre with huge enjoyment, and settled himself comfortably in his place.

"Then you don't hold with Disestablishing the Church, Mother?" he said.

"I do take no stock in Church," she replied, "begging the gentleman's pardon"—this to Gortre. "I was born and bred a Wesleyan and such I'm like to die. How should I know what they'll be doing up to London church town? This here is my first visit to England to see my daughter, and it'll be the last I've a mind to take. You should come to Cornwall, my dear, and then you'll see if religion's over and done away with."

"But you've heard of all as they've just found out at Jerusalem, surely? It's known now that Christ never was what He made out to be. He won't save no more sinners,—it's all false what the Bible says, it's been proved. I suppose you've heard about that in Cornwall?"

"I was down to the shop," said the old lady, with the gentle contempt of one speaking to a foolish child. "I was down to the shop December month, and Mrs. Baragwaneth showed me the Western Morning News with a picture and a lot of talk saying the Bible was ontrue, and Captain Billy Peters, of Treurthian mine, he was down-along too. How 'a did laugh at 'un! 'My dear,' he says, ''tis like the coast guards going mackerel-seining. Night after night have they been out, and shot the nets, too, for they be alwass seein' something briming, [239] thinking it a school o' fish, and not knowing 'tis but moonshine. It's want of experience that do make folk talk so.'"

"That's all very well, Mother," answered the man, slightly nettled by the placid assurance of her tone. "That's all pretty enough, and though I don't understand your fishing terms I can guess at your meaning. But here's the proof on one side and nothing at all on t'other. Here's all the learned men of all countries as says the Bible is not true, and proving it, and here's you with no learning at all just saying it is, with no proof whatever."

"Do 'ee want proof, then?" she answered eagerly, the odd see-saw of her voice becoming more and more accentuated in her excitement. "I tell 'ee ther's as many proofs as pilchards in the say. Ever since the Lard died—ah! 'twas a bitter nailing, a bitter nailing, my dear!"—she paused, almost with tears in her voice, and the whole atmosphere of the little compartment seemed to Basil to be irradiated, glorified by the shining faith of the old dame—"ever since that time the proofs have been going on. Now I'll tell 'ee as some as I've see'd, my son. Samson Trevorrow to Carbis water married my sister, May Rosewarne, forty years ago. He would drink something terrible bad, and swear like a foreigner. He'd a half-share in a trawler, three cottages, and money in the bank. First his money went, then his cottages, and he led a life of sin and brawling. He were a bad man, my dear. Every one were at 'un for an ongodly wastrel, but 'a kept on. An' the Lard gave him no children; May could not make a child to him, for she were onfruitful, but he would not change. All that folk with sense could do was done, but 't were no use."

"Well, I know the sort of man," said the workman, with conviction. His interest was roused, that unfailing [240] interest which the poorer classes take in each other's family history.

"Then you do know that nothing won't turn them from their evil ways?"

"When a chap gets the drink in him like that," replied the artisan, "there's no power that will take him from it. He'd go through sheet iron for it."

"And so would Samson Trevorrow, my dear," she continued. "One night he came home from Penzance market, market-peart, as the saying is, drunk if you will. My sister said something to 'un, what 't was I couldn't say, but he struck her, for the first time. Next morning was the Sunday, and when she told him of what he'd done overnight, he was shamed of himself, and she got him to come along with her to chapel. 'T was a minister from Bodmin as prached, and 'ee did prache the Lard at Sam until the Word got hold on 'un and the man shook with repentance at his naughty life. He did kneel down before them all and prayed for forgiveness, and for the Lard to help 'un to lead a new life. From that Sabbath till he died, many years after, Sam never took anything of liquor, he stopped his sweering and carrying on, and he lived as a good man should. And in a year the Lard sent 'un a son, and if God wills I shall see the boy this afternoon, for he's to meet the train. There now, my son, that be gospel truth what I tell 'ee. After that can you expect any one with a grain of sense to listen to such foolish truck as you do tell? The Lard did that for Samson Trevorrow, changed 'un from black to white, 'a did. If the Queen herself were to tell me that the Lard Jesus wasn't He, I wouldn't believe her."

As Gortre drove from Euston through the thronged veins of London towards the Inn, he thought much and with great thankfulness of the little episode in the train. Such simple faith, such supreme conviction, was, he [241] knew, the precious possession of thousands still. What did it matter to these sturdy Nonconformists in the lone West that savants denied Christ? All over England the serene triumph of the Gospel, deep, deep down in the hearts of quiet people, gave the eternal lie to Schuabe and his followers. Never could they overcome the Risen Lord in the human heart. He began to realise more and more the ineffable wonder of the Incarnation.

111

Before he had arrived at Chancery Lane the London streets began to take hold of him once more with the old familiar grip. How utterly unchanged they were! It seemed but a day since he had left them; it was impossible at the moment of re-contact to realise all that had passed since he had gone away.

He was to have an immediate and almost terrifying reminder of it. The door of the chambers was not locked, and pushing it open, he entered.

Always most sensitive to the atmosphere of a room, moral as well as material, he was immediately struck by that of the chambers, most unpleasantly so, indeed. Certain indications of what had been going on there were easily seen. Others were not so assertive, but contributed their part, nevertheless, to the subtle general impression of the place.

The air was stale with the pungent smell of Turkish tobacco and spirits. It was obvious that the windows had not been as freely opened as their wont. A litter of theatre programmes lay on one chair. On another was a programme of a Covent Garden ball and a girl's shoe of white satin, into which a fading bouquet of hothouse flowers had been wantonly crushed. The table was covered with the débris of a supper, a pâté, some long-necked bottles which had held Niersteiner, a hideous box of pink satin and light blue ribbons half full of glacé plums and chocolates.

[242] The little bust of the Hermes of Praxiteles, which stood on one of the bookcases, had been maltreated with a coarseness and vulgarity which hurt Basil like a blow. The delicate contour of the features, the pure white of the plaster, were soiled and degraded. The cheeks had been rouged up to the eyes, which were picked out in violet ink. The brows were arched with an "eyebrow pencil" and the lips with a vivid cardinal red.

Basil put down his portmanteau and grew very pale as he looked round on these and many other evidences of sordid and unlovely riot. His heart sank within him. He began to fear for Harold Spence.

Even as he looked round, Spence came into the room from his bed-chamber. He was dressed in a smoking jacket and flannel trousers. Basil saw at once that he had been drinking heavily. The cheeks were swollen under the pouch of the eye, he was unshaven, and his manner was full of noisy and tremulous geniality.

There are men in whom a week or two of sudden relapse into old and evil courses has an extraordinarily visible effect. Spence was one of them. At the moment he looked as the clay model compares with the finished marble.

Gortre was astounded at the change, but one thing the modern London clergyman learns is tact. The situation was obvious, it explained itself at once, and he nerved himself to deal with it warily and carefully.

Spence himself was ill at ease at they went through the commonplaces of meeting. Then, when they were both seated by the fire and were smoking, he began to speak frankly.

"I can see you are rather sick, old man," he said. "Better have it out and done with, don't you think?"

"Tell me all about it, old fellow," said Gortre.

"Well, there isn't very much to tell, only when I came back from Palestine after all that excitement I felt [243] quite lost and miserable. Something seemed taken away out of one's life. Then there didn't seem much to do, and some of the old set looked me up and I have been racketing about town a good bit."

"I thought you'd got over all that, Harold; because, putting it on no other grounds, you know the game is not worth the candle."

112

"So I had, Basil, before"—he swallowed something in his throat—"before this happened. I didn't believe in it at first, of course, or, at least, not properly, when I got Hands's letter. But when I got out East—and you don't know and won't be able to understand how the East turns one's ideas upside down even at ordinary times—when I got out there and saw what Hands had found, then everything seemed slipping away. Then the Commission came over and I was with them all and heard what they had to say. I know the whole private history of the thing from first to last. It made me quite hopeless—a terrible feeling—the sort of utter dreariness that Poe talks of that the man felt when he was riding up to the House of Usher. Of course, thousands of people must have felt just the same during the past weeks. But to have the one thing one leaned upon, the one hope that kept one straight in this life, the hope of another and happier one, cut suddenly out of one's consciousness! Is it any wonder that one has gone back to the old temptations? I don't think so, Basil."

His voice dropped, an intense weariness showed in his face. His whole body seemed permeated by it, he seemed to sink together in his chair. All the mental pain he had endured, all the physical languor of fast living, that terrible nausea of the soul which seizes so imperiously upon the vicious man who is still conscious of sin; all these flooded over him, possessed him, as he sat before his friend.

[244] An enormous pity was in Basil's heart as he saw this concrete weakness and misery. He realised what he had only guessed at before or seen but dimly. He would not have believed this transformation possible; he had thought Harold stronger. But even as he pitied him he marvelled at the Power which had been able to keep the man pure and straight so long. Even this horrid débâcle was but another, if indirect, testimony to the power of Faith.

And, secondly, as he listened to his friend's story, a deep anger, a righteous wrath as fierce as flame burned within him as he thought of the two men who, he was persuaded, had brought this ruin upon another. In Spence he was able to see but a single case out of thousands which he knew must be similar to it. The evil passions which lie in the hearts of all men had been loosened and unchained; they had sprung into furious activity, liberated by the appalling conspiracy of Schuabe and Llwellyn.

It is noticeable that there was by this time hardly any doubt in Gortre's mind as to the truth of his suspicions.

"I understand it all, old man," he said, "and you needn't tell me any more. I can sympathise with you. But I have much to tell you—news, or, at least, theories, which you will be astounded to hear. Listen carefully to me. I believe that just as you were the instrument of first bringing this news to public notice, so you and I are going to prove its falsity, to unearth the most wicked conspiracy in the world's history. Pull yourself together and follow me with all your power. All hope is not yet gone."

Basil saw, with some relief, the set and attentive face before him, a face more like the old Spence. But, as he began to tell his story, there flashed into his mind a sudden picture of the old Cornish woman in the train, and he marvelled at that greater faith as his eye fell upon the foul disorder of the room.

[245]
CHAPTER X

THE TRIUMPH OF SIR ROBERT LLWELLYN

In the large, open fireplaces of the Sheridan Club dining-room, logs of pine and cedar wood gave out a regular and well-diffused warmth. Outside, the snow was still falling, and beyond the long windows, covered with their crimson curtains, the yellow air was full of soft and silent movement.

The extreme comfort of the lofty, panelled dining-room was accentuated a hundred-fold, to those entering it, by the chilly experience of the streets.

The electric lights burnt steadily in their silk shades, the gleams falling upon the elaborate table furniture in a thousand points of dancing light.

At one of the tables, laid for two people, Sir Robert Llwellyn was sitting. He was in evening dress, and his massive face was closely scrutinising a printed list propped up against a wine-glass before him. His expression was interested and intent. By his side was a sheet of the club note-paper, and from time to time he jotted down something upon it with a slender gold pencil.

The great archæologist was ordering dinner for himself and a guest with much thought and care.

Crême d'asperge à la Reine

in his neat writing, the letters distinct from one another—almost like an inscription in Uncial Greek character, one might have fancied.

[246]Turbot à l'Amiral promised well; the plump, powerful fingers wrote it down.

Poulardes du Mans rôties with petits pois à la Française with a salade Niçoise to follow; that would be excellent! Then just a little suprème de pêches, à la Montreuil, which is quite the best kind of suprème, then some Parmesan before the coffee.

"Quite a simple dinner, Painter," he said to the steward of the room,—the famous "small dining-room" with its alcoves and discreet corners,—"simple but good. Of course you will tell Maurice that it is for me. I want him to do quite his best. If you will send this list off to the kitchens with a message, we will go into the wines together."

They went carefully into the wines.

"Remember that we shall want the large liqueur glasses," he said, "with the Tuileries brandy. In fact, I think I'll take a little now, as an apéritif."

The man bowed confidentially and went away. He returned with a long bottle of curious shape with an imperial crown blown in the glass. It was some of the famous brandy which had been lately found bricked up in a cellar close to the Place Carrousel, and was worth its weight in gold.

On the tray stood one of the curious liqueur glasses lately introduced into the club by Sir Robert. It was the shape of a port-wine glass, but enormously large, capable of holding a pint or more, and made of glass as thin as tissue paper and fragile as straw. The steward poured a very little of the brandy into the great glass and twirled it round rapidly by the stem. This was the most epicurean device for bringing out the bouquet of the liqueur.

Llwellyn sipped the precious liquid with an air of the most intense enjoyment. His face glowed with enthusiasm.

[247] "Wonderful, wonderful!" he said in a hushed voice. "There, take it away and bring me an olive. Then I will go down-stairs and wait for my friend in the smoking-room. You will serve the soup at five minutes past eight."

He got up from the table and moved silently over the heavy carpet to the door.

It was about seven o'clock. At eight Constantine Schuabe was coming to the Sheridan Club to dine.

Sir Robert sat in the smoking-room with a tiny cigarette of South American tobacco, wrapped in maize leaf and tied round the centre with a tiny cord of green silk. His face expressed nothing but the most absolute repose. His correspondence with life was at that moment as complete as the most perfect health and discriminating luxury could make it.

He stretched out his feet to the blaze and idly watched the reflection in the points of his shining boots.

The room was quite silent now. A few men sat about reading the evening papers, and there was a subdued hum of talk from a table where two men were playing a casual game of chess, in which neither of them seemed much interested. A large clock upon the oak mantel-shelf ticked with muffled and soothing regularity.

Llwellyn picked up a sixpenny illustrated paper, devoted to amusements and the lighter side of life, and lazily opened it.

His eye fell upon a double-page article interspersed with photographs of actors and actresses. The article was a summing-up of the year's events on the lighter stage by an accepted expert in such matters. He read as follows:

"The six Trocadero girls whom I remember in Paris recently billed as 'The Cocktails,' never forget that [248] grace is more important in dancing than mere agility. They are youthful looking, pretty and supple, and their manœuvres are cunningly devised. The diseuse of the troupe, Mdlle. Nepinasse, sings the Parisian success, Viens Poupoule, with considerable 'go' and swing. But in hearing her at the 'Gloucester' the other night I could not help regretting the disappearance of brilliant Gertrude Hunt from the boards where she was so great an attraction. Poupoule, or its English equivalent, is just the type of song, with its attendant descriptive dance, in which that gay little lady was seen at her best. In losing her, the musical-comedy stage has lost a player whose peculiar individuality will not easily be replaced. Gertrude Hunt stood quite alone among her sisters of the Profession. Who will readily forget the pert insouciance, the little trick of the gloved hands, the mellow calling voice? It has been announced that this popular favourite has disappeared for ever from the stage. But there is a distinct mystery about the sudden eclipse of this star, and one which conjecture and inquiry has utterly failed to solve. Well, I, in common with thousands of others, can only sigh and regret it. Yet I should like to think that these lines would meet her eye, and she may know that I am only voicing the wishes of the public when I call to her to come back and delight our eyes and ears as before."

By the side of the paragraph there was a photograph of Gertrude Hunt. He stared at it, his mind busy with memories and evil longing. The bold, handsome face, the great eyes, looked him full in the face. Never had any woman been able to hold him as this one. She had become part of his life. In his mad passion for the dancer he had risked everything, until his whole career had depended upon the good-will of Constantine Schuabe. [249] There had been no greater pleasure than to satisfy her wishes, however tasteless, however vulgar. And then, hastening back to her side with a fortune for her (the second he had poured into the white grasping hands), he had found her with the severe young priest. A power which he was unable to understand had risen up as a bar to his enormous egoism. She had gone, utterly disappeared, vanished as a shadow vanishes at the moving of a light.

And all his resources, all those of the theatre people with whom she had been so long associated, had utterly failed to trace her.

The Church had swallowed her up in its mystery and gloom. She was lost to him for ever. And the fierce longing to be with her once more burnt within him like the unhallowed flame upon the altar of an idol.

As he regarded the chaos into which the Church was plunged he would laugh to himself in horrid glee. His indifference to all forms of religious congregations had gone.

115

He felt an active and bitter hatred now hardly less than that of Schuabe himself. And all the concentrated hatred and incalculable malice that his poisoned brain distilled was focussed and directed upon the young curate who had been the means and instrument of his discomfiture. He had begun to plan schemes of swift revenge, laughing at himself sometimes for the crude melodrama of his thoughts.

As a waiter with his powdered hair and white silk stockings showed Schuabe into the smoking-room, the Jew saw with surprise the flushed and agitated face of his host, so unlike its usual sensual serenity. He wondered what had arisen to disturb Llwellyn, and he made up his mind that he would know it before the evening was over.

Schuabe, on his part, seemed depressed and in poor spirits.[250] There was a restlessness, quite foreign to his usual composure, which appeared in little nervous tricks of his fingers. He toyed with his wine-glass and did poor justice to the careful dinner.

"Everything is going on very well," Llwellyn said. "My book is nearly finished, and the American rights were sold yesterday. The Council of the Free Churches have appointed Dr. Barker to write a counterblast. Who could have foreseen the stir and tumult in the world? Everything is toppling over in the religious world. I have read of your triumphal progress in the North—this asparagus soup is excellent."

"I don't feel very much inclined to talk of these things to-night," said Schuabe. "To tell the truth, my nerves are a little out of order, and I have been doing too much. I've got in that ridiculous state in which one is constantly apprehending some sinister event. Everything has gone well, and yet I'm like this. It is foolish. How humiliating a thought it is, Llwellyn, that even intellects like yours and mine are entirely dependent upon the secretions of the liver!"

He smiled rather grimly, and the disturbance of the regular repose and immobility of his face showed depths of weary unhappiness which betrayed the tumult within.

He recovered himself quickly, anxious, it seemed, to betray his thoughts no further.

"You seemed upset when I came into the club," he said. "You ought to be happy enough. Debts all gone, fifty thousand in the bank, reputation higher than ever, and all the world listening to everything you've got to say." He smiled rather bitterly, as Llwellyn raised a glass of champagne to his lips.

"Exactly," said Llwellyn. "I've got everything I wanted a few months ago, and one of the principal inducements for wanting it has gone."

[251] "Oh! you mean that girl?" answered Schuabe, contemptuously. "Well, buy another. They are for sale in all the theatres, you know."

"It's all very well to sneer like that," replied Llwellyn. "It's nothing to me that you're about as cold-blooded as a fish, but you needn't sneer at a man who is not. Because you enjoy yourself by means of asceticism you have no more virtue than I have. I am fond of this one girl; she has become necessary to my life. I spent thousands on her, and then this abominable young parson takes her away—" He ground his teeth savagely, his face became purple, he was unable to finish his sentence.

Curiously enough Schuabe seemed to be in sympathy with his host's rage. A deadly and vindictive expression crept into his eyes, which were nevertheless more glittering and cold than before.

"Gortre has come back to London. He has been here nearly a week," said Schuabe, quickly.

The other started. "You know his movements then? What has he to do with you?"

"More than, perhaps, you think. Llwellyn, that young man is dangerous!"

"He's done me all the harm he can already. There is nothing else he can do, unless he elopes with Lady Llwellyn, an event which I should view with singular equanimity."

116

"At any rate, I take sufficient interest in that person's movements to have them reported to me daily."

"Why on earth——?"

"Simply because he guesses, or will guess, at the truth about the Damascus Gate sepulchre!"

Llwellyn grew utterly white. When he spoke it was with several preliminary moistenings of the lips.

"But what proof can he have?"

[252] "Don't be alarmed, Llwellyn. We are perfectly safe in every way. Only the man is an enemy of mine, and even small enemies are obnoxious. He won't disturb either of us for long."

The big man gave a sigh of relief. "Well, you manage as you think best," he said. "Confound him! He deserves all he gets—let's change the subject. It's a little too Adelphi-like to be amusing."

"I am going to hear Pachmann in the St. James's Hall. Will you come?"

Llwellyn considered a moment. "No, I don't think I will. I'm going out to a supper-party in St. John's Wood later—Charlie Fitzgerald's, the lessee of the Piccadilly. I shall go home and read a novel quietly. To tell the truth, I feel rather depressed, too. Everything seems going too well, doesn't it?"

Schuabe's voice shook a little as he replied shortly.

For a brief moment the veil was raised. Each saw the other with eyes full of the fear that was lurking within them.

For weeks they had been at cross purposes, simulating a courage and indifference they did not feel.

Now each knew the truth.

They knew that the burden of their terrible secret was beginning to press and enclose them with its awful weight. Each had imagined the other free from his own terror, that terror that lifts up its head in times of night and silence, the dread Incubus that murders sleep.

The two men went out of the club together without speaking. Their hearts were beating like drums within them; it was the beginning of the agony.

Llwellyn, his coat exchanged for a smoking jacket, lay back in a leather chair in his library. Since his return from Palestine he had transferred most of his belongings [253] to a small flat in New Bond Street. He hardly ever visited his wife now. The flat in Bloomsbury Court Mansions had been given up when Gertrude Hunt had gone.

In New Bond Street Sir Robert lived alone. A housekeeper in the basement of the buildings looked after his rooms and his valet slept above.

The new pied à terre was furnished with great luxury. It was not the garish luxury and vulgar splendour of Bloomsbury Court—that had been the dancer's taste. Here Llwellyn had gathered round him all that could make life pleasant, and his own taste had seen to everything.

As he sat alone, slightly recovered from the nervous shock of the dinner, but in an utter depression of spirits, his thoughts once more went back to his lost mistress.

It was in times like these that he needed her most. She would distract him, amuse him, where a less vulgar, more intellectual woman would have increased his boredom.

He sighed heavily, pitying himself, utterly unconscious of his degradation. The books upon the shelves, learned and weighty monographs in all languages, his own brilliant contributions to historical science among them, had no power to help him. He sighed for his rowdy Circe.

The electric bell of the flat rang sharply outside in the passage. His man was out, and he rose to answer it himself.

A friend probably had looked him up for a drink and smoke. He was glad; he wanted companionship, easy, genial companionship, not that pale devil Schuabe, with his dreary talk and everlasting reminder.

He went out into the passage and opened the front door. A woman stood there. [254] She moved, and the light from the hall shone on her face.

The eyes were brilliant, the lips were half parted.

It was Gertrude Hunt.

They were sitting on each side of the fire.

Gertrude was pale, but her dark beauty blazed at him.

She was smoking a cigarette, just as in the old time.

A little table with a caraffe of brandy and bottles of seltzer in a silver stand stood between them.

Llwellyn's face was one large circle of pleasure and content. His eyes gleamed with an evil triumph as he looked at the girl.

"Good Heavens!" he cried, "why, Gertie, it's almost worth while losing you to have you back again like this. It's just exactly as it used to be, only better; yes, better! So you got tired of it all, and you've come back. What a little fool you were ever to go away, dear!"

"Yes, I got tired of it," she repeated, but in a curiously strained voice.

He was too exhilarated to notice the strange manner of her reply.

"Well, I've got any amount of ready cash now," he said joyously. "You can have anything you like now that you've given up the confounded parsons and become sensible again."

She seemed to make an effort to throw off something that oppressed her.

"Now, Bob," she said, "don't talk about it. I've been a little fool, but that's over. What a lot you've got to tell me! What did you do all the time you were away? Where did you raise the 'oof from? Tell me everything. Let's be as we were before. No more secrets!"

[255] He seemed to hesitate for a moment.

She saw that, and stood up. "Come and kiss me, Bob," she said. He went to her with unsteady footsteps, as if he were intoxicated by the fury of his passion.

"Tell me everything, Bob," she whispered into his ear.

The man surrendered himself to her, utterly, absolutely.

"Gertie," he said, "I'll tell you the queerest story you ever heard."

He laughed wildly.

"I've tricked the whole world by Jove! cleared fifty thousand pounds, and made fools of the whole world."

She laughed, a shrill, high treble.

"Dear old Bob," she cried; "clever old Bob, you're the best of them all! What have you done this time? Tell me all about it."

"By God, I will," he cried. "I'll tell you the whole story, little girl." His voice was utterly changed.

"Yes, everything!" she repeated fiercely.

Her body shook violently as she spoke.

The man thought it was in response to his caresses.

And the face which looked out over the man's shoulder, and had lately been as the face of Delilah, was become as the face of Jael, the wife of Heber the Kenite.

"No more secrets, Bob?"

118

"No more secrets, Gertie; but how pale you look! Take some brandy, little girl. Now, I'm going to make you laugh! Listen!"

CHAPTER XI

PROGRESS

Sir Michael Manichoe, Father Ripon, and Harold Spence were sitting in Sir Michael's own study in his London house in Berkeley Square. A small circular table with the remains of a simple meal showed that they had dined there, without formality, more of necessity than pleasure.

When a small company of men animated by one strenuous purpose meet together, the same expression may often be seen on the face of each one of them. The three men in the study were curiously alike at this moment. A grim resolution, something of horror, a great expectation looked out of their eyes.

Sir Michael looked at his watch. "Gortre ought to be here directly," he said. "It won't take him very long to drive from Victoria. The train must be in already."

Father Ripon nodded, without speaking.

There was another interval of silence.

Then Spence spoke. "Of course it is only a chance," he said. "Gertrude Hunt may very likely be able to give us no information whatever. One can hardly suppose that Llewellyn would confide in her."

"Not fully," said Father Ripon. "But there will be letters probably. I feel sure that Gortre will come back with some contributory evidence, at all events. We must go to work slowly, and with the greatest care."

"The greatest possible care," repeated Sir Michael. [257] "On the shoulders of us four people hangs an incredible burden. We must do nothing until we are sure. But ever since Gortre's suspicions have been known to me, ever since Schuabe asked you that curious question in the train, Ripon, I have felt absolutely assured of their truth. Everything becomes clear at once. The only difficulty is the difficulty of believing in such colossal wickedness, coupled with such supreme daring."

"It is hard," said Father Ripon. "But probably one's mind is dazzled with the consequences, the size, and immensity of the fraud. Apart from this question of bigness, it may be that there is, given a certain Napoleonic type of brain, no more danger or difficulty in doing such gigantic evil than in doing evil on a smaller scale."

"Perhaps the size of the operation blinds people—" Spence was continuing, when the door opened and the butler showed Gortre into the room.

He wore a heavy black cloak and carried a Paisley travelling rug upon his arm.

The three waiting men started up at his approach, with an unspoken question on the lips of each one of them.

Gortre began to speak at once. He was slightly flushed from his ride through the keen, frosty air of the evening. His manner was brisk, hopeful.

"The interview was excessively painful, as I had anticipated," he began. "The result has been this: I have been able to get no direct absolute confirmation of what we think. On the other hand, what I have heard establishes something and has made me morally certain that we are on the right track. I think there can be no doubt about that. Again, there is a strong possibility that we shall know much more very shortly."

"Have you had anything to eat?" asked Sir Michael.

"No, sir, and I'm hungry after my journey. I'll [258] have some of this cold beef, and tell you everything that has happened while I eat."

He sat down, began his meal, and told his story in detail.

"I found Miss Hunt," he said, "in her little cottage by the coast-guard watch-house, looking over the sea. Of course, as you know, she is known as Mrs. Hunt in the village. Only the rector knows her story—she has made herself very beloved in Eastworld, even in the short time she has been there. I asked her, first of all, about her life in general. Then, without in any way indicating the object of my visit—at that point—I led the conversation up to the subject of the Palestine 'discovery.' Of course she had heard of it, and knew all the details. The rector had preached upon it, and the whole village, so it seems, was in a ferment for a week or so. Then, in both Church and the Dissenting chapels—there are two—the whole thing died away in a marvellous manner. The history of it was extremely interesting. Every one came to service just the same as usual, life went on in unbroken placidity. The fishermen, who compose the whole population of the village, absolutely refused to believe or discuss the thing. So utterly different from townspeople! They simply felt and knew intuitively that the statements made in the papers must be untrue. So without argument or worry they ignored it. Miss Hunt said that the church has been fuller than ever before, the people coming as a sort of stubborn protest against any attack upon the faith of their fathers. For her own part, when she realised what the news meant or would mean, Miss Hunt had a black time of terror and struggle. She is a woman with a good brain, and saw at once what it would mean to her. Her own words were infinitely pathetic. 'I went out on the sands,' she said, 'and walked for miles. Then when I [259] was tired out I sat down and cried, to think that there would never be any Jesus any more to save poor girls. It seemed so empty and terrible, and I'd only been trying to be good such a short time. I went to evensong when I got back; the bell was tolling just as usual. And as I sat there I saw that it couldn't be true that Jesus was just a good man, and not God. I wondered at myself for doubting, seeing what He'd done for me. If the paper was right, then why was it I was so happy, happier than ever before in my life—although I am going to die soon? Why was it that I could go away and leave Bob and the old life? why was it that I could see Jesus in my walks, hear the wind praying— feel that everything was speaking of Him?' That was the gist of what she said, though there was much more. I wish I could tell you adequately of the deep conviction in her voice and eyes. One doesn't often see it, except in very old people. After this I began to speak of our suspicions as delicately as possible. It was horribly difficult. One was afraid of awakening old longings and recalling that man's influence. I was relieved to find that she took it very well indeed. Her feelings towards the man have undergone a complete change. She fears him, not because he has yet an influence over her, but with a hearty fear and horror of the life she was living with him. When I told her what we thought, she began at once by saying that from what she knew of Llwellyn he would not stop even at such wickedness as this. She said that he only cared for two things, and kept them quite distinct. When he is working he throws his whole heart into what he is doing, and he will let no obstacle stand in his way. He wants to constantly assure himself of his own pre-eminence in his work. He must be first at any cost. When his work is over he dismisses it absolutely from his thoughts, and [260] lives entirely for gross, material pleasures. The man seems to pursue these with a horrid, overwhelming eagerness. I gather that he must be one of the coldest and most calculating sybarites that breathes. The actual points I have gathered are these, and I think you will see that they are extremely important. Llwellyn was indebted enormously to Schuabe. Suddenly, Miss Hunt tells me, when Llwellyn's financial position began to be very shaky, Schuabe forgave him the old debts and paid him a large sum of money. Llwellyn paid off a lot of the girl's debts, and he told her that the money had come from that source. It was not a loan this time, he said to her, but a payment for some work he was about to do. He also impressed the necessity of silence upon her. While away he wrote several times to her—once from Alexandria, from one or two places on the Continent, and twice from the German hotel, the 'Sabíl,' in Jerusalem."

There was a sudden murmur from one or two men who were listening to Gortre's narrative. He had long since forgotten to eat and was leaning forward on the table. He paused for a moment, drank a glass of water, and concluded:

"This then is all that I know at present, but it gives us a basis. We know that Sir Robert Llwellyn was staying privately at Jerusalem. Miss Hunt was instructed to write to him under the name of the Rev. Robert Lake, and she did so, thinking that his incognito was assumed owing to the kind of pleasures he was pursuing, and especially because of his recent knighthood. But in a week's time Miss Hunt has asked me to go down to Eastworld again, as she has hopes of getting other evidence for me. She will not say what this is likely to consist of, or, in fact, tell me anything about it. But she has hopes."

"This is of great importance, Gortre," said Sir Michael; [261] "we have something definite to go upon."

"I will start again for Jerusalem without loss of a day," said Spence, his whole face lighting up and hardening at the thought of active occupation.

"I was going to suggest it, Mr. Spence," said Sir Michael. "You will do what is necessary better than any of us; your departure will attract less notice. You will of course draw upon me for any moneys that may be necessary. If in the course of your investigations it may be—and it is extremely probable—may be necessary to buy the truth, of course no money considerations must stand in the way. We are working for the peace and happiness of millions. We are in very deep waters."

Father Ripon gave a deep sigh. Then, in an instant, his face hardened and flushed till it was almost unrecognisable. The others started back from him in amazement. He began to tremble violently from the legs upwards. Then he spoke:

"God forgive me," he said in a thick, husky voice. "God forgive me! But when I think of those two men, devils that they are, devils! when I regard the broken lives, the suicides, the fearful mass of crime, I——"

His voice failed him. The frightful wrath and anger took him and shook him like a reed—this tall, black-robed figure—it twisted him with a physical convulsion inexpressibly painful to witness.

For near a minute Father Ripon stood among them thus, and they were rigid with sympathy, with alarm.

Then, with a heavy sob, he turned and fell upon his knees in silent prayer.

[262]
CHAPTER XII

A SOUL ALONE ON THE SEA-SHORE

The little village of Eastworld is set on a low headland by the sea, remote from towns and any haunt of men. The white cottages of the fisherfolk, an inn, the church, and a low range of coast-guard buildings, are the only buildings there. Below the headland there are miles upon miles of utterly lonely sands which edge the sea in a great yellow scimitar as far as the eye can carry, from east to west.

121

Hardly any human footsteps ever disturb the vast virgin smoothness of the sands, for the fisherfolk sail up the mouth of a sluggish tidal river to reach the village. All day long the melancholy sea-birds call to each other over the wastes, and away on the sky-line, or so it seems to any one walking upon the sands, the great white breakers roll and boom for ever.

Over the flat expanses the tide, with no obstacle to slacken or impede its progress, rushes with furious haste—as fast, so the fisherfolks tell, as a good horse in full gallop.

It was the beginning of the winter afternoon on the day after Gortre had visited Eastworld.

There was little wind, but the sky hung low in cold and menacing clouds, ineffably cheerless and gloomy.

A single figure moved slowly through these forbidding solitudes. It was Gertrude Hunt. She wore a simple coat and skirt of grey tweed, a tam-o'-shanter cap of crimson wool, and carried a walking cane.

[263] She had come out alone to think out a problem out there between the sea and sky, with no human help or sympathy to aid her.

The strong, passionate face was paler than before and worn by suffering. Yet as she strode along there was a wild beauty in her appearance which seemed to harmonise with the very spirit and meaning of the place where she was. And yet the face had lost the old jaunty hardihood. Qualities in it which had before spoken of an impudent self-sufficiency now were changed to quiet purpose. There was an appeal for pity in the eyes which had once been bright with shamelessness and sin.

The woman was thinking deeply. Her head was bowed as she walked, the lips set close together.

Gortre's visit had moved her deeply. When she had heard his story something within her, an intuition beyond calm reason, had told her instantly of its truth. She could not have said why she knew this, but she was utterly certain.

Her long connection with Llwellyn had left no traces of affection now. As she would kneel in the little windy church on the headland and listen to the rector, an old friend of Father Ripon's, reading prayers, she looked back on her past life as a man going about his business in sunlight remembers some horrid nightmare of the evening past. She but rarely allowed her thoughts to dwell upon the former partner of her sin, but when she did so it was with a sense of shrinking and dislike. As the new Light which filled her life taught, she endeavoured to think of the man with Christian charity and sometimes to pray that his heart also might be touched. But perhaps this was the most difficult of all the duties she set herself, although she had no illusions about the past, realised his kindness to her, and also that she had been at least as bad as he. But now there [264] seemed a great gulf between them which she never cared to pass even in thought.

Her repentance was so sincere and deep, her mourning for her misspent life so genuine, that it never allowed her the least iota of spiritual pride—the snare of weaker penitents when they have turned from evil courses. Yet, try as she would, she could never manage to really identify her hopes and prayers with Llwellyn in any vivid way.

And now the young clergyman, the actual instrument of her own salvation as she regarded him, had come to her with this story in which she had recognised the truth.

In sad and eloquent words he had painted for her what the great fraud had meant to thousands. He told of upright and godly men stricken down because their faith was not strong enough to bear the blow. There was the curate at Wigan, who had shot himself and left a heart-breaking letter of mad mockery behind him; there were other cases of suicide. There was the surging tide of crime, rising ever higher and higher as the clergy lost all their influence in the slums of London and the great towns. He told her of Harold Spence, mentioning him as "a journalist friend of mine," explaining what a good fellow he was, and how he had overcome his temptations with the aid of religion and faith. And he described his own return to Lincoln's Inn, the disorder, and Harold's miserable story. She could picture it all so well, that side of life. She knew its every detail. And, moreover, Gortre had said "the evil was growing and spreading each day, each hour." True as it was that the myriad lamps of the Faithful only burned the brighter for the surrounding gloom, yet that gloom was growing and rolling up, even as the clouds on which her unseeing eyes were fixed as she [265] walked along the shore. Men were becoming reckless; the hosts of evil triumphed on every side.

The thought which came to her as Gortre had gradually unfolded the object of his visit was startling. She herself might perhaps prove to be the pivot upon which these great events were turning. It was possible that by her words, that by means of her help, the dark conspiracy might be unveiled and the world freed from its burden. She herself might be able to do all this, a kind of thank-offering for the miraculous change that had been wrought in her life.

Yet, when it was all summed up, how little she had to tell Gortre after all! True, her information was of some value; it seemed to confirm what he and his friends suspected. But still it was very little, and it meant long delay, if she could provide no other key to open this dark door. And meanwhile souls were dying and sinking....

She had asked Gortre to come to her again in a week.

In that time, she had said, she might have some further information for him.

And now she was out here, alone on the sands, to ask her soul and God what she was to do.

The clouds fell lower, a cutting wind began to moan and cry over the sand, which was swept up and swirled in her face. And still she went on with a bitterness and chill as of death in her heart.

She knew her power over her former lover,—if that pure word could describe such an unhallowed passion,—knew her power well. He would be as wax in her hands, and it had always been so. From the very first she had done what she liked with him, and there had always been an undercurrent of contempt in her thoughts that a man could be led so easily, could be made the doll and puppet of his own passion. Nor did she doubt [266] that her power still remained. She felt sure of that. Even in her seclusion some news of his frantic attempts to find her had reached her. Her beauty still remained, heightened indeed by the slow complaint from which she was suffering. He knew nothing of that. And, as for the rest—the rouge-pot, the belladonna—well, they were still available, though she had thought to have done with them for ever.

The idea began to emerge from the mist, as it were, and to take form and colour. She thought definitely of it, though with horror; looked it in the face, though shuddering as she did so.

It resolved itself into a statement, a formula, which rang and dinned itself repeatedly into her consciousness like the ominous strokes of a bell heard through the turmoil of the gathering storm,—

"If I go back to Bob and pretend I'm tired of being good, he will tell me all he's done."

Over and over again the girl repeated the sentence to herself. It glowed in her brain, and burnt it like letters of heated wire. She looked up at the leaden canopy which held the wind, and it flashed out at her in letters of violet lightning. The wind carved it in the sand,—

123

"If I go back to Bob and pretend I'm tired of being good, he will tell me what he has done."

Could she do this thing for the sake of Gortre, for the sake of the world? What did it mean exactly? She would be sinning terribly once more, going back to the old life. It was possible that she might never be able to break away again after achieving her purpose; one did not twice escape hell. It would mean that she sinned a deadly sin in order to help others. Ought she to do that! Was that right?

The wind fifed round her, shrieking.

Could she do this thing?

[267] She would only be sinning with her body, not with her heart, and Christ would know why she did so. Would He cast her out for this?

The struggle went on in her brain. She was not a subtle person, unused to any self-communing that was not perfectly straightforward and simple. The efforts she was making now were terribly hard for her to endure. Yet she forced her mind to the work by a great effort of will, summoned all her flagging energies to high consideration.

If she went back it might mean utter damnation, even though she found out what she wanted to find out. She had been a Christian so short a time, she knew very little of the truth about these matters.

In her misery and struggle she began more and more to think in this way.

Suddenly she saw the thing, as she fancied, and indeed said half aloud to herself, "in a common-sense light." Her face worked horribly, though she was quite unconscious of it.

"It's better that one person, especially one that's been as bad as I have, should go to hell than hundreds and thousands of others."

And then her decision was taken.

The light died out of her face, the hope also. She became old in a sudden moment.

And, with one despairing prayer for forgiveness, she began to walk towards her cottage—there was a fast train to town.

She believed that there could hardly be forgiveness for her act, and yet the thought of "the others" gave her strength to sin.

And so, out of her great love for Christ, this poor harlot set out to sin a sin which she thought would take Him away from her for ever.

END OF BOOK II

[269]
BOOK III

" ... Woman fearing and trembling"
[271]
CHAPTER I

WHAT IT MEANT TO THE WORLD'S WOMEN

In her house in the older, early-Victorian remnants of Kensington, Mrs. Hubert Armstrong sat at breakfast. Her daughter, a pretty, unintellectual girl, was pouring out tea with a suggestion of flippancy in her manner. The room was grave and somewhat formal. Portraits of Matthew Arnold, Professor Green, and Mark Pattison hung upon the sombre, olive walls.

Over the mantel-shelf, painted in ornamental chocolate-coloured letters, the famous authoress's pet motto was austerely blazoned,—

"The decisive events of the world take place in the intellect."

Indeed, save for the bright-haired girl at the urn, the room struck just that note. It would be difficult to imagine an ordinary conversation taking place there. It was a place in which solid chunks of thought were gravely handed about.

Mrs. Armstrong wore a flowing morning wrap of dark red material. It was clasped at the smooth white throat by a large cameo brooch, a dignified bauble once the property of George Eliot. The clear, steady eyes, the smooth bands of shining hair, the full, calm lips of the lady were all eloquent of splendid unemotional health, assisted by a careful system of hygiene.

She was opening her letters, cutting the envelopes carefully with a silver knife.

[272] "Shall I give you some more tea, Mother?" the daughter asked in a somewhat impatient voice. The offer was declined, and the girl rose to go. "I'm off now to skate with the Tremaines at Henglers," she said, and hurriedly left the room.

Mrs. Armstrong sighed in a sort of placid wonder, as Minerva might have sighed coming suddenly upon Psyche running races with Cupid in a wood, and turned to another letter.

It was written in firm, strong writing on paper headed with some official-looking print.

THE WORLD'S WOMAN'S LEAGUE
London Headquarters,
100 Regent Street, S. W.
secretary, miss paull

"My Dear Charlotte,—I should be extremely glad to see you here to-day about lunch time. I must have a long and important talk with you. The work is in a bad way. I know you are extremely busy, but trust to see you as the matters for conference are urgent. Your affectionate Sister,

"Catherine Paull."

Miss Paull was a well-known figure in what may be called "executive" life. Both she and her elder sister, Mrs. Armstrong, had been daughters of an Oxford tutor, and had become immersed in public affairs early in life. While the elder became a famous novelist and leader of "cultured doubt," the younger had remained unmarried and thrown herself with great eagerness into the movement which had for its object the strengthening of woman's position and the lightening of her burdens, no less in England than over the whole world.

The "World's Woman's League" was a great unsectarian [273] society with tentacles all over the globe. The Indian lady missionaries and doctors, who worked in the zenanas, were affiliated to it. The English and American vigilance societies for the safe-guarding of girls, the women of the furtive students' clubs in Russia, the Melbourne society for the supply of domestic workers in the lonely up-country stations of Australia, all, while having their own corporate and separate existences, were affiliated to, and in communication with, the central offices of the League in Regent Street.

The League was all-embracing. Christian, non-Christian, or heathen, it mattered nothing. It aimed at the gigantic task of centralising all the societies for the welfare of women throughout the globe.

On the board of directors one found the names and titles of all the humanitarians of Europe.

125

The working head of this vast organisation was the thin, active woman of middle age whose name figured in a hundred blue-books, whose speeches and articles were sometimes of international importance, whose political power was undoubtable—Miss Catherine Paull.

The most important function of the League, or one of its most important functions, was the yearly publication of a huge report or statement of more than a thousand pages. This annual was recognised universally as the most trustworthy and valuable summary of the progress of women in the world. It was quoted in Parliament a hundred times each session; its figures were regarded as authoritative in every way.

This report was published every May, and as Mrs. Hubert Armstrong drove to Regent Street in her brougham she realised that points in connection with it were to be discussed, possibly with the various sectional editors, possibly with Miss Paull alone.

As was natural, so distinguished an example of the [274] "higher woman" as Mrs. Armstrong was a great help to the League, and her near relationship to the secretary made her help and advice in constant request.

The office occupied two extensive floors in the quadrant, housing an army of women clerks, typewriters, and a literary staff almost exclusively feminine. Here, from morning till night, was a hum of busy activity quite foreign to the office controlled by the more drone-like men. Miss Paull contrived to interest the most insignificant of her girls in the work that was to be done, making each one feel that in the performance of her task lay not only the means of earning a weekly wage, but of doing something for women all over the world.

In short, the League was an admirable and powerful institution, presided over by an admirable and earnest woman of wonderful organising ability and the gift of tact, that extreme tact necessary in dealing with hundreds of societies officered and ruled by women whose official activities did not always quell that feminine jealousy and bickering which generally militate against success.

It was some weeks since Mrs. Armstrong had seen her sister or communicated with her. The great events in Jerusalem, the chaos into which the holders of the old creeds had been thrown, had meant a series of platform and journalistic triumphs for the novelist. Her importance had increased a thousand-fold, her presence was demanded everywhere, and she had quite lost touch with the League for a time.

As she entered her sister's room she was beaming with satisfaction at the memory of the past few weeks, and anticipating with pleasure the congratulations that would be forthcoming. Miss Paull, in the main, agreed with her sister's opinions, though her extraordinarily [275] strenuous life and busy activities in other directions prevented her public adherence to them.

Moreover, her position as head of the League, which included so many definitely Christian societies, made it inadvisable for her to take a prominent controversial part as Mrs. Armstrong did.

The secretary's room was large and well lit by double windows, which prevented the roar of the Regent Street traffic from becoming too obtrusive.

Except that there was some evidence of order and neatness on the three great writing-tables, and that the books on the shelves were all in their places, there was nothing to distinguish the place from the private room of a busy solicitor or merchant.

Perhaps the only thing which gave the place any really individual note was a large brass kettle, which droned on the fire, and a sort of sideboard with a good many teacups and a glass jar full of what seemed to be sponge cakes.

126

The two women greeted each other affectionately. Then Miss Paull sent away her secretary, who had been writing with her, expressing her desire to be quite alone for an hour or more.

"I want to discuss the report with you, Charlotte," said Miss Paull, deftly pouring some hot water into a green stone-ware teapot.

She removed her pince-nez, which had become clouded with the steam, and waited for Mrs. Armstrong to speak.

"I expected that was it when I got your note, dear," said the novelist. "I am sorry I have been so much away of late. But, of course, you will have seen how my time has been taken up. Since all Our contentions have been so remarkably established, of course one is looked to a great deal. I have to be everywhere just at present. John Mulgrave has been through three more editions during the last fortnight."

"Yes, Charlotte," answered the sister, "one hears of [276] you on all sides. It is a wonderful triumph from one point of view."

Mrs. Armstrong looked up quickly, with surprise in her eyes. There was a strange lack of enthusiasm in the secretary's tone. Indeed, it was even less than unenthusiastic; it hinted almost of dislike, nearly of dismay.

It could not be jealousy of the blaze of notoriety which had fallen upon Mrs. Armstrong, the lady knew her sister too well for that. For one brief moment she allowed herself the unworthy suspicion that Miss Paull had been harbouring Christian leanings, or had, in the stress and worry of overwork, permitted herself a sentimental adherence to the Christ-myth.

But it was only for a single moment that such thoughts remained in her brain. She dismissed them at once as disloyal to her sister and undignified for herself.

"I don't quite understand, Catherine," she said. "Surely from every point of view this glorious vindication of the truth is of incalculable benefit to mankind. How can it be otherwise? Now that we know the great teacher Jesus——"

She was beginning somewhat on the lines of her public utterances, with a slightly inspired look which, though habit had made mechanical, was still sincere, when her sister checked her with some asperity.

"That is all well and good," she said, her rather sharp, animated features becoming more harsh and eager as she spoke. "You, Charlotte, are at the moment concerned with the future and with abstractions. I am busied with the present and with facts. However I may share your gladness at this vindication, in my official capacity, and more, in the interests of my life work, I am bound to deplore what has happened. I deplore it grievously."

Placid and equable as was her usual temper of mind, [277] Mrs. Armstrong was hardly proof against such a sweeping assertion as this.

Her face flushed slightly.

"Please explain," she said somewhat coldly.

"That is why I wanted you to come to-day," answered Miss Paull. "I very much fear you will be more than startled at what I have to tell you and show you. My facts are all ready—piteous, heart-breaking facts, too. We know, here, what is going on below the surface. We are confronted by statistics, and theories pale before them. Our system is perfect."

She made a movement of her arm and pointed to a small adjacent table, on which were arranged various documents for inspection.

The novelist followed the glance, curiously disturbed by the sadness of the other's voice and the bitterness of her manner. "Show me what you mean, dear," she said.

127

Miss Paull got up and went to the table. "I will begin with points of local interest," she said, "that is, with the English statistics. In regard to these I will call your attention to a branch of the Social Question. First of all, look at the monthly map for the current month and the one for the month before the Palestine Discovery."

She handed two outline maps of Great Britain and Ireland to her sister.

The maps were shaded in crimson in different localities, the colour being either light, medium, or dark. Innumerable figures were dotted over them, referring to comprehensive marginal notes. Above each map was printed:

series d.—crimes against women

And the month and year were written in below in violet ink.

Mrs. Armstrong held the two maps, which were [278] mounted on stiff card, and glanced from one to the other. Suddenly her face flushed, her eyes became full of incredulous horror, and she stared at her sister. "What is this, Catherine?" she said in a high, agitated voice. "Surely there is some mistake? This is terrible!"

"Terrible, indeed," Miss Paull answered. "During the last month, in Wales, criminal assaults have increased two hundred per cent. In England scarcely less. In Ireland, with the exception of Ulster, the increase has been only eight per cent. I am comparing the map before the discovery with that of the present month. Crimes of ordinary violence, wife-beating and such like, have increased fifty per cent., on an average, all over the United Kingdom. We have, of course, all the convictions, sentences, and so forth. The local agents supply them to the British Protection Society, they tabulate them and send them here, and then the maps are made in this office ready for the annual report."

"But," said Mrs. Armstrong with a shocked, pale face, "is it certain that this is a case of cause and effect?"

"Absolutely certain, Charlotte. Here I have over a thousand letters from men and women interested in the work in all the great towns. They are in answer to direct queries on the subject. In order that there could be no possibility of any sectarian bias, the form has been sent to leading citizens, of all denominations and creeds, who are interested in the work. I will show you two letters at random."

She picked out two of the printed forms which had been sent out and returned filled in, and gave them to Mrs. Armstrong. One ran:

"Kindly state what, in your opinion, is the cause of [279] the abnormal increase of crimes against women in Great Britain during the past month, as shown by the annexed map.

"Name.   Rev. William Carr,
"Vicar of St. Saviour's,
"Birmingtown.
"The recent 'discovery' in Palestine, which appears to do away with the Resurrection of Christ, is in my opinion entirely responsible for the increase of crime mentioned above. Now that the Incarnation is on all hands said to be a myth, the greatest restraint upon human passion is removed. In my district I have found that the moment men give up Christ and believe in this 'discovery,' the moment that the Virgin birth and the manifestation to the Magdalen are dismissed as untrue, women's claim to consideration, and reverence for women's chastity, in the eyes of these men disappear.
"William Carr."

128

Mrs. Armstrong said nothing whatever, but turned to the other form. In this case the name was that of a Manchester alderman, obviously a Jew—Moses Goldstein, of Goldstein & Hildesheimer, chemical bleachers.

In a flowing business hand the following remarks were written:

"Regrettable increase of crime due in my opinion to sudden wave of disbelief in Christian doctrines. Have questioned men in my own works on the subject. Record this as fact without pretending to understand it. Crimes of violence on increase among Jewish workmen also. Probably sympathetic reaction against morality, though as a strict Jew myself find this doubly distressing.

"Moses Goldstein."

"The famous philanthropist," murmured Mrs. Armstrong.

[280] The lady seemed dazed. Her usual calm volubility seemed to have deserted her.

"This is a terrible blow," said Miss Paull, sadly, "and day by day things are getting worse as figures come in. It seems as if all our work has been in vain. Men seem to be relapsing into the state of the barbaric heathen world. But there is much more yet. I will read you an extract from Mrs. Mary P. Corbin's letter from Chicago. You will remember that she is the organising secretary of the United States branch of the League."

She took up a bundle of closely typewritten sheets.

"'The Friend to Poor Girls' Society' in this city reports a most painful state of things. The work has suddenly fallen to pieces and become totally disorganised. Many of the girls have left the home and returned to lives of prostitution—there seems to be no restraining influence left. In a few cases girls have returned, after two or three weeks of sin, mere wrecks of their former selves. A—— S—— was a well-known girl on the streets when she was converted and brought to the home. Five weeks ago she went away, announcing her intention of resuming her former life. She has just returned in a dying condition from brutal ill-usage. She says that her former experience was nothing to what she has lately endured. Her words are terribly significant: 'I went back as I thought it was no use being good any more now that there isn't any Jesus. I thought I'd have a good old time. But it's not as it was. Hell's broke loose in the streets. The men are a million times worse than they were. It's hell now.'

"Another awful blow has been struck at the purity work. The state of the lower parts of Chicago and New York City has become so bad that even the municipal authorities have become seriously alarmed. Unmentionable [281] orgies take place in public. Accordingly a bill is to be rushed through Congress licensing so many houses of ill-fame in each city ward, according to the Continental system."

She laid down the letter. "There is no need to read more than extracts," she said. "The letter is full of horrors. I may mention that the law against polygamy in the Mormon State of Utah is on the point of being repealed, and there can be no doubt that things will soon be as bad as ever there. Here is a letter from the Bishop of Toomarbin, who is at present in Melbourne, Australia. A Bill is preparing in the House of Legislature to make the divorce laws for men as easy and simple as possible, while women's privileges are to be greatly curtailed in this direction. In Rhodesia the mine-captains are beginning to flog native women quite unchecked by the local magistrates. English magistrates——"

"Stop, dear," said Mrs. Armstrong, with a sudden gesture almost of fear. There was a craven, hunted look in the eyes of this well-known woman. Her face was blanched with pain. She sat huddled up in her chair. All the stately confidence was gone. That proud bearing of equality, and more than equality, with men, which was so noticeable a characteristic of her port and manner, had vanished.

The white hand which lifted a cup of scalding tea to her lips trembled like a leaf.

The sisters sat together in silence. They sat there, names famous in the world for courage, ability, resource. To these two, perhaps more than to any others in England, had been given the power of building up the great edifice of women's enlightened position at the present day.

And now?

[282] In a moment all was changed. The brute in man was awake, unchained, and loose. The fires of cruelty and lust were lit, they heard the roaring of the fires like the roaring of wolves that "devour apace and nothing said."

Mrs. Armstrong was terribly affected. Her keen intelligence told her at once of coming horrors of which these were but the earliest signs.

The roaring of a great fire, louder and more menacing, nearer ... nearer.

Christ had gone from the world never to return—Christ Whom the proud, wishful, worldly woman had not believed in.... They were flogging girls, selling girls ... the fires grew greater and greater ... nearer!

mary, pity women!
[283]
CHAPTER II

CYRIL HANDS REDUX

For the first two weeks after Hands's return he was utterly bewildered by the rush of events in which he must take part and had little or no time for thought.

His days were filled by official conferences with his chiefs at the Exploring Society, from which important but by no means wealthy body he had suddenly attained more than financial security.

Meeting succeeded meeting. Hands was in constant communication with the heads of the Church, Government, and Society. Interviewers from all the important papers shadowed him everywhere. Despite his protests, for he was a quiet and retiring man, photographers fought for him, and his long, somewhat melancholy face and pointed fair beard stared at him everywhere.

He had to read papers at learned societies, and afterwards women came and carried him off to evening parties without possibility of escape.

The Unitarians of England started a monster subscription for him, a subscription which grew so fast that the less sober papers began to estimate it day by day and to point out that the fortunate discoverer would be a rich man for life.

Everywhere he was flattered, caressed, and made much of. In fact, he underwent what to some natures is the grimmest torture of a humane age—he became the man of the hour. Even by Churchmen and others most [284] interested in denying the truth of the discovery, Hands was treated with consideration and deference. His own bona fides in the matter was indubitable, his long and notable record forbade suspicion.

Of Gortre Hands saw but little. Their greeting had been cordial, but there was some natural restraint, one fearing the attitude of the other. Gortre, no less than Hands, was much away from the chambers, and the pair had few confidences. Hands felt, naturally enough under the circumstances, that he would have been more comfortable with Spence. He was surprised to find him absent, but all he was able to glean was that the journalist had suddenly left for the Continent upon a special mission. Hands supposed that Continental feeling was to be thoroughly tested, and that the work had fallen to Spence.

Meanwhile the invitations flowed in. The old staircase of the inn was besieged with callers. In order to escape them, Hands was forced to spend much time in the chambers on the other side of the landing, which belonged to a young barrister, Kennedy by name, who was able to put a spare sitting-room at his disposal. This gentleman, briefless and happy, was somewhat of the Dick Swiveller type, and it gave him intense pleasure to reconnoitre the opposite "oak" through the slit of his letter-box, and to report and speculate upon those who stood knocking for admission.

How he loathed it all!

The shock and surprise of it was not one of the least distressing features.

Far away in the ancient Eastern city he had indeed realised the momentous nature of the strange and awful things he had found. But of the consequences to himself he had thought nothing, and of the effects on the world he had not had time to think.

[285] Hands had never wished to be celebrated. His temperament was poetic in essence, retiring in action. He longed to be back under the eye of the sun, to move among the memorials of the past with his Arab boys, to lie upon the beach of the Dead Sea when no airs stirred, and, suddenly, to hear a vast, mysterious breaker, coming from nowhere, with no visible cause, like some great beast crashing through the jungle.

And he had exchanged all this for lunches at institutions, for hot rooms full of flowers and fools of women who said, "Oh, do tell me all about your delightful discovery," smiling through their paint while the world's heart was breaking. And there was worse to come. At no distant date he would have to stand upon the platform at the Albert Hall, and Mr. Constantine Schuabe, M.P., Mrs. Hubert Armstrong, the writing woman—the whole crowd of uncongenial people—would hand him a cheque for some preposterous sum of money which he did not in the least want. There would be speeches——

He was not made for this life.

His own convictions of Christianity had never been thoroughly formulated or marked out in his brain. All that was mystical in the great history of Christ had always attracted him. He took an æsthetic pleasure in the beautiful story. To him more than to most men it had become a vivid panoramic vision. The background and accessories had been part of his daily life for years. It was as the figure of King Arthur and his old knights might be to some loving student of Malory.

And although his life was pure, his actions gentle and blameless, it had always been thus to him—a lovely and poetic picture and no more. He had never made a personal application of it to himself. His heart had never been touched, and he had never heard the Divine Voice calling to him.

[286] At the end of a fortnight Hands found that he could stand the strain no longer. His nerves were failing him; there was a constant babble of meaningless voices in his ear which took all the zest and savour from life. His doctor told him quite unmistakably that he was doing too much, that he was not inured to this gaiety, and that he must go away to some solitude by the sea and rest.

The advice not only coincided with his own wishes, but made them possible. A good many engagements were cancelled, a paragraph appeared in the newspapers to say that Mr. Hands's medical adviser had insisted upon a thorough rest, and the man of the moment disappeared. Save only Gortre and the secretary of the Exploring Society, no one knew of his whereabouts.

In a week he was forgotten. Greater things began to animate Society—harsh, terrible, ugly things. There was no time to think of Hands, the instrument which had brought them about.

The doctor had recommended the remotest parts of Cornwall. Standing in his comfortable room at Harley Street, he expatiated, with an enthusiastic movement of his hand, upon the peace to be found in that lost country of frowning rocks and bottle-green seas, where, so far is it from the great centres of action, men still talk of "going into England" as if it were an enterprise, an adventure.

Two days found him at a lonely fishing cove, rather than village, lodging in the house of a coast-guard, not far from Saint Ives.

A few whitewashed houses ran down to the beach of the little natural harbour where the boats were sheltered.

On the shores of the little "Porth," as it was called, the fishermen sat about with sleepy, vacant eyes, waiting for the signal of watchmen on the moor above—the [287] shrill Cornish cry of "Ubba!" "Ubba!" which would tell them the mackerel were in sight.

Behind the cove, running inland, were the vast, lonely moors which run between the Atlantic and the Channel. It is always grey and sad upon these rolling solitudes, sad and silent. The glory of summer gorse had not yet clothed them with a fleeting warmth and hospitality. As far as the eye could reach they stretched away with a forlorn immensity that struck cold to Hands's heart. Peace was here indeed, but how austere! quiet, but what a brooding and cruel silence!

Every now and again the roving eye, in its search for incident and colour, was caught and arrested by the bleak engine-house of some ancient deserted mine and the gaunt chimney which pointed like a leaden finger to the stormy skies above. Great humming winds swept over the moor, driving flocks of Titanic clouds, an Olympian army in rout, before their fierce breath.

Here, day by day, Hands took his solitary walk, or sometimes he would sit sheltered in a hollow of the jagged volcanic rocks which set round about the cove a barrier of jagged teeth. Down below him a hard, green sea boiled and seethed in an agony of fierce unrest. The black cormorants in the middle distance dived for their cold prey. The sea-birds were tossed on the currents of the wild air, calling to each other with forlorn, melancholy voices. This remote Western world resounded with the powerful voices of the waves; night and day the gongs of Neptune's anger were sounding.

In the afternoon a weary postman tramped over the moor. He brought the London newspapers of the day before, and Hands read them with a strange subjective sensation of spectatorship.

So far away was he from the world that by a paradox of psychology he viewed its turmoil with a clearer eye. [288] As poetry is emotion remembered in tranquillity, as a painter often prefers to paint a great canvas from studies and memory—quiet in his studio—rather than from the actual but too kinetic scene, so Hands as he read the news-sheets felt and lived the story they had to tell far more acutely than in London.

He had more time to think about what he read. It was in this lost corner of the world that the chill began to creep over him.

The furious sounds of Nature clamoured in his ears, assaulting them like strongholds; these were the objective sounds.

But as his subjective brain grew clear the words his eyes conveyed to it filled it with a more awful reverberation.

The awful weight grew. He began to realise with terrible distinctness the consequences of his discovery. They stunned him. A carved inscription, a crumbling tomb

132

in half an acre of waste ground. He had stumbled upon so much and little more. He, Cyril Hands, had found this.

His straining eyes day by day turned to the columns of the papers.

CHAPTER III

all ye inhabitants of the world, and dwellers on the earth, see ye,
when he lifteth up an ensign on the mountains.—isaiah xviii: 3

Hands awoke to terrible realisation.

The telegrams in the newspapers provided him with a bird's-eye view, an epitomised summary of a world in tumult.

Out of a wealth of detail, culled from innumerable telegrams and articles, certain facts stood out clearly.

In the Balkan States, always in unrest, a crisis, graver than ever before, suddenly came about. The situation flared up like a petrol explosion.

A great revival of Mohammedan enthusiasm had begun to spread from Jerusalem as soon as Europe had more or less definitely accepted the discovery made by Cyril Hands and confirmed by the international committee.

It was no longer possible to hold the troops of the Sultan in check. It was openly said by the correspondents that instructions had been sent from Yildiz Kiosk to the provincial Valis in both European and Asiatic Turkey that Christians were to be exterminated, swept for ever from the world.

Telegrams of dire importance filled the columns of the papers.

Hands would read in one Daily Wire:

[290] "Paris (From our own Correspondent).—The Prince of Bulgaria has indefinitely postponed his departure, and remains at the Hotel Ritz for the present. It is impossible for him to progress beyond Vienna. Dr. Daneff, the Bulgarian Premier, has arrived here. In the course of an interview with a representative of Le Matin he has stated the only hope of saving the Christians remaining in the Balkan States lies in the intervention of Russia. 'The situation,' Dr. Daneff is reported to have said, 'has assumed the appearance of a religious war. The followers of Islam are drunk with triumph and hatred of the "Nazarenes." The recent discoveries in Jerusalem simply mean a licence to sweep Christians out of existence. The exulting cries of "Ashahadu, lá ílaha ill Allah" have already sounded the death-knell of our ancient faith in Bulgaria.' M. Daneff was extremely affected during the interview, and states that Prince Ferdinand is unable to leave his room."

Never before in the history of Eastern Europe had the future appeared so gloomy or the present been so replete with horror.

The massacres of bygone years were as nothing to those which were daily flashed over the wires to startle and appal a world which was still Christian, at least in name.

An extract from a leading article in the Daily Wire shows that the underlying reason and cause was thoroughly appreciated and understood in England no less than abroad.

"In this labyrinth of myth and murder," the article said, "a sudden and spontaneous outburst of hatred, of Mussulman hatred for the Christian, has now—owing to the overthrow of the chief accepted doctrine of the [291] Christian faith—become a deliberate measure of extermination adopted by a barbarous Government as the simplest solution of the problem in the Near East. The stupendous fact which has lately burst

133

upon the world has had effects which, while they might have been anticipated in some degree, have already passed far beyond the bounds of the most confirmed political pessimist's dream.

"From the fact of the Jerusalem discovery, ambitious agitators have hurried to draw their profit. Politicians have not hesitated to provoke a series of massacres, and by playing upon the worst forms of Mussulman fanaticism to organise that ghastliest system of crime upon the largest and most comprehensive scale. The whole thing is, moreover, immensely complicated by the utter unscrupulousness of that association universally notorious as the Macedonian Committee. These people, who may be described as a company of aspirants to the crown of immortality earned by other people's martyrdom, have themselves assisted in the work of lighting the fires of Turkish passion, and they have helped to provoke atrocities which will enable them to pose before the eyes of the civilised world as the interesting victims of Moslem ferocity."

Thus Hands read in his rock cave above the boiling winter sea. Thus and much more, as the cloud grew darker and darker over Eastern Europe, darker and darker day by day.

In a week it became plain to the world that Bulgarians, Servians, and Armenians alike had collapsed utterly before the insolent exultation of the Turks. The spirit of resistance and enthusiasm had gone. The ignorant and tortured peoples had no answer for those who flung foul insults at the Cross.

[292] As reflected in the newspapers, the public mind in England was becoming seriously alarmed at these horrible and daily bulletins, but neither Parliament nor people were as yet ready with a suggested course of action. The forces of disintegration had been at work; it seemed no longer possible to secure a great body of opinion as in the old times. And Englishmen were troubled with grave domestic problems also. More especially the great increase of the worst forms of crime attracted universal attention and dismay.

Then news came which shook the whole country to its depths. Men began to look into each other's eyes and ask what these things might mean.

Hands read:

"Our special correspondent in Bombay telegraphs disquieting news from India. The native regiments in Bengal are becoming difficult to handle. The officers of the staff corps are making special reports to headquarters. Three native officers of the 100th Bengal Lancers have been placed under arrest, though no particulars as to the exact reason for this step have been allowed to transpire."

This first guarded intimation of serious disaffection in India was followed, two days afterwards, by longer and far more serious reports. The Indian mail arrived with copies of The Madras Mail and The Times of India, which disclosed much more than had hitherto come over the cables.

Long extracts were printed from these journals in the English dailies.

Epitomised, Hands learned the following facts. From a mass of detail a few lurid facts remained fixed in his brain.

[293] The well-meant but frequently unsuccessful mission efforts in Southern India were brought to a complete and utter stand-still.

By that thought-willed system of communication and the almost flame-like mouth-to-mouth carnage of news which is so inexplicable to Western minds, who can only understand the workings of the electric telegraph, the whole of India seemed to be throbbing with the news of the downfall of Christianity, and this within a fortnight of the publication of the European report.

134

From Cashmere to Travancore the millions whispered the news to each other with fierce if secret exultation.

The higher Hinduism, the key to the native character in India, the wall of caste, rose up grim and forbidding. The passionate earnestness of the missionaries was met by questions they could not answer. In a few days the work of years seemed utterly undone.

Europeans began to be insulted in the Punjaub as they had never been since the days before the Mutiny. English officers and civilians also began to send their wives home. The great P. and O. boats were inconveniently crowded.

In Afghanistan there was a great uneasiness. The Emir had received two Russian officers. Russian troops were massing on the north-west frontier. Fanatics began to appear in the Hill provinces, claiming divine missions. People began to remember that every fourth man, woman, and child in the whole human race is a Buddhist. Asia began to feel a great thrill of excitement permeating it through and through. There were rumours of a new incarnation of Buddha, who would lead his followers to the conquest of the West.

Troops from all over India began to concentrate near the Sri Ulang Pass in the Hindu-Kush.

Simultaneously with these ominous rumours of war [294] came an extraordinary outburst of Christian fanaticism in Russia. The peasantry burst into a flame of anger against England. The priests of the Greek Church not only refused to believe in the Palestine discovery, but they refused to ignore it, as the Roman Catholics of the world were endeavouring to do.

They began to preach war against Great Britain for its infidelity, and the political Powers seized the opportunity to use religious fanaticism for their own ends.

All these events happened with appalling swiftness.

In the remote Cornish village Hands moved as in a dream. His eyes saw nothing of his surroundings, his face was pallid under the brown of his skin. Sometimes, as he sat alone on the moors or by the sea, he laughed loudly. Once a passing coast-guard heard him. The man told of it among the fishermen, and they regarded their silent visitor with something of awe, with the Celtic compassion for those mentally afflicted.

On the first Sunday of his arrival Hands heard the deep singing of hymns coming from the little white chapel on the cliff. He entered in time for the sermon, which was preached by a minister who had walked over from Penzance.

Here all the turmoil of the world beyond was ignored. It seemed as though nothing had ever been heard of the thing that was shaking the world. The pastor preached and prayed, the men and women answered with deep, groaning "Amens." It all mattered nothing to them. They heeded it no more than the wailing wind in the cove. The voice of Christ was not stilled in the hearts of this little congregation of the Faithful.

This chilled the recluse. He could find no meaning or comfort in it.

That evening he heard the daughter of the coast-guard with whom he lodged singing. It was a wild [295] night, and Hands was sitting by the fire in his little sitting-room. Outside the wind and rain and waves were shouting furiously in the dark.

The girl was playing a few simple chords on the harmonium and singing to them. "For ever with the Lord."

An untuneful voice, louder than need be, but with what conviction!

Hands tried to fix his attention on the newspaper which he held.

He read that in Rhodesia the mine capitalists were moving for slavery pure and simple. It was proposed openly that slavery should be the penalty for law-breaking for natives. This was the only way, it asserted, by which the labour problem in South Africa could be solved.

"Life from the dead is in that word,

'Tis immortality."

It seemed that there was small opposition to this proposal. It would be the best thing for the Kaffir, perhaps, this wise and kindly discipline. So the proposal was wrapped up.

"And nightly pitch my moving tent

A day's march nearer home."

Hands saw that, quite suddenly, the old horror of slavery had disappeared.

This, too, was coming, then? This old horror which Christians had banished from the world?

"So when my latest breath

Shall rend the veil in twain."

[296] Hands started. His thoughts came back to the house in which he sat. The girl's voice touched him immeasurably. He heard it clearly in a lull of the storm. Then another tremendous gust of wind drowned it.

Two great tears rolled down his cheeks.

It was midnight, and all the people in the house were long since asleep, when Hands picked up the last of his newspapers.

It was Saturday's edition of the London Daily Mercury, the powerful rival of the Wire. A woman who had been to Penzance market had brought it home for him, otherwise he would have had to wait for it until the Monday morning.

He gazed wearily round the homely room.

Weariness, that was what lay heavy over mind and body—an utter weariness.

The firelight played upon the crude pictures, the simple ornaments, the ship worked in worsted when the coast-guard was a boy in the Navy, the shells from a Pacific island, a model gun under a glass shade. But his thoughts were not prisoned by these humble walls and the humble room in which he sat. He heard the groaning of the peoples of the world, the tramp of armies, the bitter cry of souls from whom hope had been plucked for ever.

He remembered the fair morning in Jerusalem when, with the earliest light of dawn, he had gone to work with his Arab boys before the heat of the day.

From the Mosque of Omar he had heard the sonorous chant of the muezzin.

"The night has gone with the darkness, and the day approaches with light and brightness!

"Praise God for securing His favour and kindness!

[297] "God is most great! God is most great! I testify that there is no god but God!

"I testify that Mohammed is the Apostle of God!

"Come to prayer!

"Come to security!

"Prayer is better than sleep!

"God is most great!

"There is no god but God!

"Arise, make morning, and to God be the praise!"

He had heard the magnificent chant as he passed by, almost kneeling with his Arabs. So short a time ago! Hardly three months—he had kept no count of time lately, but it could hardly be four months.

How utterly unconscious he had been on that radiant morning outside the Damascus Gate! He had seen the men at work, and was sitting under his sun-tent writing on his pad; he was just lighting a cigarette, he remembered, when Ionides, the foreman, had come running up to him, his shrewd, brown face wrinkled with excitement.

And now, even as he sat there on that stormy midnight, far from the world, even now the whole globe was echoing and reverberating with his discovery. He had opened the little rock chambers, and it seemed that the blows of the picks had set free a troop of ruinous spirits, who were devastating mankind.

Pandora's box—that legend fitted what he had done, but with a deadly difference.

He could not find that Hope remained. It would have been better a thousand times if the hot Eastern sun had struck him down that distant morning on his way through the city.

The awful weight, the initial responsibility rested with him.

He alone had been the means by which the world was [298] being shaken with horrors—horrors growing daily, and that seemed as if the end would be unutterable night.

How the wind shrieked and wailed!

Εγω Ιωσηφ ὁ ἀπο Αριμαθειας.

The words were written in fire on his mind!

The wind was shrieking louder and louder.

The Atlantic boomed in one continuous burst of sound.

He looked once more at the leading article in the paper.

It was that article which was long afterwards remembered as the "Simple Statement" article.

The writer had spoken the thought that was by this time trembling for utterance on the lips and in the brains of all Englishmen—the thought which had never been so squarely faced, so frankly stated before.

Here and there passages started out more vividly than the rest. The words seemed to start out and stab him.

"—So much for India, where, sprung from the same Cause, the indications are impossible to mistake.

"Let us now turn to the Anglo-Saxon sprung communities other than these Islands.

"In America we find a wave of lawlessness and fierce riot passing over the country, such as it has never known before.

"The Irishmen and Italians, who throng the congested quarters of the great cities, are robbing and murdering Protestants and Jews. The United States Legislature is paralysed between the necessity of keeping order and the impossibility of resolution in the face of this tremendous bouleversement of belief.

"From Australia the foremost prelate of the great [299] country writes of the utter overthrow of a communal moral sense, and concludes his communication with the following pathetic words:

"'Everywhere,' he says, 'I see morals, no less than the religion which inculcates them, falling into neglect, set aside in a spirit of despair by fathers and mothers, treated with contempt by youths and maidens, spat upon and cursed by a degraded populace, assailed with eager sarcasm by the polite and cultured.'

"The terrible seriousness of the situation need hardly be further insisted on here. Its reality cannot be more vividly indicated than by the statement of a single fact.

"consols are down to sixty-five

"—and therefore we demand, in the name of humanity, a far more comprehensive and representative searching into the facts of the alleged 'discovery' at Jerusalem. Society is falling to pieces as we write.

"Who will deny the reason?

"Already, after a few short weeks, we are learning that the world cannot go on without Christianity. That is the Truth which the world is forced to realise. And no essay in sociology, no special pleading on the part of Scientists or Historians, can shake our conviction that a creed which, when sudden doubts are thrown upon it, can be the means of destroying the essential fabric of human society, is not the true and unassailable creed of mankind.

"We foresee an immediate reaction. The consequences of the wave of antichristian belief are now, [300] and will be, so devastating, that sane men will find in Disbelief and its consequences a glorious recrudescence and assurance of Faith."

Hands stared into the dying fire.

A solemn passage from John Bright's great speech on the Crimean War came into his mind. The plangent power and deep earnestness of the words were even more applicable now than then.

"The Angel of Death has been abroad throughout the land: you may almost hear the beating of his wings. There is no one, as when the first-born were slain of old, to sprinkle with blood the lintel and two side-posts of our doors, that he may spare and pass on."

So they were asking for another commission! Well, they might try that as a forlorn hope, but he knew that his discovery was real. Could he be mistaken possibly? Could that congress of the learned be all mistaken and imposed upon? It was not possible. It could not be. Would that it were possible.

There was no hope, despite the newspapers. For centuries the world had been living in a fool's paradise. He had destroyed it. It would be a hundred years before the echoes of his deed had died away.

But the terrible weight of the world's burden was too heavy for him to bear. He knew that. Not for much longer could he endure it.

The life seemed oozing out of him, pressed out by a weight—the sensation was physical.

He wished it was all over. He had no hope for the future, and no fear.

The weight was too heavy. The outside dark came through the walls, and began to close in on him. His [301] heart beat loudly. It seemed to rise up in his throat and choke him.

The pressure grew each moment; mountains were being piled upon him, heavier, more heavy.

The wind was but a distant murmur now, but the weight was crushing him. Only a few more moments and his heart would burst. At last!

The dark thing huddled on the hearth-rug, which the girl found when she came down in the morning, was the scholar's body.

The newspaper he had been reading lay upon his chest.

[302]
CHAPTER IV

A LUNCHEON PARTY

Constantine Schuabe's great room at the Hotel Cecil had been entirely refurnished and arranged for the winter months.

The fur of great Arctic beasts lay upon the heavy Teheran carpets, which had replaced the summer matting—furs of enormous value. The dark red curtains which hung by windows and over doors were worked with threads of dull gold.

All the chairs were more massive in material and upholstered warmly in soft leather; the logs in the fireplace crackled with white flame, amethyst in the glowing cavern beneath.

However the winter winds might sweep over the Thames below or the rain splash and welter on the Embankment, no sound or sign of the turmoil could reach or trouble the people who moved in the fragrant warmth and comfort of this room.

For his own part Schuabe never gave any attention to the mise-en-scène by which he was surrounded, here or elsewhere. The head of a famous Oxford Street firm was told to call with his artists and undermen; he was given to understand that the best that could be done was to be done, and the matter was left entirely to him.

In this there was nothing of the parvenu or of an ignorance of art, as far as Schuabe was concerned. [303] He was a man of catholic and cultured taste. But experience had taught him that his furnishing firm were trained to be catholic and cultured also, that an artist would see to it that no jarring notes appeared. And since he knew this, Schuabe infinitely preferred not to be bothered with details. In absolute contrast to Llwellyn, his mind was always busy with abstractions, with thought and forms of thought, things that cannot be handled or seen. They were the real things for him always.

The millionaire sat alone by the glowing fire. He was wearing a long gown of camel's hair, dyed crimson, confined round the waist by a crimson cord. In this easy garment and a pair of morocco slippers without heels, he looked singularly Eastern. The whole face and figure suggested that—sinister, lonely, and splendid.

The morning papers were resting on a chair by his side. He was reading one of them.

It announced the death from heart disease of Mr. Cyril Hands while taking a few days' rest in a remote village of Cornwall. Not a shadow of regret passed over the regular, impassive face. The eyes remained in fixed thought. He was logically going over the bearings of this event in his mind. How could it affect him? Would it affect him one way or the other?

He paced the long room slowly. On the whole the incident seemed without meaning for him. If it meant anything at all it meant that his position was stronger than ever. The voice of the discoverer was now for ever silent. His testimony, his reluctant but convinced opinion, was upon record. Nothing could alter that. Hands might perhaps have had doubts in the future. He might have examined more keenly [304] into the way in which he came to examine the ground where the new tomb was hidden. Yes, this was better. That danger, remote as it had been, was over.

As his eyes wandered over the rest of the news columns they became more alert, speculative, and anxious. The world was in a tumult, which grew louder and louder every hour. Thrones were rocking, dynasties trembling.

He sank down in his chair with a sigh, passing his hand wearily over his face. Who could have foreseen this? It was beyond belief. He gazed at the havoc and ruin in terrif surprise, as a child might who had lit a little fire of straw, which had grown and devou a great city.

It was in this very room—just over there in the centre—that he had bought th brain and soul of the archæologist.

The big man had stood exactly on that spot, blanched and trembling. His mi notes of hand and promises to pay had flamed up in this fire.

And now? India was slipping swiftly away; a bloody civil war was brewing in America; Central Europe was a smouldering torch; the whips of Africa were cracking in the ears of Englishmen; the fortunes of thousands were melting away like ice in the sun. In London gentlemen were going from their clubs to their houses at night carrying pistols and sword-sticks. North of Holborn, south of the Thames, no woman was safe after dark had fallen.

He saw his face in an oval silver glass. It fascinated him as it had never done before. He gripped the leather back of a chair and stared fiercely, hungrily, at the image. It was this, this man he was looking at, some stranger it seemed, who had done all this. He laughed—a dreadful, mirthless, hollow laugh. This mass of [305] phosphates, carbon, and water, this moving, talking thing in a scarlet gown, was the pivot on which the world was turning!

His brain became darkened for a time, lost in an awful wonder. He could not realise or understand.

And no one knew save his partner and instrument. No one knew!

The secret seemed to be bursting and straining within him like some live, terrible creature that longed to rush into light. For weeks the haunting thought had grown and harassed him. It rang like bells in his memory. If only he could share his own dark knowledge. He wanted to take some calm, pale woman, to hold her tight and tell her all that he had done, to whisper it into her ears and watch the mask of flesh change and shrink, to see his words carve deep furrows in it, sear the eyes, burn the colour from the lips. He saw his own face was working with the mad violence of his imaginings.

He wrenched his brain back into normal grooves, as an engineer pulls over a lever. He was half-conscious of the simile as he did so.

Turning away from the mirror, he shuddered as a man who has escaped from a sudden danger.

That above all things was fatal. His luxuriant Eastern imagination had been checked and kept in subjection all his life; the force of his intellect had tamed and starved it. He knew, none better, the end, the extinction of the brain that has got beyond control. No, come what may, he must watch himself cunningly that he did not succumb. A tiny speck in the brain, and then good-bye to thought and life for ever. He was a visitor of the Lancashire Asylum—had been so once at least—and he had seen the soulless lumps of flesh the doctors called "patients." ... "I am the master of my fate. I am the captain of my 'oul," he repeated to himself, and even as [306] he did so, his other self sneered at the
akness which must comfort itself with a poet's rhyme and cling to an apothegm for
ustment.

Ie tried to shut out the world's alarm from his mental eyes and ears.
went back to the scenes of his first triumph. They had been sweet indeed.
vorth all the price he had paid and might be called upon to pay.
England his life's thought, his constant programme had been gloriously
y had hailed him as the prophet of Truth at first—a prophet who had
tness for years, and who had at last come into his own.
great men and vast multitudes had come to him as incense. He was to
ew religion of common sense. Why had they doubted him before,
erstitions?
and feared him in the old days, had spoken against him and his
horred and unclean, were his friends and servants now.
selves to the representative of the new power. Bishops had
f the Church, and its reconstruction upon "newer,

140

broader, more illuminated lines." They had come to him with fear—anxious, eager to confess the errors of the past, swift to flatter and suggest that, with his help, the fabric and political power of the Church might yet stand.

He was shown, with furtive eyes and hesitating lips, from which the shame had not yet been cleansed, how desirable and necessary it was that in the reconstruction of Christianity the Church should still have a prominent and influential part.

He had been a colossus among them all. But—and [307] he thought of it with anger and the old amazement—all this had been at first, when the discovery had flashed over a startled world. While the thing was new it had been a great question, truly the greatest of all, but it had been one which affected men's minds and not their bodies. That is speaking of the world at large.

As has already been pointed out, only religious people—a vast host, but small beside the mass of Englishmen—were disturbed seriously by what had happened. The price of bread remained the same; beef was no dearer.

During these first weeks Schuabe had been all-powerful. He and his friends had lived in a constant and stupendous triumph.

But now—and in his frightful egoism he frowned at the thick black head-lines in the newspapers—the whole attitude of every one was changed. There was a reflex action, and in the noise it made Schuabe was forgotten.

Men had more to think of now. There was no time to congratulate the man who had been so splendidly right.

Consols were at 65!

Bread was rising each week. War was imminent. On all sides great mercantile houses were crashing. Each fall meant a thousand minor catastrophes all over the country.

The antichristians had no time to jeer at the Faithful; they must work and strain to save their own fortunes from the wreck.

The mob, who were swiftly bereft of the luxuries which kept them in good-humour, were turning on the antichristian party now. In their blind, selfish unreason they cried them down, saying that they were responsible for the misery and terror that lay over the world.

With an absolute lack of logic, the churches were crowded again. The most irreligious cried for the good [308] old times. Those who had most coarsely exulted over the broken Cross now bewailed it as the most awful of calamities.

Christianity was daily being terribly avenged through the pockets and stomachs of the crowd!

It was bizarre beyond thinking, sordid in its immensity, vulgar in its mighty soulless greed, but TRUE, REAL, a FEARFUL FACT.

A stupendous confusion.

Two great currents had met in a maelstrom. The din of the disturbance beat upon the world's ear with sickening clamour.

Louder and louder, day by day.

And the man who had done all this, the brain which had called up these legions from hell, which had loosed these fiery sorrows on mankind, was in a rich room in a luxurious hotel, alone there. Again the shock and marvel took hold of the man and shook him like a reed.

There was a round table, covered with a gleaming white cloth, by the fire. The kidneys in the silver dish were cold, the grease had congealed. The silent servants had brought up a breakfast to him. He had watched their clever, automatic movements. Did they know whom they were attending on, what would happen—?

His thoughts flashed hither and thither, now surveying a world in torture, now weaving a trivial and whimsical romance about a waiter. The frightful activity of his brain, inflamed by thoughts beyond the power of even that wonderful machine, began to have a consuming physical effect.

He felt the grey matter bubbling. Agonising pains shot from temple to temple, little knives seemed hacking at the back of his eyes. Once again, in a wave of unutterable terror, the fear of madness submerged him.

On this second occasion he was unable to recall his [309] composure by any effort which came from within himself. He stumbled into his adjoining dressing-room and selected a bottle from a shelf. It was bromide of potassium, which he had been taking of late to deaden the clamour and vibration of his nerves.

In half an hour the drug had calmed him. His face was very pale, but set and rigid. The storm was over. He felt shattered by its violence, but in an artificial peace.

He took a cigarette.

As he was lighting it his valet entered and announced that Mr. Dawlish, his man of business, was waiting in an anteroom.

He ordered that he should be shown in.

Mr. Dawlish was the junior partner of the well-known firm of city solicitors, Burrington & Tuite. That was his official description. In effect he was Schuabe's principal man of business. All his time was taken up by the millionaire's affairs all over England.

He came in quickly—a tall, well-dressed man, hair thin on the forehead, moustache carefully trained.

"You look very unwell, Mr. Schuabe," he said, with a keen glance. "Don't let these affairs overwhelm you. Nothing is so dangerous as to let the nerves go in times like these."

Schuabe started.

"How are things, Dawlish?" he said.

"Very shaky, very shaky, indeed. The shares of the Budapest Railway are to be bought for a shilling. I am afraid your investments in that concern are utterly lost. When the Bourses closed last night dealings in Foreign Government Stock were at a stand-still. Turkish C and O bonds are worthless."

Again the millionaire started. "You bring me a record of disaster," he said.

[310] "Baumann went yesterday," continued the level voice.

"My cousin," said Schuabe.

"The worst of it is that the situation is getting worse and worse. We have, as you know, made enormous efforts. But all attempts you have made to uphold your securities have only been throwing money away. The last fortnight has been frightful. More than two hundred thousand pounds have gone. In fact, an ordinary man would be ruined by the last month or two. Your position is better because of the real property in the Manchester mills."

"Trade has almost ceased."

"Close the mills down and wait. You cannot go on."

"If I do, ten thousand men will be let loose on the city with nothing but the Union funds to fall back on."

"If you don't, you will be what Baumann is to-day—a bankrupt."

"I have eighty thousand cash on deposit at the Bank of England."

"And if you throw that away after the rest you will be done for. You don't realise the situation. It can't recover. War is inevitable. India will go, I feel it. England is going to turn into a camp. Religion is the pretext of war everywhere. Take your money from the

142

Bank in cash and lock it up in the Safe Deposit strong rooms. Keep that sum, earning nothing, for emergencies, then wait for the other properties to recover. It will be years perhaps, but you will win through in the end. The freehold sites of the mills are alone worth almost anything. It is only paper millionaires that are easily ruined. You are a great property owner. But you must walk very warily, even you. Who could have foreseen all this? I see that fellow Hands is dead—couldn't stand the sight of the mischief he'd done, I suppose. The fool! the eternal fool! why couldn't he have kept his [311] sham discovery to himself? Look at the unutterable misery it has brought on the world."

"You yourself, Dawlish, are you suffering the common fate?"

"I? Certainly not! That is to say, I suffer of course, but not fatally. All my investments are in buildings in safe quarters. I may have to reduce rents for a year or two, but my houses will not be empty. And they are my own."

"Fortunate man," said Schuabe; "but why sham discovery?"

"Out of business hours," said the solicitor, with some stiffness and hesitation, "I am a Roman Catholic, Mr. Schuabe. Good-morning. I will send the transfer round for you to sign."

The cool, machine-like man went away. The millionaire knew that his fortune was tottering, but it moved him little. He knew that his power in the country was nearly over, had dwindled to nothing in the stir of greater things around. Money was only useful as a means of power, and with a sure prescience he saw that he would never regain his old position.

The hour was over.

Whatever would be the outcome of these great affairs, the hour was past and over.

The one glowing thought which burned within him, and seemed to be eating out his life, was the awful knowledge that he and no other man had set in motion this terrible machinery which was grinding up the civilised world.

Day and night from that there was no relief.

His valet again entered and reminded his master that some people were coming to lunch. He went away and began to dress with the man's help.

The guests were only two in number. One was Ommaney, [312] the editor of the Daily Wire, the other Mrs. Hubert Armstrong.

Both the lady and gentleman came in together at about two o'clock.

Mrs. Armstrong was much changed in appearance. Her face had lost its serenity; her manner was quick and anxious; her voice strained.

The slim, quiet editor, on the other hand, seemed to be untouched by worry. Quiet and inscrutable as ever, the only change in him, perhaps, was a slight briskness, an aroma rather than an actual expression of good humour and bien-être.

They sat down to the meal. Schuabe, in his dark grey frock-coat, the careful ensemble of his dress no less than the regular beauty of his face—now smooth and calm—seemed to be beyond all mundane cares. Only the lady was ill at ease.

The conversation at first was all of the actual news of the day, as it had appeared in the morning's newspapers. Hands's death was discussed. "Poor fellow!" said Mrs. Armstrong, with a sigh; "it is sad to think of his sudden ending. The burden was too much for him to bear. I can understand it when I look round upon all that is happening; it is terrible!"

"Surely you do not regret the discovery of the truth?" said Schuabe, quickly.

"I am beginning to fear truth," said the lady. "The world, it seems, was not ripe for it. In a hundred years, perhaps, our work would have paved the way. But it is premature.

143

Look at the chaos all around us. The public has ceased to think or read. They are reading nothing. Three publishers have put up the shutters during the week."

The journalist interrupted with a dry chuckle. "They are reading the Daily Wire," he said; "the circulation [313] is almost doubled." He sent a congratulatory glance to Schuabe.

The millionaire's great holding in the paper was a secret known only to a few. In the stress of greater affairs he had half forgotten it. A swift feeling of relief crossed his brain as he realised what this meant to his tottering fortunes.

"Poor Hands!" said the editor, "he was a nice fellow. Rather unpractical and dreamy, but a nice fellow. Owing to him we had the greatest chance that any paper has ever had in the history of journalism. We owe him a great debt. The present popularity and influence of the paper has dwarfed, positively dwarfed, all its rivals. I have given the poor fellow three columns to-day; I wish I could do more."

"Do you not think, Mr. Ommaney," asked Mrs. Armstrong, "that in the enormous publication of telegrams and political foreign news, the glorious fact that the world has at last awakened to a knowledge of the glorious truths of real religion is being swamped and forgotten? After all, what will be the greatest thing in history a hundred years from now? Will it not be the death of the old superstitions rather than a mutiny in the East or a war with Russia? Will not the names of the pioneers of truth remain more firmly fixed in the minds of mankind than those of generals and chancellors?"

The editor made it quite plain that these were speculations with which he had nothing whatever to do.

"It's dead, Mrs. Armstrong," he said brutally. "The religious aspect is utterly dead, and wouldn't sell an extra copy of the paper. It would be madness to touch it now. The public gaze is fixed on Kabul River and St. Petersburg, Belgrade and Constantinople. They have almost forgotten that Jerusalem exists. I sent out twelve special correspondents ten days ago."

[314] Mrs. Armstrong sighed deeply. It was true, bitterly true. She was no longer of any importance in the public eye. No one asked her to lecture now. The mass meetings were all over. Not a single copy of John Mulgrave had been sold for a month. How differently she had pictured it all on that winter's morning at Sir Michael's; how brightly and gloriously it had begun, and now how bitter the dénouement, how utterly beyond foresight? What was this superstition, this Christianity which in its death struggles could overthrow a world?

"The decisive events of the world occur in the intellect." Yes, but how soon do they leave their parent and outstrip its poor control?

There was no need for women now. That was the bitterest thought of all. The movement was over—done with. A private in the Guards was a greater hero than the leader of an intellectual movement. What a monstrous bouleversement of everything!

Again the lady sighed deeply.

"No," she said again, "the world was not yet strong enough to bear the truth. I have sold my Consols," she continued; "I have been advised to do so. I was investing for my daughter when I am gone. Newspaper shares are the things to buy now, I suppose! My brokers told me that I was doing the wisest thing. They said that they could not recover for years."

"The money market is a thing in which I have very little concern except inasmuch as it affects large public issues," said the editor. "I leave it all to my city editor and his staff—men in whom I have the greatest possible trust. But I heard a curious piece of news last night. I don't know what it portends; perhaps Mr. Schuabe can tell me; he knows all about

144

these things. Sir Michael Manichoe, the head of the Church political party, you know has been buying Consols enormously. Keith, my [315] city editor, told me. He has, so it appears, invested enormous sums. Consols will go up in consequence. But even then I don't see how he can repay himself. They cannot rise much."

"I wonder if I was well advised to sell?" said Mrs. Armstrong, nervously. "They say Sir Michael never makes a mistake. He must have some private information."

"I don't think that is possible, Mrs. Armstrong," Ommaney said. "Of course Sir Michael may very likely know something about the situation which is not yet public. He may be reckoning on it. But things are in such hopeless confusion that no sane speculator would buy for a small rise which endured for half a day. He would not be able to unload quickly enough. It seems as if Sir Michael is buying for a permanent recovery. And I assure you that nothing can bring that about. Only one thing at least."

"What is that?" asked both Mrs. Armstrong and Schuabe together.

The editor paused, while a faint smile flickered over his face. "Ah," he said, "an impossibility, of course. If any one discovered that 'The Discovery' was a fraud—a great forgery, for instance—then we should see a universal relief."

"That, of course, is asking for an impossibility," said Mrs. Armstrong, rather shortly. She resented the somewhat flippant tone of the great man.

These things were all her life. To Ommaney they but represented a passing panorama in which he took absolutely no personal interest. The novelist disliked and feared this detachment. It warred with her strong sense of mental duty. The highly trained journalist, to whom all life was but news, news, news, was a strange modern product which warred with her sense of what was fitting.

[316] "You're not well!" said the editor, suddenly turning to Schuabe, who had grown very pale. His voice reassured them.

It was without a trace of weakness.

The "Perfectly, thank you" was deliberate and calm as ever. Ommaney, however, noticed that, with a very steady hand, the host poured out nearly a tumbler of Burgundy and drank it in one draught.

Schuabe had been taking nothing stronger than water hitherto during the progress of the meal.

The man who had been waiting had just left the room for coffee. After Ommaney had spoken, there was a slight, almost embarrassed, silence. A sudden interruption came from the door of the room.

It opened with a quick push and turn of the handle, quite unlike the deliberate movements of any one of the attendants.

Sir Robert Llwellyn strode into the room. It was obvious that he was labouring under some almost uncontrollable agitation. The great face, usually so jolly and fresh-coloured, was ghastly pale. There was a fixed stare of fright in the eyes. He had forgotten to remove his silk hat, which was grotesquely tilted on his head, showing the hair matted with perspiration.

Ommaney and Mrs. Armstrong sat perfectly still.

They were paralysed with wonder at the sudden apparition of this famous person, obviously in such urgent hurry and distress.

Then, with the natural instinct of well-bred people, their heads turned away, their eyes fell to their plates, and they began to converse in an undertone upon trivial matters.

Schuabe had risen with a quick, snake-like movement, utterly unlike his general deliberation. In a moment he had crossed the room and taken Llwellyn's arm in a [317] firm grip, looking him steadily in the face with an ominous and warning frown.

145

That clear, sword-like glance seemed to nerve the big man into more restraint. A wave of artificial composure passed over him. He removed his hat and breathed deeply.

Then he spoke in a voice which trembled somewhat, but which nevertheless attained something of control.

"I am really very sorry," he said, with a ghastly attempt at a smile, "to have burst in upon you like this. I didn't know you had friends with you. Please excuse me. But the truth is—the truth is, that I am in rather a hurry to see you. I have an important message for you from—" he hesitated a single moment before he found the ready lie—"from Lord ———. There are—there is something going on at the House of Commons which—But I will tell you later on. How do you do, Mrs. Armstrong? How are you, Ommaney? Fearfully rushed, of course! We archæologists are the only people who have leisure nowadays. No, thanks, Schuabe, I lunched before I came. Coffee? Oh, yes; excellent!"

His manner was noticeably forced and unnatural in its artificial geniality. The man, who had now entered with coffee, brought the tray to him, but instead of taking any he half filled an empty cup with Kümmel and drank it off.

His hurried explanation hardly deceived the two shrewd people at the table, but at least it made it obvious that he wished to be alone with their host.

There was a little desultory conversation over the coffee, in which Llwellyn took a too easy and hilarious part, and then Mrs. Armstrong got up to go.

Ommaney followed her.

Schuabe walked with them a little way down the corridor. While he was out of the room, Llwellyn walked [318] unsteadily to a sideboard. With shaking hand he mixed himself a large brandy-and-soda. His shaking hands, the intense greed with which he swallowed the mixture, were horrible in their sensual revelation. The mask of pleasantness had gone; the reserve of good manners disappeared.

He stood there naked, as it were—a vast bulk of a man in deadly fear.

Schuabe came back and closed the door silently. He drew Llwellyn to the old spot, right in the centre of the great room. There was a wild question in his eyes which his lips seemed powerless to utter.

"Gertrude!" gasped the big man. "You know she came back to me. I told you at the club that it was all right between us again?"

An immeasurable relief crossed the Jew's face. He pushed his friend away with a snarl of concentrated disgust.

"You come here," he hissed venomously, "and burst into my rooms to tell me of your petty amours. Have I not borne with the story of your lust and degradation enough? You come here as if the—." He stopped suddenly. The words died away on his lips.

Llwellyn was transformed.

Even in his terror and agitation an ugly sneer blazed out upon his face. His nostrils curled with evil laughter. His voice became low and threatening. Something subtly vulgar and common stole into it. It was this last that arrested Schuabe. It was horrible.

"Not quite so fast, my good friend," said Llwellyn. "Wait and hear my story; and, confound you! if you talk to me like that again, I'll kill you! Things are equal now, my Jewish partner—equal between us. If I am in danger, why, so are you; and either you speak civilly or you pay the penalty."

[319] A curious thing happened. The enormous overbearing brutality of the man, his vitality, seemed to cow and beat down the master mind.

Schuabe, for the moment, was weak in the hands of his inferior. As yet he had heard nothing of what the other had come to tell; he was conscious only of hands of cold fear knocking at his heart.

146

He seemed to shrink into himself. For the first and last time in his life, the inherited slavishness in his blood asserted itself.

He had never known such degradation before. The beauty of his face went out like an extinguished candle. His features grew markedly Semitic; he cringed and fawned, as his ancestors had cringed and fawned before fools in power hundreds of years back.

This inexpressibly disgusting change in the distinguished man had its immediate effect upon his companion. It was new and utterly startling. He had come to lean on Schuabe, to place the threads of a dreadful dilemma in his hand, to rest upon his master mind.

So, for a second or two, in loathsome pantomime the men bowed and salaamed to each other in the centre of the room, not knowing what they did.

It was Sir Robert who pulled himself together first. The fear which was rushing over him in waves gave him back a semblance of control.

"We must not quarrel now," he said in a swift, eager voice. "Listen to me. We are on the brink of terrible things. Gertrude Hunt came back to me, as you know. She told me that she was sick to death of her friends the priests, that the old life called her, that she could not live apart from me. She mocked at her sudden conversion. I thought that it was real. I laughed and mocked with her. I trusted her as I would trust myself."

[320] He paused for a moment, choking down the immense agitation which rose up in his throat and half strangled speech.

Schuabe's eyes, attentive and fixed, were still uncomprehending. Still the Jew did not see whither Llwellyn was leading—could not understand.

"She's gone!" said the big man, all colour fading absolutely from his face. "And, Schuabe, in my mad folly and infatuation, in my incredible foolishness ... I told her everything."

A sudden sharp animal moan burst from Schuabe's lips—clear, vibrant, and bestial in the silence.

His rigidity changed into an extraordinary trembling. It was a temporary palsy which set every separate limb trembling with an independent motion. He waited thus, with an ashen face, to hear more.

Llwellyn, when the irremediable fact had passed his lips, when the enormous difficulty of confession was surmounted, proceeded with slight relief:

"This might, you will think, be just possibly without significance for us. It might be a coincidence. But it is not so, Schuabe. I know now, as certainly as I can know anything, that she came to me, was sent to me, by the people who have got hold of her. There has been suspicion for some time, there must have been. We have been ruined by this woman I trusted."

"But why ... how?"

"Because, Schuabe, as I was walking down Chancery Lane not an hour since I saw Gertrude come out of Lincoln's Inn with the clergyman Gortre. They got into a cab together and drove away. And more: I learn from Lambert, my assistant at the Museum, that Harold Spence, the journalist, who is a member of his club and a friend of his, left for Palestine several days ago."

"I have just heard," whispered Schuabe, "that Sir [321] Michael Manichoe has been buying large parcels of Consols."

"The thing is over. We must——"

"Hush!" said the Jew, menacingly. "All is not lost yet. Perhaps, the strong probability is, that only this Gortre knows yet. Even if anything is known to others, it is only vague, and cannot be substantiated until the man in Palestine gets a letter. Without this woman and Gortre we are safe."

The Professor looked at him and understood. Nor was there any terror in his face, only a faint film of relief.

Five minutes afterwards the two distinguished men, talking easily together, walked through the vestibule of the hotel, down the great courtyard and into the roaring Strand.

A hotel clerk explained the celebrities to a voluble group of American tourists as they went by.

[322]
CHAPTER V

BY THE TOWER OF HIPPICUS

Harold Spence was essentially a man of action. His mental and moral health depended for its continuance upon the active prosecution of affairs more than most men's.

A product of the day, "modern" in his culture, modern in his ideals, he must live the vivid, eager, strenuous life of his times or the fibres of his brain became slack and loosened.

In the absorbing interest of his first mission to the East Spence had found work which exactly suited his temperament. It was work which keyed him up to his best and most successful efforts.

But when that was over, when the news that he had given brilliantly to the world became the world's and was no longer his, then the reaction set in.

The whole man became relaxed and unstrung; he was drifting into a sloth of the mind and body when Gortre had arrived from the North with his message of Hope.

The renewed opportunity of action, the tonic to his weak and waning faith—that faith which alone was able to keep him clean and worthy—again strung up the chords of his manhood till they vibrated in harmony.

Once more Spence was in the Holy City.

But a short time ago he was at Jerusalem as the collective eye of millions of Englishmen, the telegraph wires stretched out behind him to London.

[323] Now he was, to all official intents, a private person, yet, as the steamer cast anchor in the roadstead of Jaffa, he had realised that a more tremendous responsibility than ever before rested with him.

The last words spoken to Spence in England had been those of Sir Michael Manichoe. The great man was bidding him good-bye at Charing Cross.

"Remember," he had said, "that whatever proof or help we may get from this woman, Gertrude Hunt, will be but the basis for you to work on in the East. We shall cable every result of our investigations here. Remember that, as we think, you have immense ability and resource against you. Go very warily. As I have said before, no sum is too great to sacrifice, no sacrifice too great to make."

There had been a day's delay at Jaffa. It had been a day of strange, bewildering thoughts to the journalist.

The "Gate of the Holy Land" is not, as many people suppose, a fine harbour, a thronged port.

The navies of the ancient world which congregated there were smaller than even the coasting steamers of to-day. They found shelter in a narrow space of more or less

148

untroubled water between the shelving rock of the long, flat shore and a low reef rising out of the sea parallel to the town. The vessels with timber for Solomon's Temple tossed almost unsheltered before the terraces of ochre-coloured Oriental houses.

For several hours it had been too rough for the passengers on the French boat to land. More than a mile of restless bottle-green sea separated them from the rude ladders fastened to the wave-washed quay.

There had been one of the heavy rain-storms which at that season of the year visit Palestine. Over the Moslem minarets of the town the purple tops of the central mountains of Judah and Ephraim showed clear and far away.

[324] The time of waiting gave Spence an opportunity for collecting and ordering his thoughts, for summing up the situation and trying to get at the very heart of its meaning.

The messagery steamer was the only one in the roads. Two coasting craft with rags of light brown sails were beating over the swell into the Mediterranean.

The sky was cloudy, the air still and warm. Only the sea was turbulent and uneasy, the steamer rolled with a sickening, regular movement, and the anchor chains beat and rattled with the precision of a pendulum.

Spence sat on the india-rubber treads of the steps leading up to the bridge, with an arm crooked round a white-painted stanchion supporting the hand-rail. A few yards away two lascars were working a chain and pulley, drawing up zinc boxes of ashes from the stoke-hold and tipping them into the sea. As the clinkers fell into the water a little cloud of steam rose from them.

There were but few passengers on the ship, which wore a somewhat neglected, "off-duty" aspect. No longer were the cabins filled with drilled bands of tourists with their loud-voiced lecturing cleric in charge. Not now was there the accustomed rush to the main deck, the pious ejaculations at the first sight of Palestine, the electric knocking at the hearts even of the least devout.

Nobody came to Jerusalem now from England. From Beyrout to Jaffa the maritime plain was silent and deserted, and no tourists plucked the roses of Sharon any more.

A German commercial traveller, with cases of cutlery, from Essen, was arguing with the little Greek steward about his wine bill; a professional photographer from Alexandria, travelling with his cameras for a New York firm of art publishers; two Turkish officers smoking cigarettes; a Russian gentleman with two young sons; [325] a fat man in flannels and with an unshaven chin, very much at home; an orange buyer from a warehouse by the Tower Bridge—these were the undistinguished companions of the journalist.

The steward clapped his hands; déjeuner was ready. The passengers tumbled down to the saloon. Spence declined the loud-voiced Cockney invitation of the fruit merchant and remained where he was, gazing with unseeing eyes at the low Eastern town, which rose and fell before him as the ship rolled lazily from side to side.

There was something immensely, tremendously incongruous in his position. It was without precedent. He had come, in the first place, as a sort of private inquiry agent. He was a detective charged by a group of three or four people, a clergyman or two, a wealthy Member of Parliament, to find out the year-old movements—if, indeed, movements there had been!—of a distinguished European professor. He was to pry, to question, to deceive. This much in itself was utterly astonishing, strangely difficult of realisation.

But how much more there was to stir and confuse his brain!

He was coming back alone to Jerusalem. But a short time ago he had seen the great savants of Europe—only thirty miles beyond this Eastern town—reluctantly pronounce the words which meant the downfall of the Christian Faith.

149

The gunboat which had brought them all was anchored in this very spot. A Turkish guard had been waiting yonder on the quay, they had gone along the new road to Jerusalem in open carriages,—through the orange groves,—riding to make history.

And now he was here once more.

While he sat on this dingy steamer in this remote corner of the Mediterranean, it was no exaggeration to [326] say that the whole world was in a state of cataclysm such as it had hardly, at least not often, known before.

It was his business to watch events, to forecast whither they would lead. He was a Simon Magus of the modern world, with an electric wire and stylographic pen to prophesy with. He of all men could see and realise what was happening all over the globe. He was more alarmed than even the man in the street. This much was certain.

And a day's easy ride away lay the little town which held the acre of rocky ground from which all these horrors, this imminent upheaval, had come.

Again it seemed beyond the power of his brain to seize it all, to contain the vastness of his thoughts.

These facts, which all the world knew, were almost too stupendous for belief. But when he dwelt upon the personal aspect of them he was as a traveller whose way is irrevocably barred by sheer precipice.

At the very first he had been one mouthpiece of the news. For some hours the packet containing it had hung in the dressing-room of a London Turkish bath.

His act had recoiled upon himself, for when Gortre found him in the chambers he was spiritually dying.

Could this suspicion of Schuabe and Llwellyn possibly be true? It had seemed both plausible and probable in Sir Michael's study in London. But out here in the Jaffa roadstead, when he realised—or tried to realise—that on him might depend the salvation of the world.... He laughed aloud at that monstrous grandiloquent phrase. He was in the nineteenth century, not the tenth.

He doubted more and more. Had it been any one else it might have been possible to believe. But he could not see himself in this stupendous rôle.

The mental processes became insupportable; he dismissed [327] thought with a great effort of will and got up from his seat.

At least there was some action, something definite to do waiting for him. Speculation only blurred everything. He would be true to the trust his friends in England reposed in him and leave the rest to happen as it was fated.

There was a relief in that attitude—the Arab attitude. Kismet!

Griggs, the fruit merchant, came up from the saloon wiping his lips.

"Bit orf," he said, "waiting like this. But the sea will go down soon. Last spring I had to go on to Beyrout, the weather was that rough. Ever tried that Vin de Rishon le Zion? It's a treat. Made from Bordeaux vines transplanted to Palestine—you'll pass the fields on the way up—just had a half bottle. Hallo!—look, there's the boat at last—old Francis Karane's boat. Must go and look after my traps."

A long boat was creeping out from behind the reef. Spence went to his cabin to see after his light kit. It was better to move and work than to think.

It was early morning, the morning after Spence's arrival in Jerusalem. He slept well and soundly in his hotel room, tired by the long ride—for he had come on horseback over the moonlit slopes of Ajalon.

When at length he awoke it was with a sensation of mental and bodily vigour, a quickening of all his pulses in hope and expectation, which was in fine contrast to the doubts and hesitations of the Jaffa roads.

A bright sun poured into the room.

He got up and went to the window. There was a deep, unspoken prayer in his heart.

The hotel was in Akra, the European and Christian [328] quarter of Jerusalem, close by the Jaffa Gate, with the Tower of Hippicus frowning down upon it.

The whole extent of the city lay beneath the windows in a glorious panorama, washed as it was in the brilliant morning light. Far beyond, a dark shadow yet, the Olivet range rose in background to the minarets and cupolas below it.

His eye roved over the prospect, marking and recognising the buildings.

There was the purple dome of the great Mosque of Omar, very clear against the amber-primrose lights of dawn.

Where now the muezzin called to Allah, the burnt-offerings had once smoked in the courts of the Temple—it was in that spot the mysterious veil had parted in symbol of God's pain and death. It was in the porches bounding the court of the Gentiles that Christ had taught.

Closer, below the Antonia Tower, rose the dark, lead-covered cupola of the Church of the Holy Sepulchre.

Great emotion came to him as he gazed at the shrine sacred above all others for so many centuries.

He thought of that holy spot diminished in its ancient glory in the eyes of half the Christian world.

Perhaps no more would the Holy Fire burst forth from the yellow, aged marble of the Tomb at Easter time.

Who could say?

Was not he, Harold Spence, there to try that awful issue?

He wondered, as he gazed, if another Easter would still see the wild messengers bursting away to Nazareth and Bethlehem bearing The Holy Flame.

The sun became suddenly more powerful. It threw a warmer light into the grey dome, and, deep down, [329] the cold, dark waters of Hezekiah's Pool became bright and golden.

The sacred places focussed the light and sprang into a new life.

He made the sign of the Cross, wondering fancifully if this were an omen.

Then with a shudder he looked to the left towards the ogre-grey Turkish battlements of the Damascus Gate.

It was there, over by the Temple Quarries of Bezetha, the New Tomb of Joseph lay.

Yes! straight away to the north lay the rock-hewn sepulchre where the great doctors had sorrowfully pronounced the end of so many Christian hopes.

How difficult to believe that so short a distance away lay the centre of the world's trouble! Surely he could actually distinguish the guard-house in the wall which had been built round the spot.

Over the sad Oriental city—for Jerusalem is always sad, as if the ancient stones were still conscious of Christ's passion—he gazed towards the terrible place, wondering, hoping, fearing.

It was very difficult to know how to begin upon this extraordinary affair.

When he had made the first meal of the day and was confronted with the business, with the actual fact of what he had to do, he was aghast at what seemed his own powerlessness.

He had no plan of action, no method. For an hour he felt absolutely hopeless.

Sir Robert Llwellyn, so his friends believed, had been in Jerusalem prior to the discovery of the New Tomb.

151

The first duty of the investigator was to find out whether that was true.

[330] How was he to do it?

In his irresolution he decided to go out into the city. He would call upon various people he knew, friends of Cyril Hands, and trust to events for guiding his further movements.

The rooms where Hands had always stayed were close to the schools of the Church Missionary Society; he would go there. Down in the Mûristan area he could also chat with the doctor at the English Ophthalmic Hospice; he would call on his way to the New Tomb.

It was at The Tomb that he might learn something, perhaps, yet how nebulous it all was, how unsatisfying!

He set out, down the roughly paved streets, through the arched and shaded bazaars—places less full of colour and more sombre than the markets of other Oriental cities—to the heart of the city, where the streets were bounded by the vision of the distant hills of Olivet.

The religious riots and unrest were long since over. The pilgrims to the Church of the Holy Sepulchre were less in number, but were mostly Russians of the Greek Church, who still accepted the Church of the Holy Sepulchre as the true goal of their desires.

The Greeks and Armenians hated each other no more than usual. The Turks were held in good control by a strong governor of Jerusalem. Nor was this a time of special festival. The city, never quite at rest, was still in its normal condition.

The Bedouin women with their unveiled faces, tattooed in blue, strode to the bazaars with the butter they had brought in from their desert herds. They wore gaudy head-dresses and high red boots, and they jostled the "pale townsmen" as they passed them; free, untamed creatures of the sun and air.

As Spence passed by the courtyard of the Church [331] of the Holy Sepulchre a crowd of Fellah boys ran up to him with candles ornamented with scenes from the Passion, pressing him to buy.

The sun grew hotter as he walked, though the purple shadows of the narrow streets were cool enough. As he left the European heights of Akra and dived deep into the eastern central city, the well-remembered scenes and smells rose up like a wall before him and the rest of life.

He began to walk more slowly, in harmony with the slow-moving forms around. He had been to Omdurman with the avenging army, knew Constantinople during the Greek war—the East had meaning for him.

And as the veritable East closed round him his doubts and self-ridicule vanished. His strange mission seemed possible here.

As he was passing one of the vast ruined structures once belonging to the mediæval knights of St. John, thinking, indeed, that he himself was a veritable Crusader, a thin, importunate voice came to him from an angle of the stone-work.

He looked down and saw an old Nurié woman sitting there. She belonged to the "Nowar," the unclean pariah class of Palestine, who are said to practise magic arts. A gipsy of the Sussex Downs would be her sister in England.

The woman was tattooed from head to foot. She wore a blue turban, and from squares and angles drawn in the dust before her, Spence knew her for a professional geomancer or fortune-teller.

He threw her a coin in idle speculation and asked her "his lot" for the immediate future.

152

The woman had a few shells of different shapes in a heap by her side, and she threw them into the figures on the ground.

[332] Then, picking them up, she said, in bastard Arabic interspersed with a hard "K"-like sound, which marks the nomad in Palestine, "Effendi, you have a sorrow and bewilderment just past you, and, like a black star, it has fixed itself on your forehead. A letter is coming to you from over the seas telling you of work to do. And then you will leave this country and cross home in a steamer, with a story to tell many people."

Spence smiled at the glib prophecy. Certainly it might very well outline his future course of action, but it was no more than a shrewd and obvious guess.

He was turning to go away when the woman opened her clothes in front, showing the upper part of her body literally covered with tattoo marks, and drew out a small bag.

"Stay, my lord," she said. "I can tell you much more if you will hear. I have here a very precious stone rubbed with oil, which I brought from Mecca. Now, if you will hold this stone in your hand and give me the price you shall hear what will come to you, O camel of the house!"

The curious sensation of "expectation" that had been coming over Spence, the fatalistic waiting for chance to guide him which, in this wild and dream-like business, had begun to take hold of him, made him give the hag what she asked.

There was something in clairvoyance perhaps; at any rate he would hear what the Nurié woman had to say.

She took a dark and greasy pebble from the bag and put it in his hand, gazing at his fingers for a minute or two in a fixed stare without speaking.

When at last she broke the silence Spence noticed that something had gone out of her voice. The medicant whine, the ingratiating invitation had ceased.

Her tones were impersonal, thinner, a recitative.

[333] "Ere sundown my lord will hear that a friend has died and his spirit is in the well of souls."

"Tell me of this friend, O my aunt!" Spence said in colloquial Arabic.

"Thy friend is a Frank, but more than a Frank, for he is one knowing much of this country, and has walked the stones of Jerusalem for many years. Thou wilt hear of his death from the lips of one who will tell thee of another thou seekest, and know not that it is he.... Give me back the stone, lord, and go thy way," she broke off suddenly, with seeming sincerity. "I will tell thee no more, for great business is in thy hands and thou art no ordinary wayfarer. Why didst thou hide it from me, Effendi?"

Drawing her blue head-dress over her face, the woman refused to speak another word.

Spence passed on, wondering. He knew, as all travellers who are not merely tourists know, that no one has ever been quite able to sift the fraud and trickery from the strange power possessed by those Eastern geomancers. It is an undecided question still, but only the shallow dare to say that all is imposture.[2]

And even the London journalist could not be purely materialistic in Jerusalem, the City of Sorrows.

He went on towards his destination. Not far from the missionary establishment was a building which was the headquarters of the Palestine Exploring Society in Jerusalem.

Cyril Hands had always lived up in Akra among the Europeans, but much of his time was necessarily spent in the Mûristan district.

[334] The building was known as the "Research Museum."

Hands and his assistants had gathered a valuable collection of ancient curiosities.

153

Here were hundreds of drawings and photographs of various excavations. Accurate measurements of tombs, buried houses, ancient churches were entered in great books.

In glass cases were fragments of ancient pottery, old Hebrew seals, scarabs, antique fragments of jewellery—all the varied objects from which high scholarship and expert training was gradually, year by year, providing a luminous and entirely fresh commentary on Holy Writ.

Here, in short, were the tools of what is known as the "Higher Criticism."

Attached to the museum was a library and drawing office, a photographic dark room, apartments for the curator and his wife. A man who engaged the native labour required for the excavations superintended the work of the men and acted as general agent and intermediary between the European officials and all Easterns with whom they came in contact.

This man was well known in the city—a character in his way. In the reports of the Exploring Society he was often referred to as an invaluable assistant. But a year ago his portrait had been published in the annual statement of the fund, and the face of the Greek Ionides in his turban lay upon the study tables of many a quiet English vicarage.

Spence entered the courtyard of the building. It was quiet and deserted; some pigeons were feeding there.

He turned under a stone archway to the right, pushed open a door, and entered the museum.

There was a babel of voices.

A small group of people stood by a wooden pedestal [335] in the centre of the room, which supported the famous cruciform font found at Bîâr Es-seb'a.

They turned at Spence's entrance. He saw some familiar faces of people with whom he had been brought in contact during the time of the first discovery.

Two English missionaries, one in orders, the English Consul, and Professor Theodore Adams, the American archæologist, who lived all the year round in the new western suburb, stood speaking in grave tones and with distressed faces—so it seemed to the intruder.

An Egyptian servant, dressed in white linen, carrying a bunch of keys, was with them.

In his hand the Consul held a roll of yellow native wax.

An enormous surprise shone out on the faces of these people as Spence walked up to him.

"Mr. Spence!" said the Consul, "we never expected you or heard of your coming. This is most fortunate, however. You were his great friend. I think you both shared chambers together in London?"

Spence looked at him in wonder, mechanically shaking the proffered hand.

"I don't think I quite understand," he said. "I came here quite by chance, just to see if there was any one that I knew about."

"Then you have not heard—" said the clergyman.

"I have heard nothing."

"Your friend, our distinguished fellow-worker, Professor Hands, is no more. We have just received a cable. Poor, dear Hands died of heart disease while taking a seaside holiday."

Spence was genuinely affected.

Hands was an old and dear friend. His sweet, kindly nature, too dreamy and retiring perhaps for the rush and hurry of Occidental life, had always been wonderfully [336] welcome for a month or two each year in Lincoln's Inn. His quaint, learned letters, his

154

enthusiasm for his work had become part of the journalist's life. They were recurring pleasures. And now he was gone!

Now it was all over. Never more would he hear the quiet voice, hear the water-pipe bubble in the quiet old inn as night gave way to dawn....

His brain whirled with the sudden shock. He grew very pale, waiting to hear more.

"We know little more," said the Consul, with a sigh. "A cable from the central office of the Society has just stated the fact and asked me to take official charge of everything here. We were just about to begin sealing up the rooms when you came. There are many important documents which must be seen to. Mr. Forbes, poor Hands's assistant, is away on the shores of the Dead Sea, but we have sent for him by the camel garrison post. But it will be some weeks before he can be here, probably."

"This is terribly sad news for me," said Spence at length. "We were, of course, the dearest friends. The months when Hands was in town were always the pleasantest. Of course, lately we did not see so much of each other; he had become a public character. He was becoming very depressed and unwell, terrified, I almost think, at what was going on in the world owing to the discovery he had made, and he was going away to recuperate. But I knew nothing of this!"

"I am sorry," said the Consul, "to have to tell you of such a sad business, but we naturally thought that somehow you knew—though, of course, in point of time that would hardly be possible, or only just so."

"I am in the East," said Spence, giving an explanation that he had previously prepared if it became necessary to account for his presence—"I am here on a [337] mission for my newspaper—to ascertain various points about public opinion in view of all these imminent international complications."

"Quite so, quite so," said the Consul. "I shall be glad to help you in any way I can, of course. But when you came in we were wondering what we should do exactly about poor Hands's private effects, papers, and so on. When he went on leave all his things were packed in cases and sent down here from his rooms in the upper city. I suppose they had better be shipped to England. Perhaps you would take charge of them on your return?"

"I expect you will hear from his brother, the Rev. John Hands, a Leicestershire clergyman, when the mail comes in," said Spence. "This is a great blow to me. I should like to pay my poor friend some public tribute. I should like to write something for English people to read—a sketch of his life and work here in Jerusalem—his daily work among you all."

His voice faltered. His eyes had fallen on a photograph which hung upon the wall. A group of Arabs sat at the mouth of a rock tomb. In front of them, wearing a sun helmet and holding a ten-foot surveyor's wand, stood the dead professor. A kindly smile was on his face as he looked down upon the white figures of his men.

"It would be a gracious tribute," said one of the missionaries. "Every one loved him, whatever their race or creed. We can all tell you of him as we saw him in our midst. It is a great pity that old Ionides has gone. He was the confidential sharer of all the work here, and Hands trusted him implicitly. He could have told you much."

"I remember Ionides well," said Spence. "At the time of the discovery, of course, he was very much in [338] evidence, and he was examined by the committee. Is the old fellow dead, then?"

"No," answered the missionary. "Some time ago, just after the Commission left, in fact, he came into a considerable sum of money. He was getting on in years, and he resigned his position here. He has taken an olive farm somewhere by Nabulûs, a Turkish city by Mount Gerizim. I fear we shall never see him more. He would grieve at this news."

"I think," said Spence, "I will go back to my hotel. I should like to be alone to-day. I will call on you this evening, if I may," he added, turning to the Consul.

He left the melancholy group, once more beginning their sad business, and went out again into the narrow street.

He wanted to be alone, in some quiet place, to pay his departed friend the last rites of quiet thought and memory. He would say a prayer for him in the cool darkness of the Church of the Holy Sepulchre.

How did it go?

"So when this corruptible shall have put on incorruption, and this mortal shall have put on immortality; Then shall be brought to pass the saying that is written, Death is swallowed up in victory. O death, where is thy sting? O grave, where is thy victory?"

Always all his life long he had thought that these were perhaps the most beautiful of written words.

He turned to the right, passed the Turkish guard at the entrance, and went down the narrow steps to the "Calvary" chapel.

The gloom and glory of the great church, its rich and sombre light, the cool yet heavy air, saddened his soul. He knelt in humble prayer.

When he came out once more into the brilliant sunlight [339] and the noises of the city he felt braver and more confident.

He began to turn his thoughts earnestly and resolutely to his mission.

Swiftly, with a quick shock of memory, he remembered his talk with the old fortune-teller. It was with an unpleasant sense of chill and shock that he remembered her predictions.

Some strange sense of divination had told her of this sad news that waited for him. He could not explain or understand it. But there was more than this. It might be wild and foolish, but he could not thrust the woman's words from his brain.

She knew he was in quest of some one. She said he would be told....

He entered the yellow stone portico of the hotel with a sigh of relief. The hall was large, flagged, and cool. A pool of clear water was in the centre, glimmering green over its tiles. The eye rested on it with pleasure. Spence sank into a deck-chair and clapped his hands. He was exhausted, tired, and thirsty.

An Arab boy came in answer to his hand-clapping. He brought an envelope on a tray.

It was a cable from England.

Spence went up-stairs to his bedroom. From his kit-bag he drew a small volume, bound in thick leather, with a locked clasp.

It was Sir Michael Manichoe's private cable code—a precious volume which great commercial houses all over the world would have paid great sums to see, which the great man in his anxiety and trust had confided to his emissary.

Slowly and laboriously he de-coded the message, a collection of letters and figures to be momentous in the history of Christendom.

[340] These were the words:

"The woman has discovered everything from Llwellyn. All suspicions confirmed. Conspiracy between Llwellyn and Schuabe. You will find full confirmation from the Greek foreman of Society explorations, Ionides. Get statement of truth by any means, coercion or money to any amount. All is legitimate. Having obtained, hasten home, special steamer if quicker. Can do nothing certain without your evidence. We trust in you. Hasten.

"Manichoe."

156

He trembled with excitement as he relocked the code.

It was a light in a dark place. Ionides! the trusted for many years! The eager helper! The traitor bought by Llwellyn!

It was afternoon now. He must go out again. A caravan, camels, guides, must be found for a start to-morrow.

It would not be a very difficult journey, but it must be made with speed, and it was four days, five days away.

He passed out of the hotel and by the Tower of Hippicus.

A new drinking fountain had been erected there, a domed building, with pillars of red stone and a glittering roof, surmounted by a golden crescent.

Some camel drivers were drinking there. He was passing by when a tall, white-robed figure bowed low before him. A voice, speaking French, bade him good-day.

The face of the man seemed familiar. He asked him his name and business.

It was Ibrahim, the Egyptian servant he had seen at the museum in the morning.

The rooms had been sealed up, and the man had been to the Consul's private house with the keys.

[341] This man had temporarily succeeded the Greek Ionides.

Spence turned back to the hotel and bade Ibrahim follow him.

[342]
CHAPTER VI

UNDER THE EASTERN STARS: TOWARDS GERIZIM

The night was cold and still, the starlight brilliant in the huge hollow sapphire of the sky.

Wrapped in a heavy cloak, Spence sat at the door of one of the two little tents which composed his caravan.

Ibrahim the Egyptian, a Roman Catholic, as it seemed, had volunteered to act as dragoman. In a few hours this man had got together the necessary animals and equipment for the expedition to Nabulûs.

Spence rode a little grey horse of the wiry Moabite breed, Ibrahim a Damascus bay. The other men, a cook and two muleteers, all Syrians of the Greek Church, rode mules.

The day's march had been long and tiring. Night, with its ineffable peace and rest, was very welcome.

On the evening of the morrow they would be on the slopes of Ebal and Gerizim, near to the homestead of the man they sought.

All the long day Spence had asked himself what would be the outcome of this wild journey. He was full of a grim determination to wring the truth from the renegade. In his hip pocket his revolver pressed against his thigh. He was strung up for action. Whatever course presented itself, that he would take, regardless of any law that there might be even in these far-away districts.

His passport was specially endorsed by the Foreign [343] Office; he bore a letter, obtained by the Consul, from the Governor of Jerusalem to the Turkish officer in command of Nabulûs.

He had little doubt of the ultimate result. Money or force should obtain a full confession, and then, a swift rush for London with the charter of salvation—for it would be little less than that—and the engine of destruction for the two terrible criminals at home.

157

As they marched over the plains the red anemone and blue iris had peeped from the herbage. The ibex, the roebuck, the wild boar, had fled from the advancing caravan.

Eagles and vultures had moved heavily through the sky at vast heights. Quails, partridges, and plovers started from beneath the horses' feet.

As the sun plunged away, the owls had begun to mourn in the olive groves, the restless chirping of the grasshoppers began to die away, and as the stars grew bright, the nightingale—the lonely song-bird of these solitudes—poured out his melody to the night.

The camp had been formed under the shade of a clump of terebinth and acacias close to a spring of clear water which made the grass around it a vivid green, in pleasant contrast to the dry, withered herbage in the open.

The men had dug out tree roots for fuel, and a red fire glowed a few yards away from Spence's tent.

A group of silent figures sat round the fire. Now and then a low murmur of talk sounded for a minute and then died away again. A slight breeze, cool and keen, rustled in the trees overhead. Save for that, and the occasional movement of one of the hobbled horses, no sound broke the stillness of the glorious night.

It was here, so Spence thought, that the Lord must have walked with His disciples on the journey between Jerusalem and Nazareth.

[344] On such a night as this the little group may have sat in the vale of El Makhna in quiet talk at supper-time.

The same stars looked down on him as they did on those others two thousand years ago. How real and true it all seemed here! How much easier it was to realise and believe than in Chancery Lane!

Why did men live in cities?

Was it not better far for the soul's health to be here alone with God?

Here, and in such places as these, God spoke clear and loud to the hearts of men. He shuddered as the thought of his own lack of faith came back to him.

In rapid review he saw the recent time of his hopelessness and shame. How utterly he had fallen to pieces! It was difficult to understand the pit into which he was falling so easily when Basil had come to him.

Now, the love of God ran in his veins like fire, every sight and sound spoke to him of the Christus Consolator.

It was more than mere cold belief, a love or personal devotion to Christ welled up in him. The figure of the Man of Sorrows was very near him—there was a great fiery cross of stars in the sky above him.

He entered the little tent to pray. He prayed humbly that it might be even thus until the end. He prayed that this new and sweet communion with his Master might never fade or lessen till the glorious daylight of Death dawned and this sojourning far from home was over.

And, in the name of all the unknown millions whom he was come to this far land to aid, he prayed for success, for the Truth to be made manifest, and for a happy issue out of all these afflictions.

"And this we beg for Jesus Christ, His sake."

Then much refreshed and comforted he emerged once more into the serene beauty of the night.

[345] He lit his pipe and sat there, quietly smoking. Presently Ibrahim the Egyptian began to croon a low song, one of the Egyptian songs that soldiers sing round the camp-fires.

158

The man had done his term of compulsory service in the past, and perhaps this sudden transition from the comfortable quarters in Jerusalem to the old life of camp-fire and plein air had its way with him and opened the springs of memory.

This is part of what he sang in a thin, sad voice:

Born in Galiub, since my birth, many times have I seen the Nile's waters overflow our fields.

And I had a neighbour, Sheikh Abdehei, whose daughter's face was known only to me:

Nothing could be compared to the beauty and tenderness of Fatmé.

Her eyes were as big as coffee cups, and her body was firm with the vigour of youth.

We had one heart, and were free from jealousies, ready to be united.

But Allah curse the military inspector who bound my two hands,

For, together with many more, we were marched off to the camp.

I was poor and had to serve, nothing could soften the inspector's heart.

The drums and the trumpets daily soon made me forget my cottage and the well-wheel on the Nile.

The long-drawn-out notes vibrated mournfully in the night air.

Sadly the singer put his hand to one side of his head, bending as if he were wailing.

The quaint, imaginative song-story throbbed through many phases and incidents, and every now and again the motionless figures round the red embers wailed in sympathy.

At last came the end, a happy climax, no less loved by these simple children of the desert than by the European novel reader.

... So that I was in the hospital and had become most seriously ill.

But swifter than the gazelle, the light of my life came near the hospital.

[346]

And called in at the window, "Ibrahim! my eye! my heart!"

And full of joy I carried her about the camp, and presented her to all my superiors, leaving out none, from the colonel down to the sergeant.

I received my dismissal, to return to Galiub and to marry.

Old Abdehei was awaiting us, to bless us. God be praised!

So sang Ibrahim, the converted Christian, the Moslem songs of his youth; for here, in El Makhna, the plain of Shechem, there were no missionaries with their cold reproof and little hymns in simple couplets.

The fire died away, and they slept until dawn flooded the plain.

When, on the next day, the sun was waning, though still high in the western heavens, the travellers came within view of the ancient city of Nabulûs.

There was a great tumult of excitement in Spence's pulses as he saw the city, radiant in the long afternoon lights, and far away.

Here, in the confines of this distant glittering town, lay the last link in the terrible secret which he was to solve.

On either side the purple slopes of the mountains made a mighty frame to the terraced houses below. Ebal and Gerizim kept solemn watch and ward over the city.

The sun was just sinking as they rode into the suburbs. It was a lovely, placid evening.

The abundant cascades of water, which flow from great fissures in the mountain and make this Turkish town the jewel of the East, glittered in the light.

Below them the broad, still reservoirs lay like plates of gold.

159

They rode through luxuriant groves of olives, figs, and vines, wonderfully grateful and refreshing to the eye after the burnt brown herbage of the plain, towards the regular camping-ground where all travellers lay.

In the cool of the evening Spence and Ibrahim rode through the teeming streets to the Governor's house.

[347] It was a city of fanatics, so the Englishman had heard, and during the great Moslem festivals the members of the various, and rather extensive, missionary establishments were in constant danger. But as the two men rode among the wild armed men who sat in the bazaars or pushed along the narrow streets they were not in any way molested.

After a ceremonious introduction and the delivery of the letter from the Governor of Jerusalem, Spence made known his business over the coffee and cigarettes which were brought immediately on his arrival.

The Governor was a placid, pleasant-mannered man, very ready to give his visitor any help he could.

It was represented to him that the man Ionides, who had but lately settled in the suburbs, was in the possession of some important secrets affecting the welfare of many wealthy residents in Jerusalem. These, it was hinted, were of a private nature, but in all probability great pressure would have to be put upon the Greek in order to receive any satisfactory confession.

The conversation, which was carried on in French, ended in an eminently satisfactory way.

"Monsieur will understand," said the Governor, "that I make no inquiry into the nature of the information monsieur wishes to obtain. I may or may not have my ideas upon that subject. The Greek was, I understand, intimately connected with the recent discoveries in Jerusalem. Let that pass. It is none of my business. Here I am a good Moslem, Allah be praised! it is a necessity of my official position."

He laughed cynically, clapped his hands for a new brass vessel of creaming coffee and continued:

"A political necessity, Monsieur, as a man of the world, will quite understand me. I have been in London, at the Embassy, and I myself am free from foolish [348] prejudices. I am not Moslem in heart nor am I Christian—some coffee, Monsieur?—yes! Monsieur also is a man of the world!"

Spence, sitting cross-legged opposite his host, had smiled an answering cynical smile at these words. He shrugged his shoulders and threw out his hands. Everything depended upon making a good impression upon this local autocrat.

"Eh bien, monsieur avait raison-même—that, I repeat, is not my affair. But this letter from my brother of Jerusalem makes me of anxiety to serve your interests. And, moreover, the man is a Greek, of no great importance—we are not fond of the Greeks, we Turks! Now it is most probable that the man will not speak without persuasion. Moreover, that persuasion were better officially applied. To assist monsieur, I shall send Tewfik Pasha, my nephew, and captain commandant of the northern fort, with half a dozen men. If this dog will not talk they will know how to make him. I suppose you have no scruples as to any means they may employ? There are foolish prejudices among the Western people."

Spence took his decision very quickly. He was a man who had been on many battle-fields, knew the grimness of life in many lands. If torture were necessary, then it must be so. The man deserved it, the end was great if the means were evil. It must be remembered that Spence was a man to whom the very loftiest and highest Christian ideals had not yet been made manifest. There are degrees in the struggle for saintliness; the journalist was but a postulant.

He saw these questions of conduct roughly, crudely. His conscience animated his deeds, but it was a conscience as yet ungrown. And indeed there are many instruments in an orchestra, all tuneful perhaps to the conductor's beat, which they obey and understand, yet [349] not all of equal eminence or beauty in the great scheme of the concert.

The violin soars into great mysteries of emotion, calling high "in the deep-domed empyrean." The flutes whisper a chorus to the great story of their comrade. Yet, though the plangent sounding of the kettle-drums, the single beat of the barbaric cymbals are in one note and unfrequent, yet these minor messages go to swell the great tone-symphony and make it perfect in the serene beauty of something directed and ordained.

"Sir," said the journalist, "the man must be made to speak. The methods are indifferent to me."

"Oh, that can be done; we have a way," said the Governor.

He shifted a little among his cushions. A certain dryness came into his voice as he resumed:

"Monsieur, however, as a man of the world, will understand, no doubt, that when a private individual finds it necessary to invoke the powers of law it is a vast undertaking to move so ponderous a machine?... also it is a privilege? It is not, of course, a personal matter—ça m'est égal. But there are certain unavoidable and indeed quite necessary expenses which must be satisfied."

Spence well understood the polite humbug of all this. He knew that in the East one buys justice—or injustice—as one can afford it. As the correspondent of that great paper over which Ommaney presided, he had always been able to spend money like water when it had been necessary. He had those powers now. There was nothing unusual to him in the situation, nor did he hesitate.

"Your Excellency," he said, "speaks with great truth upon these points. It is ever from a man of your Excellency's penetration that one hears those dicta which [350] govern affairs. I have a certain object in view, and I realise that to obtain it there are certain necessary formalities to be gone through. I have with me letters of credit upon the bank of Lelain Delaunay et Cie., of Jaffa, Jerusalem, and Athens."

"A sound, estimable house," said the Governor, with a very pleased smile.

"It but then remains," said Spence, "to confer with the secretary of your Excellency as to the sum which is necessary to pay for the legal expenses of the inquiry."

"You speak most sensibly," said the Turk. "In the morning I will send the captain commandant and the soldiers to the encampment. My secretary shall accompany them. Then, Monsieur, when the little preliminaries are arranged, you will be free to start for the farm of this dog Ionides. It is not more than four miles from your camp, and my nephew will guide you there. May Allah prosper your undertaking."

"—And have you in His care," replied Spence. "I will now have the honour to wish your Excellency undisturbed rest."

He rose and bowed. The Turkish gentleman rose also and shook hands in genial European fashion.

"Monsieur," he said, with an expansive smile, "Monsieur is without doubt a thorough man of the world."

That night, in the suburbs of the city, sweet and fragrant as the olive groves and fig trees were, cool and fresh as the night wind was, Spence slept but little.

He could hear the prowling dogs of the streets baying the Eastern moon, the owls hooted in the trees, but it was not these distant sounds, all mellowed by the distance,

161

which drove rest and sleep away. It was the imminent sense of the great issues of the morrow, a wild and fierce excitement which forbade sleep or rest and filled his veins with fire.

[351] He could not quite realise what awful things hung upon the event of the coming day. He knew that his brain could not contain the whole terror and vastness of the thought.

Indeed, he felt that no brain could adequately realise the importance of it all.

Yet even that partial realisation of which he was capable was enough to drive all peace away, the live-long night, to leave him nothing but the plangent, burning thought.

He was very glad when the cool, hopeful dawn came.

The nightmare of vigil was gone. Action was at hand. He prayed in the morning air.

Presently, from the city gates, he saw a little cavalcade drawing near, twelve soldiers on wiry Damascene horses, an officer, with the Governor's secretary riding by his side.

Those preliminaries of a signed draft upon the bank, which cupidity and the occasion demanded, were soon over.

These twelve soldiers and their commandant cost him two hundred pounds "English"; but that was nothing.

If his own words were ineffective, then the cord and wedge must do the rest. It had to be paid for.

The world was waiting.

On through the olive groves and the vines laden with purple. On, over the little stone-bridged cascades and streams—sweet gifts of lordly Ebal—round the eastern wall of the town, crumbling stone where the mailed lizards were sleeping in the sun; on to the low roofs and vivid trees where the Greek traitor had made his home!

At length the red road opened before them on to a burnt plain which was the edge and brim of the farm.

It lay direct and patent to the view, the place of the great secret.

[352] Ionides was waiting for them, under a light verandah which ran round the house, before they reached the building.

He had seen them coming over the plain.

A little elderly olive-skinned man, with restless eyes the colour of sherry, bowed and bent before them with terrified inquiry in every gesture.

His gaze flickered over the arms and shabby uniforms of the soldiers with hate and fear in it mingled with a piteous cringing. It was the look which the sad Greek boatmen on the shores of the Bosphorus wear all their lives.

Then he saw Spence and recognised him as the Englishman who had been the friend of Hands, and was at the meetings of the Conference.

The sight of the journalist seemed to affect him like a sudden blow. The fear and uneasiness he had shown at the first sight of the Turkish soldiers were intensified a thousand-fold.

The man seemed to shrink and collapse. His face became ashen grey, his lips parched suddenly, for his tongue began to curl round them in order to moisten their rigidity.

With a great effort he forced himself to speak in English first, fluent enough but elementary, and then in a rush of French, the language of all Europe, and one with which the cosmopolitan Greek is ever at home.

The captain gave an order. His men dismounted and tied up the horses.

162

Then, taking the conduct of the affair into his own hands at once, he spoke to Ionides with a snarling contempt and brutality that he would hardly have used to a strolling street dog.

"The English gentleman has come to ask you some questions, dog. See to it that you give a true answer [353] and speedy. For, if not, there are many ways to make you. I have the warrant of his Excellency the Governor to do as I please with you and yours."

The Greek made an inarticulate noise. He raised one long-fingered, delicate hand to his throat.

Spence, as he watched, could not help a feeling of pity. The whole attitude of the man was inexpressibly painful in its sheer terror.

His face had become a white wedge of fear.

The officer spoke again.

"You will take the English pasha into a private room," he said sternly, "where he will ask you all he wishes. I shall post two of my men at the door. Take heed that they do not have to summon me. And meanwhile bring out food and entertainment for me and my soldiers."

He clapped his hands and the women of the house, who were peering round the end of the verandah, ran to bring pilaff and tobacco.

Spence, with two soldiers, closely following the swaying, tottering figure of Ionides, went into a cool chamber opening on to the little central courtyard round which the house was built.

It was a bare room, with a low bench or ottoman here and there.

But, on the walls, oddly incongruous in such a setting, were some framed photographs. Hands, in a white linen suit and a wide Panama hat, was there; there was a photograph of the museum at Jerusalem, and a picture cut from an English illustrated paper of the Society's great excavations at Tell Sandahannah.

It was odd, Spence thought gravely, that the man cared to keep these records of his life in Jerusalem, crowned as it was with such an act of treachery.

He sat down on the ottoman. The Greek stood before him, cowering against the wall.

[354] It was a little difficult to know how he should begin; what was the best method to ensure a full confession.

He lit a cigarette to help his thoughts.

"What did Sir Robert Llwellyn give you?—how much?" he said suddenly.

Again the look of ashen fear came over the Greek's face. He struggled with it before he spoke.

"I am sorry that your meaning is not plain to me, sir. I do not know of whom you speak."

"I speak of him whom you served secretly. It was with your aid that the 'new' tomb was found. But before it was found you and Sir Robert Llwellyn were at work there. I have come to obtain from you a detailed confession of how the thing was done, who cut the inscription?—I must know everything. If not, I tell you with perfect truth, your life is not safe. The Governor has sent men with me and you will be made to speak."

He spoke with a deep menace in his tone, and at the same time drew his revolver from the hip pocket of his riding-breeches and held it on his knee.

He had begun to realise the awful nature of this man's deed more and more poignantly in his presence. True, he was the tool of greater intelligences, and his guilt was not so heavy as theirs. Nevertheless, the Greek was no fool, he had something of an education, he had not done this thing blindly.

163

The man crouched against the wall, desperate and hopeless.

One of the soldiers outside the door moved, and his sabre clanked.

The sound was decisive. With a broken, husky voice Ionides began his miserable confession.

How simple it was! Wild astonishment at the ease with which the whole thing had been done filled the journalist's brain.

[355] The tomb, already known to the Greek, the slow carving of the inscription at dead of night by Llwellyn, the new coating of hamra sealing up the inner chamber.

And yet, so skilfully had the forgeries been committed, chance had so aided the forgers, and their secret had been so well preserved that the whole world of experts was deceived.

In the overpowering relief of the confession Spence was but little interested in the details, but at length they were duly set down and signed by the Greek in the presence of the officer.

By midnight the journalist was far away on the road to Jerusalem.

[356]
CHAPTER VII

THE LAST MEETING

In Sir Robert Llwellyn's flat in Bond Street the electric bell suddenly rang, a shrill tinkle in the silence.

Schuabe, who sat by the window, looked up with a strained, white face.

Avoiding his glance, Llwellyn rose and went out into the passage. The latch of the door clicked, there was a murmur of voices, and Llwellyn returned, following a third person.

Schuabe gave a scarcely perceptible shudder as this man entered.

The man was a thick-set person of medium height, clean shaven. He was dressed in a frock-coat and carried a silk hat, neither new nor smart, yet not seedy nor showing any evidences of poverty. The man's face was one to inspire a sensitive or alert person with a sudden disgust and terror for which a name can hardly be found. It was an utterly abominable and black soul that looked out of the still rather bilious eyes.

The eyes were much older than the rest of the face. They were full of a cold and deliberate cruelty and, worse even than this, such a hideous knowledge of unmentionable crime was there! The lips made one thin, wicked curve which hardly varied in direction, for this man could not smile.

He belonged to a certain horrible gang who infest the West End of London, bringing terror and ruin to all [357] they meet. These people haunt the bars and music halls of the "pleasure" part of London.

It were better for a man that he had never been born—a thousand times better—than that he should go among these men. Black shame and horrors worse than death they bring with both hands to the bitter fools who lightly meet them unknowing what they are.

Constantine Schuabe, in the moment when he saw this man—knowing well who and what he was—knew the bitterest moment of his life.

Vast criminal that he was himself, mighty in his evil brain, ... he was pure; certain infamies were not his.... He spat into his handkerchief with an awful physical disgust.

"This is my friend, Nunc Wallace," said Llwellyn, pale and trembling.

The man looked keenly at his two hosts. Then he sat down in a chair.

164

"Well, gentlemen," he said in correct English, but with a curious lack of timbre, of life and feeling in his voice—he spoke as one might think a corpse would speak—"I'm sorry to say that it's all off. It simply can't be done at any price. Even I myself, 'King of the boys' as they call me, confess myself beaten."

Schuabe gave a sudden start, almost of relief it seemed.

Llwellyn cleared his throat once or twice before he could speak. When the words came at length there was a nauseous eagerness in them.

"Why not, Wallace? Surely you and your friends—it must be something very hard that you can't manage."

The words jostled each other in their rapid utterance.

"Give me a drink, Sir Robert, and I'll tell you the reason," said the man.

Then, with an inexpressible assumption of confidence and an identity of interests, which galled and stung the [358] two wretched men till they could hardly bear the torture of it, he began:

"You see, it's like this; we can generally calculate on 'putting a man through it' if he's anything to do with racing on the Turf. I've seen a man's face kicked liver colour, and no one knew who did it. But this parson was a more difficult thing altogether. Then it has been very much complicated by the fact of his friend coming back.

"The idea was to get into the chambers on the evening of this Spence's arrival and put them both through it. In fact, we'd arranged everything fairly well. But two nights ago, as I was in the American bar, at the Horsecloth, a man touched me on the arm. It was Detective Inspector Melton. He knows everything. 'Nunc,' he said, 'sit down at one of these little tables and have a drink. I want to say a few words to you.' Well, of course I had to. He knows every one of the boys.

"'Now, look here,' he said straight out. 'Some of your crowd have been watching the Rev. Basil Gortre of Lincoln's Inn; also, you've had a man at Charing Cross waiting for the continental express. Now, I've nothing against you yet, but I'll just tell you this. The people behind you aren't any guarantee for you. It's not as you think. This is a big thing. I'll tell you something more. This Mr. Gortre and this Mr. Spence you're waiting for are guarded night and day by order of the Home Secretary. It's an international affair. You can no more touch them than you can touch the Prince of Wales. Is that clear? If it's not, then you'll come with me at once on suspicion. I can put my finger on Bunny Watson'— he's my organising pal, gentlemen—'inside of an hour.'"

He stopped at last, taking another drink with a shaking [359] hand, watching the other two with horribly observing eyes.

His cleverness had at once shown him that he had stumbled into something far more dangerous than any ordinary incident of his horrid trade. A million pounds would not have made him touch the "business" now. He had come to say this to his employers now.

The unhappy men became aware that the man was looking at them both with a new expression. There was wonder in his cold eyes now, and a sort of fear also. When Llwellyn had first sought him with black and infamous proposals, there had been none of this. That had seemed ordinary enough to him, the reason he did not inquire or seek to know.

But now there was inquiry in his eyes.

Both Schuabe and Llwellyn saw it, knew the cause, and shuddered.

There was a tense silence, and then the creature spoke again. There was a loathsome confidential note in his voice.

165

"Now, gentlemen," he said, "you've already paid me well for any little kindness I may have been able to try to do for you. I suppose, now that the little job is 'off,' I shall not get the rest of the sum agreed upon?"

Schuabe, without speaking, made a sign to Llwellyn. The big man got up, went to a little nest of mahogany drawers which stood on his writing-table, and opening one of them, took from it a bundle of notes.

He gave them to the assassin. "There, Nunc," he said; "no doubt you've done all you could. You won't find us ungrateful. But I want to ask you a few questions."

The man took the notes, counted them deliberately, and then looked up with a gleam of satisfied greed [360] passing over his face—the gleam of a pale sunbeam in hell.

"Ask anything you like, sir," he said; "I'll give you any help I can."

Already there was a ring almost of patronage in his voice. The word "help" was slightly emphasised.

"This inspector, who is he exactly? I mean, is he an important person?"

"He is the man who has charge of all the big things. He goes abroad when one of the big city men bunk to South America. He generally works straight from the Home Office; he's the Government man. To tell the truth, I was surprised to meet him in the Horsecloth. One of the others generally goes there. When he began to talk, I knew that there was something important, more than usual."

"He definitely said that he knew your—backers?"

"Yes, he did; and what's more, gentlemen, he seemed to know too much altogether about the business. I don't pretend to understand it. I don't know why a young parson and a press reporter are being looked after by Government as if they were continental sovereigns and the Anarchists were trying to get at them—no more than I know why two such gentlemen as you are wanting two smaller men put through it. But all's well that ends well. I'm satisfied enough, and I'm extremely glad that I got this notice in time to stop it off. But whatever you do, gentlemen, give up any idea of doing those two any harm. You couldn't do it—couldn't get near them. Give it up, gentlemen. Somehow or other, they know all about it. Be careful. Now I'm off. Good-day, gentlemen. Look after yourselves. I fear there is trouble brewing somewhere, though it won't come through me. They can't prove anything on our side."

[361] He went slowly out of the room, back into the darkness of the pit whence he came, to the dark which mercifully hides such as he from the gaze of dwellers under the heavens.

Only the police of London know all about these men, and their imaginations are not, perhaps, strong enough to let the horror of contact remain with them.

When he had gone, Llwellyn sank heavily into a chair. He covered his face with his hands and moaned.

"Oh, fool that I was to try anything of the sort!" hissed Schuabe. "I might have known!"

"What is the state of things, really, do you suppose?" said Llwellyn.

"Imminent with doom for us!" Schuabe answered in a deep and melancholy voice. "It is all clear to me now. Your woman was set on to you by these men from the first. They are clever men. Michael Manichoe is behind them all. She got the story. Spence has been sent to verify it. He has got everything from Ionides. The Government has been told. These things have been going on during the last few hours. Spence has cabled something of his news, perhaps not all. He will be back to-day, this afternoon. He will have left Paris by now, and almost be nearing Amiens. In that train, Llwellyn, lies our

166

death-warrant. Nothing can stop it. They will send the news all over the world to-night. It will be announced in London by dinner-time, probably."

Llwellyn groaned again. In this supreme hour of torture the sensualist was nearer collapse than the ascetic. His life told heavily. He looked up. His face was green-grey save where, here and there, his fingers had pressed into, and left red marks upon, the cheeks, which had lost their firmness and begun to be pendulous and flabby.

[362] "What do you think must be the end?" he said.

"The end is here," said Schuabe. "What matters the form or manner of it? They may bring in a bill and hang us, they will certainly give us penal servitude for life, but probably we shall be torn in pieces by the mob. There is only one thing left."

He made an expressive gesture. Llwellyn shuddered.

"All is not necessarily at an end," he said. "I shall make a last effort to get away. I have still got the clergyman's clothes I wore when I went to Jerusalem. There will be time to get out of London before this evening."

"All over the continent and America you would be known. There is no getting away nowadays. As for me, I shall go down to my place in Manchester by the mid-day train. There is just time to catch it. And there I shall die before they can come to me."

He got up and strode away out of the flat with a set, stern face. Never a passing look did he give to the man he had enriched and damned for ever. Never a gesture of farewell.

Already he was as one in the grave. Llwellyn, left to himself in the silent, richly furnished flat, fell into hysterical sobbing.

His big body shook with the vehemence of his unnatural terror. His moans and cries were utterly without dignity or pathos. He was filled with the immense self-pity of the sensualist.

It is the added torture which comes to the evil-liver.

In the hour of blackness, every moment of physical gratification or sin adds its weight to the terrible burden which must be borne.

This man felt that he was lost. Perhaps all hope was not quite dead. He called on all his courage to make a last attempt at escape.

[363] He must leave this place at once. He would go first to his house in Upper Berkeley Street, Lady Llwellyn's house! His wife.

Something strange and long forgotten moved within him at that word. What might not his life have been by her side, a life lived in open honour! What had he done with it all? His great name, his fame, were built up slowly by his long and brilliant work. Yet all the time that fair edifice was being undermined by secret workers. The lusts of the flesh were deep below the structure, their hammers were always slowly tapping—and now it was all over.

He drove up to his own door, unlocked it, and went up the stairs to his own rooms.

Though he had not been near them for weeks, he saw—with how keen a pang of regret—that they were swept and tidy, ready for his coming at any time.

He rang the bell.

[364]
CHAPTER VIII

DEATH COMING WITH ONE GRACE

The door opened softly. A long beam of late winter sunshine which had been pouring in at the opposite window and striking the door with its projection of golden powder suddenly framed, played over, and lighted up the figure of Lady Llwellyn.

Sir Robert stood in the middle of the pleasant room and looked at her.

The sunlight showed up the grey pallor of her face, the lines of sorrow and resignation, the faded hair, the thin and bony hands.

"Kate," he said in a weak voice.

It was the first time he had called her by her name for many years.

The tired face lit up with a swift and divine tenderness.

She made a step forward into the room.

He was swaying a little, giddy, it seemed.

She looked him full in the face and saw things there which she had never seen before. A great horror was upon him, a frightful awakening from the long, sensual sloth of his life.

Moving, working, in that great countenance, generally so impassive, uninfluenced by any emotion—at least to her long watchings—except by a moody irritation, she saw Doom, Fate, the Call of the Eumenides.

It came to the poor woman in a sudden wave of illuminating certainty.

[365] She knew the end had come.

And yet, strangely enough, she felt nothing but a quickening of the pulses, a swift embracing pity which was almost a joy in its breaking away of barriers.

If the end were here, it should be together—at last together.

For she loved this cruel, sinning man, this lover of light loves, this man of purple, fine linen, and the sparkling deadly wines of life.

"Kate!"

He said it once more.

Her manner changed. Shrinking, timidity, fear, fled for ever. In her overpowering rush of protecting love all the diffidences of temperament, all the bars which he had forced her to build around her instincts, were swept utterly away.

She went quickly up to him, folded him in her arms.

"Robert!" she said, "poor boy, the end has come to it all. I knew it must come some day. Well, we have not been happy. I wonder if you have been happy? No, I don't think so. But now, Robert, you have me to comfort you with my love once more, my poor Robert, once more, as in the old, simple days when we were young."

She led him to a couch.

He trembled violently. His decision of movement seemed to have gone. His purpose of flight had for the moment become obscure.

And now, into this man's heart came a remorse and regret so awful, a realisation so sudden and strong, so instinct with a pain for which there is no name, that everything before his eyes turned to burning fire.

The flames of his agony burnt up the veils which had for so long obscured the truth. They shrivelled and vanished.

[366] Too late, too late, he knew what he had lost.

The last agony wrenched his brain round again to another and more terrible contemplation.

His thoughts were in other and outside hands, which pulled his brain from one scene to another as a man moves the eye of the camera obscura to different fields of view.

Incredible as it may seem, for the first time Llwellyn realised what he had done—realised, that is, in its entirety, the whole horror and consequences of that action of his which was to kill him now.

He had not been able to see the magnitude and extent of his crime before—either at the time when it was proposed to him, except at the first moment of speech, or after its committal.

His brain and temperament had been wrapped round in the hideous fact of sensuality, which deadens and destroys sensation.

And now, with his wife's thin arms round him, her withered cheek pressed to his, her words of glad love, a martyr's swan song in his ears, he saw, knew, and understood.

Through the terror of his thoughts her words began to penetrate.

"I know, Robert—husband, I know. The end is here. But what has happened? Tell me everything, that I may comfort you the more. Tell me, Robert, for the dear Christ's sake!"

At those words the man stiffened. "For the dear Christ's sake!"

Suddenly, in the disorder and tumult of his tortured brain, came, quite foolishly and inconsequently, a quotation from an old French romance—full of satire and the keen cynicism of a period—which he had been reading:

[367] "'Tres volontiers,' repartit le démon.
'Vous aimez les tableaux changeans;
Je veux vous contenter.'"

Yes! the devil who was torturing him now had shown him many moving aspects of life. Les tableaux changeans!

But now, at last, here was the worst moment of all.

"For the dear Christ's sake, tell me, Robert!"

How could he tell this?

This was his last moment of peace, his last chance of any help or hope.

He had begun to cling to her, to mingle foolish tears with hers—the while his fired brain ranged all the halls of agony.

For if he told her—this gentle Christian lady, to whom he had been so unkind—then she would never touch him more.

The last hours—there was but little time remaining—would be alone. Alone!

This new revelation that her love was still his, wonder of mysteries! this came at the last moments to aid him.

A last grace before the running waters closed over him. Was he to give this up?

The thought of flight lay like a wounded bird in his brain. It crept about it like some paralysed thing. Not yet dead, but inactive. Though he knew how terribly the moments called to him, yet he could not act.

The myriad agonies he was enduring now, agonies so various and great that he knew Hell had none greater, these, even these were alleviated by the wonder of his wife's love.

The terrible remorse that was knocking at his heart could not undo that.

He clung to her.

"Tell me all about it, Robert. I will forgive you, [368] whatever you have done. I have long ago forgiven everything in my heart. There are only the words to say."

She rested her worn, tired head on his shoulder. The sunbeams gave it a glory.

Again the man must suffer a terrible agony. She had asked him to tell her all his trouble in a voice full of gentle pleading.

169

Whose voice did her voice recall to him; what fatal hour? A coarser voice, a richer voice, trembling, so he had thought, with love for him.

"Tell me everything, Bob!" It was Gertrude's voice.

The day of his undoing! The day when his horrid secret was wrested from him by the levers of his own passions. The day which had brought him to this. Finis coronat opus!

But the agony within him was the agony of contrast.

The great fires round his soul had burnt his lust away. There was no more regret or longing for the evil past. All the joys of a sensual life seemed as if they had never been. Now, the pain was the pain of a man, not who knows the worst too soon, but who knows the best too late!

A vivid picture, a succession of thoughts following each other with such kinetic swiftness that they became welded in one single picture, as one may see a vast landscape of wood and torrent, champaign and forest, in one flash of the storm sword, came to him now.

And, at the last, he saw himself seated at a great table in a noble room. There were soft lights. Silver and flowers were there. Round the board sat many men and women. On their faces was the calm triumph of those who had succeeded in a fine battle, won an intellectual strife. The faces were calm, powerful, serene. They were the salt of society. He saw his own face in [369] a little mirror set among the flowers. His face was even as their faces. Self-reverence had dignified it, self-knowledge and self-control had turned the lines to kindly marble, defiant of time.

At the other end of the table sat a calm and gracious lady, richly dressed in some glowing sombre stuff. She was the grave and loving matron who slept by his side.

Full of honour, full of the glorious satisfaction of a great work well done, a life lived well; hand in hand, a noble and notable pair, they were making their fine progress together.

"I am waiting, Robert, dear!"

Then he knew that he must speak. In rapid words, which seemed to come from a vast distance, he confessed it all.

He told her how Schuabe had tempted him with a vast fortune, how he was already in his power when the temptation had come. How his evil desires had so gripped him, his life of sin had become like air itself to him.

He told of the secret visit to Palestine and the forgery which had stirred the world.

As he spoke, he felt, in some subtle way, that the life and warmth were dying out of the arms which were round him.

The electric current of devotion which had been flowing from this lady seemed to flicker and die away.

The awful story was ended at last.

Then with a face in which the horror came out in waves, inexpressibly terrible to see, with each beat of the pulses a wave of unutterable horror, she slowly rose.

Her arms fell heavily to her sides, all her motions became automatic, jerky.

Slowly, slowly, she turned.

Her feet made no noise as she moved over the room. [370] Her garments did not rustle. But she walked, not as an elderly woman, but a very old woman.

The door clicked softly. He was left alone in the comfortable room.

Alone.

170

He stood up, tottered a few steps in the direction she had gone, and then, with a resounding crash which shook the furniture in a succession of quick rattles, his great form fell prone upon the floor.

He lay there, head downwards, with the sunshine pouring on him, still and without any reactionary movement.

The afternoon was begun. London was as it had been for days. The uneasiness and unrest which were now become the common incubus of its inhabitants neither grew nor lessened.

The afternoon papers were merely repetitions of former days. Great financial houses were tottering, rumours of wars were growing every hour, no country was at rest, no colony secure. Over the world lawlessness and rapine were holding horrid revel.

But, and long afterwards, this fact was noticed and commented on by the historians: on this especial winter's afternoon there was no ultra-alarming shock, speaking comparatively, to the general state of things.

In the pale winter sunshine men moved heavily about their business, the common burden was shared by all, but there was no loud trumpet note during those hours.

About four o'clock some carriages drove to Downing Street. In one sat Sir Michael Manichoe, Father Ripon, Harold Spence, and Basil Gortre.

In another was the English Consul at Jerusalem, who had arrived with Spence from the Holy City, Dr. Schmöulder from Berlin, and the Duke of Suffolk.

[371] The carriages stopped at the house of the Prime Minister and the party entered.

Nothing occurred, visibly, for an hour, though urgent messages were passing over the telephone wires.

In an hour's time a cab came driving furiously down the Embankment, round by the new Scotland Yard and St. Stephen's Club, into Parliament Street.

The cab contained the Editor of the Times. Following his arrival, in a few seconds, a number of other cabs drove up, all at a fast pace. Each one contained a prominent journalist. Ommaney was among the first to arrive, and Folliott Farmer was with him.

It was nearly an hour when these people left Downing Street, all with very grave faces.

A few minutes after their departure Sir Michael and his party came out, accompanied by several ministers, including the Home Secretary and the Chief Commissioner of Police.

Though the distance to Scotland Yard is only a few hundred yards, the latter gentleman jumped into a passing hansom and was driven rapidly to his office.

This brings the time up to about six o'clock.

It was quite dark in Sir Robert's room. A faint yellow flicker came through the window, which was not curtained, from a gas lamp in the street. A dull and distant murmur from the Edgeware Road could be dimly heard, otherwise the room was quite silent.

Llwellyn did not lie where he had fallen. His swoon had lasted long and no one had come to succour him. But the end was not just yet. The merciful oblivion of passing from a swoon into death was denied him.

He had come to his senses late in the afternoon, about the time that the large party of people had emerged on [372] foot and in carriages from the narrow cul-de-sac of Downing Street.

He had felt very cold, an icy-cold. There had come a terrible moment. The physical sensation was swamped and forgotten in one frightful flash of realisation. He was alone, the end was at hand.

Alone.

Instinctively he had tried to rise. He was lying face downwards at the return of sensation. His legs would not answer the message of his brain when he tried to move them so that he might rise. They lay like long dead cylinders behind him. He was able to drag himself very slowly, for a yard or two, until he reached an ottoman. He could not lift the vast weight of his body into the seat. It was utterly beyond his strength. He propped his trunk against the seat. It was all he was able to accomplish. Icy-cold sweat ran down his cheeks at the exertion. After he had finished moving he found that all strength had left him.

He was paralysed from the waist downwards. The rest of his body was too weak to move him.

Only his brain was working with a terrible activity, there alone in the chill dark.

There came into his molten brain the impulse to pray. Deep down in every human heart that impulse lies.

It is a seed planted there by God that it may grow into the tree of salvation.

The effort was sub-conscious. Almost simultaneously with it came the awful remembrance of what he had done.

A name danced in letters of flame in his brain—JUDAS.

He looked round for some means to end this unbearable torture. He could see nothing, the room was very cold and dark, but he knew there was a case of razors on a table by the window.

[373] When he tried to move he found that he could not. The paralysis was growing upwards.

Then this was to be the end?

A momentary flood of relief came over him. His blood seemed warm again.

But the sensation died rapidly away, the physical and mental glow alike.

He remembered those cases, frequent enough, when the whole body loses the power of movement, but the brain survives, active, alive, helpless.

And all the sweat which the physical glow had induced turned to little icicles all over his body, even as the thought froze in his brain.

An hour went by.

Alone in the dark.

His tongue was parched and dry. A sudden wonder came to him—could he speak still?

Without realising what word he used as a test he spoke.

"Kate."

A gaunt whisper in the silence.

Silence! How silent it was! Yet no, he could hear the distant rumbling of the traffic. He became suddenly conscious of it. Surely it was very loud?

It must be this physical change which was creeping over him. His head was swimming, disordered.

Yet it seemed strangely loud.

And louder, as he began to listen intently. He could not move his head to catch the sound more clearly, but he was beginning to hear it well enough now.

No traffic ever sounded quite like that. It was like an advancing tide, thundering, as a horse gallops, over flat, level sands.

A great sea rushing towards—towards what?

Then he knew what that sound was.

[374] At last he knew.

He could hear the individual shouts that made up the enormous mass of menacing sound.

The nation was coming to take its revenge upon its betrayer.

Mob law!

They had found him out. It was as Schuabe had said—the great conspiracy was at an end. The stunning truth was out, flying round the world with its glad message.

Yet, though once more the dishonoured Cross gleamed as the one solace in the hearts of men whose faith had been weak, though at that moment the glad news was racing round the world, yet the evil was not over.

The Prince of the Powers of the air had reigned too long. Not lightly was he to relinquish his sceptre and dominion.

They were in the erst-while quiet street below. The whole space was packed with the roaring multitude. The cries and curses came up to him in one roaring volume of sound, sounds that one looking over the brink of the pit of hell might hear.

A heavy blow upon the stout door of the old well-built house shook the walls where the palsied Judas lay impotent.

Another crash! The room was much lighter now, the crowd below had lights with them.

Crash.

The door opened silently. Lady Llwellyn came swiftly into the room.

She wore a long white robe. Her face was lighted as if a lamp shone behind it.

In her hand was the great crucifix which was wont to hang above her bed.

When Christ died and bade the dying thief ascend [375] with him to Paradise, can we say that His silence condemned the other?

Her face was all aglow with love.

"Robert!" she said. Her voice was like the voice of an angel.

Her arms are round him, her kisses press upon him, the great crucifix is lifted to his dying eyes.

A great thunder on the stairs, furious voices, the tide rising higher, higher.

Death.

[376]
CHAPTER IX

AT WALKTOWN AGAIN

The news came to Walktown, the final confirmation of what had been so long suspected, in a short telegram from Basil, dispatched immediately he had left Downing Street.

Mr. Byars and Helena had been kept well acquainted with every step in the progress of the investigation.

Ever since Gortre had left Walktown, after his holiday visit, his suspicions had been ringing in the vicar's ears.

Then, when the matter had been communicated to Sir Michael and Father Ripon, when Spence had started, and Mr. Byars knew that all the powers of wealth and intellect were at work, his hopes revived.

The vicar's faith had never for a single moment wavered.

In the crash of the creeds his deep conviction never wavered.

The light burned steadily before the altar.

He had been one of the faithful thousands, learned, simple, Methodist, ritualist, who knew that this thing could not be.

Nevertheless his courage had been failing him. Life seemed to have lost its sweetness, and often he humbly wondered when he should die, hoping that the time was not too long—not without a tremulous belief that God would recognise that he had fought the good fight and kept the faith.

[377] In his own immediate neighbourhood the consequences of the "Discovery" nearly broke his heart. He had no need to look beyond Walktown. Even the great political events which were stirring the world had left him unmoved. His own small corner of the vineyard, now, alas! so choked with rank, luxuriant growth, was enough for this faithful pastor. Here he saw nothing but vice suddenly rearing its head and threatening to overwhelm all else. He heard the Holy Names blasphemed with all the inventions of obscene imaginations, assailed with all the wit of full-blooded men amazed and rejoiced that they could stifle their consciences at last. And this after all his life-work among these folk! He had given them of his best. His prayers, his intellect, much of his money had been theirs.

How insolently they had exulted over him, these coarse and vulgar hearts!

When Basil had first told Mr. Byars of his suspicions the vicar can hardly have been blamed for regarding them sadly as the generous effects of a young and ardent soul seeking to find an immediate way out of the impasse.

The elder man knew that fraud had been at work, but he suspected no such modern and insolent attempt as Basil indicated. It was too much to believe. Gortre had left him most despondent.

But his interest had soon become quickened and alive, as the private reports from London reached him.

When he knew that great people were moving quietly, that the weight of Sir Michael was behind Gortre, he knew at once that in all probability Basil's suspicions were right.

A curious change came over the vicar's public appearances and utterances. His sermons were full of fire, almost Pauline in their strength. People began to flow and flock into the great empty church at Walktown. Mr. Byars's fame spread.

[378] Then, swiftly, after the first week or two, had come the beginning of the great financial depression.

It was felt acutely in Manchester.

All the wealthy, comfortable, easy-going folk who grudgingly paid a small pew-rent out of their superfluity became alarmed, horribly alarmed. The Christianity which had sat so lightly upon them that at first opportunity they had rushed into the Unitarian meeting-houses became suddenly a very desirable thing.

In the fall of Christianity they saw their own fortunes falling. And these self-deceivers would be swept back upon the tide of this reaction into the arms of the Anglican mother they had despised.

The vicar saw all this. He was a keen expert in, and student of, human affairs, and withal a psychologist. He saw his opportunity.

His words lashed and stung these renegades. They were made to see themselves as they were; the preacher cut away all the ground from under them. They were left face to face with naked shame.

What puzzled and yet uplifted the congregation at St. Thomas's was their vicar's extraordinary certainty that the spiritual darkness over the land was shortly to be removed.

It was commented on, keenly observed, greatly wondered at.

"Mr. Byars speaks," said Mr. Pryde, a wealthy solicitor, "as if he had some private information about this Palestine discovery. He is so confident that he magnetises one into his own state of mind, and Byars is not a very emotional man either. His conviction is real. It's not hysteria."

And, being a shrewd, silent man, the solicitor formed his own conclusions, but said nothing of them.

The church continued full of worshippers.

[379] When the news from Basil came, the vicar was sitting before the fire in his lighted study. He had been expecting the telegram all day.

His brain had been haunted by the picture of that distinguished figure with the dark red hair he had so often met.

Again he saw the millionaire standing in his drawing-room proffering money for scholarships. And in Dieppe also!

How well and clearly he saw the huge figure of the savant in his coat of astrachan, with his babble of soups and entrée!

Try as he would, the vicar could not hate these two men. The sin, the awful sin, yes, a thousand times. Horror could not be stretched far enough, no hatred could be too great for such immensity of crime.

But in his great heart, in his large, human nature there was a Divine pity for this wretched pair. He could not help it. It was part of him. He wondered if he were not erring in feeling pity. Was not this, indeed, that mysterious sin against the Holy Ghost for which there was no forgiveness? Was it not said of Judas that for his deed he should lie for ever in hell?

The telegram was brought in by a neat, unconcerned housemaid.

Then the vicar got up and locked the inner door of his study. He knelt in prayer and thanksgiving.

It was a moment of intense spiritual communion with the Unseen.

This good man, who had given his vigorous life and active intellect to God, knelt humbly at his study table while a joy and happiness not of this earth filled all his soul.

At that supreme moment, when the sense of the glorious [380] vindication of Christ flooded the priest's whole being with ecstasy, he knew, perhaps, a faint foreshadowing of the life the Blessed live in Heaven.

For a few brief moments that imperfect instrument, the human body, was permitted a glimpse, a flash of the eternal joy prepared for the saints of God.

The vicar drew very near the Veil.

Helena beat at the door; he opened to her, the tall, gracious lady.

She saw the news in her father's face.

They embraced with deep and silent emotion.

Two hours later the vicarage was full of people.

The news had arrived.

Special editions of the evening papers were being shouted through the streets. Downing Street had spoken, and in Manchester—as in almost every great city in England—the Truth was pulsing and throbbing in the air, spreading from house to house, from heart to heart.

Every one knew it in Walktown now.

175

There was a sudden unanimous rush of people to the vicarage.

Each big, luxurious house all round sent out its eager owners into the night.

They came to show the pastor, who had not failed them in the darkness, their joy and gratitude now that light had come at last.

How warm and hearty these North-country people were! Mr. Byars had never penetrated so deeply beneath the somewhat forbidding crust of manner and surface-hardness before.

Mingled with the sense of shame and misery at their own lukewarmness, there was a fine and genuine desire to show the vicar how they honoured him for his steadfastness.

[381] "You've been an example to all of us, vicar," said a hard-faced, brassy-voiced cotton-spinner, a kindly light in his eyes, his lips somewhat tremulous.

"We haven't done as we ought to by t' church," said another, "but you'll see that altered, Mr. Byars. Eh! but our faith has been weak! There'll be many a Christian's heart full of shame and sorrow for the past months this night, I'm thinking."

They crowded round him, this knot of expensively dressed people, hard-faced and harsh-spoken, with a warmth and contrition which moved the old man inexpressibly.

Never before had he been so near to them. Dimly he began to think he saw a wise and awful purpose of God, who had allowed this iniquity and calamity that the faith of the world might be strengthened.

"We'll never forget what you've done for us, Mr. Byars."

"If we've been lukewarm before, vicar, 't will be all boiling now!"

"Praise God that He has spoken at last, and God forgive us for forgetting Him."

The air was electric with love and praise.

"Will you say a prayer, vicar?" asked one of the churchwardens. "It seems the time for prayer and a word or two like."

The company knelt down.

It was a curious scene. In the richly furnished drawing-room the group of portly men and matrons knelt at chairs and sofas, stolid, respectable, and middle-aged.

But here and there a shoulder shook with suppressed emotion, a faint sob was heard. This, to many of them there, was the greatest spiritual moment they had ever known. Confirmation, communion, all the episodic mile-stones of the professing Christian's life had been [382] experienced and passed decorously enough. But the inward fire had not been there. The deep certainty of God's mysterious commune with the brain, the deep love for Christ which glows so purely and steadfastly among the saints still on earth—these were coming to them now.

And, even as the fires of the Paraclete had descended upon the Apostles many centuries before, so now the Holy Spirit began to stir and move these Christians at Walktown.

The vicar offered up the joy and thanks of his people. He prayed that, in His mercy, God would never again let such extreme darkness descend upon the world. Even as He had said, "Neither will I again smite any more every thing living, as I have done."

He prayed that all those who had been cast into spiritual darkness, or who had left the fold of Christ, might now return to it with contrite hearts and be in peace.

Finally, they said the Lord's Prayer with deep feeling, and the vicar blessed them.

And for each one there that night became a precious, helpful memory which remained with them for many years.

Afterwards, while servants brought coffee, always the accompaniment to any sort of function in Walktown, the talk broke out into a hushed amazement.

176

The news which had been telegraphed everywhere consisted of a statement signed by the Secretary of State and the archbishops that the discovery in Palestine was a forgery executed by Sir Robert Llwellyn at the instigation of Constantine Schuabe.

"Ample and completely satisfying evidence is in our possession," so the wording ran. "We render heartfelt gratitude to Almighty God that He has in His wisdom [383] caused this black conspiracy to be discovered. The thanks of the whole world, the gratitude of all Christians, must be for those devoted and faithful men who have been the instruments of Providence in discovering the Truth. Sir Michael Manichoe, the Rev. Basil Gortre, the Rev. Arthur Ripon, and Mr. Harold Spence have alone dispelled the clouds that have hung over the Christian world."

It was a frightful shock to these people to know how a great magnate among them, a business confrère, the member for their own division, an intimate, should have done this thing.

As long as the world lasted the Owner of Mount Prospect who had spoken on their platforms would be accursed. It was too startling to realise at once; the thought only became familiar gradually, in little jerks, as one aspect after another presented itself to their minds.

It was incredible that this antichrist had been long housed among them but a mile from where they stood.

"What will they do to him?"

"Who can say! There's never been a case like it before, you see."

"Well, the paper doesn't say, but I expect they've got them safe enough in London—Mr. Schuabe and the other fellow."

"Just to think of our Mr. Gortre helping to find it out! Pity we ever let him go away from the parish church."

"They can't do less than make him a bishop, I should think."

"Miss Byars, you ought to be proud of your young man. There's many folk blessing him in England this night."

And so on, and so forth; simple, homely speeches, not [384] indeed free from a somewhat hard commercial view, but informed with kindliness and gratitude.

At last, one by one, they went away. It was close upon midnight when the last visitor had departed.

The vicar read a psalm to his daughter:

"Lord, now lettest thou thy servant depart in peace, according to thy word. For mine eyes have seen thy salvation, which thou hast prepared before the face of all people."

Basil was to come to them on the morrow for a long stay.

[385]
EPILOGUE

IN THREE PICTURES

Note.—The three pictures all synchronise. The episodes they portray take place five years after the day upon which Sir Robert Llwellyn died.—G. T.

I. The Grave

Two figures walked over the cliffs.

177

The day was wild and stormy. Huge clouds, bursting with sombre light, sailed over the pewter-coloured sea. The bleak magnificence of the moor stretched away in endless billows, as sad and desolate as the sea on which no sail was to be seen.

The wayfarers turned out of the struggle of the bitter wind into a slight depression. A few scattered cottages began to come into the field of their vision.

Soon they saw the whitewashed buildings of a coast-guard station and the high, square tower of a church.

"So it's all settled, Spence," said one of the men, a tall, noble-faced man, dressed as a clerk in Holy Orders.

"Yes, Father Ripon," Spence said. "They have offered me the paper. It was one of poor Ommaney's last wishes. Of course, we were injured in our circulation by the fact that we were the first to publish the news of the great forgery. But in two years Ommaney had brought the paper to the front again. He was wonderful, the first editor of his age.

"I was there with Folliott Farmer and the doctors [386] when he died. Fancy, it was the first time I had ever been in his flat, though we had worked together all these years! The simplest place you ever saw. Just a couple of rooms, where he slept all the daytime. No luxury, hardly even comfort. Ommaney had no existence apart from his work. He'd saved nearly all his very large salary for many years. I am an executor of his will. He left a legacy to Farmer, and to me also, and the rest to the Institute of Journalists. But I am persuaded that he did not care in the least what happened to his money. He never did. He wasn't mean in any way, but he worked all night and slept all day, and simply hadn't any use for money. A good-hearted man, a very brilliant editor, but utterly detached from any personal contact with life."

Father Ripon's keen face, still as eager and powerful as before, set into lines of thought.

He sighed a little. "A modern product," he said at length. "A modern product, a sign of the times. Well, Spence, a power is entrusted to you now such as no priest can enjoy. I pray that your editorship of this great paper will be fine. Try to be fine always. I believe that the Holy Spirit will be with you."

They rose up towards the moor again. "There's the church," said Spence, "where she lies buried. Gortre sees that the grave is kept beautiful with flowers. It was an odd impulse of yours, Father, to propose this visit."

"I do odd things sometimes," said the priest, simply. "I thought that the sight of this poor woman's resting-place might remind you and me of what has passed, of what she did for the world—though no one knows it but our group of friends. I hope that it will remind us, remind you very solemnly, my friend, in your new responsibility, of what Christ means to the world. The shadows of the time of darkness, 'When it Was Dark' [387] during the 'Horror of Great Darkness,' have gone from us. And this poor sister did this for her Saviour's sake."

They stood by Gertrude Hunt's grave as they spoke.

A slender copper cross rose above it, some six feet high.

"I wonder how the poor girl managed it," said Spence at length; "her letter was wonderfully complete. Sir Michael—Lord Fencastle, I mean—showed it me some years ago. She was wonderfully adroit. I suppose Llwellyn had left papers about or something. But I do wonder how she did it."

"That," said Father Ripon, "was what she would never tell anybody."

"Requiescat in pace," said Spence.

"In Paradise with Saint Mary of Magdala," the priest said softly.

Quem Deus Vult Perdere.

The chaplain of the county asylum stood by the castellated red brick lodge at the end of the asylum drive, talking to a group of young ladies.

The drive, which stretched away nearly a quarter of a mile to the enormous buildings of the asylum, with their lofty towers and warm, florid architecture, was edged with rhododendrons and other shrubs.

The gardens were beautifully kept. Everything was mathematically straight and clean, almost luxurious, indeed.

The girls were three in number, young, fashionably dressed. They talked without ceasing in an empty-headed stream of girlish chatter.

They were the daughters of a great ironfounder in the district, and would each have a hundred thousand pounds.

[388] The chaplain was showing them over the asylum.

"How sweet of you, Mr. Pritchard, to show us everything!" said one of the girls. "It's awfully thrilling. I suppose we shall be quite safe from the violent ones?"

"Oh, yes," said the chaplain, "you will only see those from a distance; we keep them well locked up, I assure you."

The girls laughed with him.

The party went laughing through the long, spotless corridors, peeping into the bright, airy living-rooms, where bodies without brains were mumbling and singing to each other.

The imbecile who moved vacantly with slobbering lip, the dementia patient, the log-like, general paralytic—"G. P."—things which must be fed, the barred and dangerous maniac, they saw them all with pleasant thrills of horror, disgust, and sometimes with laughter.

"Oh, Grace, do look at that funny little fat one in the corner—the one with his tongue hanging out! Isn't he weird?"

"There's one actually reading! He must be only pretending!"

A young doctor joined them—a handsome Scotchman with pleasant manners.

For a time the lunatics were forgotten.

"Well, now, have we seen all, Doctor Steward?" one of the girls said. "All the worst cases? It's really quite a new sensation, you know, and I always go in for new sensations."

"Did ye show the young leddies Schuabe?" said the doctor to the chaplain.

"Bless my soul!" he replied, "I must be going mad myself. I'd quite forgotten to show you Schuabe."

"Who is Schuabe?" said the youngest of the sisters, a girl just fresh from school at Saint Leonards.

[389] "Oh, Maisie!" said the eldest. "Surely you remember. Why, it's only five years ago. He was the Manchester millionaire who went mad after trying to blow up the tomb of Christ. I think that was it. It was in all the papers. A young clergyman found out what he'd been trying to do, and then he went mad—this Schuabe creature, I mean, not the clergyman."

"Every one likes to have a look at this patient," said the doctor. "He has a little sleeping-room of his own and a special attendant. His money was all confiscated by order of the Government, but they allow two hundred a year for him. Otherwise he would be among the paupers."

The girls giggled with pleasurable anticipation.

179

The doctor unlocked a door. The party entered a fairly large room, simply furnished. In an arm-chair a uniformed attendant was sitting, reading a sporting paper.

The man sprang up and saluted as he heard the door open.

On a bed lay the idiot. He had grown very fat and looked healthy. The features were all coarsened, but the hair retained its colour of dark red.

He was sleeping.

"Now, Miss Clegg, ye'd never think that was the fellow that made such a stir in the world but five years since. But there he lies. He always eats as much as he can, and goes to sleep after his meal. He's waking up now, sir. Here, Mr. Schuabe, some ladies have come to see you."

It got up with a foolish grin and began some ungainly capers.

"Thank you so much, Mr. Pritchard," the girls said as they left the building. "We've enjoyed ourselves so much."

[390] "I liked the little man with his tongue hanging out the best," said one.

"Oh, Mabel, you've no sense of humour! That Schuabe creature was the funniest of all!"

THE THIRD PICTURE

A Sunday evensong. The grim old Lancashire church of Walktown is full of people. The galleries are crowded, every seat in the aisles below is packed.

This night, Easter night, the church looks less forbidding. The harsh note is gone, something of the supreme joy of Holy Easter has driven it away.

Old Mr. Byars sits in his stall. He is tired by the long, happy day, and as the choir sings the last verse of the hymn before the sermon he sits down.

The delicate, intellectual face is a little pinched and transparent. Age has come, but it is to this faithful priest but as the rare bloom upon the fruits of peace and quiet.

How the thunderous voices peal in exultation!

Alleluia!

Christ is risen! The old man turned his head. His eyes were full of happy tears. He saw his daughter, a young and noble matron now, standing in a pew close to the chancel steps. He heard her pure voice, full of triumph. Christ is risen!

From his oak chair behind the altar rails Dean Gortre came down towards the pulpit.

Young still—strangely young for the dignity which they had pressed on him for two years before he would accept it—Basil ascended the steps.

Christ is risen!

The organ crashed; there was silence.

[391] All the lights in the church were suddenly lowered to half their height.

The two candles in the pulpit shone brightly on the preacher's face.

They all saw that it was filled with holy fire.

Christ is risen!

"if christ be not risen your faith is vain"

The church was absolutely still as the words of the text rang out into it.

The people were thinking humbly, with contrite hearts, of the shame five years ago.

"Would that our imagination, under the conduct of Christian faith, could even faintly realise the scene when the Human Soul of Our Lord came with myriads of attendant angels to the grave of Joseph, to claim the Body that had hung upon the cross.

180

"To-night, with the promise and warrant of our own resurrection that His has given us, our thoughts involuntarily turn to those we call the dead. We feel that this Easter is for them also an occasion of rejoicing, and that the happiness of the earthly Church is shared by the loving and beloved choir behind the veil.

"Christ is risen! Away with the illusions which may have kept us from Him. Let us also arise and live. For, as the spouse sings in the Canticles, 'The winter is past, ... the time of the singing of birds is come; ... arise, my love, my fair one, and come away!'"

Christ is risen!

FOOTNOTES:

[1] This article has already been seen in the preceding chapter.

[2] This particular instance of the Nurié woman is not all fiction. An incident much resembling it actually occurred to a well-known writer on the intimate life of Eastern peoples. For the purposes of the narrative the locale has been changed from the Jaffa Road—where the event took place—to Jerusalem itself.

THE END

Made in United States
Troutdale, OR
09/25/2024

23147394R00102